A Monkee In My Life

Jerri Keele

DEDICATION

This book is dedicated to
my grandfather, Harry "Jack" Rundle,
whose stories and poems were the
first I heard and the first I read,
thus opening up the little author in me,
who grew and grew.

All proceeds from this book benefit
The Davy Jones Equine Memorial Foundation.

ACKNOWLEDGMENTS

Thank you to all who assisted me in this project –

Colleen Gruver
Brian Keele
Andrea Gilbey
Ginny Fleming

Note: This is a novel of fiction, a work of fantasy

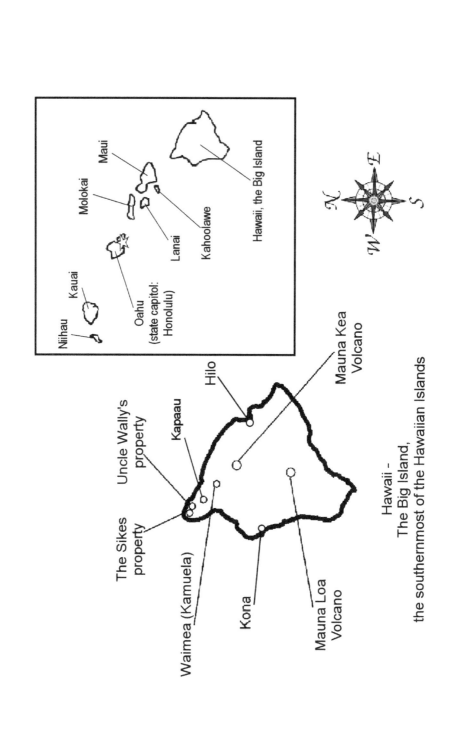

Niihau

Kauai

Oahu
(state capitol:
Honolulu)

Molokai

Maui

Lanai

Kahoolawe

Hawaii, the Big Island

N E
W S

The Sikes
property

Uncle Wally's
property

Kapaau

Hilo

Mauna Kea
Volcano

Waimea (Kamuela)

Kona

Mauna Loa
Volcano

Hawaii –
The Big Island,
the southernmost of the Hawaiian Islands

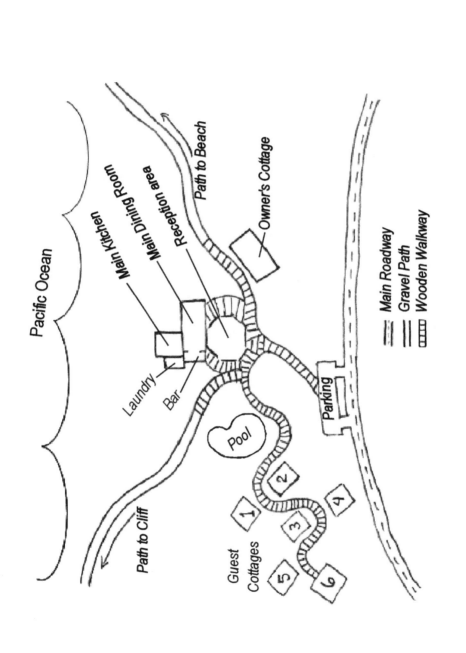

Pacific Ocean

Main Kitchen

Main Dining Room

Reception area

Path to Beach

Owner's Cottage

Laundry

Bar

Parking

Pool

Path to Cliff

Guest
Cottages

1

2

3

4

5

6

Main Roadway
Gravel Path
Wooden Walkway

ONE

Poltergeists and Polka Dots

Where do I even begin? "At the beginning," people often say. But the beginning is so long ago, and of course the middle is a mess, so I really am at a loss. Therefore, let me go back just a little bit to catch you up. As usual, it all started with breakfast. Well, not *with* breakfast, but *at* breakfast.

I had my laptop out and was checking our email for the inn as I nibbled at my oatmeal topped with fresh strawberries I'd plucked from our vegetable and fruit garden. The garden had been the brainstorm of Kalei, our chef, and Albert, our groundskeeper, in order to make better use of a good-sized but unused plot of soil behind the main kitchen building. They'd gone to a lot of trouble to put on a big show in order to convince me of the benefits of touting our own harvests in the inn's promotional material, as if I would have objected to homegrown fresh produce nearly all year round. But I digress. You'll find that I do that a lot.

In between bites I responded to queries about our inn and directed any actual booking info to Bennie's separate email, as he maintained the reservations. Bennie is my right-hand guy here at Hale Mele, which loosely translates to *House of Song*, the inn I inherited when my Uncle Wally was murdered by the once-owner of a nearby hotel.

Anyway, I switched over to my personal email account and weeded out the spam, the subscriptions I no longer had time to read, and the ads that somehow slipped through the filters, in order to read the messages from my few friends outside the inn. There, about halfway down the list, was a name I recognized from many years ago. Annie Thompson had been my mother's closest childhood friend. They'd connected early on and sealed that bond over the 1960s television show *The Monkees*. Every single Monday night, my mother Willow had joined Annie and her family for dinner, and then they all gathered to watch the show. That's when both girls fell madly in love with a cute lad from Manchester, England, named Davy Jones.

Shortly after *The Monkees* television show went off the air, Annie

1

gave up her dream of marrying Davy and chose her longtime beau just one month after high school graduation. They were married in an open field near the commune where my parents lived. Annie's husband Erik Haas had received a full scholarship to an Ivy League school so off they went to live on the East Coast, leaving my parents Willow and Jude behind. Mom never made another friendship as close as they'd had but occasionally Annie would bring her two children back to the Berkeley area to visit family, and Willow was always included in these reunions.

Annie had named her daughters after characters in that famous television show that she and Willow had still loved and watched whenever the reruns appeared, but Annie's kids were luckier than I with their monikers: Bettina, the princess from the episode "Royal Flush," and Vanessa from the pilot episode titled "Here Come The Monkees." Sadly, Vanessa passed away at the tender age of twelve, the victim of a drunk driver. This left an embittered Bettina alone to endure the schoolyard bullies who teased her about her name. It's not easy being the offspring of Monkees or Beatles obsessed fans. These days though, I cherish my names because my late parents chose them. You see, I am Macca Lennon Daydream Liberty. Yeah, it's a heavyweight name, but it's mine and my parents' together, in a way.

By the time I was born, Bettina had a daughter who she named Taylor. What was Bettina's inspiration for this name? Her husband's mother's family name was just that…Taylor. Simple, yeah? And although my dad had moved us to the Los Angeles area because of a lucrative job offer, whenever Annie, Bettina, and Taylor came to visit family in Berkeley, my mother and I would make the drive to be with them.

Bettina had always come across as sullen and a little prickly, while Taylor and I, being the same age, got along well enough. I could never have been besties with her though, for there was something about her that warned me to keep her at arm's length. Although we enjoyed many of the same things, the same games, the same heroes, she never really let me get close. I wasn't too bothered about it because our shared interest in Barbie dolls, hopscotch, and The Backstreet Boys didn't require a closeness to be enjoyed together. Yeah, don't hate me for The Backstreet Boys. I was a kid. I cringe now though when I think about it.

So there I was, munching my breakfast and reading an email from Annie Thompson-Haas. She had been a long-distance supporter ever since my parents and then my aunt and uncle had all died, but our visits had been few and far between. Until now that is, for it appeared she wanted to visit along with her daughter and granddaughter just like old times. I squealed, loudly, thus disturbing my big orange cat, Chester, who was sleeping on my lap. He was quick to admonish me.

Really? Can't a guy get his 23 hours of sleep? He "spoke" to me in my mind. Yeah, this was a fairly new development, one I hadn't quite gotten used to yet. He yawned and dug his front claws into my thighs as he stretched and rearranged himself.

"Sorry big guy." I gave him a little pet and a scratch on the side of his face. "Annie is coming to visit!"

Whoopee. I'm going back to sleep.

"Sweet dreams, Chester, you old sourpuss." I glanced over at my empty breakfast bowl and tamped down the urge to get up to attend to the breakfast dishes. After all, I was suffering from that well-known malady, Feline Paralysis. I had a cat on my lap.

Davy shimmered in, the air around him electric. "You squealed! Is everything okay?" my beloved ghostly friend asked, his face pinched with concern.

"But I didn't squeal 'goldfish' this time." I frowned, referring to our agreed upon emergency code word.

Davy's friend Mr. Pinckney, a ghost we'd met at the library some months before, appeared like a blip, disappeared, then reappeared in horizontal lines for a moment until he managed to fully show his pudgy self. "Still working on that shimmer, I see." I smirked at the ex-librarian as Davy leaned over my shoulder to read my email from Annie.

"Oh! This is brilliant!" He smiled and kissed the side of my head. "I know you miss your friends."

His smile was contagious. "Yeah. She's the last link to my mother, and I haven't seen her or her family in years."

"Who is Annie?" Mr. Pinckney timidly inquired.

"Macca's mother's best friend," Davy responded quickly.

"Oh." He gave a small smile. "That's nice."

Mr. Pinckney had few friends in life, and even fewer in the afterlife. Frankly, Davy and I were pretty much it. Oh yeah, that's THE Davy Jones of The Monkees, and not that slimy, squirm-inducing character from the pirate movies. He came to me when my Uncle Wally died, and has been my closest and dearest friend ever since. We once shared a chaste kiss in the early days, and we had little flirtations here and there, not to mention frequent cuddling, but I was slowly coming to terms with the fact that I could never have a true relationship with a ghost. I mean, how would I even go about that?

"You two will need to be careful while they're here," I warned the both of them.

"We will, Babe. Aren't we always careful?"

Visions of the few times other people had spotted him flitted into my memory, like a slideshow on hyper-drive. "Um, not really. Let's work on that, okay?"

He gave my ponytail a playful tug and grinned. "Don't you worry."

And that's just it; as soon as those words were spoken, I began to worry. I do it so well. I'm an expert. If I could hire out my services as a worrier, I'd be rich. My mind wandered to the imaginary ad I could put in the classifieds. "Give me your problems and I'll worry them away for you, $10 per day." If only it worked that way.

I shifted in my chair which caused Chester to grumble before he hopped off my lap and trotted out of the room, presumably to find a quieter place to continue his nap. I brushed his orange fur off my shorts, closed the laptop, and stood. I'd have to respond to Annie later when I had some privacy.

"I've got work to do, guys," which didn't silence their voices even in the slightest. I rinsed my dishes, placed them in the small dishwasher, and then picked up the laptop on the way out. Davy followed closely on my heels, as he usually did, and Mr. Pinckney was right behind him. Macca's Ghost Train chugged along, but only one set of footsteps sounded on the wooden walkways that wound around the grounds and joined at the main building.

Davy and Mr. Pinckney were yammering on about all sorts of things that I tended to block out. I was getting better at ignoring the constant sound of their chatter. Davy though was so close that he kept stepping on my flip-flops, causing me to have to repeatedly re-insert my toes into the flimsy beach sandals. I saw Bennie watching me from the open reception area, so I couldn't turn around and snap at the two ghostly gents about following too closely.

"Aloha, Bennie," I said as I stepped over the threshold and then stopped abruptly. Macca's Ghost Train suddenly derailed as Davy bumped into me, causing Mr. Pinckney to bump into him. I was chewing him out in my mind because I knew he could hear my thoughts, but he was oblivious and began to sing his usual Elton John song in a loud falsetto.

"B-b-b-Bennie and the Jetsssssss…" He really did know how to annoy me, thus earning his nickname: The Pest. Davy and Mr. Pinckney then disappeared to find other things with which to entertain themselves. What exactly do ghosts do? I hadn't figured that out yet. They knew though that haunting the guests was completely unacceptable, or kapu, as they say locally. Forbidden.

"Aloha, Macca," Bennie responded with a wide grin, oblivious to the impromptu serenade that had gone on behind me. I was grateful that

Bennie could neither hear nor see my ghostly shadows. "Beautiful morning," he continued.

"As usual." I returned his grin and placed my laptop over on the empty bar. I returned to the front and retrieved a cup of Bennie's special Kona brew which was available to guests and staff all day. "Bennie, could you do me a favor and let me know if we have any availability for the week of the 31st of next month? I have friends who would like to visit."

"You have friends?" He always teased me about my social life, or lack thereof.

I stuck my tongue out. "Yes, a few."

He chuckled and tapped on the keyboard, then scrolled with the mouse until he saw the schedule. He nodded his head a few times. "We've got Number 6 available that whole week. Shall I put a hold on it?"

"Please." I turned to walk toward my laptop at the bar and called over my shoulder to him. "And thank you."

Sitting on the bar stool and plunking my cup of coffee beside my laptop, I reopened my email and whipped off a reply to Annie. I let her know that not only did we have a bungalow, but I was truly looking forward to their visit. Taking a drink of Kona, I relished the brief whisper of chocolate from the cocoa nibs Bennie always added.

I found myself humming happily as I went about my morning tasks around the inn. *My inn.* I was still getting used to the notion that Hale Mele had been my sole inheritance upon my Uncle Wally's passing. Sight unseen but devastated by his death, I had packed up a few belongings, sold or donated the rest, and moved with Chester here to Hawai'i. Of course Davy followed us, and I will forever be grateful for that. I haven't looked back since. I didn't miss the crowds, the smog, or the noise of Los Angeles.

Although I was the owner and thus the innkeeper, I had the most stellar crew around me. Husband and wife duo, Kalei and Lani created magic in the kitchen, and they even performed during our weekly home style luau, bringing their Hawaiian heritage to life every Saturday night. This had always been a high point for me; I had not missed a show yet, and I didn't plan to. Now that Lani was pregnant though, her expanding belly made dancing awkward, so she had convinced one of her fellow dance troupe members to stand in for her until after the birth of the baby. Lani still performed with her at times, but as more of a supporting act.

Ming was one of the quieter members of our little innkeeping family. I had always hated housekeeping, but Ming seemed to go about it quite happily. I asked her many times what kept her going, and she always answered in her very shy manner, "I take great satisfaction in seeing something made right again, clean and pristine." Yep. She amazed me. Last year we'd put our heads together and switched all maintenance supplies to more organic, cruelty-free, and environmentally friendly products, some homemade even. I hadn't thought it possible, but Ming seemed even happier. I could frequently hear her singing or humming very quietly as she went about her tasks.

Another quiet staff member, Albert, was also very private. I hadn't yet gotten him to open up to me, but we had a mutual respect for each other, and that was enough for now. I hoped he'd warm up some as time went on. Albert kept the grounds tidy and trimmed, and he also helped out with the imu oven behind the kitchen whenever Kalei was roasting.

Sam was our young beach boy, the vision of every preconceived notion of a surfer. Long dark blond hair, bleached even lighter after a day of surfing, evenly tanned, and perhaps a little less worldly than the rest of our Hale Mele family. I found his naiveté refreshing though. He was like the little brother I wished I had. Sam maintained our tiny gift shop, and occasionally helped tend bar. But mostly he pitched in wherever help was needed, always going above and beyond to keep us up and running.

Our assistant manager, Bennie, was an expert user of the hotel software, coordinator of reservations, keeper of the paperwork, bartender, and all around good guy. He was openly warm to guests and visitors alike, and even allowed the senior guests to drag him up on the dance floor or rope him into a card game. He, along with whomever else was on hand at the time, had no issue with picking up a pile of guests' luggage and carting it along to their bungalows. There was no real pecking order among the employees; instead, it was a true team effort.

Our mascots for the inn were either furry or feathered. There was Chester, of course, who wandered around and endeared himself to the guests, and there was also Susie, a ghost dog who made himself seen to all guests. It was not unusual to walk through the pool area and see one or both of the furbabies getting treats or pets from the guests. And Susie — yes, a boy dog with a girl's name — was actually Davy's from decades past. When he came looking for his previous master, it was a sweet reunion, and since the dog showed he knew how to avoid being seen "disappearing," guests were none the wiser to his spectral identity.

We had two feathered friends, an African Grey parrot named Winston, and a large Derbyan parakeet we named Marley. Winston's original owner had been a fan of the former Prime Minister of the United Kingdom and taught the bird many Churchill quotes. However, Davy and Bennie had separately decided to bring the parrot's vocabulary into the twenty-first century by teaching him more varied phrases and songs. Our Winston was a love. He had a very large cage on the lanai outside the reception area, but he only spent the nights inside it. During the day he had the freedom to fly at will; I refused to clip his wings as so many other parrot owners did. He stayed close to home, being a smart bird and understanding where the food and affection were. A stand-alone perch stood on the other side of the reception lanai, and he could usually be found right there upon it. Why? It was near a food dish, of course. Yes, our Winston was a bit of a glutton.

Earlier this year Winston met Marley, a lady bird so named because she whistled Bob Marley tunes all the time. I caught Davy teaching her to whistle "Daydream Believer" though. That should be interesting if she decided to add it to her reggae repertoire. When she first showed up I notified online bird clubs, and I put notices in newspapers and on the vet's bulletin board, but we were never able to find her previous owner, so she slowly became part of our family.

Below the cliffs, our most stunning creature sometimes hid in the thick and deep tropical foliage at the south end of the beach. Glory-Gunn, or Glory for short, was Davy's adopted ghost horse and quite a magnificent beast. Together they often rode the shoreline early in the morning. I'd had the pleasure of joining them once, but since Glory was ghostly, with no means of explaining away his appearances and disappearances, I had refrained since then. He was a very sweet giant teddy bear of a horse who made Davy happy, and that was enough for me.

Deep in thought, I was hauling my own load of personal laundry back to my bungalow after I'd helped Ming with some chores when I saw that the mail was arriving. That is, Mr. Ian Woon, our ancient yet retired letter carrier, was bringing our mail to us. It took him several minutes of hunched-over shuffling to navigate the stairs from the parking area where his daughter, our official letter carrier for the area, waited in the car for him. Mr. Ian Woon reached the bottom step and shifted the small bundle of mail under his arm before beginning the next part of his journey to the reception desk. Many a time one of us had tried to help him, but he was a proud gentleman who just wanted to do the job from which he'd been forced into mandatory retirement. Fortunately the local postmaster turned a blind eye to the fact that Mr. Woon's daughter allowed him to ride with her and deliver mail to his old friends as long as he was able.

"Aloha, Mr. Woon," I called to him as usual. "How are you doing this fine morning?"

"Aloha, Miss Liberty." His voice was surprisingly loud and clear. I thought back to the first time I had heard him speak and how shocked I was that the grizzled body, failing with age, was at polar opposites to his speech. He stopped and tilted his bent body just enough to look into my eyes. "Did ya hear the one about the postal worker who was always stamping her feet, whenever they would letter?" He cackled then, and I had to join in his mirth. The elderly gentleman entertained us each day with a new joke, and it was nothing short of delightful.

"That's a good one, Mr. Woon," I said through my laughter. "Bennie will love it," I stated, for it was true. Bennie and Mr. Woon had been friends for years.

Mr. Ian Woon waved goodbye and then resumed his shuffle toward the reception desk to deposit the mail. I continued on to my bungalow, deposited my laundry basket in my bedroom, and then ran back to the main kitchen. Lani was bent over the work table, vigorously kneading a large pile of purple dough that she would magically turn into poi rolls for dinner. She had four industrial-sized trays of banana macadamia nut muffins cooling on the counter. I scooped up six of them and deposited them in a paper bag.

"For Mr. Woon." I smiled her way and she nodded, grunting with the efforts of forcing the dough to surrender. Each of us had offered to take over for her when it was time to knead dough, especially during her pregnancy, but she claimed it was therapeutic, and I tended to agree.

I jogged past Mr. Woon and Bennie, took the steps to the parking area two at a time and saw Tina Woon, Mr. Woon's daughter, sitting in their idling car, the windows down. "Aloha, Tina." I smiled and extended the bag of muffins across the empty passenger seat. "Fresh from the oven. Lani is baking enough for an army and made sure there was plenty for your family as well."

She beamed and took the bag from me. "Mahalo, Miss Liberty! Papa loves them and so do we. Please tell Lani mahalo as well?" I nodded and waved, then bounded back down the stairs to finish my morning tasks.

In the afternoon there was time to return to my own bungalow to put clean laundry away. I left the front door open because Chester was meandering toward me, presumably to nap on the deck in the warm sunshine. Out of the corner of my eye I saw the ceiling fan high in the middle of the living room rotating lazily. This was normal. However, the scene was stolen by one of my old ratty socks, a black number with purple polka dots that was stuck on the end of one of the blades. The toe flapped gently as the air current lifted it and then let it drop, over and over again. I snickered. "Okay, who's the wise ghost?"

Davy shimmered in. "I cannot tell a lie; it was me."

I snickered again. "But... why?"

"I always hated those socks."

"What did they ever do to you?"

"They taunt me."

I burst into laughter and walked away, shaking my head and shrugging. I loved this man-ghost for his friendship, his wisdom, his loyalty, and his ability to make me laugh. And two could play this game. I just needed to find the ideal comeback.

The following day, as I sat briefly on my deck with a mug of hot tea in my hands, an idea came to me. I felt my lips stretch into a grin as I sipped and plotted. I just had to find the right time to implement the perfect retaliation.

He had taken to sleeping in the extra bedroom occasionally since my run-in with Lani's crazy brother a few months before. Davy frequently complained about my unchecked impulsiveness. "Your parents would never forgive me," he stated recently, "if something happened to you."

I was fine with that, and I liked having him in that room, which is where my plan had begun to develop. When I was sure Davy and Mr. Pinckney were off doing whatever ghosts do when they're not apparating, I used some double-stick tape to adhere open envelopes to the top of the ceiling fan blades. Inside the envelopes was about two month's worth of "dots" from punching holes in our invoices and packing lists for our files. It only took a few grunts, groans, and suppressed giggles to put them in place, and then I tiptoed out.

That evening I pretended to be sleepy and turned in early to read my book in bed. I listened until Mr. Pinckney had gone and Davy had retired to the extra room and felt like a little kid giggling quietly while trying to concentrate on my book.

When I was certain he must be asleep, I tiptoed through the dark bungalow and silently eased his door open just enough to reach my hand in and flip the switch to the ceiling fan. Then I high-tailed it back to my room and waited. I must have eventually fallen asleep, for when I awoke, the sun was peeking in the window. The house was peaceful so I made a pot of tea and left it to steep for a few minutes. It was just as I popped bread in the toaster that I heard Davy yelling from his room, banging about, and swearing fiercely. I plastered an innocent look on my face and peeked out of the kitchen to see him swing his door open wildly.

"Oh my gosh." I feigned shock and put my hand to my mouth to cover the grin that was on my lips. There stood Davy dressed in garish pajamas made of a dark silky fabric embellished with giant multi-colored dots. The absurd scene was punctuated by the smaller paper polka dots clinging to the fabric and his hair. He spit a few times and sodden dots fell to the floor. "What happened?"

His eyes narrowed. "Don't you play coy with me! I know you had a hand in this, woman!" He bent over and shook out his hair, dots floating all around.

"I'm not cleaning that up," I warned, beginning to giggle.

"I'm not either." He glared for a few seconds, but soon began to giggle right alongside me. "Okay. That was good, Babe. You did well; I admit it, but I'm still not cleaning it up."

"Maybe Mr. Pinckney did it. He can clean it up." I smirked and returned to the kitchen to pour tea.

Davy grumbled something, but I couldn't make out the words. He knew it had been me, but I was determined to maintain an air of innocence regardless.

The following day, there was another sock on the ceiling fan, right next to mine. This one was black, green, and blue argyle, and it was clearly one of Davy's.

"Now what could that innocent sock have possibly done to deserve such a fate?" I asked loudly. Davy shimmered in, a smug expression firmly planted on his face.

"It simply flew to the ceiling." He shrugged. "It was out of my control. Maybe we have a poltergeist." He smirked and I could already see the wheels in his mind working to pin the blame on Mr. Pinckney, just for chuckles. I firmly believed at that moment that Davy needed a new hobby.

Later that evening Mr. Pinckney joined us in a poof and a blip. "When are you going to master that entrance, Mr. Pinckney?" I couldn't help but smile as I waited for his fidgeting to pick up momentum.

"Oh dear." He wrung his timid hands as he whined his timid words.

"Oi! Mate!" Davy put a frown on his face. "You been messin' around wi' me? Who put that sock up there?" He pointed to his own that was circling over our heads with its pal, my polka dotted sock.

"Oh my!" The balding ghost looked on in horror as the sock parade continued far above us. There was no way I could reach them without a ladder, so I just joined in the fun, keeping my straight face firmly in place. Mr. Pinckney snapped his eyes away from the merry-go-round of stinky footwear and looked wide-eyed at Davy. "I didn't do it! Do you think…" he gulped before continuing in a whisper, "we have a bully spirit?"

"A poltergeist, you mean?" I joined in the fun.

"No." He jerked his head back and forth to look at the two of us, jowls flapping like a St. Bernard. "I mean one of the bully spirits that hate me."

"Nonsense!" Davy admonished him and gave him a slap on the back. "It's just a poltergeist. Far more annoying than a bully, mate."

"Oh that's good," Mr. Pinckney murmured, and then realized what it meant. "Oh no! I've never met a poltergeist! Are they truly worse than… bullies?"

"They're meaner," Davy began. "Bullies are just arses who are too cowardly to do anything more than make other people's lives as miserable as their own."

"I used to think they only existed on a schoolyard," Mr. Pinckney whispered conspiratorially.

"Sadly, many adults in this world are bullies. They're especially prevalent on the internet where they can hide behind anonymous personas," I tried to soothe him.

"I'm so relieved I never used the internet much," Mr. Pinckney continued. "It was too new when I was a librarian."

"It's a wonderful tool," I continued, "if the user has even an ounce of integrity. It's a shame that so many do not possess any these days."

Davy bumped my shoulder gently with his own. I guess I was laying it on a little thick, but I'd always been disgusted by bullying. I tended to get on my soapbox when the subject arose. Just a little. Okay, maybe a lot.

"How should one… deal with bullies?" Mr. Pinckney had stopped fidgeting and was waiting earnestly for my reply.

"By ignorin' 'em," Davy jumped in. "Just ignore 'em. It really makes 'em stew a bit."

That's our Davy, direct and on point. But Mr. Pinckney seemed satisfied.

TWO

A Prickly Porcupine and a Tiara

When the day came that Annie, Princess Bettina, and Taylor were scheduled to arrive, Ming and I had cleaned Number 6 to within an inch of its foundation. We added extra chocolate macadamia nut cookies to the welcome basket, along with the touring information for the areas they had indicated were within their interests. I stowed two bottles of champagne, the drink of Annie and Bettina's choice, in the fridge to chill.

Annie had been quite the artist in her youth, and when her husband died in 2012 she'd taken up the art of watercolor yet again, honing her skills. I'd seen the photos of her work on an artists' website. With this in mind I'd collected a few suggestions from the local artisans about the best viewpoints and scenic areas that would allow Annie to set up an easel and paint.

Annie had told me that they wanted to visit the Volcanoes National Park, so I found information about a relatively short trail that was a special favorite of several artists I'd met. The 'Iliahi Trail wound around one side of Kilauea Caldera, passing the steam vents and allowing spectacular views along the way. I also gathered brochures about Waipi'o Valley — one of my very favorites — as well as Parker Ranch, Kona Coast, the botanical gardens, and Papakolea Green Sand Beach. Annie told me they knew there would not be enough time to see it all, but they'd try their best. Even though it's called the Big Island, visitors are still often surprised at its size and how much time it takes to travel. Many roads are narrow and indirect, and there are scenic distractions along the way that often derail even the most well planned itinerary.

I knew Annie had booked a flight from Honolulu to Kona that would land late that morning. Considering the time required for the collection of luggage, picking up of the rental car, possible traffic, and perhaps at least one occurrence of getting lost, I figured they'd arrive mid afternoon. I wasn't too far off either, because I heard the thudding of luggage down the steps as we cleaned up after the lunch service. I felt a squeal building inside my throat as I trotted out of my bungalow and met them on the path to the reception area. Although she had aged since the last time I'd seen her, Annie was still the tall and striking beauty that I remembered from my past. Her silvery hair was chin length with soft curls encompassing her head, and a halo-like glow when the sunlight was behind her. She dropped the handle of her suitcase and opened her arms, her grin matching the one I knew was spreading on my own face. We embraced, giggling and squealing with happiness. Just behind her was her granddaughter Taylor, wearing an identical grin. I pulled her into the hug, and it was then I saw the sullen face of Bettina. I opened my arms again to gather her as well, but she was stiff and barely touched any of us. Princess Bettina of the Kingdom of the Prickly Porcupine had not changed much over the years, except that her hair was graying as well. Looking at the three women, I could see the strong resemblance across the generations, like familial time lapse photography.

"I've missed you so much!"

"How have you been?"

"Oh, you look wonderful!"

We all spoke at once, uttering nearly the same things, except for the Princess, who remained mostly silent, save for a few perfunctory greetings. I led them into the reception area and made brief introductions to Bennie, along with Lani and Kalei who had been nearby cleaning up the lunch service in the dining area.

Once the trio was checked in, Bennie was joined by Sam to help bring the rest of their luggage down from their car in the parking lot. Meanwhile, I showed them to Number 6 and they were duly impressed with the accommodations, the view, and the decor.

"This is lovely, sweetheart." Annie held tightly to my hand. "Have you done much of this yourself?"

"With the help of Ming, yes. I redecorated all the bungalows over the last year. It's been a lot of fun, and I want to do right by Uncle Wally's vision for this place."

"Well..." She tucked a strand of my unruly hair back and my heart lurched as a memory of my mother invaded it. "I think he would be quite proud."

"Thank you." I felt suddenly choked with shyness. Perhaps it was the sudden lump in my throat.

Bettina and her daughter took the second bedroom with the twin beds, giving the elder woman the master bedroom with a queen-sized set up.

"Shall I leave you to get settled? We can meet up a little later." I smiled at each one of them.

"How about an hour from now?" Annie squeezed my hand. "That gives us time to unpack and freshen up a bit."

I told them where my own bungalow was and we agreed to meet there. Annie kissed my forehead and I left them to unpack.

Lani and Kalei had helped me prep a few snacks to lay out in my bungalow, along with a pitcher of Kalei's wonderful iced tea, a bottle of champagne, and plenty of freshly cut fruit. I had cleaned the place from top to bottom, or so I thought. The ceiling fan some sixteen feet above caught my eye as it lazily spun the two socks around, the argyle and the polka dot. I just hoped they wouldn't notice the anomaly.

Fortunately, the paper sprinkles from Davy's room had been vacuumed this morning by none other than myself. I refused to let him know it was me though. I was ready to proclaim that we had a clean freak poltergeist rather than admit I couldn't stand to look at the mess any longer.

My front door was open when I heard someone say, "Knock knock." I looked up to find Taylor coming in. We hugged again and I led her to the kitchen where the snacks and the drinks were.

"Iced tea or champagne? I also have beer and wine."

"Oh, I'd love a cold beer." She wiped her brow.

"We'll go on the deck when your mother and grandmother get here, and there we'll be able to catch a breeze."

"Whew, good. I'm not acclimated yet. New England is a lot cooler."

"I can imagine." I really couldn't, never having been farther east than Palm Springs, California, but I knew how to make basic small talk. I popped open a bottle of Fire Rock Pale Ale, from Kona Brewing Company. "You want a glass or the bottle?"

"Oh, no ceremonies for me; the bottle is good. Keeps it colder and maintains that great fizz."

I nodded and handed it to her. "This is a local beer, but I was beginning to see it in California stores before I moved here. I hope you like it."

She took a long drink and then read the label as she swallowed. "That's great; really hits the spot." She frowned a little, studying the label before smiling, "I can almost taste a hint of coffee flavor. It's pretty good." She lifted the bottle and saluted me with it.

"Will Annie and Bettina be long, do you know?"

"No. They're having one of their usual arguments, but they should be here any minute."

And just as I was about to respond, they appeared in the doorway. I greeted them with hugs again, and noticed Bettina was still cool and aloof. I'd always thought of her as a sort of Pandora's box for she seemed to keep her personality and emotions locked up rather than risk the release of all her inner demons.

I offered drinks again and was not surprised when they chose champagne. I popped the cork and poured two glasses. I had iced tea myself, since I still had work to do later.

14

"Let's go enjoy the breezes on the deck," I suggested. I had placed the snacks on the table outside and was pleased to see the ladies fill some plates before taking their seats.

"Oh, this is such a beautiful spot, sweetheart," Annie proclaimed as she admired my view. Chester ambled out and hopped up on the railing to watch the birds.

"That's Chester, my buddy. He came over from Los Angeles with me and he's been a real trooper."

"Hi Chester!" Annie stood and approached him to give him a few pets, which he gladly accepted.

She's just okay. I think there's something off about the three of them though, he told me in my head. I only nodded slightly.

Annie leaned against the railing, facing us. "So, do you like it here?"

"I do; I really do. I feel like I've finally found my home, and I've settled into a new and comfortable group of friends and sort of a chosen family. I haven't been this happy since I was a kid."

"Oh Macca, that is exceptional news! She reached out and touched my arm. "I must admit, I have been skeptical. I'm quite relieved to see what you've got here, and to hear that you're happy."

She sat back down with the rest of us and began to sample the snacks she'd plated for herself.

"Tell me what you've all been up to lately." I leaned forward, eager to hear of their lives.

Annie waved her hand dismissively but responded in a very casual manner anyway. "Oh, I'm still dabbling in painting and enjoying my retirement. I volunteer at the art museum, and I'm part of a group of ladies who occasionally play bridge together. Other than that, not much."

"It sounds like a busy schedule to me." I offered a smile and turned to Bettina. "Are you still teaching piano?"

"Yes. Sometimes."

"Unfortunately, her husband recently left her for another woman." Annie spoke gently, but I felt it was odd that she would divulge such personal information on behalf of her daughter. I detected a fleeting look of resentment on Bettina's face.

"I'm so sorry, Bettina." I reached out and put my hand on top of hers. "I truly am." I wasn't lying or even just trying to placate her; I was truly appalled, even though I'd always admired Stu for sticking with a woman who could be so sullen and moody at times. At first touch she flinched, but then I saw her give just a hint of a smile and a nod.

"I'll be fine, but thank you. We hadn't been getting along lately

15

anyway." She spoke so quietly, and again I thought I saw her accept my touch as comfort, but it flitted away as quickly as it had come so I withdrew my hand.

"And Taylor graduated university," Annie began before giving a very subtle sneer, "and now works as a secretary in an elementary school."

"It's just temporary, Gran," Taylor wrinkled her nose but didn't flinch at her grandmother's jab. "I want to get my master's degree in early childhood education."

"Yes," Annie continued, "so you can teach kindergartners. You have your bachelor's and your teaching certificate. Isn't that enough?"

"It's not enough for me." She faced off against her elder, her voice rising. "I'm also considering a PhD whether you like it or not."

Whoa… there was some serious family crap going on here, and I suddenly felt more than a little uncomfortable.

"Honestly, I think you've found your true profession: student," Annie continued. Bettina remained silent, eyes cast down into her champagne.

Ouch. I cleared my throat and stood up to break the tension. "Okay..." I quickly tried to change the subject. "How about a tour of the place?"

My three guests reluctantly rose from their seats. "Mother, really, this is neither the time nor the place," Bettina hissed through clenched jaws, finally responding to the verbal attack on her daughter.

Annie paused briefly before shaking her head; the glum look on her face was replaced with a forced smile. "Forgive me, Macca," she sighed. "I just don't know what gets into me these days."

Bettina glared first at her mother then turned that same expression on her daughter which was also disconcerting.

"Yes, let's have the grand tour, sweetheart." Annie set her glass and plate on the small side table. Bettina followed suit, but Taylor took her time, much like a diva bathing in the applause and waiting for her encore to be demanded by the audience. She finished the last few sips of her beer and then leisurely nibbled at a strawberry before she deigned to join us for the tour.

Stay away from the food, Chester, I sent the mental message to the snoozing feline.

Hmph. One eye opened first and he glared at me. *I am not an unruly kitten.* He stretched and closed his eyes again.

I led them through the maze of walkways surrounding the common areas and the cottages of Hale Mele, beaming with pride at the well equipped main kitchen, the vegetable and fruit garden, and the small imu oven that Kalei and Albert had built into the ground.

We meandered along the cliff path and came upon the five rustic outdoor rocking chairs we'd recently acquired. Placed by the large grassy lawn, they offered spectacular views of the Pacific.

Despite my protests, Davy occasionally played tricks on guests by setting one or more to rocking. On the occasions when I happened to hear guests commenting on the strong breezes, I would send a mental message to his inner-incorrigible child to knock it off.

"What a grand view," Annie exclaimed as she took a seat. Bettina and Taylor joined her, admiring the lovely spot as well. I stood nearby and felt a blush rise up my neck as the two empty chairs began to rock. *Davy!* I admonished him in my thoughts, but his only response was laughter which faded away as if he were running down the path.

"That wind sure picked up quickly," Taylor remarked as she watched the rockers gently sway. Bettina peered past her daughter to watch as well.

I'm going to get you for this, Davy, I sent one last message but it appeared to fall on deaf ears. Or… spirits, as the case may be.

"Yes indeed," I acknowledged. "Shall we continue our tour then?" I was anxious to avoid further discussion of the mysterious rocking chairs.

When my guests were on their feet again we looped back to the pool area with the little outside bar, which had been my very first upgrade.

Before we were to head down to the beach, I led them to the Whispering Bench which bore plaques commemorating loved ones gone. Annie stood mesmerized as I demonstrated the whispering aspect of it, with first Bettina and then Taylor sitting at the other end while I whispered at my end. The two women actually giggled when they clearly heard me welcoming them to Hale Mele with my whisper. I beamed with pride until I looked up at Annie and saw tears in her eyes.

"This is beautiful." She caressed the plaque with her index finger while she brushed the tears away with her other hand. "Davy, Willow, Jude… your Uncle Wally and Aunt Fran..." She gulped, unable to finish her sentence.

I leaned close and put my arm around her waist. We hugged each other, and she kissed the top of my head. "I miss her too," she whispered. All I could do was nod, for there was a lump in my throat that matched her obvious emotions.

"I think she'd like this bench," Annie added once her emotions were under control, and she gave me a squeeze. It was at that point that I noted the look on Bettina's face, somewhere between jealousy and hatred actually. Was it directed at me or her mother? I couldn't tell, but it made me just uneasy enough to gently pull away from Annie.

"Well," I spoke just a little too brightly and inwardly cringed. "Shall we walk down to the beach?"

"Of course, dear." Annie touched my cheek very briefly. Bettina stood abruptly and Taylor eased off the bench to join my odd little line of followers as I wound around the paths back in the direction of my bungalow to the stairs just below my deck.

"So, it's a full circle around the bungalows and the pool area," I chattered, my imaginary tour guide hat firmly in place. "Then behind the kitchen and common areas, to the stairs. Oh, and we have outdoor showers both at the top of the stairs here, and over behind the laundry area." I knew I was rambling but couldn't stop myself. There was a weird dynamic to the little family extension I'd once thought was part of my own. Now though, I realized I didn't know these people anymore. Our "glue" in the form of my mother was gone, causing the fragile seams between families to fray.

As they plodded down the stairs behind me, I raised my voice in the wind so they could hear me explain the cove below. "Few people can surf here because there really aren't very big waves. At dawn and dusk though you'll find a few die-hards attempting to catch a wave. Mostly it's good for swimming, wading, and body surfing. Even a boogie board is fun now and then." I was still rambling and mentally kicked myself.

We tossed our shoes and sandals aside at the bottom of the stairs and took in the lovely sea breeze.

"Oh, this is amazing." Taylor had her arms out and was slowly spinning, breathing deeply. "I could see myself doing yoga here in the mornings!"

"The trek down and back up the stairs is enough exercise for me," Bettina muttered, yet she appeared quite physically fit. I kept my mouth shut though. These people seemed like strangers to me, a very odd collection at that, and I just wanted a few hours alone to let it all sink in. I glanced down the beach and saw Davy and Glory in… well, in all their glory, at the far end. I sucked my breath in and turned to look at my little party. They were peering about yet seemed completely unaware of both the man and the horse. How did he do that? And why did I always forget to ask Davy these crucial questions?

"Macca, this is beautiful." Taylor beamed, taking in the sea air and the lush tropical growth at the base of the cliff. "How do you keep yourself from hanging out here all day?" She was chuckling, and it helped to ease the previous tension.

"It's not easy but I really do want Uncle Wally's vision to be successful so I work hard. I even got certified in hotel management when I first moved here."

"Oh, you didn't use one of those fake universities, did you?" Annie's brow wrinkled in concern.

I smiled, trying desperately not to laugh. "No. There are extension courses from various qualified universities. My alma mater offers a program as a matter of fact."

"Oh good, because I've heard so many horrible stories of people getting ripped off."

I could see it would be of no use to go into detail, so I just smiled and grasped her hand. "Believe me, I'm internet savvy and very familiar with the online world so I'm well aware of which universities are legitimate. And besides, I'm not looking to get a degree, but simply wanted to know more about the industry I suddenly found myself in."

"We were so sad to hear of your uncle's tragic death. I know you're doing the best you can."

Whoa. Backhanded compliment, but I just shrugged my shoulders. "It was difficult but I'm happy now, and the customers are satisfied so far." I smiled my brightest, even though her words seemed to tug at my heart.

Don't worry Dear, I heard my mother's voice in my head. *Annie has had an unfortunate turn of events that have left her unable to shut her mouth when she should.* I bit my lower lip to keep from laughing at Mom. She and Dad weren't supposed to communicate with me for fear it would be too upsetting. Whoever or whatever had made such a decision sure didn't know anything about my relationship with my parents, but that's why Davy had appeared in my life instead, and I sure couldn't complain too much about that. Thinking of my ghostly friend caused me to wonder; I squinted and checked the far end of the beach with a wave of relief as I noticed the absence of both man and horse.

"So..." I turned back to Annie, Bettina, and Taylor. "Would you like to relax a little before dinner?"

"I would," Bettina spoke quickly.

"I suppose we're all a little jet lagged, sweetheart," Annie chimed in.

I grabbed my flip flops and held them in my hand as I led us back up the steps. At the top, I rinsed my feet in one of the outdoor showers. "It keeps the sand-clogged drains in the bungalows to a minimum," I explained and waited as they followed my lead.

"Very good idea." Annie was the next. Taylor followed her, and

Bettina begrudgingly did as her mother and daughter had done, but not without grumbling about the inconvenience.

Me? I was craving a few minutes alone to decompress. This just didn't feel like the same family I'd known for most of my life. Or perhaps my memories had been skewed by all the other challenges I'd overcome on my own.

Once I'd seen the trio head back to their bungalow, I flopped down on my sofa and watched the socks twirl around on the ceiling fan. I identified with them right then, lazily spinning out of reach. My thoughts turned to the person in my life who'd put them up there and I couldn't help but smile. He was still my rock. My Sock Rock, in this case.

Davy shimmered in, plopped on the other end of the sofa, and placed my feet in his lap, giving them a little massage. "So, how was it?"

"Horrible."

He gave one breathy chuckle. "Care to elaborate?"

I slapped both hands over my face and groaned. "What the hell happened to that family? They're just so... unpleasant to each other!"

"Even Annie? You said she was like a second mum to you at one time."

"Maybe her husband's death soured her. There's just something not right between those women. And it's difficult to wrap my head around it." I sat up slowly, swinging my bare feet off his lap and onto the floor. "I think it's going to be a long week."

Davy gently massaged the back of my neck and just let me talk for awhile. Imagine that, a silent Davy. But he was an exceptional listener.

"Annie is still very sweet and loving with me," I began, "but with Bettina and Taylor she's very... rough. Or something. Bordering on unkind. I'm not sure how Taylor, in particular, can stand it. Bettina has always been full of darkness, but at least Taylor was enough of a friend to me in earlier years."

"*Enough of a friend?* Define that, please."

I frowned and turned my head to look more closely at his sweet and kind face, and it made me pause, grasping desperately for a few fleeting memories from my childhood. They were elusive at best though, and I shook my head. "I'm not sure what made me say that, except that there are some deeply buried recollections of my playing with her that fit that phrase. I just can't seem to remember them right now. It's like playing keep-away. The memories are there; I know they are, but they won't let me retrieve them." I groaned before continuing. "It's maddening."

"Give me a day or so and I'll do some prodding, not only with you, but also your parents. Maybe they can shed some light on it."

"Oh! That's right! Mom's voice came to me while I was with the Troublesome Trio."

"Really? What did she say?"

I tried to focus again, and this time the short-term memory came back to me. "She said that I shouldn't worry, and that Annie's recent unpleasant turn of events had taken away her ability to keep her mouth shut at times. That's not exactly the whole issue though. It's not just Annie. Bettina seems even more morose than I remembered."

"Wouldn't you be if you were named Bettina and you weren't the princess that was promised with the name?"

"Whoa. Could that be it? She never got her tiara, so to speak? The one she thinks was owed to her?" I shook my head. "You know how I hate tiaras," I continued with the metaphor, "and the tantrums that come with them. This is just another reason why."

"Unfortunately there are a lot of people in the world who feel many things are owed to them." He rubbed his face. "Some of them just grab what they think they should have, regardless of the feelings of others, and some just carry a dark cloud for the rest of their lives. But then there's you." He smiled and brushed a strand of hair off my face; the tender touch was like balm after being with my guests. "You, who tossed away any idea of a tiara and never looked back."

"I've never expected one really. I never felt like I wanted to be a princess. I wanted to be a superhero."

He laughed, his head back, the muscles in his neck showing. "You are a superhero. That's one of the many things I love about you."

I leaned back on the sofa and let him hold me for as long as he wanted. I needed real family contact and he fit the bill quite perfectly.

"Thank you," I whispered and relaxed against him. Chester chose that moment to wander in from the deck and settle on our combined laps.

I don't like those people. They're not coming back, right? It was times like this that I was relieved that others couldn't hear him.

"Sorry, Chet. They're here for a week. Just try to steer clear. You'll get a nice reward at the end; I promise."

Well, okay then. He rested his head on a paw and closed his eyes. *But I'm holding you to that promise.*

I gave his little cheek a scratch and smoothed the fur on top of his head. He began to purr.

"Cats are such good medicine." Davy smiled at his little orange friend. "And dogs, horses, chickens, rabbits, and anything else with fur or feathers."

"What? No scales?"

He shrugged. "Never really been my thing, but I wouldn't turn one away."

"And that, my friend, is one of the things I love about *you*."

That night I joined my three guests at dinner, rounding out their party to four. I had warned them though that I might have to excuse myself now and then if I was needed in the kitchen or for setting up the entertainment, for this was our Saturday Luau Night at Hale Mele. I helped Lani and Kalei with the dinner prep and also Sam with his bar prep before all of our guests began to arrive for the evening. Our long-standing guests, the Morrison family, were the first arrivals. Rick and Jack herded their brood in — the twins Ella and Ethan, and baby Noah, just beginning to walk. Jack held Noah's hands and let him guide his little pudgy feet toward the table I pointed to, one that had become their regular in the many months they'd been here.

"How is the house coming along?" I asked after greeting them. Rick was the architect half of the couple and had experienced delays in the delivery of supplies as they built their new family home just south of our inn.

"Slow but steady." Rick smiled, helping Ella and Ethan onto their booster seats while Jack guided Noah's happily thrashing legs into the wooden highchair. "We'll be out of your hair sometime next month."

"Or next year," Jack chided him gently, a grin on his lips.

I laughed, idly touching each of the children's sweet heads. "You are not in our hair. On the contrary, we're going to miss you all when you move into that lovely home, but we know you'll be happy there. And..." I looked pointedly at them one at a time. "We fully expect to see you here occasionally. We know where you'll be living, so we can come pester you if you don't," I teased. I'd come to love this family who had been with us so long.

"And we fully expect to have you over for dinner as well, so it's mutually beneficial." Jack grinned, taking his seat.

"It's a deal." I took drink orders and served them up. When I saw Annie, Bettina, and Taylor arrive, I excused myself and welcomed the trio to the table I had saved. Other guests were being guided in by Sam as well. Although it was hectic having only one mealtime, it worked out better in the end for the entertainment afterward. One dinner, one show.

I took drink orders and delivered them before pouring myself a glass of Pinot Grigio and taking a seat between Annie and Taylor. "Did you get a chance to rest?"

"We did." Annie smiled as she lifted her champagne glass and we followed her lead. "To Macca, her beautiful inn, her wonderful staff, and her future happiness."

"Aww, thank you." I felt my cheeks warm. We clinked glasses and took the requisite post-toast sips.

"This is great." Taylor was smiling as she looked around the semi-open-air dining area. The windows had no glass, only storm shutters that were all thrown open to the evening breezes. Behind us, the entire wall of floor-to-ceiling shutters were open, leading out to the pool area and the day bar. The landscaping lights put a soft glow on the scene, back-lighting the room we were in, and complementing the soy candles flickering in glass globes on each table. Ceiling fans circled lazily above us, sans socks amazingly enough, and Sam had turned the background music low for ambiance.

"Thank you." I smiled back at her. "I do hope you'll all enjoy the food and the show as well."

"I'm starving." Annie finished her champagne and I poured another. "And I know it will be good. We heard several other guests raving about it!"

I beamed with pride. Hale Mele was our baby, the staff and mine together.

"You're joining us tomorrow, right?" Taylor asked, taking another drink of her beer.

"To Kona? Of course! I wouldn't miss it for the world. I've only been there once before, you know."

"You rarely get a day off do you, sweetheart?" Annie could be so warm and loving toward me at times, and my heart squeezed a bit, wishing the older woman would extend that to her own family as well.

"Oh, I get the occasional day off here and there. I recently spent the day with friends in Waipi'o Valley."

"We'd hoped to be able to go there this trip, but I'm afraid Mom and Gran have filled up our week with volcanoes and the botanical garden, after Kona of course." Taylor finished her beer and took another one that was chilling in the small rustic galvanized bucket Sam had filled with ice and placed on a stand beside her.

"But I know you'll have such a great time," I picked up the previous conversation, "and you'll just have to return some day to cover more of the island. There is so much to see here, and even though travel is slow, there's something to see around every bend in every road."

"It sounds so enticing," Annie spoke between sips of champagne. "We decided to stay local Monday, and then head to the volcanoes Tuesday."

"That gives you time to soak up a little sun, perhaps drive down to the Waipi'o Lookout, since there's no time for the valley itself, or enjoy the local towns. Parker Ranch and Waimea are close by as well."

"Perhaps you and Taylor can examine a map for us and point out where those are, dear," she added.

"I'd be happy to! We can map it out tomorrow."

Dinner was ready to be spread out in typical luau fashion by way of a lush buffet of pork, vegetables, and fish, all roasted in Kalei's beloved imu oven, along with a large assortment of fruits, salads, and breads as well. The dessert table held a variety of puddings, cakes, fruit sauces, and of course Lani's lovely cookies. Tonight's array included coconut macadamia nut bars and peanut butter chocolate cookies with thinly sliced almonds. For the kids, big and small, there were tiny chilled bowls of ice cream — chocolate, mango, and passion fruit, all nestled on a huge pile of ice.

After dinner, I switched to drinking hot tea and happily held Noah in my lap at my own table while Jack and Rick helped Ella and Ethan choose their very special dessert items. When the twins were back in their seats and digging into their chosen treats under Rick's watchful eye, Jack crouched by Noah and me.

"Hey bud, want some dessert?" Noah reached out to his dad. I mean, what kid doesn't learn the meaning of "dessert" early on in his or her life, right? I chuckled as Noah turned and blew me a little kiss before leaving.

I turned back to Annie, Bettina, and Taylor. "I love that family so much."

"They've been here for a long time then? How do you manage that?" Annie sipped her champagne, eyeing me over the top of her glass.

I shrugged, sipping my tea. "It's easy. They're paying customers who have opened their family to us, and we enjoy every second of it. We all hit it off from the very beginning. Plus, Lani and Kalei are learning about being parents from Jack and Rick. It's a perfect set-up, really." I knew the grin on my face added to my words, but then I realized Annie wasn't smiling.

"But they're gay." She frowned. "Don't you object to that?"

I had to laugh. "Object to what? Happiness? Hell no. Everyone has the right to be loved and to love back. Love is love." I truly thought I'd see steam coming from her ears, a la Daffy Duck or something. She simply glowered and drank more champagne. *Yeah, drink up, Judgmental Josephine*, I thought. How on earth was I going to manage an entire day with this crew? I suddenly wished I was drinking something stronger than tea, but knowing my assistance would be needed in cleaning up, I abstained. Oh, but once I was in the comfort of my own place? I was having a drink. Of what, I didn't know. Didn't care either. I'd earned the pleasure of the numbing reward.

Just before showtime, I excused myself from my extended but dysfunctional family yet again and helped clear the plates and the leftover food, although there wasn't much of the latter. Lani and her friend Malina were in the back laundry area getting their costumes on.

Kalei and I had become quite adept at clearing and cleaning just enough to make space for the show. He retrieved his "instruments," a small drum, some sticks, a large shell, and a couple of gourds filled with seeds. He cued up the music and brought out the big basket of leis that Makala and her friends at Hale Maluhia had been commissioned to make for us each week. Our standing order had spurred a business for the inhabitants of the homeless camp and brought in funds that helped provide a little extra assistance for all their residents.

While Malina slowly began the show, Lani, with her modified costume to cover the bit of pregnant tummy she was now showing, took the basket of leis around the dining room and presented one to each guest, ceremoniously placing it around their neck and giving them her thousand watt smile with a kiss on each cheek.

One of Makala's special touches was that she made the small, children's sized leis in a manner that they'd break away easily if the young ones got them caught on something. It was the little things that parents appreciated, but it had been Makala's idea and we made sure our guests knew that. We'd become one of many champions of the homeless and were reaching out to bring wider attention to their plight.

My daydreaming was interrupted by Bettina's comment. She indicated Lani's fairly conservative costume, which covered her from shoulder to knee. "That woman in the green dress... is she pregnant?"

"Yes." I turned back to Bettina. "I'm going to be an 'anake. I feel so blessed!"

"What's 'anake mean?" Taylor played with her after dinner drink, a strong blend Sam had made.

"I'll be one of the baby's aunties. I'm just so excited!"

My enthusiasm was met by blank stares. I fiddled with my spoon.

"My dear..." Annie began as if she was talking to a four-year-old. "Anyone can be tagged as an aunt, but unless it's blood relations, it really means nothing."

Wow. Just... wow. "But you're not a blood relation to me, and yet I feel like you're family." However unfortunate that may have seemed at the time.

"Well..." She stroked my hand and my skin crawled. "I knew your mother for years before you were born, but we're just…friends."

I sat, stunned and sickened. I simply shook my head, unable to come up with a response. But then I remembered my mother's words in my head. I took a deep breath and spoke through clenched teeth. "Well I chose to open my heart to additional family, and *they* are very important to me."

After a very long pause, Annie withdrew her hand from mine and spoke under her breath. "Very well, sweetheart. As you wish." But her words were empty; I could see it in her eyes. If I could just get through this week with them, I could wash my hands of this small and toxic extended family… I mean friends. They didn't represent me, it wasn't what I was all about, nor what my parents had raised me to be. One trip to Kona, a final visit when they returned from the volcanoes, and I'd be done, I promised myself.

The show was enchanting as usual, and even the prickly trio seemed to enjoy it, as evidenced by their boisterous applause at the end.

"That big man sure is sexy," Taylor stage whispered to me, and I chuckled.

"And most definitely, extremely, irrevocably married and in love with his wife." I winked.

"Damn," she joked, but there was something in her eyes that made me think that love and marriage might not be a formidable barrier in her little world. Fortunately, I didn't see the need to worry because I hadn't been exaggerating about Kalei and Lani. Sometimes when they looked at each other it was as if no one else existed in the world. *Someday I'll have a Kalei of my own*, I thought to myself.

Yes you will, Davy responded in my thoughts, causing me to blush and smile.

THREE

White Knuckles and Watercolors

Sunday dawned earlier than desired. I had to scramble to help get the food together for Hale Maluhia, so I jumped in the shower and high-tailed it to join Kalei and Lani in the main kitchen. We gathered all the containers and baskets and loaded them into their car. They had agreed to deliver and serve the homeless settlement this week to allow me time to go to Kona with Annie, Bettina, and Taylor.

I bolted back down the stairs from the parking area in order to meet with my guests. They were sitting by the pool waiting for me. Annie had her small portable easel, her tiny case of paints, and a miniature canvas ready to go. In comparison, Bettina had a pretty large and quite impressive camera hanging from a strap on her shoulder.

"Aloha," I called to them.

"Good morning," they chimed together.

"I'm ready if you are. I just need to grab my purse." I ran to my bungalow, gave Chester a pat, picked up my purse, and ran back to my guests.

Since Roomba was so tiny we took their rental car. My little Smart Car barely held two people and a few groceries. The compact car they'd rented would be much more comfortable. Annie and Bettina chose the back seat in order for me to navigate from the front passenger seat as Taylor drove. I'd only been to Kona once, but the route was still fresh in my memory.

I pointed out the numerous points of beauty along the way. Taylor was quite the aggressive driver and I found myself gripping the arm-rest, my knuckles white, trying desperately not to react too strongly.

In Kona we found a central spot to park and began to stroll up and down Ali'i Drive. Annie and Bettina were particularly interested in the art galleries. After three or four of them though, Taylor and I opted to sit on one of the benches outside to enjoy the sunshine and the cooling breeze.

"You're so lucky to live here," she spoke softly, seemingly in awe of the sights and the weather.

"I do love it. Perpetual spring and summer, in a way."

"I'm sick of East Coast winters, frankly. I could see living here."

I cringed inwardly at the thought of her being here permanently, especially if it meant I'd be seeing her mother and grandmother more. None of them fit my idea of a happy family.

"But I'm stuck there," she continued with a heavy sigh.

"You're never stuck anywhere, really. It's up to you to make the changes you desire." What was I saying? And why was I encouraging her? I mentally kicked myself.

"Oh, I'm stuck all right. I haven't told Mom and Gran, but I got accepted into a graduate program at Columbia."

"Wow! Congratulations Taylor. That's fantastic news!"

"Thank you. Just... don't let them know yet, okay?"

"Cross my heart! Your secret is safe with me."

"You heard how Gran reacted to the idea of me continuing my education. I'm just not ready to tell them."

I nodded, understanding completely. "Does this mean you'll be moving to Manhattan?"

"Yes." Her eyes were suddenly bright. "I'm going to share a small apartment with two other students. I'm really looking forward to experiencing the New York lifestyle! It's far more exciting than Connecticut."

Inwardly I cringed at the thought of battling the crowds, the noise, and the smells of a big city. Los Angeles had been more than enough for me, and it was a far cry from the masses in New York City, or so I'd heard.

Annie and Bettina emerged from the art gallery just then and joined us on the bench, eagerly soaking up the sunshine.

"Oh, this is so relaxing," Annie sighed, a tinge of contentment in her voice and a small smile on her face. That was the Annie I remembered and longed for.

"These galleries are marvelous! There is some surprisingly artistic talent here on the island." Bettina seemed to have found her reason to converse. "I was very impressed with some of the photography."

"Bettina is taking up the art of the camera, you know." Annie touched my arm. "I love to see my family doing creative things."

"I took a class at the local community college back home." Bettina scooted around in her seat to address us better. "I'm hooked. To take a piece of equipment, point the lens at a subject, and create a stunning work of shadow and light? It hit me. I've got the camera bug."

I chuckled. "It's a good bug to have! I'd love to see some of your work."

"I can show you back at the inn. They're not great, but I do seem to be picking it up, if slowly."

"There's plenty of time, dear." Annie patted her daughter's hand. "What do you do for creativity, Macca?"

28

Whoa. She had me there. "Um… nothing much, really. I've never really been much of an artist or anything. I used to knit, but lost that desire a long time ago."

"That's too bad." She looked at me with… what? Pity? I kept myself damned busy doing things. I brushed her off in my thoughts and shrugged.

"Everyone has different desires." I smiled, daring her to take the subject further. She simply nodded and sat back against the bench. Score one for me.

We wandered up and down the road again, hopping into a store now and then. I picked up a few trinkets for the staff and a couple of little gifts for Davy and Mr. Pinckney. I was both surprised and disappointed that my two ghostly shadows had been keeping themselves hidden even from me lately. I missed Davy especially.

We stopped for cups of Kona, carrying the drinks into the park and sitting under a big tree. We watched the fishing boats come and go for a bit, as Annie dabbed at her watercolors, applying them to her canvas. Bettina wandered with her camera while Taylor and I chatted amiably. We didn't have much in common, but seemed to find plenty of things to say. I was surprised that I was having a rather nice time considering that I'd dreaded this day.

When the sun began to produce too much glare, Annie packed up her things and led our little group into a small East Indian gift shop that had caught her eye. My senses were pleasantly assaulted by the heady fragrance of incense. I found myself sniffing the samples and ended up choosing a box of amber resin, some sandalwood, and of course, the old standard 1960s Nag Champa. All I needed now were beads to hang in a doorway and I could recreate my parents' old apartment where I was born. I crack myself up at times. It's a small audience.

"Oh look, dear," Annie called to me as I grabbed a shopping basket for my treasures. "They have these lovely little cross stitch kits! Wouldn't that be a wonderful way for you to dabble creatively?"

I peered at the small package that couldn't have measured more than five inches square. It was a pineapple. A pineapple? How cliché can you get. She shuffled through the other packages in the display basket and tossed a few to the side to dig deeper. One of the discarded packages caught my eye though. It was a tiny representation of a beach much like ours near Hale Mele, complete with rainbow and a man and woman walking hand in hand along the surf. I peered closer and saw that the man was wearing red trunks and had longish dark hair, while the light brown-haired woman was in a blue bikini. I couldn't help but smile. It was sort of a sign. I looked around me as I felt a presence. There, in the corner, was my sweet friend hiding behind the fringed throws and clothing. He was pointing to an embroidered sun dress and waggling his eyebrows.

"You would look great in this, Babe," he called to me.

I found myself blushing and turned my attention to Annie, trying to block out my pesky ghost. "Annie, I really like this one." I showed her the cross stitch kit of the couple on the beach.

"Oh." She held it briefly. "How quaint. May I buy it for you? As a gift. Maybe it will open up that creativity that I know you have inside."

"Okay, thank you." Her constant innuendo implying there was so much wrong with my life for which she needed to intervene was starting to irritate me. However, she placed the little kit inside her own shopping basket and I headed over to check out the dress Davy had been pointing at. It was a lovely sleeveless gauzy number, light cocoa in color with dark brown and taupe embroidery, and it had a soft ruffle at the hem and a lightweight muslin lining. The embroidery on the neckline and hem included rustic beads made from coconut shells, so the tag read. I held it up to me and saw that it would fit nicely and wasn't too short, but was full of flowing femininity. It was a far cry from my normal tee shirts and shorts.

"Ohh," I sighed happily. "I love this. I've never had anything like this," I whispered, acting as if I were talking to myself. I glanced at the price tag and blanched. It was marked down to $45, but that was still a lot of money. It was then that Davy nudged me and pointed to a sign that said 50% off markdowns. "Whoa."

He grinned then. "$22.50. It's you." I grinned right back and folded it into my little shopping basket. "And thanks for the incense," he added as he shimmered away.

Annie was already paying for her items when I joined her. "What did you find, dear?"

"This lovely little dress." I held it against myself again and showed her.

"Oh, that is very pretty indeed! Taylor! Bettina! Did you see the dresses over there?" All three women made a beeline to the area where Davy had shimmered away and were pawing through the remaining clothing, leaving me to pay for my purchases in peace.

By the time we exited the shop, they'd bought themselves several shirts and skirts and were chattering happily about their "finds" as I thanked Davy in my thoughts.

You're welcome, Babe, I heard him reply as we all walked along the sidewalk.

We ended up at a waterfront restaurant for a late lunch and were seated outside on the deck under a banana leaf canopy. I had a fresh market salad, while Annie and Bettina had fish sandwiches, and Taylor had a burger. The food was good, the company on their better behavior, and the view of the harbor exquisite. It was busy at this hour with fishing tourists returning from their chartered excursions which provided us with welcome entertainment.

"This iced tea is nowhere near as good as what your chef makes," Annie chuckled.

"I agree. I don't know what Kalei's magic is, but the recipe is a family secret he's guarded for years."

After lunch we hit a couple of bookstores and I picked up a history book about the Kona Coast to add to my collection. I found myself reading more and more on the culture and history of Hawai'i. It was fascinating and I couldn't seem to get enough. I often felt I was transported back to King Kamehameha's era.

The drive home felt relaxed and even a bit lazy. I invited Annie, Bettina, and Taylor to join me in my bungalow for a light dinner later that night. Back at the inn, the trio returned to their own bungalow to rest and put away their purchases. I hung up my new dress and then checked in with Bennie; there were no issues to be addressed. I rather figured there wouldn't be, but it never hurts to check. Ming had left me a note that she needed a few extra supplies. I put them on my list and then sat in my living room for a few minutes with Chester snuggled on my lap. I stared out the sliding glass door, letting my mind wander until it went comfortably blank.

Winston fluttered to the deck railing and peered inside at me, jolting me out of my zone, so I joined him on the deck and let him sit on my shoulder. "How have you been, Mr. Winston?"

Cheer up Sleepy Jean, he sang in his cute little chirpy way. Marley, rarely far behind Winston, fluttered onto the deck and watched us. Susie suddenly appeared on the deck and plunked his body down on the large pillow I kept for him near my chair. He let out a contented sigh and groan. A soan? A grigh? Anyway, it was an endearing sound, and I reached down to give his head a little pat. Marley whistled a couple bars of a Bob Marley song just as Chester stretched and joined us, settling on my lap. I was surrounded by blissfully unconditional love.

The sun was low behind the treetops when I finally extricated myself from all the critters and went into my little kitchen to begin dinner. Annie, Bettina, and Taylor would arrive soon and I wanted to get a jump on things. We'd had such a big lunch, and fairly late too, that I decided on a vegetable frittata with a side salad of spring greens. I began chopping onions, garlic, tomatoes, zucchini, and basil for the frittata and got the eggs out to let them come to room temperature. I placed my spring greens in a bowl and peeled a couple of tangerines, separating the wedges and scattering them over the greens. I mixed up a small amount of orange vinaigrette, as Lani had shown me, and let it sit until the last minute. Setting out champagne glasses for Annie and Bettina, I then poured a glass of Sauvignon blanc for myself. Light and herbaceous, it would fit just perfectly with our meal, in case any of the others wanted a glass as well. As for me, I just drank what I was in the mood for, usually.

I heard a knock on the door and set my glass down to let my guests in. Passing by the open sliding glass door, I could see that Winston and Marley were sitting together on the deck railing, happily chattering away. Susie was still on his bed, but Chester had taken refuge from my impending guests. *I don't like them very much*, he'd told me just a few moments before, as he'd casually walked past, headed for my room.

Annie, Bettina, and Taylor stood on the other side of the door, Annie holding a brightly wrapped package in her arms which she held out to me.

"I brought you something that I made a while back. I think it belongs with you more than with me."

"Why thank you!" I took the package and held it in my hands for what seemed like a long time, since it wasn't often that I received a gift for no reason, and I wanted to savor it for a few minutes.

"Open it, silly!" Annie teased gently.

I gently tore off the wrapping and found a twelve-inch square stretched canvas done in watercolor. While the subject of the piece was a mother and child, it was the grouping of evergreen trees in the background that held my eye, for it was the same stand of trees near our old home in the Berkeley area. A lump began to form in my throat. That same lump began to quiver when I switched my gaze to the mother and small child. At once I recognized that it was a soft, hazy representation of my own mother and me. I could see her long blond hair hanging loosely around her shoulders, and I was nestled in the crook of her arm, my white cotton dress with pink ribbons blended against her softly embroidered blouse over a blue and white gauze skirt… the same skirt I still wore occasionally. In the distance, a young man walked toward the mother and child, and I could tell by his clothing that he represented my father. I felt flushed, my eyes burning with unshed tears.

"It's just simply the most beautiful thing in the whole world," I whispered, pulling my gaze away from the canvas to peer into the bright green eyes of the woman my mother once considered to be her best friend. "I…" I gulped, unable to find the words.

Annie's smile was the old one that I remembered from my youth. She lifted her hand to my face and cupped my cheek. "You're welcome." Her whisper matched mine, and I was grateful that I didn't have to say more. My thoughts were jumbled, my words lost in the depth of emotion. The tears finally came, rolling down my cheeks and dropping hotly onto my hands that still clutched this most magnificent gift. And although it was an unframed canvas, I felt it was perfectly finished — raw nature and beauty just like my parents had been. I moved to the wall that was the first visible area near the front door and removed an old print of Uncle Wally's, putting this canvas in its new and very special place of honor. I knew Uncle Wally wouldn't mind. I would see this every day and every night, as would any guests who visited. I stood gazing at the canvas for a long while, my arms hanging limply at my side. I could nearly feel my mother's arms around me, could sense that strength in her protective embrace, drawing upon the energy of the evergreen trees beyond. As irritating as Annie could be, this piece of art proved to me that she truly knew my mother, and therefore provided a terribly important link I needed. I was suddenly able to cast aside the irritation I'd felt and instead bask in the love.

Silently, I turned to Annie and hugged her hard and long. She hugged me right back, and without either of us speaking a single word, we felt the connection. She pulled away just slightly and cupped the back of my head. "I love you," she whispered.

"I love you too."

"All right, all right." Taylor stepped up with her grandmother's glass of champagne in one hand and my glass of white wine in the other. "Enough of this, or you'll have us all bawling."

I was grateful for the brash interruption and the sudden return to jarring reality as she slipped my wine into my hand. I took a too-big gulp and heaved a sigh of what? Relief? No, more like exhaustion. Emotions were tiring, and I'd had more than my fair share in my life, dammit.

All too brightly, I turned to my three guests and apologized for them having to get their own drinks. "Forgive me for my lapse in properly carrying out my host duties, but let's take our drinks out onto the deck. It's a magical evening." I gave the painting one last glance.

Outside, Susie allowed himself to be petted. Actually, let's face it, he luxuriated in the attention. Marley and Winston bobbed their heads as Marley whistled one of my favorite Bob Marley tunes, "One Love." We were having a mini-party on the deck.

I brought out a small basket of poi chips, another of Lani's little treats, and a bowl of spicy mango salsa. Then I pulled out the local map and we joined together to make plans for them for the next day.

The evening was going splendidly. I excused myself for a few minutes to get the frittata going, and at the end, to dress the salad. I served both on the deck, four plates that included a large wedge of the egg and vegetable concoction with a big pile of greens with tangerines and orange dressing.

We ate amidst amicable small talk, and the meal was enjoyable for a bit until Taylor decided to share her news. I quickly grabbed the champagne, some beers, and my wine as Taylor made her revelation. I made sure to keep all glasses filled and beers available, all the while watching the faces of Annie and Bettina. I thought for sure Bettina was going to explode, but she surprised me by keeping her cool. The second surprise was Annie's cool... no... chilly... actually freezing response.

"Very well, Taylor. Do what you think you must, but don't come crying to me for validation or funds. You're on your own."

Although I could see Taylor was steaming, she attempted a casual tone. "Actually, Gran, I'm not. Dad has promised to help me."

"Oh, really." Annie's voice dripped with disdain.

"Yes, really. He believes in me."

She simply snorted derisively. I glanced at Bettina, who was making lazy circles with the condensation on the table before her as she twirled her glass. She suddenly plunked that same glass down hard on the table.

"Dammit Taylor. You couldn't wait until after the holiday? Why is it all about you, every single day?"

Bettina stood, drained her glass, and left.

I was dumbfounded, glancing back and forth between Annie and Taylor. Their expressions, however, were unreadable. This family was a series of see-saw moves. Up, down, up, down, until someone was bound to fall off. It was exhausting to me, but I didn't know what to do. I just sat there, sipping my wine and craving popcorn for some reason.

Annie then turned her scathing look on her granddaughter. "Really, Taylor? You felt the need to spoil a perfectly lovely evening?"

"I'm sick of walking on eggshells! No matter what I do, I'm wrong. I'm out of here." She stomped off, leaving me alone with Annie.

"I apologize for the girls," she said to me, and belittling the two women, who were well on the other side of girlhood.

I simply nodded, not wanting to feed her inner fire.

"Well, I guess I'll be going. I need to patch us together yet again. Thank you for the lovely dinner."

"No problem," I muttered to her as she disappeared.

Davy shimmered in as I stacked the dishes to cart them to my little kitchen.

"Whoa. What is *up* with those women?"

Letting loose with a heavy sigh of exasperation, I took my stack of dishes to the sink. "I have no idea. It's like living in a den of porcupines."

He laughed in that wondrously infectious manner and I couldn't help but grin. He wandered to the new watercolor addition on my wall and gazed at it. "This is good," he mumbled.

"It really is. But it's too bad that the heart of the artist is dead."

"Yeah, I could see it was a white-knuckle day."

"You saw us and heard it all?"

"Oh yeah. I just didn't make my presence known, except to try to convince you to buy that dress. You did, didn't you?"

I grinned. "I did. It's beautiful. I haven't even tried it on yet, but it doesn't matter because it makes me happy even on the hanger."

"What? You haven't modeled it? Do it now! *Now*, Babe! I demand it." He was being cute and he knew it. So... I trotted to my room to put the dress on. As it fell onto my shoulders and down to the tops of my knees I gasped and then sighed happily. It was not only beautiful, but it felt so... floaty. So sexy, too. I did a little twirl and bent down, just to be sure it didn't show too much if I wore it for dinner service one night. When it met my requirements, I sashayed into the living room where Davy sat in one of the chairs. He whistled, long and loudly.

"Oh my word," he breathed. "You are... gorgeous."

I felt my face flush but managed a tiny little "Thank you."

He stood and took my hand, pulling me close into sort of a ballroom dancing pose. He waved his hand and music began to play. How *did* he do that? Tony Bennett sang "The Way You Look Tonight" and we slowly danced cheek to cheek. All the ugliness of the evening fell away and I felt warm and loved.

FOUR

Fried Spam and a Juggling Ghost

Monday morning dawned clear and bright, and I was looking forward to returning to my normal life after spending the previous day with the Devil Trio. I showered, dressed in my standard shorts, tee shirt, and the requisite flip flops, and fed Chester before heading to the reception area. Bennie was on the phone, so I made a beeline to the coffee urn and poured a cup of his Kona, adding a generous splash of half and half. This time I got a heavier hit of chocolate in my first sip, but it was gone by the time I took my second.

"Sorry, Macca." Bennie turned after he'd hung up the phone. "I accidentally dumped twice as many cocoa nibs in the brew today. I blame it on Winston and Marley. They distracted me." He gave an impish grin.

I peered at the two birds who sat together on the outdoor perch, looking innocent. "What did they do?"

"They stole my donut! Evil little mongooses with wings."

I roared with laughter because it was the very last thing I'd expected to hear. Those birds never acted out like that. "Well, I blame their bad behavior on the Terrible Trio staying with us. The dark cloud of gloom has tainted our little mascots."

He laughed with me. "It's been difficult then?"

I blew out a huge breath I hadn't realized I'd been holding. Tension does weird things to the human body. "Yep. Horrible. I'm looking forward to the weekend."

He looked sheepishly at me. "Um… it's only Monday."

"Shhh! I don't want to hear that!" I even stuck my tongue out at him. Yes, my apparently mis-chosen family had that effect on me too, I guess. He simply shook his head and turned back to the computer, grinning.

"New booking for next week," Bennie casually informed me. "Their timing was great because the guy calling seemed to expect me to say we were full up. I swear, I could almost feel him high-fiving me when I told him we had a vacancy."

"Oh," I exclaimed, chuckling at the visual before recovering. "Finally some good news."

"But that means your family has to check out on the promised date."

"Oh, they will, believe me, even if I have to drive them to the airport myself!" I nearly skipped off to do my chores, the thought of the Devil Trio's checkout date giving me something to look forward to.

Ming had the day off, so I got the service cart out and pushed it down the wooden walkway. I was grateful that we'd replaced the wheels on the cart with larger balloon-type mini-tires, making it easier to push the beast along the bumpy walkway. I stopped at Number 1 and knocked. "Housekeeping," I called out, then unlocked the door. Our guests had indeed departed, so I began to clean the bungalow and replace the linens. I kept doing this at each bungalow, with the exception of Number 3, still occupied, and Number 4 which was the Morrison family. Since they were staying long-term, they had asked that we only clean their bungalow once a week, and we were more than happy to abide by such a request.

When I got to Number 6, where The Trio was staying, I held my breath when I knocked and called out, "Housekeeping!" No answer to my knock made me smile in relief, but when I opened the door I was met by a disaster scene. Clothes were strewn everywhere, empty glasses and dishes all over nearly every surface, and linens bunched up on the floors and the furniture. "Oh my..." I couldn't even finish my thoughts. I dialed Bennie's cell from my own and asked him to join me at Number 6. He was there in just a minute and stood transfixed in the open doorway.

"What the hell happened?"

"I... I'm not sure. Is this a crime scene? It sure looks like it." I surveyed the bedrooms and found similar disarray. "Should I call the police?"

"No. Why don't you call one of their cells and just casually ask when they think they'll be back."

"Oh! Good idea." I scrolled through my directory and called Annie's cell first. No answer, and off to voicemail. I left a short message that I was just checking on them. I tried Taylor's next, because Bettina was just my least favorite of the group. She answered just before it went to voicemail.

"Hi Taylor. It's Macca. Just checking on you all. How are things going?"

"Hi Macca! We're just now at Waipi'o Lookout. It's fabulous!" It was hard to hear all of what she was saying, cell service being spotty in many areas.

"So you're all okay then?"

"Oh yes. We'll head down to Parker Ranch from here and be back to the inn this afternoon."

"Okay." This was so surreal. "I'll see you later." I disconnected the call and turned to Bennie in shock. "They're fine. I guess they're just total slobs." I shook my head and began to clean up.

"I'll help you." The poor guy really didn't have to, but I surely appreciated it.

"Thank you, and… I'm sorry. I'm so sorry." Channeling Doctor Who, I wondered if I should shout, "Allons-y!"

"We've had slobs before." He chuckled and it was infectious. I found myself laughing right beside him. Yeah, they were slobs, but this was just downright rude too.

We spent the better part of an hour just picking things up and either carting them to the main kitchen for cleaning or the laundry for washing. I cleaned the mini-kitchen, the bathroom, and all the surfaces in the living areas. I was wiped out and hadn't even tackled the vacuuming or replacing the linens yet. Bennie took a stack of sheets from me and began in the master bedroom. I took the second bedroom and we finished nearly evenly. I had worked up quite a sweat and stood wiping my brow as Bennie pulled out his cell and placed a call.

"Ming," he responded when the other end was apparently answered. "Number 6… Did they leave a pig sty yesterday?"

I could only hear his side of the conversation, but as he stood there nodding, I knew the worst: they were indeed disgusting. "Please tell her I'm so very sorry," I whispered.

He relayed the message to her and then grinned before saying goodbye. He slipped his phone into his pocket and chuckled. "She says you owe her an extra day off."

"And she can have it… after they leave." We both giggled but vowed to help Ming clean this bungalow each day. It was far more than could be expected of one person.

By the time we finished, the guests in Number 3 had gone for the day so I shooed Bennie back to his other duties and tackled it solo. It was a breath of fresh air compared to what we'd just seen.

After restocking the service cart and putting it away for the day, I trudged to my own bungalow and took a quick, cooling shower. It was heavenly. Chester pushed the door open while I was wrapping the towel around me.

"Hey big guy. How are you doing today?"

I'm ready for them to go home. I don't like them. I don't like how they treat you or anyone else.

"I know sweetie. We've got several more days though. Thankfully they'll be gone for a night down at the volcanoes."

Oh, that will be the time to celebrate then. He swished his tail in irritation as he perched on the toilet lid. I felt his pain.

After my shower I worked on the mountain of laundry from the day's cleanup. As sweat dripped down my face, my chest, and my back, a brief thought flashed through my mind. *Why on earth did I take a shower before doing this huge task?* Ming would probably laugh at me, for she was an old hand and would have known to wait. Oh well, maybe I'd learn the real ropes someday.

As I was transferring wet linens to one of the dryers, and more dirty linens into the washers, Chester found me and wound his soft and furry body around my bare legs.

"Hello Chet. How ya doin'?"

I feel like I'm in a scene from Poltergeist, he said in my head as usual. *They're baaaack.* I admit it; I groaned. Loudly.

And then it hit me. "Hey! Who let you watch *Poltergeist* anyway, young man?" I think I heard him snicker as he sashayed away, presumably to find a quiet place to hide. I realized then that I hadn't seen much of Susie, Winston, or Marley today either, proving once again that animals are smarter than humans.

I heard Annie asking Bennie my whereabouts and wondered if I could quietly close the laundry room door to hide out for a while, but it was too late; he directed her right to me. I was bent over the dryer, pulling towels out and folding them before stacking them on the shelves behind me.

"Macca! What on earth are you doing?"

I blinked a few times at the incredibly stupid question. "Working. How was your day?" I tried to put on a cheery face; I really did.

She paused for a long moment before answering. "We had a very nice time." Her frown was still on her face as she watched me methodically fold and stack, fold and stack. "You clean and do laundry too?"

"On Ming's day off, yes. The only way any of us gets any time off is to pitch in and cover. We all know how to do the others' jobs, except we leave the cooking to Kalei for safety's sake." It may seem like I was joking, but it had been discussed a lot among all of us at the inn. We may laugh, but it's serious business cooking for actual customers.

"It just seems so… menial." She wrinkled her brow and puckered her lips as if that word left a bad taste in her mouth.

"That it is. I'm living the good life." My sarcasm button had been pushed. I stacked the last of the towels and moved more laundry between washer and dryer, which I would repeat until it was all done or I died on the spot, whichever came first. On the upside, I saw my upper arms were toning nicely since I'd moved here. Gotta find the bright spot in everything, right?

"Well, we're going to relax by the pool if you want to join us." She was slowly shaking her head in dismay and I laughed out loud then.

"Yeah, when I've won the laundry battle I may join you."

Still perplexed, she watched me for a few beats before turning to leave, calling over her shoulder, "Okay. Hope to see you soon." She sounded unsure.

"Snob," I muttered under my breath after she'd gone, and then I chuckled. When at last I was done with the Mt. Everest equivalent of laundry, I changed into my swimsuit and went out to the pool, joining Annie, Bettina, and Taylor. Annie had set up her easel and was working to capture the colors of a flowering plumeria on a small canvas.

"Nice." I watched her for a moment and then dove smoothly into the cool water. I swam a few laps and climbed out again, bringing my towel to a chair next to the women. "So, tell me about your adventures today!"

"I wish we had time to actually go down into Waipi'o Valley," Taylor whined. "It was spectacular from the lookout!"

"Maybe next time." Bettina actually smiled briefly, then seemed to wipe it away when she realized she'd nearly cracked her grumpy facade.

"Oh, do you think there will be a next time?" Taylor sat up straight, shoving her sunglasses on top of her head and facing her mother.

"I'm pretty sure. Your Gran says she has many subjects to paint yet."

Taylor clapped her hands in glee, very much like a five-year-old might do. It was just a little ridiculous. No, a lot. When would this young woman, so close to my own age, grow up? Or, did I grow up too early due to the circumstances with my parents? Life questions that I didn't have the stamina to address at the time.

"Annie," I included the elder woman in the conversation, "you would find so many fantastic things to paint in the valley! The waterfalls are astounding!"

"I read that there are several. Is that right?" Annie turned, slipping her reading glasses down to the tip of her nose and peering over the top.

"Yes! Beautiful falls at the back of the valley, and also at the mouth, pouring into the sea. It's breathtaking!"

"I would love to be able to try to paint a waterfall! I haven't had much practice with falling water."

"Judging by the colors and shadows on the painting you gave me, I think you would do a superb job of it!"

She grinned and gave me a little wink. "Thank you, dear!" She swiveled back to her canvas and dabbed at a little color on her palette to apply to her project.

"We also enjoyed the Parker Ranch area. The horse farms are fun," Taylor added. "I love the classic white ranch fencing, with the green grass and the horses in the pastures. Very pretty. And we did a little shopping at Waimea, and had lunch at a lovely little Hawaiian food truck with picnic tables and benches beside it. Imagine that!"

Wow, stooping to the local level, I thought, and inwardly giggled. Food trucks were a huge draw across the Hawaiian islands, and the local fare was fresh and frankly addictive. I was partial to several trucks' vegetarian takes on local food, like a tempeh katsu sandwich with sundried tomato tapenade. I would go out of my way for that one.

"I had a fried spam sandwich today," Taylor exclaimed, clearly enamored with the most iconic local *meat*, as it were. "It was fab!" Whoa, flashback to the 60s, of which neither of us were familiar. Well, to be fair, I probably had a leg up on her because Davy (oh how I was missing him lately) often shared his memories of the 60s, including the standard line borrowed from his bandmate, "I'm told I had a really good time."

I listened for a long time while they expounded on their adventures, and even though it sounded like they'd had a great time, I was quite happy not to have been with them. Laundry was no longer the worst job at the inn.

By late afternoon I was yawning, the physical labor of the day breaking down my stamina. We agreed to meet for dinner and I escaped to the privacy of my bungalow. After quickly showering off the chlorine from the pool I stretched out on the bed for a rest. Chester joined me, followed closely by Davy. Mr. Pinckney shimmer-jolted-blipped in, saw us, muttered an "oh dear" and blipped-jolted-nearly shimmered out. Davy chuckled deep in his throat, snuggling next to the cat and me.

"I've missed you," I whispered.

"I'm right here now." I held onto his arms around me and we dozed for about an hour, Chester's purrs providing the perfect lullaby.

When I awoke, a stream of drool had pooled on my pillow.

"So attractive," Davy teased. I wiped my face on the sleeve of my tee-shirt. "Also attractive," he chuckled.

"Shut up," I croaked, my voice still full of sleep. He shimmered away then, his laughter trailing behind and lingering briefly in the air after his disappearance.

Just before I needed to be in the kitchen to help with last minute dinner service preparations, I donned my new sundress and bronze flip flops. I added my usual earrings and pulled the hair at the crown of my head back in a clip, letting the length fall on my shoulders and down my back as I said goodbye to Chester. *I really need a haircut*, I thought to myself and hurried to help Kalei and Lani. We did a quick set-up and the guests began to arrive a few minutes early, as usual.

When I saw Annie, Bettina, and Taylor arrive, I showed them to their table and brought their drinks, including a glass of wine for myself. Settling into the fourth chair, I waited nervously for one of them to complain about something. I didn't have to wait long.

"Mother, we could have eaten out you know."

"I know," Annie brushed her daughter off, "but we should spend time with Macca. We won't be here for a couple of days, after all."

Oh, I nearly squirmed with anticipation. "I think you'll like the dinner here, Bettina. It's not a buffet tonight like Luau night." I stood and fetched the freshly printed menus, for every night was different depending on the availability of local fish, meat, and produce. I handed the sheets to each of them and waited for the next complaint. Instead, I was met with sounds of pleasure as one by one they spied something on the menu that enticed them.

"Oh, this looks good," Taylor began, smiling widely. "I'm going to have the sweet and sour rib platter!"

"That sounds good," Annie began, "but I think I'll try the... Ono! I've never had Ono, but the preparation sounds interesting. What kind of fish is that?"

"It's also called Wahoo on the mainland. It's a flaky white fish, one of the favorites in the islands."

"You've never tried it though?" she asked, but I think she knew the answer. She'd never been keen on the fact that my parents had raised me vegetarian.

"No, but our guests rave about it, and it's not always available. If Kalei has it, I strongly recommend it, and I know you won't be disappointed."

Bettina was listening and glancing at the menu. "I think I want to try the Ono, but maybe the seafood Cobb salad would be better. Hmmm." She peered eagerly at the menu. Then she looked up at me. "What are you having?"

"Actually, I'm having the roasted mushroom and crispy kale fettuccine."

"That sounds interesting, but I am really in the mood for seafood." She bit at her lower lip.

"You're welcome to have a taste of my pasta, Bettina."

Her face brightened. "Oh, that would be perfect! I'm just curious. Your chef has remarkable talents."

I beamed. "Yes, I agree. Thank you. And I'll be sure to tell him how pleased you are."

She grinned, but it was fleeting, as if she realized she shouldn't have a reason to smile or be happy. It tugged at my heart and made me wonder what had happened to her to make her so wary.

When our food arrived, I fetched an extra plate and dished up a few forkfuls of my pasta, passing it across to Bettina.

"Oh my." She took a bite, being sure to get mushroom, kale, and pasta on the fork. "That is heavenly. So velvety, but with a bit of crunch."

I grinned, feeling pleased that she enjoyed it. It was definitely one of my favorite dishes on Kalei's menu.

"This fish, Ono is it?" Annie looked up at me, chewing slowly.

"Yes, Ono or Wahoo."

"It's really good!"

"Now I wish I'd ordered something more exotic," Taylor spoke between mouthfuls. "The ribs are great, but I should have tried a new dish."

"You'll have a few more opportunities before we have to leave." Annie smiled over her glass of champagne. This was by far one of the best conversations I'd had with this family since they arrived. I was relieved to feel a little lightness around me at last, and then they had to go and spoil it.

"I sure don't feel like packing anything up for tomorrow's trip to the volcano," Taylor complained.

"You don't have to go with us, you know." Annie looked sideways at her granddaughter.

"Mother, really." Bettina sounded weary. Then she turned her attention to her own daughter. "It'd be easier if you didn't throw your stuff around, you know."

"Poor Macca had to clean up after you today," Annie joined the attack on the younger woman. "Did you know that?"

Taylor looked stricken and turned to me. "Is that true?"

I took a sip of my iced tea and set the glass down before responding with a simple "Yes."

She put her hand up to her face, a theatrical move. "I'm so sorry. The entire place was a mess." She turned to her grandmother before adding, "Including your room, Gran."

"Well, we were in a hurry this morning," she scoffed. I had trouble holding in a derisive snort, and I fear a tiny bit of it escaped. All three of them looked at me.

"Sorry." I feigned choking on my tea to provide cover. I knew the truth though. All three of them were slobs, with no regard for "hired help" as I'm sure they referred to us.

They continued bickering over little things for far longer than was comfortable so I excused myself to help Lani. Believe me, cleaning the kitchen was more pleasant than listening to them. By the time I returned to my seat, the three women were silent. Very silent.

"Is everything okay?" Why did I even ask that?

"Yes," Annie murmured, but it wasn't. They weren't speaking to each other but were gathering their things to leave the dining area.

"What time are you leaving in the morning?"

"Early." Bettina was her normal glum self again.

"Then I should say goodnight so you can get some sleep." I stood and gathered our dishes. "And I'll see you Wednesday evening when you return." I tried to be bright and cheery but I doubt it was very convincing.

They rose and quietly bid their farewells. I was so happy to be rid of them, even if it was just for a short while. I bussed more dishes, taking them to Lani. She and I scrubbed, soaked, and ran things through the large dishwasher. It was emotionally cleansing for me to see the dinnerware emerge pristine.

"Rough evening?" Lani bumped my shoulder playfully with her own.

"Extremely. You know how there's birth family, and then there's chosen family, like you? Well, there's also family chosen by prior members of your family who turn out to be mischosen. Is that even a word?" I pulled my brow into a frown, my "thinking" face, but gave up within seconds and shrugged. "Well, it is now."

Lani laughed. "I love it when you make up words. And yes, I do understand." And then I saw her eyes soften. "They are your last connection to your parents, aren't they?"

I nodded, and my throat suddenly constricted.

"I'm so sorry for that." She wiped her soapy hands and then turned to hug me. I swear, she nearly hugged the stuffing out of me. I didn't know she had such strength. I wrapped my arms around the petite woman and squeezed right back.

"Thank you. My newly chosen family is wonderful. After this week, I will most likely divorce myself from the old."

"I think that's a difficult decision, but I support whatever you do. Really. You're so kind and genuine. They don't deserve you."

"Oh my gosh." I found myself swiping soapy hands across my cheeks to catch the tears that were rolling down. "I love you guys so much. Thank you."

44

We hugged again, and I felt such resolve, such strength and fortitude in her embrace. "Kalei doesn't even want to be in the same room as them," she whispered and giggled. "He says they're toxic."

"Yes!" I pulled away to look at her and we both giggled. "Toxic. That's perfect."

"You don't need toxicity in your life. You've been through enough."

I clasped both her hands in mine. "Thank you. You have no idea how much that means to me."

"Hey!" Kalei's voice boomed as he came in from the walk-in cooler. "What's going on here? You're supposed to be sudsing, not blubbering!" His teasing tone was so endearing.

"Go back to your cooler, big man," Lani teased back. "We're having a girl-moment here."

"Oh! Yikes! I'm outta here." He made a cartoon-like movement and skedaddled out the back door, presumably to make sure the imu oven was securely locked down for the night.

Lani just shook her head. "That kane... cracks me up and irritates me all within eleven minutes or less."

I chuckled and we turned back to the last of the clean-up. My heart felt lighter though.

I didn't relax until Winston and Marley were properly ensconced in their shared cage and I was back in my bungalow with Chester on my lap and Susie next to me on the sofa. I took a deep breath, slowly let it out, and closed my eyes. So cleansing. Susie stretched beside me and I buried my fingers in the thick fur around his neck. He groaned in pleasure. Chester then stretched, but curled up again, his head resting against my stomach. I smoothed the fur along his head, neck, and back and he slow-blinked at me... twice... before closing his eyes. I picked up my book and settled in to read.

It wasn't even ten minutes though before I felt Davy's shimmer and Mr. Pinckney's shimmer-jolt-blip. "You really need to work on that." I smiled at the librarian ghost.

"Oh dear." Mr. Pinckney wrung his hands and fidgeted. "I'm just not as talented as Davy, I guess."

Davy playfully punched his friend's shoulder. "You're gettin' it, man! Just keep practicing! Do you know how long it took me to learn to juggle?"

"No. How long?" the timid voice whined, not recognizing that it had been a rhetorical question.

"Long. Let's just say long," he deadpanned. Even Davy seemed to lose patience with Mr. Pinckney at times.

"Okay." The timid ghost settled into a chair, hovering just a few inches above it. Davy picked up three of Chester's cat toys and began to juggle. Slowly at first, then picking up speed.

"It's all in the hand-eye coordination," he said, his words keeping the beat of the toys moving in and out of his hands.

"Whoa…" Mr. Pinckney's eyes were round as he watched.

I shook my head. "This is lovely entertainment, but Susie, Chester, and I were just settling down to relax for the evening."

"Pffft." Davy caught his juggled cat toys one at a time and placed them on the coffee table. "Relax? You don't need to relax! Let's go have some fun!"

"Um. No. It's been a rough day and I'm completely done."

He stopped and peered at me for several beats before responding. "Yeah, you're looking a bit worse for wear there, Babe."

"Gee, thanks. You look great too." Pushing that sarcasm button again.

Davy turned to his ghostly buddy. "Hey, let's go find some entertainment then."

"I don't know." He wrung his hands. "Last time you suggested that we ended up being seen by all those little kids at the concert in the park."

"Oh, come on. What's a little mischief? The kids were fine."

"What's this now…" I began to ask then decided I really didn't want to know any details in case I was ever interviewed by police about said event. I shook my head and picked up my book again. "Bye, you two. See you later." They shimmer-blipped out and the bungalow was quiet again.

I became engrossed in my book again in no time, the characters coming to life while feasting and dancing in my imagination. "Don't order the turkey leg!" I yelled at the main character who was attending a fair. "Get the falafel!" And with that exclamation I might have crossed the line of sanity in some people's eyes, I'm sure. "Oh dangit! Now I'm hungry." I snapped the book shut, carefully moved the sleeping cat from my lap to the sofa, and shuffled to the kitchen. Grabbing a banana in its naturally zippered package, I made a cup of tea and took both back to the sofa. Crossing my legs under me, I nibbled at my banana and picked up the book again. The animals hadn't stirred. Susie stretched and settled once more. Chester hadn't even moved a whisker the entire time. This was the perfectly peaceful end to yet another crazy day in my life.

FIVE

Barking Sea Lions and a Honking Moose

Tuesday dawned bright and cheery and so did I. The threesome were well on their way to Volcanoes National Park, and I was relieved I was not with them. It wasn't only because they were driving me nuts, but also that I wasn't sure I could be trusted to *not* push them into the crater. "Oh, look at the pretty lava rock. Look closer! Closer!" Boom! I smiled to myself. We all need that tiny release, in our imagination only of course, in order to let loose those pent up feelings of frustration and anger. What divides the good people from the bad is that most of us would never act upon it. However, the memory of two people who did try to snuff out my light over the past couple of years flashed behind my eyes and I was flooded with guilt for having such thoughts.

So, I rolled out of bed, showered, and dressed in bright pink shorts, a pink and white polka dot tank top, and white flip flops. Instant cheer. I tied my hair up in a knot and began my lovely day by feeding Chester. I left the sliding glass door cracked so he could wander after his meal, and I headed for the reception area. Bennie hadn't yet arrived so I pulled the cover off of Winston and Marley's cage and let them out while I filled their dishes with fresh water and food. Watching them commence their morning ritual of "waking up" put a grin on my face. They would stretch one wing, groom their feathers, stretch the other wing, groom more feathers, and then finish with a big yawn. At last they fluttered over to their open perch to watch me.

I'm a pretty boy.

"Yes you are, Winston. And Marley? You're a pretty girl."

Marley whistled a reggae tune, even putting a bit of a back beat to it. Or would it be back beak? I found it hilarious that she could be a one-bird band at times. I cleaned out their cage, replacing the bottom covering and giving the perches just a bit of smoothing. They eyed me carefully from the safety of their open air domain.

"You're very suspicious," I teased and Marley bobbed her head. "Okay, be good," I reminded them as I began to open up the doors and swing all the storm shutters open to catch the refreshing morning breeze. I did the same in the dining area before returning to the front desk.

Checking my inbox, I found notes from Kalei about kitchen supplies, so I added the info to my purchase order folder. I would work on those once Bennie arrived to start the most important part of every morning: the big pot of his special blend of Kona coffee. I knew he added a pinch of cinnamon and a couple of cocoa nibs, but I had previously tried to duplicate his recipe without success. Knowing he was due any minute, I left it for him. On his days off, we had to make do with plain old Kona, and most of us grumbled the entire time, but it was all in good humor; it just proved that we loved his brew.

I heard Bennie talking to the birds before he came inside, where he greeted me as well. "Good morning, Macca!" He was almost always cheerful and today was no different. "Your guests aren't here today and tomorrow, yes?" Ahh, the reason for his cheerfulness was the same as mine.

"Good morning! And yep, they're gone! I feel like singing and dancing," I responded.

He did a hilarious little pirouette and ended with a mock leap and a very unsteady arabesque on one leg. I found myself giggling the entire time, dissolving into a fit of laughter at his final pose.

"Bravo!" I shouted and clapped through my laughter. He took an exaggerated bow then, and when he stood straight he was laughing too. Suddenly he hugged me close and kissed me on the lips. And the interesting part is that I wasn't the one to pull away first; he was.

"Oh my gosh." He was out of breath and blushing. "I'm so sorry." He ducked his head and rushed out of the reception area. I was left stunned and unsure of not only his actions but also my reaction. I can't say I didn't like it. I can't say I wished he hadn't done it either. I grabbed up my file of purchase orders and hurried to take refuge in my own bungalow. Shutting the door behind me, I leaned against it, breathing heavily. Bennie and I had been skirting at something for months, but I wasn't sure what it was or exactly how I felt about it.

"Oh my... oh dear," I muttered, shaking my head, yet remembering the feeling of his lips upon mine. I groaned in frustration. What the hell was I supposed to do? How should I handle this? And most importantly, what did I want? I stood there for the longest time, just holding up the front door with my back. Chester wandered in and rubbed his soft fur against my bare legs, but I was not easily distracted.

What's wrong, Mom?

"Nothing, Chet. All is... Oh hell! All is a jumbled mess." I finally moved away from the door, giving it a brief glance as if it might burst open any second. I dropped my file on the coffee table and plunked onto the sofa. "Davy?"

No response, no shimmer, not even a blip from Mr. Pinckney. "Davy?" I called again. I didn't want to use our emergency word, goldfish, so I just sat back on the sofa for a few minutes, stroking Chester and gazing out the open sliding glass door to the deck, the tropics, and the ocean beyond. "Davy?" Still nothing.

My eyes glazed over as I stared out to sea, briefly noticing Susie snoozing on the deck. Out of the corner of my eye I spied a subtle movement. I turned my head to try to find it again and at last I caught sight of a large and gorgeous swallowtail hovering on the other side of the sliding glass door. I felt a frown crease my forehead as I focused on its movement and tilted my head. The graceful butterfly seemed as if it were in grayscale, but now and then the sun caught a glint of iridescent blue and gold on the hind wings. I was mesmerized by the slow flutter of its wings and allowed my eyes to follow its movements easily. However, when it maneuvered through the open glass door, I held my breath. This was... different. It fluttered toward me and around me, alighting briefly on my knee before taking a lazy flight again. Hovering close to my face, I could feel the slight current of air around its wings. Suddenly it took flight again and was out the door and gone.

"Whoa," I said to no one. "That was weird, and kind of wonderful too."

Really? Chester peered up at me with a lazy look on his face. *You didn't get that?*

"Get what?"

Chester grumbled then. *You humans. You've low intellect and it's only our lack of thumbs that keep us from taking over the planet.*

I chuckled before replying. "Right. Keep on dreaming, bud."

Really? You don't see that the butterfly was from Davy? You didn't connect that, oh mighty human?

I gasped then, for it did make sense, yet I'd never experienced such a thing. "But... why?"

He can't always come to you when you call, you know. He has many responsibilities to people that look to him, that call to him, that honor him.

He was right, and I had been a fool. All this time I'd thought I was unique, but in actuality, he probably visited many people like he did me.

He only visits you the way he does: up close and personal, but he stays involved with many others. Many. He sends signs and he watches and encourages. But you? You actually get to have him in a very special manner. And don't get me wrong... he loves it. You give him joy. But I swear, I will deny I ever said any of this.

"Really?"

Yes. I will deny it to my dying day.

"No, I mean... I'm really the only one?"

For now, yes. It can change though. Don't ever take it for granted.
"I never have and I promise I never will."
Good. Now, can I get back to my nap? Please?
I chuckled and gave him a gentle shoulder massage.
Oh my, that's good. That will do the trick. Thank you. That's the spot that you put flea medicine on and it always itches. Ahhhh….
And he was asleep, or so I thought. "Thank you Chester… from the bottom of my heart."
How about the top of it instead?
"Everyone's a comedian." I smoothed his fur. "But thank you, little guy. I love you. Now go back to sleep."
Love you too. Just don't expect me to say that all the time.
I chuckled and peered out the window again, willing the swallowtail to reappear. Instead, the air was calm and clear.

I hid out in my bungalow for as long as I could before deciding to take a nice long run to clear my head.

"Come on, Susie," I called to him. "Run with me?"

He eagerly got to his feet as I donned socks and running shoes. We then hit the path via the back way in order to better avoid Bennie. As I passed the main building I could see through the open shutters to the front desk and felt great relief when I saw him there working on the computer. Skirting behind the building, we picked up speed on the path. Susie was such a great running companion. He kept after me when I got distracted or slowed down, pushing me to keep going. His huge tongue lolled out the side of his open mouth. My feet slapped the pavement on the path between Hale Mele and the neighboring property, and Susie's paws beat a rhythm beside me. As I neared the neighboring resort I pushed on, spurred to get beyond the cliff where Mr. Sikes had tried to do me in. Susie and I kept going, and I felt my troubles drop away as the adrenaline and endorphins kicked in.

"Way to go, boy," I encouraged Susie, and he looked up at me with that goofy dog grin that always made me smile. We ran until we hit the property line of the Royal Aina Resort, and then I pushed myself harder along the perimeter. I knew Sikes' ex-wife was trying to sell the large hotel complex and I hoped for her success. She'd helped bankroll so many of our own upgrades for the inn, as a sort of apology for her now ex-husband's evil doings.

We turned around and headed back at the same pace. I found myself slowing a little, so we took a shorter route home. Susie didn't object. As I ran past the rocking chairs in the grassy area, one by one they rocked gently, as if standing up to do "The Wave" to cheer me on. I chuckled breathlessly and sent Davy a message in my mind. *Thank you. I'd bow but… you know.* I heard his breathy laugh fade away in the distance so I pressed on to the end.

Back in the bungalow Susie went for the water bowl and I hit the jug of water I kept in the fridge. I could hear both of us swallowing huge amounts of the refreshing liquid.

"Water is life," I said to Susie. "Remember that." He looked up grinning, water pouring from his jowls. "Gee, thanks. I have to clean that up, you know." I gave him a two-handed scratch on the sides of his head and kissed his snout. He plopped himself down on his bed and stretched out, panting. "Yeah, me too, big guy."

I hit the shower and dressed in a new set of shorts and a tank, then flopped onto the sofa. I didn't care if my hair went in a million different directions; I was just going to tie it up in a knot anyway.

After a good twenty minutes of just zoning out, I got to my feet, grabbed my purchasing file and laptop, and sat in my favorite chair on the deck. Such a rough life, working in the sunshine with an incredible view before me. And avoiding Bennie. But I didn't want to think too hard about that right now.

It took a good hour to manage our various orders from equally varying vendors. As I made sure my purchase orders were organized and saved to the inn's account I could see that Bennie was currently putting other types of the inn's files there as well so I quickly finished my business before shutting down.

"You're being ridiculous, Macca. Even seeing his username is freaking you out? Coward," I scolded myself. Susie lifted his head to peer at me, but seemed satisfied I was not in any danger and laid down again. I responded to a few email inquiries, including one from my attorney, Alex Baldwin. He was inviting me to join him and his wife along with the Parker Kulas for dinner. Delighted, I responded and put the date, a few weeks off, on my calendar. I had just recently had the two couples to the inn for dinner, and Kalei had gone all out on the luau spread for that particular Saturday. We'd all had a grand time, joking, teasing, laughing, eating, and drinking. It had been a memorable evening and now they were reciprocating yet again. It was nice to have that to look forward to.

I was successful at avoiding being alone with Bennie for the rest of the day as I went about my business tasks.

When I awoke Wednesday morning, the uneasy feeling that Annie, Bettina, and Taylor would be returning hit me like a punch in the gut. I really just wanted them to go home already. I dreaded the bickering and odd conversations. One good thing about the day though was that I didn't have to help Ming clean their bungalow, as they hadn't been there since the previous morning. Yesterday's clean up efforts had been the same epic chore, for they had trashed their rooms yet again. How can people willingly live like slobs? It was beyond my comprehension. I was in no way a neat-freak, but their house-hygiene was deplorable. Poor Ming. I really did owe her an extra day off, and I promised her that she could take it whenever she wanted.

I was helping her with laundry toward the middle of the afternoon when my cell phone rang.

"Macca." I heard Bennie's voice on the other end when I answered it. "Detective Green is here to see you."

"What? Why?"

"He didn't say. Can you come to the front desk though? Please?"

I sighed. The last thing I wanted to do was meet with Detective Green; no good could come from it, as our history had shown. "Okay. Give me just a second."

I apologized to Ming and headed to the reception area, already beginning to fume. I didn't appreciate interruptions when we were busy with the inn.

"Macca." The detective extended his hand and I shook it. "How have you been?"

"Good, and you?" What? Was this some weird social call?

"Good. Busy as usual, as I'm sure you are too."

I nodded. "What can I do for you?"

"Is there someplace we can talk privately?"

I frowned and wondered if there was another murder he was going to try to pin on me. "Sure." I led him to the dining area that had already been set for the meal service later in the evening.

Sitting opposite each other, he pulled out his ever-present notebook and opened it up.

"You have family visiting? Is that correct?" He was alternating between peering at the details in his notebook and watching me as well.

"Actually, they're friends of my family. They're down at the volcanoes." And then my stomach did a flip. "Why? What's happened?" I heard my voice rising in panic.

"I'm so sorry to report that there's been a development at Volcanoes National Park."

I silently gripped the edge of the table, waiting for the rest of his news to come.

"Mrs. Annie Thompson-Haas is missing."

I sucked in my breath and felt sick. "Oh my gosh," I muttered. "What happened?"

"As far as I can tell, there was an argument and the trio split up, planning to meet back at their hotel. When it was evident that Mrs. Haas didn't return by this morning, her granddaughter, Miss Taylor Lundgren, called the local police."

"Oh my gosh." I breathed and leaned back in my chair. I felt a shimmer behind me, followed by very warm hands on my shoulders. Davy gently pressed his chin to the top of my head.

"I'm right here, Babe," he whispered. He squeezed my shoulders and gently kissed where his chin had been, but I felt numbed. He crouched down beside me, his head even with my shoulder. Below the tabletop he held my hand and squeezed. I squeezed back and the sudden relief that I wasn't as numb as I imagined brought my attention back to the detective.

"Is…" I had to swallow a few times to clear my throat. I tried again. "Is there a search party looking for her?"

He glanced back down at his notes for an hour. Actually it was just a second or two. "Yes, and they're calling in a K-9 unit as well."

"Oh my gosh." Why did I keep saying that? And then my first thought was something I'd seen on television — *cadaver dog*. I felt the tears roll down my cheeks. Detective Green pulled a freshly laundered linen handkerchief from his breast pocket and handed it over to me. Who used those anymore? And more importantly, why didn't *everyone* use them? "Thank you." I took the handkerchief with shaking hands and wiped my eyes and cheeks. I refused to blow my nose on such a beautiful piece of well-cared for cloth. I saw myself folding it and placing it on the table, but I was surprised that it was actually my hands performing the task. I was distracted, to say the very least.

I felt Davy shimmer away from one side of me and reappear at the other. He patted my thigh, holding fast to my other hand now. "I'm still here. You see me, right?"

I slid my eyes toward him and he nodded.

"What should I do?" I let my eyes wander over to the detective, truly asking for earthbound guidance.

"There isn't anything you can do at this point. But you may eventually be needed down at VNP."

"VNP?"

"I'm sorry." He truly looked remorseful. "Volcanoes National Park."

"Oh, that's right." I hadn't had the wherewithal to connect the popular acronym at first. "What hotel were they staying at? I can't seem to recall right now." Had they even told me?

"Lava Rock Inn, adjacent to the area where Mrs. Haas went missing."

I stared at him a moment longer before the tears began to leak down my face yet again. Reaching for his handkerchief again, I dried my eyes. A sudden and rather weird thought came to me that since I don't wear makeup these days I wouldn't truly soil his hankie. I found this to be both funny and irreverent, until the reality hit me in the chest like a fist. Annie was missing.

"Did anyone find her easel, canvas, and supplies?" I don't know why I asked, but I did. Perhaps it was the memory of the enormously sentimental gift she'd given me. Or maybe it was just my way of dealing with the ugliness of the situation. I had a sudden desire for both her and her personal belongings to be safe. I was clinging to the woman who was my last connection with my beloved mother, and actually, could anyone blame me for feeling that way? Once again, I felt all alone in the world. Alone. Again. Naturally. Wait... wrong singer.

I heard Davy chuckling right there beside me. He rocked back on his heels in his crouched position, and ended up plopping on his bum. Usually I hated that he could hear my thoughts, but his reaction was hilarious. I found myself trying so hard to ignore him, but his antics were a welcome distraction. What could I do? I buried my face in my hands so Detective Green could not see that I was holding back irreverent laughter, but as soon as the memory of Annie flooded back, I was sobered again. And I admired the fact that Davy was able to recover enough to attend to the dire issues at hand. He stood behind me and gripped my shoulders again. That comfort was real and palpable. I took a deep and cleansing breath, blowing it out slowly before taking another.

"How can I help?" I knew I was repeating myself even as the words spilled from my lips.

"At this time there's nothing for you to do." The detective closed his notebook. "I'm just making the notification. We'll contact you when we have more information."

And then it dawned on me. "But why did they call you in the first place?"

"Miss Lundgren stated their home base for their holiday is here, and when local LEOs looked you up in their DB..."

"Wait. LEOs? DB?"

"Law Enforcement Officers, and DB is database."

"I know what DB is, but why was I in it?"

"Your rap sheet was in it."

"My rap sheet? Wait... I have a rap sheet?" I heard my voice rise an octave as I sat up straight in my chair.

54

"Yes, because you were arrested in the Chad…" He was indicating my homeless friend who'd been murdered not too long ago, but I cut him off.

"I know the case, and you've got someone sitting in jail awaiting trial. The charges against me were dropped. I was, and still am, innocent. So why do I have a rap sheet?"

"Everyone who has been arrested has a rap sheet, regardless of innocence proven later."

"I think this is despicable. Anyone whose charges have been dropped should no longer have this thing you call a rap sheet."

"Well, RAP stands for Record of Arrests and Prosecutions, so…"

"I know what that stands for too. I'm not stupid."

"We're getting off subject here, Macca." Detective Green could be so condescending at times.

"That's Ms. Liberty to you, thank you. I always refer to you as Detective Green. You owe me the same respect, and a whole lot of apologies too." I stood. "Keep me advised about Annie then." I turned on my heel and headed for my bungalow. I had much to process. I put in a call to Alex Baldwin to ask about the rap sheet, but he was out of the office, so I left a detailed message with his secretary. Then I tried to call Annie, Bettina, and Taylor on their individual cell phones, but they all went directly to voicemail. My final call was to Bennie to let him know the situation so that he could advise the rest of the team since I was too upset to do so myself. Davy shimmered beside me on the sofa, his arm around my back.

"You handled that well, Babe. Green's just a halfwit."

I turned to look at him and the tears spilled again. This time I didn't have that fancy handkerchief, so I lifted the hem of my tank top and used that.

"Babe…" He grinned as he watched. "You really need to stop doing that. I mean, it's a nice view and all but…"

"I'm in no mood."

"I know." He took my tear-drenched hand and held it in his own. "I'm sorry." He pulled a linen handkerchief out of his pocket and handed it to me. It wasn't as pristine as Detective Green's, but it was Davy's. I used it to wipe my face and then kept it clutched in my fist.

"Thank you."

"Don't mention it. I heard you like linen…" his voice trailed off. "And now, if you're going to be okay, I'll just sort of nip on down to the volcanoes and see what's going on. I'll report back when I have news, and only then, okay?"

I nodded and wiped my damp eyes again. Mr. Pinckney blipped in, then out again, and finally materialized. He still needed to work on that.

"I'm so sorry, Ms. Liberty." Mr. Pinckney spoke quietly, but it was a heartfelt message.

"Thank you." I handed the handkerchief back to Davy and he tucked it in his pocket.

"Okay Mate," Davy addressed his ghostly friend. "Let's go. We have much work to do."

"I'm ready." Mr. Pinckney dropped his fidgety hands to his sides and stood tall. Davy reached out to touch the librarian's shoulder and they both shimmer-blipped out. I was left alone and it was terrifying. Not only was I alone in my home, but I felt completely alone in the world. I had to think hard about family and hold fast to the pictures of them in my mind. I found myself shivering and hugging my arms around my body. Susie appeared on the deck and wiggled his way through the partially closed sliding glass door to settle on the floor beside me with his giant head resting upon my foot. Not to be outdone, Chester trotted through the open door too and hopped up to snuggle by my side.

"Thank you, both of you," I whispered, trying to get around the lump in my throat while the tears burned behind my eyes again. I reached down and gave Susie several very gentle but loving strokes, then sat back against the cushions and patted the sofa to give permission to the large dog to join me. He hopped up easily and settled with his head against my side. I put one hand on Chester and the other on Susie. I don't know how long we sat there like that, but they were the warmth and heart that I needed in my time of grief.

I didn't move from the sofa, nor did I pull away from Susie and Chester, but I watched my phone on the coffee table before me, willing it to come to life with an important call. The daylight was slipping away when I heard the familiar ringtone Davy had installed long ago, "Daydream Believer." I felt my heart constrict until I saw the call was from Alex.

"Macca!" His voice carried the urgency of my concerns but was warm and comforting at the same time. "I've made a few calls on your behalf, not only for the rap sheet issue, but to find out what is actually going on at VNP.

"Oh thank you, Alex. I just feel so helpless! And frankly, the rap sheet pisses me off, but right now, the safety and well-being of Annie, Bettina, and Taylor are the most important."

"Well, I can't get much information regarding the three ladies except that Bettina and Taylor are at the police station and are being taken care of."

"Taken care of? Are they under arrest?"

"No." I heard hesitation in his voice. "But they're considered 'persons of interest' at this time, so they won't be let go just yet."

"Oh my gosh," I moaned quietly, rubbing my face.

"I will be kept advised of the situation though, having already tipped my hand that, should they request counsel, we're on it."

"Oh thank you, Alex! Thank you so much!"

"As for your rap sheet, the record was supposed to have been expunged. Rob and I are already on it and we'll let you know how that goes. For now, he's got the paperwork going to present to a judge tomorrow."

I began to cry again, the lump in my throat silencing me. "Thank you," I managed to whisper.

"That's what we're here for, Macca." His voice was gentle, like the Alex I'd come to know. His booming barrister speech was gone and I felt comforted and secure again. "You'll be okay? Is there anyone who can be with you?"

"I think so. Thank you." I thought of Lani or Kalei. I knew Davy was busy doing important stuff on our behalf.

"Okay, I'll call you when I know more."

"Thank you." As we ended the call I noted the time showing on my phone and quickly dislodged the critters to head over to help with dinner service. I was relieved to have tasks to get lost in.

Later that night I returned to my place and sat on the sofa again staring out the window into the darkness, lost in thought. My mind was playing like one of those old View-Master toys; slide the lever and a new scene clicks into sight. Slide the lever, faster and faster, and you get a sort of stop action retrospective of your life. I could almost hear the ka-thunk-ka of the lever. The beach with mom, singing songs with both my parents, dinner with Annie and my parents, and onward, the years speeding up until the final slide which was an imagined scene of Annie's easel, half-painted canvas, and her watercolors in their case, all tossed aside on a trail along the crater in a public park. How could this happen?

I stood quickly and moved over to view the painting Annie had just given me. I studied the beautiful representation of my mother and me and the tears slid down my cheeks again. "Mom, I'm so sorry." I covered my face with my hands. It was then I felt warm, sweet-smelling arms around me. The fragrance? Fresh lavender. One of Mom's favorites. I turned in her arms and we held each other tight.

"Shhh, Monkee Paw," Mom soothed me with my childhood nickname and the tears seemed to evaporate; all was right in the world for just those few precious seconds. "Annie is gone," she whispered.

I pulled back just enough to peer into her eyes. "No! It just can't be." And then it hit me that my mother was there with me. I held tightly to her, burying my face in her neck and losing myself in her fragrance.

"It is, sweetheart. I'm sorry."

"Who hurt her?" I demanded. "Who would do this?"

She shook her head as it pressed against mine. "That I can't say."

"You can't say or you won't?"

She held me away from her, gently grasping me by the shoulders so firmly that I thought she was still alive. She looked so deeply into my eyes that I could feel a warmth penetrate and grow, glowing down to my toes.

"I can't. I don't know. She doesn't know either."

I gasped. "So, she's *with* you?"

Mom nodded. "She is."

Fresh tears erupted. "I can't do this. I've seen too much violence, too much hatred."

"Listen to me right now. You're strong, you're young, and you are so, *so* smart. You can do this. You can see the truth, and you can help the authorities. I know you can, and we're counting on you. And Davy, too. Lean on him, but also, be his partner. Be his Dr. Watson…"

"To his Sherlock Jones." I heard my voice trail off and my eyes found a spot on the floor to watch as everything glazed over. Then I snapped back to mom. "You can visit me now? You're here! Is this going to happen again? I'm not ready to lose you too… again."

She smoothed the hair off my face and tucked a few stray strands into the clip at the top of my head. "No, we're not supposed to be here, but we felt the urgency around you," she frowned. "But I've missed you so much, Monkee Paw." She smiled into my eyes. "You have important work to do, so we'll appear when we're needed, if we can, but only if we think we can help. Okay?"

"We?"

Brief confusion washed over me when I felt a shimmer, not unlike Davy's signature shimmer, but a little less… showboat. And there behind my mom, and before me now stood my dad. As if I hadn't cried enough tears, they came again in a rush much like the Kaluahine Falls. I couldn't stop. Dad pulled me to him and I could smell his fragrance too… incense and woodfire smoke. A heady combination especially with Mom's lavender. With just those familiar scents I was sucked back to my childhood. The love, the happiness, and the peace was thick as Mom and Dad enveloped me in a massive parental hug. I didn't want it to end… ever; I wanted to be eight years old again and feel forever protected.

"You can't," Dad whispered, proving that it wasn't just Davy who could hear my thoughts. "You need to move on. But we'll always be with you in some way, because you're very special. You have a gift. Use it."

"A gift? What? My cat can talk to me and Ghost Davy has become my best friend?" I heard my voice rising in a near manic state, but I couldn't stop. "Not to mention his new ghostie friend Mr. Pinckney! How many more? And what does it prove? What can I do?" I was hysterical then. It was only their joint hug that was holding me up on my own feet. I'm not sure how, but I was suddenly seated on the sofa, Dad on my left, Mom on my right, and we all held onto each other's hands. I held on tightly, hoping to keep them with me forever.

Dad spoke first. "Yes, you can hear Chester speak, and you can see various 'ghosts.' Next, you will begin to develop the ability to see truth, to see it beyond what others see, if you'll only let it happen. The bigger issue will be finding a way to advise people of authority without pointing blame back at yourself, or causing too much of the spotlight to be pointed at you."

"Wait. What?"

"Focus, Monkee Paw," Mom spoke in a hushed voice.

"I'm trying, but I'm feeling lost... and confused."

"And overwhelmed," Dad added.

"Yes."

"We can help just a little bit with that, Monks." Dad rubbed his thumb on my hand that he held so warmly. "You'll have to rely on Davy for more."

I gulped, resisting change as usual. That was my thing. Just let me go merrily along on my daily schedule. Meeting and making friends with new guests was as far a stretch as I was willing to go. I hated change. I always did. Change unravels the very fabric of the space-time continuum and could destroy the entire universe! I mean... what do you think Doc Brown would say? Yeah, I know, but I do tend to get a little crazy when my world tilts. *You've got to start thinking fourth dimensionally!* Go away, Doc Brown. This is not your movie. But then I remembered this wasn't a movie at all; it was my life. I realized the biggest change I'd ever made was packing it all up and moving here to Hawai'i, and if I had to do it all again I would without hesitation, for this was where I belonged. So I guess change isn't always bad. It's just often unexpected, and that was my real issue — the lack of control.

Shaking myself out of my head, I heard Dad chuckling next to me. "You've always been such a gas," he said.

"Gee, I'm so happy to have been a source of amusement for you, Dad. I'm sure there's nothing else in your otherworldly existence that you could possibly find humorous." Yep, my sarcasm button was now stuck in the *on* position. I'd need to bend open a giant imaginary paper clip to pry it up again. Yeah, put that one in your bong, Dad, and smoke it.

"Don't be rude," Mom scolded.

"I'm sorry," I sighed before realizing what I'd said. "Wait! I am *not* sorry. I am not sorry at all! I didn't ask for this, and I don't want it."

I pushed away, turning to look down as they sat on the sofa together, nearly as one. Really? Couldn't they stay apart for just a few minutes? For their only child's sake? Apparently not, because I saw them hold each other's hands and gaze lovingly at one another. Really? I stomped my foot. Yeah, it was a throwback to my youth, but I swear they were bringing out all the old bad behavior in me. I marched to the kitchen and poured myself not one, not even two, but three fingers of bourbon! I took a sip and relished the heat and the burn. I dropped a single maraschino cherry in all its sickly, syrupy sweetness into the glass and swirled it. Taking another sip, I sighed, for it was perfect. Heat, headiness, and the tiniest nip of nectar. Letting the alcohol warm me from my throat down to my stomach, I closed my eyes for several seconds, nearly forgetting my parents were still there.

"Are you drinking?" Mom asked, suddenly beside me again with Dad.

"Yep." I took another defiant sip.

"We didn't raise you to rely on alcohol," she added and I laughed. Actually, it sounded more like a sea lion barking, but hey, potayto, potahto.

"You only raised me for nine years, so excuse me if I have many more years of experience without you." I turned to the window over the sink and peered out as I took another sip. I could see their reflections in the glass, but when I opened my eyes after another sip, they were gone. "Good. Walk a mile in my shoes, people," I muttered, and then I began to cry, my forearms resting against the kitchen sink as my head dipped low over the basin. I could feel the sobs building strength and erupting from my lips as I sobbed. Again.

Still bent over the sink, I detected a shimmer behind me, and a warmth enveloped my body as Davy held me so tenderly. I could tell it was him by his fragrance as well: clean soap and mild spice. He said nothing. He didn't even make any shushing noises. He just let me wail, and when my tears began to ebb, he turned me around to face him and held me tightly. I felt rainbows arc and angels sing, and then the angels turned and beat the crap out of the rainbows. I began to giggle.

"You liked that, yeah?" He nudged my chin up with his finger and I nodded, suddenly realizing he was the one who had controlled my vision and turned it into the bizarre. He got me. He really did. It turned out I was a *Monty Python* girl and wanted to be surrounded by the bizarre. So? I also loved *The X-Files*, *Harry Potter*, and *Doctor Who*. Did that mean I wore a tin foil hat, carried a wand, and expected to travel in a blue time machine? No, but I did have a more unusual view of life than some people. Many have called it refreshing. Some have probably wanted to call for the men with the special coats where the sleeves tied in the back, but although I had been worried about that tacky fashion accessory for years now, nothing had materialized. I warned myself, though… don't get cocky.

"I'm not happy with my parents," I whimpered into his shoulder.

"I know. They had the ugly task of delivering news I knew you wouldn't want to hear. I refused. But, being your parents, they took the responsibility on and embraced it. I'm sorry they're so out of practice."

"I felt like I was witnessing some horrendous political coup and they took a stance against me."

"They didn't. They just did what needed to be done. And remember, they didn't cause this. They're just the messengers. Others have done the same for me. Sometimes we're too close to our children, our families, and it's easier for someone else to step in and handle the unpleasant bits. But your parents didn't want anyone else to tell you once I refused."

"Yeah?" So eloquent. I sniffed and wiped my nose and my face on my arm. Not pretty, but he'd already warned me against the continued use of my shirt hem.

"You and I are very open with each other, right?"

I nodded and pulled a tissue from the box behind him and blew my nose, sounding like a honking moose or something. Yeah, so attractive… notsomuch. "Why didn't you want to tell me?"

"Because you've had enough pain over the years. It was cowardly of me, but I just couldn't bear to be the messenger I was sure you'd want to shoot."

I nodded and grabbed a paper towel because it was more effective than using a tissue or my arm to wipe my face.

"Feeling better?" He touched my cheek briefly.

"No. I'm angry, and frustrated, and scared. Are *you* feeling better?"

He stood there looking at me with a completely blank look upon his face. "Nope. You scare me."

I froze and stared at him for at least three beats before responding. "Well, good then. We're on the same page. I'm scared; you're scared; we're all scared of something."

I swung around and scrubbed imaginary dirt from the pristine sink. He took me by the arms and turned me back to him.

"No, you scare me because you're impulsive. Of course that's also why I admire you. So consider my dilemma for a moment, please? How do I keep you safe?"

I gently pulled myself away and wiped the kitchen counter. "You won't need to. I have no intention of getting into trouble again."

He laughed then, that infectious raspy chuckle of his. Even I cracked a smile myself and met his eyes. "Yeah, even as the words came out of my mouth I didn't believe them myself." But he continued to laugh so I smacked his arm, laughing with him and at myself.

I picked up my neglected glass of bourbon and took another sip. "Care to join me?" I asked him, but he had already taken down a glass from the cupboard and was pouring himself a generous amount. "I guess so." I giggled and he took a good swig.

"Gotta catch up." He smiled and emitted a generous burp which got me to giggling again. We took our drinks to the sofa and each took an end, our legs meeting in the middle. He examined my bare feet before reaching down and pulling off his boots and socks, tossing them carelessly under the coffee table.

"Comfy?"

"Very." He raised his glass and I mirrored him. "To…" and he hesitated.

"Wait. Don't tell me I'm witnessing the impossible! You're… speechless?" I grinned and he poked my feet with his own, his boyish smile brightening the room.

"It doesn't happen often. Gimme a sec…" He pulled those distinctive eyebrows together for a moment and then smiled again. "To loved ones."

"I like that. To loved ones," I repeated and we drank. And we drank some more. At some point he fetched the bottle and refreshed our drinks, but I can't recall the details.

"Hey." He flopped on the sofa, "It's fun to drink and not worry about a hangover," he chuckled.

"For you maybe!" I sipped. It was a good night to risk the hangover.

"Meh. You'll swear off booze, bumble around for a few hours, pop some aspirin, and forget by the end of tomorrow."

"Sadly, you're right. Will I ever learn?"

"Pfft." A little bourbon sprayed from his lips. "No, but you'll be fine." He took a big gulp again.

"I will? And you're sure about this?"

"Well, if you behave and stop being so impulsive, yes. You'll be fine."

I rolled my eyes. "Yes Dad."

"Hey! I am not your dad!" He licked his lips. "And I happen to know for a fact that if you stop getting yourself into trouble you'll have three kids, two dogs, and two cats." He froze.

I froze too.

"Holy cow! I wasn't supposed to tell you any of that!" The stricken look on his face was comical. "You won't remember, right?"

"Right." I smirked. But I would. And it felt good. We drank well into the night and then fell asleep on the sofa.

SIX

Fetal Positions and Swallowtails

As expected, I was just a tiny bit hung-over the next morning. Actually, I was a whole lot hung-over and chugging Kona like it was plain water. Okay, okay, it's basically bean water, but it's stronger, and necessary. I was channeling the Juan Valdez of Hawai'i, whoever that might be, and I briefly wondered who really did develop the Kona bean. I pulled my laptop open and researched... anything to distract me from how crappy I felt. I spent a good twenty minutes reading about my chosen subject. The first coffee plant was brought to Kona in 1828 by some guy named Samuel Ruggles, but it was Henry Greenwell who developed the brand, Kona. Well, thank you Hank!

Okay, enough procrastinating. I carried my third cup of Kona into the bathroom with me and took a long and luxurious hot shower; water catchment system be damned... just for today. I think the hangover was also emotional. Too much had happened the previous night and I needed to wash it away.

Once I was dressed and my coffee cup cleaned, I headed to the reception area, just a little bit late, but we don't punch time clocks so who's counting, right?

"Morning." Bennie greeted me with a little too much cheer... and volume. I winced. "Rough night, eh?"

"You have no idea." The coffee called to me so I poured another cup for myself before grabbing all the items in my inbox and perching on a barstool to begin the business day.

"Macca," Bennie called to me. "We have a family checking in today. A mom, dad, young child, and a baby."

"Okay. Thanks for the heads up."

"Their baby is a special needs kid. They noted that on their reservation request."

I looked over at him. "Do they need anything extra from us then?"

"Not so far. They asked for a crib in their bungalow."

I nodded. "Let me know what they say when they arrive. If I'm alive."

"Wow. You really did have a rough night."

"You'd never believe it if I told you. Really." I sipped more coffee and organized the requests in my hand, entering the details on my laptop. Lani and Kalei walked by, bags of produce in their hands.

"Farmers' market," the big man said, indicating the bags and handing me the receipts.

"Thank you." Even my own voice was too loud. I followed them into the kitchen, got the industrial-sized bottle of ibuprofen down from the shelf, and popped two more with a large glass of water. I knew the couple were watching me, but I ignored them because talking hurt too much and I didn't want to vomit either. Oh, I swore I'd never drink again. We always do, right? Pffft. Even I knew *that* wouldn't last.

I trudged back to my laptop and my coffee, read my email and held my face over the steaming brew in between sips.

Just before lunch service was to begin I returned to my bungalow to eat something. Scrambling a couple of eggs, I added some spring greens and mushrooms before sitting down to eat. The first bite was the hardest, but after that I began to feel a lot better. When I was washing up my dishes my phone dinged in my pocket. A text from Bennie told me our new guests had arrived so I wandered over to meet them.

At the front desk, the couple were checking in. Standing between them was a little girl I guessed to be five or six years old. In the woman's arms was a baby whose little shirt said "Daddy's Boy." When he saw me, he smiled and kicked his legs, holding his pudgy hands out to me.

"Well hello, little guy!" I held one of his hands and he squirmed, giggling and kicking more. I then turned to his mother. "Hello. My name is Macca."

The mother's face lit up with recognition. "You must be the owner. My name is Catherine Wallace and this is our son Grant and our daughter Lily." She indicated the girl between them. "And this is my husband Zack." He shook my hand.

"It's very nice to meet you all, and welcome to Hale Mele!" Little Grant still reached out for me so I asked, "May I?" Catherine grinned and held her son out to me. He came readily into my arms and held on tightly, molding his tiny body against mine. "Such a jolly little guy you are!"

"He's nearly always happy," Zack agreed, watching us with pride.

"He's beautiful." I gazed at him and then his older sister caught my eye. "And you are too, Lily! How old are you?"

She smiled sweetly, showing one missing tooth in front. "I'm thix yearth old. I'm in firtht grade!"

"You are? Well aren't you a smart girl!" When she blushed, I turned back to their parents. "How was your flight?"

"Nice and short," Catherine answered. "We live in Honolulu."

"Oh, that's convenient," I chuckled. "Have you been to the Big Island before?"

"Yes," Zack spoke as he put his identification and credit card away that Bennie had just passed back to him, "but we heard about your inn from some friends."

"They didn't stay here," Catherine added quickly, "but friends of theirs are here for an extended period while their house is being built."

"Oh! You mean the Morrison family! Do they know you're coming?"

"No. We don't really know them; we just know *of* them, through the mutual friends."

"You'll like them." I gently swayed with Grant as I spoke. "Another very nice family."

"I did have a question." Catherine seemed a little nervous. "Do you know of a babysitting service? We might want to go out one night while we're here, but only if we're sure the kids will be in good hands."

I turned toward Bennie and he nodded approval to me, "Bennie's sister does a lot of babysitting for us. From what I've heard and seen, she's very good with children."

"We have quite a big family so she's had a lot of practice." Bennie grinned.

Catherine looked between the two of us and then deferred to her husband, who nodded before jumping in for his wife. "Grant has some… eating challenges. We just want to be sure she can handle a child with Down syndrome." He seemed almost apologetic.

"She's a smart cookie and is studying child development." Bennie told them, his pride evident. "And she's specializing in children with special needs."

"Oh, thank you!" Catherine grasped her husband's hand as relief registered on her face.

"She's coming this evening to sit for the Morrison kids. I'll introduce you, if you'd like," Benny's grin as he spoke was evidence of his pride for his sister.

"We would definitely like to meet her." Zack kept watching his son in my arms. I got the feeling they didn't often let the little guy out of their sight. Part of me actually wanted to spend time with both these children, but especially little Grant who had stolen my heart. His beautiful eyes stared up at me with wonder.

"I think I'm in love," I whispered to Grant. Although he had no idea what I'd said, he smiled. "Yes, you're a sweet little guy, aren't you?" I suddenly realized the room had grown silent. I looked up and all eyes were on us. "Oh, sorry. I got lost in the moment." I handed Grant back to his mom, but I noticed they were all smiling at me, so I didn't feel too horribly embarrassed, just a little self-conscious.

"Please don't be sorry." Catherine grinned as she settled her son on her hip. "He has that effect on many people."

"He'th my baby brother," Lily proudly exclaimed. "But I will thare him with you if you want."

"Oh my." I put my hand out to her and she took it. "I'm so touched. That's a very generous thing to do. I know I will enjoy both your company and Grant's." I turned back to Catherine and Zack. "Is Lily a great help then?"

They chuckled. "She is an excellent helper!" Zack picked his daughter up and swung her over his shoulder like a sack of potatoes, grinning as she squealed in delight. I could see the pride on all their faces.

Bennie stood up then. "Shall we show you all to your bungalow then?" He gave me a playful nudge as he passed by to pick up their bags.

"Thanks, but we have more in the rental car, too."

"We'll help you bring them down after we show you to your home away from home." I picked up their diaper bag and we led our guests to their bungalow.

It only took a couple of trips up the stairs to the parking lot for Bennie and Zack to get all of their belongings out of the car. Meanwhile, I stayed behind with Catherine and the kids and helped her organize things and set up the rollaway crib we provided. "You can roll it to whichever room you want it in," I showed her.

"Thank you! When we stay in hotels we usually keep it next to our bed, but I like the option to move it around, especially during the day."

"Oh good! And Ming and I will be taking care of you during your stay. We don't service the bungalows until we're sure you've gone out, or in the case of staying in for the day, we'll ask beforehand so we don't disrupt your family time."

"Thank you. And I understand there's a luau on Saturday night?"

"Yes! I know you'll enjoy that. Kalei and Lani make fabulous food and then put on a show afterward. Lani is pregnant though, so she has enlisted the help of one of her dance troupe members to round out the show."

"Oh, how lovely! Is this her first child?"

"Yes. She and Kalei are over the moon, as am I. I've already been named 'Anake Macca. It's a mouthful but I'm loving it already."

She touched my arm affectionately as we laughed. When all their bags had been brought in, Bennie and I excused ourselves.

"Feel free to call, day or night, if you need anything, okay? We're available. Just call the front desk and it will be routed to one of us. In that respect, we never close," I teased.

"Oh, thank you," Catherine said again.

We'd given a lot of thought to a parent's worries about things such as kids getting sick or running out of necessary supplies. So we had defined ourselves as a full service inn, and the entire team embraced the concept.

As Bennie and I headed back to the front desk, we chatted as if that impromptu kiss had never occurred.

"I like them... a lot," he began but I jumped in.

"I'm in love with that baby," I gushed. I'll admit it.

"I'd say that baby was pretty much in love with you too."

We were laughing just like old times and I felt a genuine relief. I hated when our little world experienced ripples.

"You'll be sure to connect them with your sister?"

"I will," he promised with a smile. I left him at the front desk and he returned to his work as I continued on to my own bungalow.

Once inside my little sanctuary I thought again of Annie... and then considered Bettina and Taylor. I was suspicious of Bettina, frankly. She had just seemed so disagreeable for most of the time they'd been here, and she and Annie had been at each other the whole time. I sat on the deck and stared out to the vast Pacific Ocean, my favorite view to use for focusing my thoughts. So many unanswered questions, so many interrupted lives.

I tried to imagine what went on with those three women while they were at the volcano. Was Annie just the random target of a stranger? Was there an accident? Or could it be something more nefarious like a family argument gone too far? And if so, was it Bettina? Or Taylor? Or even a group effort? I shuddered at the thought of it all.

I was wondering where Davy was and if he'd found out any details when my phone sang out to me. The display told me it was Alex, my diligent attorney.

"Macca," he said after we'd exchanged short greetings. "Rob is heading down to meet with the police tomorrow morning."

"Did Bettina and Taylor request an attorney?"

"Not yet, and phone calls are getting us nowhere."

"Oh dear." I rubbed my face. "You know I can't pay him, but that family is very well off financially."

"Don't you fret. He'll get things under control. I know you must be beside yourself with worry."

"Yeah. It's the not knowing that's so unsettling, and wondering if..." I could not divulge that I knew Annie was dead, so I stopped for a few seconds to collect my thoughts before continuing. "...if Annie is lying somewhere, injured and alone."

Whew. Dodged that one. This is exactly what Mom and Davy had both meant about keeping myself out of trouble. I needed to learn to be a little less impulsive. Hell, I needed to learn to be a *lot* less impulsive. I needed to think before I spoke, and especially before I acted.

Yes you do, a very Mancunian accent sounded in my head, and I turned from my phone to stick out my tongue at the universe.

"I know, Macca." Alex brought me out of my reverie. "We'll try to get some information."

"You can't even know how much I appreciate this. Thank you, Alex."

"Hey, what are friends for, right?"

I could hear the smile in his words and my mood lifted. "Right. But I thank you from the bottom of my heart."

"You're welcome, and either Rob or I will call you when we know something, okay? Promise not to worry too much for now?"

I smiled. "I'll try. You're the best."

"Nah, just trying to help out a good friend." His words warmed me and we bid goodbye for the time being.

Setting my phone down on the little table by my chair, I gazed out to sea again. It was comforting to imagine being on a lovely boat with Chester and Davy, just sailing away to a happier place. But then I considered all I'd be leaving behind, not only the inn, but the people connected to it as well. Tears pooled in my eyes. I was just so tired that my emotions seemed tied to a yo-yo string. I was sure that the remnants of the lingering hangover weren't helping either. I ran my hands over my face and stood up, ready to return to work despite the tremendous desire to crawl into bed and assume the fetal position.

Thursday morning dawned bleak, followed by the equally bleak Thursday afternoon. It was nearly time to set up for dinner service when I stopped to have a cup of tea and my phone sang again; it was Rob Parker Kula calling this time. Still sitting at my little kitchen table, I answered.

"Rob!" I was maybe just a little eager to hear from him, then remembered my manners. "Hello. How are you?"

"I'm frustrated. I'm afraid I keep running into walls of silence down here. Mrs. Lundgren and her daughter have been held since last night. Police have limited time to bring charges or release them and the clock is ticking. Both women have denied needing counsel, which worries me, but there isn't anything I can do. So I'm heading back; I left my business cards for them just in case."

"Wow. I'm so sorry you drove all that way for nothing, but thank you."

"It wasn't for nothing because they know now that they can contact me."

"They haven't found Annie… yet?" I almost said "Annie's body" but caught myself in time.

"No. The search parties can only work in the daylight because of the terrain."

I sighed. From exasperation? Fear? Or anger? Perhaps it was all three, and none of the anger was directed at any one person, but rather at the situation itself.

"I'm sorry, Macca." Rob was reading my sigh as directed at him, I could tell.

"No, no. It's just frustrating as you said. You've gone above and beyond, Rob. I thank you."

"Okay. I'll let you know if I hear more. The detectives in charge also have my card, with instructions to call me if there are any developments. Oh! One thing I nearly forgot. They've got a warrant to search the ladies' bungalow. Has anyone touched it?"

"Well, we cleaned it just after they left on Tuesday, but that's it."

"Very understandable. Oh, and Detective Green will be joining them when they search, as a liaison."

"Oh, terrific." Yep, my sarcasm button was still stuck firmly in the "on" position, and I had little desire to get it fixed.

"I know. He's not your favorite person."

"When are they coming? Do you know?"

"Friday morning."

That was just tomorrow. "Good. I'd rather get it done and get them out of here."

"I know you've had more than your fair share of police presence since moving here."

I sighed again, resigned to my fate. "I'm a magnet I guess." I chuckled and he joined with light laughter himself.

"And I promise we're on target to get your record expunged. It was a clerical mistake in the prosecutor's office."

"That's great news, and thank you!"

When we disconnected our call, I dropped my phone on the table and got up to pour a little iced tea for myself. My throat was dry from a combination of emotion and the warmth of the day.

I called the team to meet me in the dining area so I could bring them up to date on the situation with Annie, Bettina, and Taylor, and they were quick to rally around. Since the trio had been due to check out in a couple days, we'd already booked the next guests into that bungalow. I decided that Bettina and Taylor would have to move in with me if they were kept here on the island longer than Saturday morning. That gave little time to take action. Once the police released their belongings, Bennie, Albert, and I could move them into my bungalow. I really hoped, though, that they'd be winging their way home to Connecticut on Saturday, but I felt in my heart that this would not play out in that manner.

After the others had gone back to their duties, Bennie stayed behind. "Are you okay, Macca?"

I nodded. "Yeah. I've had time to accept that my life is in a total state of flux." I chuckled and he smiled but it didn't reach his eyes; there was sadness instead. He understood.

"No, I mean… are you really okay?" He stared into my eyes as though he could see right through to my soul. I felt my eyes burn with tears held back, followed by that stupid lump in my throat that had been haunting me.

"Not really," I whispered. He left his chair and came to sit beside me.

"Tell me? Please?"

What the hell was I supposed to say? "Bennie, I'm not sure that I can tell you everything."

"Why not?" He tilted his head and for some reason, the innocence behind the gesture set me at ease.

"There are several reasons." I gulped, but kept going. "One, I'm not sure you will like everything you hear, and two, I'm not sure you will believe everything I say."

He leaned back in his chair, his eyebrows arching in skepticism. "Try me."

I blew out all the air I'd been holding and looked around desperately. "Let's go somewhere more private, okay?"

He nodded and rose to his feet, ready to follow me. Hesitating for just a moment, I stood and led him to the back deck of my bungalow, that refuge that overlooked tropical foliage and the sea beyond. As I began to take my usual seat, I pointed to the chair angled beside mine and he joined me.

"Iced tea?"

"No. Just truth. All of it." His eyes still bore into mine with concern.

"Okay." I bought time, trying desperately to decide what to say, and how much to tell him. "I see ghosts," I finally blurted. He blinked several

71

times, but remained silent. "And Chester speaks to me... in my head... but it's him, really."

He nodded once. "And?"

I sucked in my breath and pulled back some. "What do you mean 'and'?"

"I think it's time you told me the whole story."

Whoa. I felt my heart drop. "The whole story?" Repeating his words bought me a little more time to think.

"Macca..." He sighed and squirmed in his chair. "There have been so many odd occurrences since you arrived, and I have tried not to pry even though there have been many times I've wanted to."

Whoa... Whatever I decided to tell him next could dramatically change things between us. I was mesmerized and kept listening.

"But I sense there is something bigger going on," he continued. "You're like the middle ring of a three-ring circus. If I'd been appalled by that, I would have left long ago. But the fact that I've stayed should prove to you that I'm willing to walk beside you, share whatever this is, and embrace it too."

"Wow." It came out as a whisper, but he heard it.

He just sat there, staring at me. His handsome face was nearly unreadable, but his gentle brown eyes spoke volumes. In a rush, I realized I could indeed trust him with my very life. It was a heady feeling. "I'll wait until you're ready," he continued. "If you're not comfortable telling me now, right at this minute, I'll go back to the front desk and go on about my work...and my life, but I hope you realize that I'm here for you. I've always been here, and I always will be."

He began to rise, presumably to leave, but I reached out for his hand and held it. "No, stay. Please."

He took his seat again, elbows on the armrests and hands clasped in front. Waiting.

I gulped a few times then squarely faced him. "As I said, I see ghosts. They live with me... sometimes. They appear when I need them, and they appear when they want to annoy me." I wondered how much I should tell him. I had to give that some thought before proceeding. "We're... close."

Well, that's pretty lame. I heard that familiar Mancunian accent in my head. I shook my head to rid myself of that voice just long enough to think straight and continue.

"Go on," Bennie gently encouraged.

"One ghost has become my best friend." I winced, waiting to hear derisive laughter, but Bennie just watched me, waiting for me to continue, so I did just that. "He's helped me a lot actually. He left you a note to call 911... twice now."

Bennie nodded but remained silent.

"So..." I took a deep breath. "He will always be with me. I think it's why I cut myself off from people at times. I mean, how do you explain that you've got an invisible friend with you nearly every day, you know?"

Bennie examined his fingernails as though he'd never seen them, then took a deep breath before speaking. "I knew things were odd, but I had no explanation. It's a relief to know."

"Then... you believe me?"

He frowned. "Why wouldn't I?"

"Because it's a pretty far out story, frankly. I still can't believe it myself at times."

He smiled then. "Well, I believe you. What's his name, this ghost?"

"Davy. David."

His eyes widened. "The name on the Whispering Bench?"

I nodded and looked out at the tall trees that grew from so far below that the tops were easily visible from the deck.

He whistled long and low. "Who are the others?"

"A librarian from just south of here, a horse, and Susie."

"Oh my God," he gasped. "Susie is a ghost? Why can everyone see him?"

"Because he wants them to; he wants to help people, wants to love them. And be loved, too."

"Susie." There was wonderment in his voice. At hearing his name, the dog appeared beside Bennie, nudging the man's hand to encourage petting. Bennie was startled, but only briefly. He rubbed Susie's head and neck. "Where are they now? Davy and the librarian, I mean."

"I'm pretty sure they're trying to find Annie and sort of spying on the cops who are questioning Taylor and Bettina."

"Wow. Sleuthing spirits. I think there's a story in that," he teased.

"Good. I'll let you write it," I replied dryly.

"Oh, I'm sorry," he fidgeted. "I didn't mean to make light of the situation. But there's something I've never told anyone," he began, suddenly shy.

I tilted my head toward him, waiting for him to share. When he remained silent, I encouraged him. "Fair is fair. I shared my secret. Spill it," I said lightly.

"I write screenplays. I haven't sold one yet, but I keep trying."

"You write?" I was shocked. And impressed. And I told him so.

"That's fantastic, Bennie!"

He blushed as a smile spread across his face. "Would you like to read one someday?"

I put my hand to my chest, so touched. "I'd be honored. And you know I love to read!"

"I do! It's sort of the joke around here that whenever you're not working, your nose is stuck in a book."

I chuckled then, beginning to feel lighter and a lot more relaxed. "That's how I was raised. My father read philosophy and history, and my mother read anything she could get her hands on. We didn't have much money, so we spent each weekend at the library. I picked up the reading habit out of self defense, almost." I chuckled.

"When in Rome, right?"

"Exactly." I felt very shy again. He reached out to hold my hand and we sat in silent comfort for several minutes. "I think we just shared a 'moment' didn't we?" I grinned like a schoolgirl..

"I think you're right." He squeezed my hand and shyly ducked his head as if to study his shoes. "And I kind of hope there will be more."

I gulped. "Bennie, I need to be honest with you. I don't know if I'm ready."

"I know that. I could tell. And I'll be honest with you. I will wait. As long as you need."

I let out a long and shaky breath. "I... I think I'd like that... but if you decide you can't wait any longer, I will understand."

He squeezed my hand again. "You'll soon learn that I'm extremely patient. In fact, my family says it infuriating."

We chuckled together and sat in comfortable silence for a very long while, watching the birds, the swaying trees, and a persistent but familiar swallowtail butterfly. *Thank you*, I told Davy. The butterfly hovered around us before disappearing into the vegetation.

SEVEN

Misguided Pasties and Water Wings

Friday morning I was up early. Davy was in our little kitchen already making tea; he had something in the oven as well.

"What's cookin'?"

"Oi! Where's the rest of that question?"

"What's cookin' please?"

He shot me a look as if to say, "Really?" But I was playing with him. He shook his head and made tsk tsk sounds.

"Oh all right," I gave in so easily to him sometimes. "What's cookin' good lookin' then."

He chuckled. "That's better. Thought me looks was slippin' for a bloomin' second there."

"Bum-di-bum," I teased.

His chuckle turned into a raspy laugh. "I'm here all week, ladies and gents."

"So, what *is* in the oven?"

"Oh! I nicked a bit of Lani's bread dough from the freezer."

"So... bread?"

"No. I made a sort of dumpling-thing... filled with leftover vegetables and hard boiled eggs. A misguided pasty. Walking on the wild side. Needing an intervention, maybe."

That made me laugh again as I'd read about the English dish but never knew it was pronounced *pah-stee*. So now I knew. "Where did you get the leftovers?"

He had the good sense to look guilty then. "Also from the kitchen."

"You're incorrigible, you know. I sure hope nobody saw bread dough, veggies, and hard boiled eggs floating through the air."

"Nope. It was before anyone was stirring. Even the mice were still asleep."

"Har de har."

"Really. It was the dark o' the morn," he added in a thick accent.

"Good, but we still need to be careful even though Lani, Kalei, and now Bennie know of your existence. I don't want to be the newest stop on the Haunted Tours agenda, you know?"

"Pfft. You and me both."

"You're okay that Bennie knows?"

"Of course! He's a good kid."

"He's my age."

"Like I said, he's a good kid."

I stuck my tongue out at him, further validating his comment. It was yet another facepalm moment recorded in my memory for eternity. My life seemed to be full of them.

Davy splashed milk into two cups, followed by fresh hot tea. I picked one up and sipped. He added sugar in his own cup as usual. I shuddered at the thought. Sweets were not my thing, unless it was something special like Kalei and Lani's desserts, or a malasada, to which I'd only recently been introduced by the Baldwins and the Parker Kulas. I'd had Los Angeles versions of beignets, which I was told were not very much like those you'd find in Louisiana, but were still spectacular. However, they did not hold a candle to a malasada. Just thinking of the luscious pillowy pastries made my mouth water.

"Are your stolen goods nearly done?"

"Ha! Everyone's a comedian. Some are just better than others," he quipped. "Bum-di-bum."

"I've missed you lately."

"Yeah?"

I nodded. "Yeah. Stop disappearing for such long periods, okay?"

He set down the hot pads and turned to me. "Well, do you want me to stay with you or find out what's going on with your family?"

I thought for a long time before answering. "Both."

"You are one demanding woman," he teased again.

"Get used to it."

He raised his eyebrows playfully… and folks, when Davy Jones raises his eyebrows, you notice. That's a *lot* of eyebrow. "Is this the new Macca, spilling her guts to Bennie, sharing a kiss and all?" He was grinning, but it was a scary subject to me because I still had no clue which direction I wanted my relationship with Bennie to take, other than being friends. I wasn't good at these things. After all, I hadn't had much practice.

Lost in my ruminations, I ignored Davy's verbal jab because I wasn't ready to discuss it yet. "The police are coming this morning to go through Annie, Bettina, and Taylor's things. So what have you found out? And is Mr. Pinckney beside you when you haunt the police station?"

He smirked as he saw through my diversionary tactic but let it go. "Yeah. Mr. Pinckney is a good detective actually. We haven't seen much yet, except that Bettina and Taylor have both remained relatively quiet, only answering the most basic of questions. The only issue is that they were separated from each other for about thirty minutes during the estimated period where Annie disappeared. That's what the cops are focusing on."

"Do the police think one of them killed Annie?"

"Officially, they still consider her only missing, but yeah. They do. Both women have been remarkably silent."

"Oh my gosh." I put my hand to my face. "My worst fears may be coming true."

"I'm sorry, Babe." He moved to my side at the kitchen table and draped his arm across my shoulders, giving me a warm squeeze.

"I know it's not very charitable of me." I leaned against him for comfort. "But I just want this nightmare to be over."

He dragged a chair next to mine, sat, and held me close, all in one fluid motion. "You have every right to be wigged out from this. You've had more than your fair share of this kind of trauma. I swear, if Bettina or Taylor had a hand in this, they will feel the full force of my haunting. Poltergeist? They ain't seen nothin' yet."

I rested my head on his strong shoulder and closed my eyes, emotional fatigue washing over me. "Is it bedtime yet?"

He spoke through a derisive snort. "It's just now breakfast time. Sorry."

"Damn." I sat up then and sipped my tea. Davy got up and fetched the dumpling-thingies from the oven. When he placed one in front of me, I drooled a little. I think. I picked it up and felt just how hot it still was, so I set it back down and sipped my tea a bit longer, but I kept eyeing the pillowy wonder on the plate. When I saw Davy pick up his own little dumpling, I tried mine and decided he must have asbestos fingers. Either that or ghosthood made him impervious to burns.

"What time are the fuzz supposed to be here?" Stuffing his pasty bite into his cheek in order to speak, he looked like a hamster. I giggled not only at that, but also at his use of a term for police that was clearly a holdover from the sixties.

"I'm not sure. They don't give us mere peasants any details."

"They'd get a lot more cooperation if they were open and honest with people, you know."

"Perhaps. But I don't want to worry about cops."

He eyed me then. "Yeah. Hard to worry about them when there may be something more insidious happening in your own family."

I could only nod, taking another sip of tea. I finally found the dumpling thing to be cool enough to pick up so I bit into it. The buttery crisp exterior gave way to even more buttery chewiness, the vegetables perfectly complementing the dough. "Oh geez, please marry me," I addressed the pasty bite being savored in my mouth, a perfectly chewy dough filled with warmed vegetables.

"I take that to mean you like it?" He was teasing again, but I didn't want to use eating time to answer so I simply nodded emphatically, stuffing a stray crumb between my lips. I waited until I'd swallowed every last morsel.

"You could make those for me regularly, you know." I licked my finger and dabbed at all the crumbs on my plate. When I looked up he was staring at me, amused. "What?"

"I love a woman who loves her food, but really…"

I frowned then. "Hey, I was hungry and it tasted good. Take your compliment for what it was: a compliment."

I stood and bussed and rinsed our dishes, stowing them in the small dishwasher at my side. I stopped washing for a bit, wondering why we bother to use a dishwasher if we've already thoroughly rinsed the plates? Wouldn't it be easier to just hand wash them, dry them, and put them away? But I guess if you've got a large family, it's different. Or if you have such an endless supply of dishes that it doesn't matter if half of them are sitting in the dishwasher waiting for it to be full before running the machine. Yes, I spend a lot of time thinking about things that don't need thinking… about. Or something. It's also called procrastinating. I'm not always a procrastinator, but I do carry the recessive gene.

My phone dinged right then and I slid it out of my pocket to view the activity; it was Bennie with a text. Detective Green and his cohorts from the south of the island were here. "Oh goody." I really did need to get that sarcasm button fixed.

"The coppers? Let's make a run for it, Bonnie!" Davy teased.

"Okay Clyde," I deadpanned. "You go first. I'll follow… maybe."

He stuck his tongue out at me and motioned me to the door. I tucked my chin in and led the way. My stomach lurched when I saw the grouping of police at the end of the walkway near Annie, Bettina, and Taylor's bungalow.

"Hello, Detective." We shook hands before he then turned and introduced his southern counterparts. I say "southern" because even though it's only a few miles south, traveling along the main roads was so slow at times that many considered we had different regions on the island. Of course no one would ever dream of adding more roads or — gasp — a "freeway" that would destroy the beautiful land.

The southern contingency had brought along their crime scene experts as well. I led them to the bungalow that Annie, Bettina, and Taylor were still technically occupying and stood on the outskirts while the three detectives went in to do their duties. Me? I pulled my phone out and caught up on a hot game of Scrabble I was playing with Kate Baldwin, Alex's wife. Wow. She'd played "jury," an ominous turn. I was able to play off the "j" and came up with "just." So there.

I glanced up, peered through the open door to the bungalow, and saw they were basically tearing everything apart. I texted Bennie quickly.

Don't let Ming back here.
She'd be upset at the mess.

He responded quickly.

She's busy with other stuff.
I'll watch for her.

Yes, we text in full words and full sentences. Why? Because we're usually texting about stuff that is important to the inn and the guests. Why on earth would we risk misunderstanding a shortcut word if it meant incorrect data or instructions were being shared. Uncle Wally had put that practice in play a few years ago and the staff had agreed back then. They still agreed today, and so did I. Directions are important and information is crucial. Don't shortcut it just to shave off a few letters or seconds. Life is not lived on Twitter, where character count is limited. Really.

Stepping off my imaginary soapbox, I peeked through the open door again and saw that they had pulled out sofa cushions and chair pillows. I cringed. It looked like they were destroying our furnishings. OUR furnishings. Not Annie's, Bettina's, or Taylor's, but *our* furnishings. Our inn. I glanced up to the skies and sent a silent message to the universe to please let them find what they need and make them go away.

Nothing. I sighed and looked at my phone again. No messages. No emails. No texts. And worse, no updated word game. *Okay*, I thought to myself, *a game of spades is my last resort*. I sighed and waited for it to load.

While I waited, I heard squeals of delight from the pool and glanced up to see three fathers in the water with three kids and two babies all floating or swimming about. The Morrison and Wallace families had found each other and were enjoying their new bond. Catherine Wallace stood on the side taking video of the sweet sight. I spied her husband holding little Grant, his pudgy legs and arms splashing as he giggled in delight. Their daughter Lily and the Morrison twins appeared quite adept at swimming, but were still under the watchful eyes of their dads. When the twins caught sight of me, they gestured eagerly for me to join them. I waved and called to them, "Sorry sweeties; I'm working. Maybe later!"

My phone buzzed, reminding me that my game of Spades was ready, so I studied my cards to make my bid. Of course Detective Green chose that exact minute to interrupt. I shot a surreptitious glance to the skies again.

"They're nearly finished," he spoke quietly to me.

"Thanks." I let my phone hang down to my side, despite the fact that I was anxious to get back to my game, just to escape this little nightmare of police procedure. Detective Green glanced from the phone hanging by my side to my face and back again.

"Okay then." He wandered back inside, and I raised the phone to make my bid… six. I had the ace, king, and queen of spades. What could go wrong? Famous last words. I glanced up to see the police rifling through small suitcases. They really weren't tidy at all, and I felt anger bubbling up inside, so I took a deep breath and resumed my game. I played my cards cautiously, but then the AI seemed to rally and thoroughly trounced me. I'd bid six and won only four tricks. I closed the game, for this was not the positive distraction I needed today. I shoved my phone into the pocket of my shorts and leaned against the railing, arms crossed against my chest. I'd about had it with this police search when Rob showed up.

"Is everything okay?" He sidled up and leaned against my part of the railing that I happened to be propping up.

"On the surface, yes."

"And below?"

I turned to him and blew out a huge breath of frustration. "They have no respect for people's belongings, nor for our inn. I want to throttle them!"

"Throttle?" He was amused, I could see it in his eyes.

"Yeah. Throttle." I lifted my chin in defiance.

He put one hand on my arm and spoke quietly but authoritatively "Let it go. Let them do their job. We'll just ask for compensation for damages." And then he winked and pulled back to look at me before snickering. "Of course they'll laugh us right out." His eyes twinkled. "But it's always good to keep them on their toes. That's what we do. And when that great day comes that all cops are required to wear body cams to complement their dash cams? We'll be in a place that is *maybe* 10% better than it is now."

Wow. I'd never heard him talk like this. I just nodded and listened as he continued, fascinated to hear his opinions.

"Mind you, not every cop is corrupt, but one bad cop is enough to taint the system, and all good cops who don't stand up to bad cops are pretty much complicit."

And that is exactly where we agreed. I'd heard too many accounts of people being treated like trash, not just here in the islands but all over the country. So many lives lost. It had to be addressed. And then it dawned on me that Rob was cleverly distracting me until the cops and the crime scene experts had finished. The sneak.

Detective Green emerged from the bungalow first. "I'm sorry," he said quietly as he passed.

"For which part?" I noticed a large dose of sneer in my voice.

"The mess." He glanced over his shoulder and then moved aside to wait for the other detectives and their crime scene crew, which I found amusing since this bungalow was anything but a crime scene. Rob ducked inside and did a quick survey of all the rooms.

When the entire police group had exited the bungalow, I stepped inside to survey the mess and let out a strangled yelp that probably could still have been heard around the world. Meanwhile, Rob cornered the detectives and gave them a piece of his mind, promising to not only bring suit, but present a formal complaint to their chief. He's a strong man, intelligent and well-spoken, so it was a pleasure to see them look appropriately contrite. I tried to hide my grin before I turned back to the mess. I began to snap photos of the chaos. Oh my. This was going to take forever to clean, and we only had until the next afternoon when the new guests arrived. Plus, we had to pack and move all of the current belongings that had not been bagged, tagged, and carted away as evidence. I felt tension and worry build in my chest until I thought my heart would just abandon ship. I pulled out my phone and sent a text to Bennie.

It's worse than I expected.

He responded nearly immediately.

I'll be right there.

I even heard his feet pounding on the wooden walkway as he neared. Meanwhile, I moved from one bedroom to the other and snapped photos from as many angles as possible.

I turned and watched as Bennie entered through the open door and looked around with an expression of shock and dismay etched on his face. "What the..." He scratched his head as he looked around. Belongings were strewn all over, fingerprint dust covered nearly every surface, and all the cupboard doors and drawers stood open. "Really?" He looked at me in amazement and I simply shrugged.

"Didn't they do this to my bungalow when I was a suspect?"

"It was nothing like this, and we were able to clean it up in about twenty minutes. This?" He opened his arms to encompass the entire scene of destruction and said no more.

"Well..." I let out a big sigh. "I guess it's time to get to work."

Ming appeared in the doorway then and let out a string of Mandarin that I could only assume was swearing, Asian style.

"I'll go get the service cart." Bennie was still shaking his head as he left. Ming and I picked up clothing and other personal belongings and did our best to return them to the proper suitcase, but it wasn't entirely obvious which items belonged to whom. I found myself grumbling under my breath the entire time, a running monologue about the indecencies perpetrated by my fellow human beings. I heard the rumble of the service cart being rolled down the walkway at breakneck speed and made a mental note to never hurry with that thing for fear of waking every single guest. Fortunately all guests were currently accounted for, either by the pool or having left for sightseeing.

"Sorry." Bennie was breathing hard as he pushed the cart to the open door. "I know it was noisy, but I was rushing."

I simply smiled and nodded. He began in the bathroom, where I'd already taken photos, and put all of the personal toiletries in a basket before placing them by the three final suitcases that lay open on the sofa before me. Once all the belongings were repacked, I zipped up the cases and rolled them to the little entryway at the front door, and then I tackled the living room area. They'd unzipped all the sofa and chair cushions and dug around in the stuffing. I had to ease the fluffy fiberfill and high density foam back in, smooth it out, and zip it back up.

With the living room set right again, I went to the kitchenette and couldn't help myself; I gasped. Why on earth would the police have pulled all the dishes out of the cupboard and the few food stuffs out of the fridge? I mean… *really*?

Bennie and Ming must have heard me, because they were suddenly standing beside me and surveying the mess as well.

"Why?" They chorused.

I just shook my head. "Your guess is as good as mine. I pulled my phone out and took the final photos to document the brutality the cops had inflicted on innocent cutlery and stoneware. "What'd they ever do to you, Detectives?" I muttered as I cleaned. I loaded the dishwasher and set it to run, putting a reminder alarm on my phone to unload it before the new guests arrived tomorrow. Ming and I then scrubbed the counters, the refrigerator, and the floor until they met our strict standards. They sparkled so brightly that I expected a choir of angels. But instead of angels I got Davy, shimmering in beside me as I dumped the trash into the sack on the service cart.

"A little too proud of your hard work then, yeah?" Davy teased me, shaking the cart while I tried to maneuver the trash into it. "What a nice little charwoman you'd make."

"Shut up," I hissed as I finally got the trash dumped. Ming squeezed past me to close herself in the bathroom with scrub brushes and rags.

"Oh, but testy. I suspect that will lower your pay."

"Yeah, and I get paid *so* much, don't I?" I whispered.

Bennie peeked his head out of the master bedroom where he'd been changing the bedclothes. "You talking to me?"

"Oh! No, Bennie. Just talking to myself. Everything is fine."

He just stood there though, unmoving, his eyes darting around suspiciously. "You're talking to *him*, aren't you? Is he here? Right now?" He stepped closer to me, his head swiveling as he tried desperately to see what I saw, but to no avail.

"Yeah." I responded quietly, not wanting Ming to hear, as I grabbed new kitchen linens. "He's here."

"I want to see him," Bennie demanded.

"It doesn't work that way, Bennie."

Davy jumped in front of him and waved his hand in front of Bennie's face. "Can ya see me now?" he teased.

"Don't be rude, Davy," I admonished him, but it only served to incense Bennie.

"I want to see him now."

I sighed and looked to my little Mancunian sidekick. "Well?"

"Oh all right." He shook his head, shimmered out for a few seconds, and then made a very dramatic, extremely theatrical, and shimmery re-entry, landing right in front of Bennie, down on one knee with his arms outstretched, Al Jolson style.

"Oh," was all Bennie could say.

"Yeah, he's real eloquent, that one." Davy's derogatory comments did nothing to put the younger man at ease. Wait… he was younger, technically, but Davy was in his 1960s persona so *he* was actually younger… oh never mind. My life was not simple. Davy popped up to a standing position, and as they stood face to face, a brief thought floated through my mind about the similarities between the two. Both were handsome but also cute at times, with shiny dark hair, smooth tanned skin, and dark eyes that could easily captivate. The fleeting thought vanished as they faced off.

"He's… shorter than I expected." Bennie studied Davy.

"Oi! 'Oo you callin' short?" He advanced on Bennie, his chin pointed up defiantly. Bennie took one step back because Davy was invading his personal space.

"Davy!"

"Wot?"

"If you can't be nice, then go somewhere else right now. We're busy cleaning up a mess." I heard the stern tone to my own voice and felt a momentary pride. Yeah, I could be commanding if I needed.

"Fine. But you haven't seen the last of me." He puffed up his chest and poked his finger at Bennie before shimmering away.

"I apologize. He's very protective of me."

"Well, I'm not trying to hurt you." Bennie stood proud. "I just want to know what I'm up against."

"Up against?"

He bit his lip and shook his head. "Never mind. Let's clean."

Ming poked her head out of the bathroom. "What's going on? Am I the only one scrubbing? What's wrong with that scenario then?"

We chuckled and apologized. The three of us spent the next hour scrubbing and setting things right again. I looked at my watch. It was past lunch time and well nearing the dinner hour.

"Geez," I moaned. "And I had so much to do today!"

"I know." Bennie patted my shoulder. "I'm way behind too."

"I finished the other bungalows before this one." Ming beamed, obviously the smartest of our now grimy trio.

We left the bungalow, the luggage all packed and ready to be moved in the morning. We said goodbye to Ming for the day, and together Bennie and I wheeled the service cart back to its hiding place.

"Thank you for all your help. I'll see you later." I waved to Bennie and found solace in my private quarters. Flopping on my sofa, I gathered my last bit of strength.

"Davy, you were an asshole!"

He shimmered in. "Yeah? And so was he. He called me short!"

"Well, you are."

He stood with his hands on his hips, his strong chin jutting out. "Yeah, maybe I am, but he's no Wilt Chamberlain."

"Who?"

"Never mind, but I promise I'll give him a Manchester Kiss if he ever calls me short again."

I narrowed my eyes as I peered at him. "Why do I think you've had a lot of practice with... brawling?"

He broke into a grin then. "Well, maybe."

"I knew it! You were rowdy in your youth."

"We were not rowdy. We were..." his voice softened in an overly dramatic moment, "often unchaperoned youth in a time when love was free, drugs were readily available, and we were totally misunderstood. Oh, and underestimated." And then he winked.

"I know." I did know, because my parents told me about the attacks on what the establishment called 'hippies' simply because they were young people trying to express themselves. They didn't have the right to vote, but they were being drafted into service for a very unpopular police action in Vietnam. Police action? No, it was war. I knew about it all too well from stories my parents had shared with me. Dad had been worrying about the draft, but then he'd showed illness and was no longer eligible. I often wondered if he would have lived longer had he seen a doctor, and maybe Mom too. But it was in the past and there was nothing I could do to change it, nor was dreaming about it a good use of my time.

"I know you know. Just reminding you." His voice softened.

"Point taken, but could you just not be so antagonistic toward Bennie?"

He frowned. "Yeah." And then he shimmered away again. I simply shook my head. I really didn't understand men any more than men understood women.

I had only meant to close my eyes for a minute or two, but it was growing dark by the time I opened them again. "Crap!" I jumped to my feet and tried to rub some life back into my face. Chester was staring at me from the coffee table.

I thought you'd forgotten about me.

"No. Sorry. Fell asleep. I'll feed you now." Dishing up some of his canned food, I set it on the floor and then added a few more pieces of kibble to his other dish and refreshed his water.

The dog drank out of that water bowl. I'd like a clean one please.

I couldn't help but laugh. "Okay, but you have become very spoiled. And…" it suddenly dawned on me, "why didn't he eat your kibble too?"

He said it smelled like cat. And then he chuckled, almost like a giggle snort. That was new.

The singing of my phone interrupted us and I saw it was Taylor so I answered. "Oh my goodness. Are you both okay?"

"Yes. We're fine," she reassured me, but her voice sounded tired. "We're staying at the hotel tonight; they've extended our reservation at no charge, which was very nice of them."

"Oh, that's good!" I knew how innkeepers sometimes did that out of goodwill when guests fell on hardship, for we had often done the same, especially when storms closed the roads or the airports. "Then what is the plan for tomorrow?"

She sighed heavily. "We're not allowed to leave the island until the police tell us we can. Will our room up there still be available?"

"No. I'm so sorry. We have new guests arriving tomorrow, but we're moving your stuff into my bungalow. You're welcome to stay as long as you need." I promised myself I wouldn't encourage them; I shuddered at the idea of permanent house guests.

"Oh, thank you Macca." She sounded so relieved, causing my heart to warm toward them just a little more. "We'll be there when we can. And thanks again. Really."

"Don't mention it. Everything is going to be fine." Ha! Famous last words. I was getting good at those.

When we disconnected our call, I ran to the dining room to help Lani and Kalei, but they seemed quite organized. Sam, however, was busy unpacking cases of alcohol at the bar. "Late arrival." He smiled apologetically.

"No problem. We'll get it all stowed in no time." I was dead on my feet, but there was business to take care of. Together we unpacked, cut the boxes down, and carted them out to the recycle bin behind the shed. We quickly washed our hands and hurried back to the bar in the dining area. Guests were starting to arrive, and a few sat at the bar already. Sam took care of their drink orders while I did the same for those who had by now taken seats at their tables.

I saw Lani bringing out appetizers for each table and a tray at the bar, but we only had time for a quick smile to greet each other. What a day. I was glad to see it coming to an end and I knew I'd sleep well.

EIGHT

Hair Nets and a Snarly Dog

Saturday morning came well before I wanted it to, but there it was. Time to get the day going. Standing under the hot shower spray, I thought about the day ahead and felt completely overwhelmed. I hadn't even had time lately to tend to my hair with my usual coconut oil treatment, so I just combed it and caught it up in a butterfly clip at the back of my head. I dressed quickly in red shorts and a red and white striped tank top. Looking in the mirror caused me to grimace. I could pass for one of those poor girls in the mall who sell hot dogs on sticks. All I was missing was the hat. Shaking my head, I rushed to the kitchen, fed the cat, dropped a piece of King's Hawaiian bread in the toaster, and put the kettle on for tea. I took two mugs down, hoping Davy would appear. We'd hit a bit of a rough patch yesterday and it wasn't sitting well with me.

Just as I was putting a tea bag into each mug, I felt him shimmer in. "Good morning, Babe." He smiled rather sheepishly.

"Good morning." I put on my cheerful voice and poured hot water over each tea bag. As the tea steeped, he held both his hands out to me, his fists closed.

"Pick a hand.. any hand."

I pointed. "The left."

"Not that one," he admonished. "I thought for sure you'd pick the right one without hesitation. Pick another."

Laughing, I chose his right hand. "That one, because last time I looked, you only had two."

He stuck his tongue out at me and opened his right hand to show a tiny gift wrapped in beautiful tissue paper printed with cherry blossoms and tied by a thin gold ribbon. "For you," he stated the obvious, but I was touched.

"Aww. What's the occasion?" I picked up the gift and untied the ribbon.

"Just because we haven't had much time together lately. And because," he wrinkled his nose, "I was quite the beast yesterday."

Smiling, I shook my head and kissed his cheek before unwrapping the tissue. Inside was a beautiful little ceramic interpretation of a bonsai cherry tree on a dark wooden base. The whole thing was less than two inches in size. "Oh, I love this! Where did you get it?"

"In Tokyo. Yesterday."

"Really? What were you doing there?"

"I had to... *visit* some important people."

My eyes darted back up to his face. "Visit?" Were there other people he spent so much time with too? I thought Chester told me I was the only one. And then I mentally kicked myself for being petty and unkind... and worst of all, selfish.

"Well, they didn't see me, but I was there and made sure they felt it."

"Oh Davy. That is so sweet, and it's just so... you." I kissed his cheek again and gave myself an even swifter mental kick for my pathetic self-pity before turning to place my lovely little gift on the window sill there in the kitchen. The sunlight peeking through the partially closed blinds made the cherry blossoms on the tree sparkle a little, so I pulled the sash and let more light in. "It's beautiful." I clapped my hands. "Thank you so much."

"Apology accepted? Such as it is..."

"No apology necessary. I was tired and you and Bennie are men." I looked at him slyly then.

"What's that supposed to mean?"

"It means that men are often boys who frequently misbehave."

"Well, I can't deny that, I guess." He opened his arms and we shared a warm and comforting hug. Maybe this day wouldn't be so awful after all.

He carried our mugs of tea to the little dining table and I cut my piece of toast in half, slathering a bit of Lani's mango butter on each before handing one of the halves off to Davy. We sat together and crunched and munched. "Wow," I said between bites. "I still think Lani should market this stuff."

"It's way too good," he agreed, shaking is head as he chewed while savoring the mango butter, his eyes closed briefly. "So..." he continued after washing the last bite down with a sip of tea. "Are The Terribles returning today?"

"Yeah. They're staying in your room. Sorry."

"No problem. If I'm here, I'll just stay with you." His wink was playful and his grin infectious. "And I'll make sure 'my' room is tidy before they get here."

"Thank you."

"As long as no one puts confetti on the ceiling fan," he teased.

Mr. Pinckney blipped into the room at that point. "We have to go." His words were aimed at Davy and seemed quite urgent.

"Why?"

88

"I can't say right now because of the oo-man-way itting-say ere-hay."

Davy's laugh was sudden and sharp, like a bark. "Like she can't understand Pig Latin, man?"

"Okay. I know Double Dutch too," Mr. Pinckney continued, leaning closer to Davy in a conspiratorial manner. "The woola-foo-malla-fan silla-fit-tilla-fing heela-feer."

I'm quite sure my face held the same expression of total confusion, shock, and dismay as Davy's. This time I was the first to laugh. "Yep. Pretty sure I have no idea what you just said."

"And... neither do I." Davy shook his head. "Okay." He stood, putting his hand on the librarian's shoulder. "Let us be off then, and we'll discuss it along the way."

"Actually," I deadpanned, "I think you're both *off* already."

"Har har har," were Davy's last words as the two of them shimmered and blipped away.

I glanced at the clock and yelled, "Crap!" I was late. I found my red flip flops and flapped off to the reception area. "Sorry Bennie," I said as I reached into my inbox.

"No problem. Nothing going on yet."

"Oh good." I grabbed a cup of his Kona and perched at the bar checking out the notes and invoices in my hand. Nothing out of the usual there, but I'd forgotten my laptop so I ran back to my place and entered all the information from there instead. Chester was just waking up, stretching and yawning in a patch of sunlight that streamed in through the open sliding glass door.

"Sleeping late today, I see." I watched him slow blink.

I was up late last night.

"Partying?" I loved teasing him.

Partying? I guess you could call it that. I take it you haven't checked your running shoes, then?

"Oh please tell me you didn't hack up a hairball in them."

I swore he smiled. My running shoes were in my bedroom and I hesitantly picked them up and peered inside each one. I screamed when something fell out of the right shoe.

I brought that just for you, his noble chest was puffed out as he wandered in. *I hope you like it.*

He watched proudly as I stared transfixed at the dead mouse lying on the floor. "Um, Chester..." I was trying to think of something to say that wouldn't offend him. "How... very kind of you," I began slowly. "And your first one. I feel so... honored." He sat there contentedly, slow-blinking. "But... hey Big Guy, could you do me a favor?"

Maybe, he dragged the word out, seemingly suspicious of my intentions. Such a cat.

"Could you just leave future... gifts... on the deck in the back, and not in my shoe?"

Of course! You should have told me before.

It was then that I realized how absolutely absurd this conversation was. "I wasn't thinking... sorry."

But do you like it? I caught it just for you.

"Um, it's very nice, yes." I deserved an award for this performance because frankly, this particular gift was pretty disgusting. Such a cute little mouse it had been at one time, I'm certain. I suppressed a shudder and stepped around the mouse and the cat to get a paper towel and a bag from the kitchen, and then I set about the unpleasant task of removing the dearly departed rodent from my home. Once it was safely in the bag, I held it far in front of me.

Wait, where are you taking it? I worked hard to bring you that!

"I just want to..." Think fast, Macca! "...show it off. That's right, I'm going to show it to the gang."

He stretched and arched his back before settling down again to nap. *Good. Now... do not disturb. It was a lot of work to catch it, and I need my beauty sleep.*

I performed a quick review of my bizarre life as I walked to the main trash behind the storage shed. I had a ghost who brought me a gift from the other side of the world. Wonderful. I had an orange cat who brought me dead rodents. Horrible. Yes, my life had plenty of balance.

"Whatcha got there?" Sam was dumping the kitchen trash when I arrived.

"Chester brought me a dead mouse."

"Aww." He smiled. "The little guy's first catch?"

I shuddered then. "Yeah, and let's hope it's his last."

"Hey, he could be doing the inn a favor if he gets good at it."

"Oh, don't even think that." I dropped the makeshift body bag into the open bin and backed away, Sam laughing at me the entire time.

"Next time just give me a holler and I'll remove it for you, okay?"

I blew out a huge breath. "Oh, thank you! I will!" I shuddered again. "I think I liked my old citified Chester better though. Ick."

Sam laughed again and shook his head.

Back in my bungalow I put my running shoes in the kitchen sink, squirting soap inside while hot water filled the basin. I considered tossing them out with the garbage as well, but running shoes don't come cheap, so I hoped a nice long soak would be good enough.

90

Just as I was returning to the front desk, our new guests arrived and we welcomed the couple celebrating their 50th wedding anniversary. They were so adorable, holding hands as they walked toward us to check in. She was about eight inches shorter than her husband, wearing her gun-metal gray hair in a little bob with one side held back by a wooden barrette, and as they neared I could see her soft doe eyes were deep brown. He had a full head of silver hair with a darker gray mustache and ice blue eyes.

"Mr. and Mrs. Willton..." Bennie smiled and stretched his hand out to them as they reached the front desk. "My name is Bennie, and this lovely lady beside me is the owner here, Macca Liberty." I stretched my hand out as well and there were handshakes crossing over each other.

"Welcome to Hale Mele." I couldn't help but smile at this sweet couple.

"It's great to be here." Mr. Willton had a deep, gravelly, but quiet voice. "And please call us Bill and Jean."

"Very nice to meet you both. Bennie tells me you're celebrating your anniversary with us."

"We are," Jean answered, "and we heard there's a wonderful luau tonight. Is that true?"

"Yes." I grinned, happy to hear that word about us was spreading. "Will you be joining us then? It's a buffet and then a show, just behind us in the dining area," I said as I gestured in the general direction.

"We wouldn't miss it for the world," Bill answered, gazing lovingly down at Jean.

I jotted their names down on the reservation list and gave them the details about the cocktail hour just before dinner.

"Oh, we'll be there. I've never been to a luau." Jean excitedly clasped her hands in front of her on one of the few occasions she let go of her husband's.

I was scribbling a note for Lani and Kalei to let them know that our guests with the big anniversary had arrived. I knew Kalei was busy tending the imu oven out back and decided to let the couple know. "Bill and Jean, if you have the time and the desire, you can get a peek at chef Kalei's imu oven. You can't miss him; he's the big guy with the long dark braid hanging down his back. A sweetheart, indeed. His wife Lani creates the baked goods and provides the show."

"Oh." Jean began to blush. "Is he of Hawaiian descent?"

"That he is, and so is his wife Lani." I grinned, always so proud of our little inn's family.

"Oh boy," Bill laughed. "Jean goes weak in the knees over

Hawaiian men."

Jean giggled and it was infectious. I leaned over and stage-whispered loud enough for everyone to hear. "He's tall, dark, and handsome."

She clapped her hands like a little kid. "Jean, dear, he's also married," her husband teased.

"I know, I know," she shushed him. "I may be be old and married, but I'm not dead, so I can at the very least look and admire."

"Yes dear." Bill winked at us. Oh, this couple was a hoot, and I was thrilled they'd be joining us for ten days.

We picked up their bags for them and stepped out to the little porch. Winston chose that moment to sing "Cheer up sleepy Jean," in his usual manner. Jean clapped her hands and giggled, and I could almost see the young woman her husband had fallen in love with many years ago.

Bennie and I led them to their bungalow and you would never have guessed that it had been the subject of a police search the previous day. I considered a bonus for each of the team members as Bennie ushered us in. As he showed them around, I opened some windows for the couple in order to catch the lovely breezes that came in off the sea, especially toward the end of each day.

"We look forward to seeing you this evening," I added as we left them to get settled.

"Ha! I'm going to like them." Bennie was smiling widely.

"Me too. They're like 19-year-olds in senior citizen bodies." He chuckled and headed back to work while I veered to the kitchen and left the reminder note for Lani and Kalei.

"I have a sudden desire to watch *Cocoon* tonight," Bennie joked as I then headed back to the reception area.

I chuckled; that was a favorite movie of mine as well. "Yes. That would be perfect."

"Care to join me?"

I felt my smile try to fade, but I forced it to stay in place. "Oh, Bennie. What a lovely invitation. It's just…"

"It's okay. I know your friends will be here and all." He appeared to ease out of that uncomfortable and most likely impulsive invitation quite casually. I heard footsteps on the stairs from the parking lot and saw that Bettina and Taylor had arrived. I felt awkward with Bennie, but he came to my rescue and simply said, "I'll see you later," before returning to work.

"Okay Bennie." And I watched his back as he turned to the computer. I blew out the breath I hadn't realized I'd been holding and stepped outside to greet my friends with open arms. It was almost like a magnet drew them into my embrace and we were all hugging silently.

"It's been horrible." Taylor was the first to pull away a little as she began to give commentary on their time with the police. "I was so afraid they were going to lock us up even though we did nothing wrong!"

Bettina was watching her daughter with a curiously grim expression on her face. "Are you both okay then?" I looked from one to the other.

"Yes," Taylor continued to gush. "So glad to be back on friendly turf."

"Were you two…" I worked hard to find the right words that would not betray that I already knew the answer, "…kept separate from each other the whole time?"

"Yes!" Taylor wailed again, looking dramatically to the sky. "I just saw Mom for the first time last night! I thought for sure she was going to be arrested."

While Taylor continued to whimper, I sensed Bettina closing up, as if retreating behind a shield. She simply shook her head very slightly at her daughter's theatrics and looked away. "Have our things been moved?" she asked me quietly.

I nodded and opened my arm to direct them to my bungalow, showing them their room and leaving them to get settled for a bit. I did hear raised voices a few times, but couldn't tell if they were from Bettina, Taylor, or both. Theirs was a pairing I was ill-prepared to understand, especially without the balance of Annie's presence. I couldn't imagine yelling at my mother, nor could I imagine her yelling at me. Of course I only knew her as a child. My lack of insight left me standing alone on the deck watching the tiny specks that were sailboats on the vast sea beyond the trees. I wondered if any hitchhiker ever tried to thumb a ride on a boat? Hmmm…

My peace was broken by Taylor stepping onto the deck beside me and letting out a great, dramatic sigh. "Parents. They can be so annoying sometimes."

I forced a smile. "I can't recall that feeling, actually," I said with an edge to my voice that even I could hear.

"Oh." She turned to me then. "I'm sorry. I always forget that your parents have been gone for so long."

That statement hurt, but it was the truth. "It's okay," I lied.

"But, you have to admit how much easier adult life is without them, right?"

I pulled back so suddenly that I imagined whiplash for a second. I could only frown at her though, for unspoken words were clogging my

93

throat. I shook my head, turned on my heel, and marched back toward the front desk where it was safe. By the time I got there I was silently seething.

"What happened?" Bennie knew me so well.

"Family," I responded and continued to stomp to the kitchen.

He nodded. "I get it. I really do." He turned his attention back to the computer screen he'd been staring at as he typed on the keyboard. Good. I wasn't ready to address anything else with him. I swung the kitchen door open.

"Hey Lani. Got any yeast dough you need to have punched down and beaten up?"

Lovely Lani, feisty little thing, laughed and pulled a bowl from the warmth above the stove. "As a matter of fact, I do. Here... have at it."

I put a Miss Lulu Lunch Lady hair-net on, washed my hands, floured a large section of the work table, and dumped the big mountain of dough onto it. I punched it down, then rolled it over and kneaded. I did this solidly for at least ten minutes, feeling more relaxed with every turn. I felt Lani give me a few little pats on my back as she passed, and it was comforting. I continued to beat the crap out of the dough until I was spent. Lani came to stand next to me and poked her finger at the dough a few times.

"Well, you beat it into submission. These will be the most tender rolls ever."

"Or the toughest." I blew out a breath as I huffed and puffed, and it made a few strands of stray hair that had escaped the hair net float up from my face before settling back down and sticking to my skin. "Exhausting work. Exactly what I needed."

"Yeah." She gave a derisive snort. "Like you don't work enough. But look — it's a beautiful mound of dough!" She thought for a few seconds before tilting her head up to look into my eyes. "Family, then?"

I nodded and she sighed. She understood.

We stepped back and looked at the giant lump of dough, the surface glistening from being worked. I plunged three fingers into it. "Look, a deflated bowling ball." We burst into laughter over the silliness of it all. Kalei wandered in, surveyed the two of us and our mound of dough, and simply shook his head before heading back outside again. We dissolved into laughter and I hugged the diminutive woman. "Oh thank you for making me feel better."

"I could tell you were needing to let out some steam. I'm just happy I had an outlet to offer you." She gently elbowed me then. "We gotta stick together, you know."

I nodded. "Yes, we certainly do." And I felt that my smile had finally reached my heart again. Pretending happiness is hard work, and I was tired of compromising myself in order to tolerate my two guests.

"It's exciting to have a couple celebrating their 50th this evening," she expertly turned the subject away from my ire. "It's hard to imagine fifty years, really," she laughed, "but we'll make something special for the Willtons."

"You always do!"

Feeling better after winning my prize fight against the mountain of dough, I headed back to my place to get ready for the evening meal and the show. Saturdays were our busiest nights, of course, and I wouldn't necessarily find much time to coddle Bettina and Taylor. I was trying to think of what to say when I opened my door and found them waiting for me, seated on the sofa.

"Macca..." Taylor began. "I'm terribly sorry for saying the things I did about your parents."

I wasn't buying it. Looking into her eyes showed me she was without the remorse that should have backed up her words. Therefore, I simply nodded.

She looked then at her mom who nodded sternly, urging her on. "And I'm very grateful to you for letting us stay with you while we wait on the police."

Still nothing in her eyes.

"Mom and I are going to go have dinner at Lomi-Lomi," she continued. "We were able to get last minute reservations and we haven't been out in several days." Her smile was bright, cheery, and totally without substance.

"Oh, okay." I surely wasn't going to object. "I'll be busy with the luau, so just make yourselves at home afterward. There are some DVDs below the television if you want."

"Don't you worry about us," Bettina said and stood up. She was so disturbingly prickly all the time that it gave me the heebie-jeebies. Was I sharing my bungalow with a murderer? Or two? I looked back and forth between the two of them and had a brief thought that I'd put my money on the older woman. She was creepy and scary, but there was also something else underneath that I could not put my finger on just yet. Did it keep me up at night? Not so far... but tonight was the first time I'd be sharing a home with them. I tried to stifle a shudder.

"Well, I hope you have a good time." They were going to a local restaurant that had gotten great reviews since opening last year. "And let me know how Lomi-Lomi is. I've never been there." My comment was casual, but they gave me a look of such intense pity that I was instantly incensed. It's not easy running a business such as this one, but I was damned proud of its success. Once they'd gone, I put down more food for Chester, who I'd seen hiding just outside the sliding glass door. He slunk in, his eyes darting back and forth.

"It's clear, Big Guy. They're gone."

They scare the shit out of me.

"Whoa. Where'd you learn to talk like that?"

He slowly turned his face to peer up at mine. *Really? You. Davy. The staff. Need I go on?*

"I guess not." I admit that I was properly humbled. "You might want to come in early and sleep in my room then, because they'll be here for a few days."

I'll hide in your closet until they leave.

Oh, that was sad. And pathetic. And then I realized he was trying to manipulate me so that I'd feel sorry for him, possibly angling for treats.

"Good," I changed course. "Enjoy the solitude." And I headed out to work.

It was with great joy and relief that I joined the staff in the dining and kitchen area to help with the prep and set-up for dinner and the show. I loved Saturday nights.

The Morrison family were the first to arrive for dinner. The twins, Ella and Ethan, were dressed in their hula finery that they'd been collecting over the course of their weeks on the island. Behind them stood their dads, Jack and Rick, with baby Noah in the latter's arms, both men in deep discussion about the imminent arrival of appliances for their new house that was nearing completion.

"Hello Morrisons!" I beamed as Ethan and Ella gave me hugs around my legs.

"Hi Macca!" Jack and I did the cheek-kissy thing, then Rick followed.

"And hello to you too, Noah!" I gave him a peck on the cheek.

"We asked the Wallace family to join us," Rick said as he bounced Noah on his hip. "Would it be possible to push some tables together?"

"Of course! I'd be delighted. Wait right here and we'll get you all set up." I motioned to Sam and we pulled a few tables together and situated two high chairs along with seven regular chairs. With a parent seated on either side of their kids, it was a perfect fit. Noah squealed with delight when he was placed in his high chair; that kid was an eater! The Wallaces arrived as we were just settling the Morrisons, and they placed Grant's baby seat on the high chair, strapping it in tightly. I stopped to greet the adults, Catherine and Zack, then patted little Lily's shoulder and asked if she was having a good time. Her enthusiastic nod spoke volumes. I couldn't very well leave them though until I greeted my little Grant.

"Hello my little bunny. How are you today?" I kissed his cheek and he clumsily touched my face, smiling widely. "I'll take that as *good* then." I took their drink orders and Sam and I served them all just as more people were arriving.

Our newest guests, Jean and Bill Willton, looked much fresher than when they'd first arrived. "Good evening," I greeted them and showed them to their table. "How was your afternoon?"

"Relaxing, thanks," Jean answered. "Our flight from Vancouver was exhausting so we took a little snooze by the pool."

"I feel great now." Bill pounded his chest and then pretended to cough like an old man.

"Oh, stop that," his wife teased and covered his hand with her own on the table. I got their drink orders taken care of, and just as I was seating our last guest, Bennie whispered in my ear.

"We have a surprise guest this evening. Their daughter and son-in-law have brought Mr. and Mrs. Ian Woon to celebrate his birthday. He's 82 years young!"

"How wonderful!" I was looking forward to enjoying the company of our postal workers in a social setting. "We finally get to meet the elusive Mrs. Woon then," I teased.

"I was beginning to think she didn't exist," he responded over his shoulder as he went to deliver drinks to other guests. I noticed then that the Woon party was just arriving.

"Mr. and Mrs. Woon." I held my hands out "It's so lovely to see you! And Happy Birthday, Mr. Ian Woon."

"Thank you! This is my wife Betty." He indicated the equally aged yet beautiful woman by his side and we exchanged greetings. "And you know my daughter Tina," he added, indicating the couple standing behind them. "And this is our son-in-law Stan the Man. Wonderful guy. He spoils us all."

"It's very nice to meet you Stan, and Mrs. Woon too. We are so honored that you chose our little place for your celebration."

I showed them to their table and Bennie joined us to say hello and take drink orders, but not before the mandatory joke from Mr. Woon. "Did you hear about the new stamp that's coming out? It's got a picture of a dog on it. It's the first stamp that can lick itself." He cackled and slapped his knee and we chuckled right along with him. "And do you know what it means when the post office is flying the flag at half mast?"

"No." I grinned. "What does it mean?" I know. I'd make a great straight man… erm… woman.

"It means they're hiring." He winked at us, and Bennie and I both burst out laughing simply because we loved Mr. Woon and his corny jokes..

"That's a great one, Mr. Woon." I patted the elderly man's shoulder.

"Ian..." Betty playfully scolded. "You need to find some new material, dear."

"I'm working on it." He fiddled with his flatware, still chuckling to himself. My attention was drawn to Lani giving me a heads up. They were ready to begin laying the buffet items, so I excused myself in order to help her. When it was ready I quietly went to each table and let the guests know that they could visit the buffet whenever they were ready.

As usual, I held Noah while his siblings went with their dads to get food. "Catherine, I'll be happy to sit with Grant too while you go to the buffet."

The smile on her face nearly lit up the room as she stood and took Lily's hand. "Thank you, Macca." I smiled and nodded, getting the feeling that the poor woman didn't often get much outside help with the kids. Of course, it really was my pleasure. I sat in Catherine's chair and talked to both Noah and Grant at the same time. There was no fussing, just happiness shown by gurgles and coos. Once everyone was seated and enjoying their meal, I stole away to the kitchen to munch on some fruit and a poi roll, keeping an eye on things through the door that was propped open just a crack.

When dessert was served, we poured a complimentary glass of champagne for all the adults who wanted, and sparkling cider for the kids and other non-drinkers. Bennie raised his glass of water and announced both the birthday and the anniversary we were celebrating while Kalei got out his ukulele. The voices were diverse as we sang "Happy Birthday" to Mr. Ian Woon, then "Happy Anniversary" to Mr. and Mrs. Willton.

Our guests seemed to be enjoying themselves, for the volume in the room had grown to large proportions. Lani's friend Malina arrived and the two young women went into the laundry area to change into their costumes. Meanwhile, Sam and I put leis around our necks and then brought out the big basket of Makala's floral creations, presenting each guest with a lei. Despite the open air room, the fragrance from all the leis combined to create a heady perfume in the warm night air.

Kalei cued the music and the show began. I watched the faces of our newer guests and couldn't help but feel more than content. All eyes were on our little makeshift stage and the lovely Lani and Malina as they danced. When the chanting began in the next dance, I saw Mrs. Woon tear up, and Mr. Woon grasped her hand so lovingly. I also saw Jean Willton become just a little overwhelmed with emotion as well; her eyes brimmed with unshed tears and darted back and forth between the dancers and Kalei, as if she couldn't quite decide which was more enchanting.

After the show, Lani presented Mr. Ian Woon and Mr. and Mrs. Willton each a beautiful beribboned box of pineapple oatmeal macadamia nut cookies. Kalei led our guests in a round of applause before turning the music on again. Bennie had gathered a few big band CDs, and when the first notes of The Glenn Miller Orchestra's "Moonlight Serenade" began, we invited the two celebrating couples up to the small dance floor. I watched the faces of the other guests as they looked on, and was touched by their obvious pleasure.

Bennie elbowed me halfway through the music and whispered, "Shall we dance?" I felt my face flush as he pulled me to the dance floor. As we slowly danced, we motioned for others to join us, and by the time the song was over, the floor was pleasantly filled with smiling couples. When the next song began, barely anyone returned to their seats, and I noticed that the Woons and the Willtons had switched partners. It was quite simply adorable. Bennie and I giggled and danced toward the kitchen to make space for others. With the liquor flowing smoothly from the bar and people enjoying the music and the dancing, we began to help with the clean up efforts.

"A successful evening, I'd say," I said once most of us were in the kitchen. "And I thank you all."

I was exhausted by the end of the evening and eagerly returned to my bungalow once the kitchen and dining room had been cleaned up. Sam kept the bar open, as usual, for those that wanted to linger and revel in the happy mood created by great food and equally great entertainment.

I'd almost forgotten that I had roommates. I sure hoped it was only for a few days, but I was well aware of the slow pace of police department investigations.

Light spilling from the front window let me know Bettina and Taylor were home, and I wondered if they were going to trash my place the way they had their own. I opened the door to find them sitting on the sofa watching television.

"Hi." Taylor looked over her shoulder at me. "It sounds like the guests are having a fine old time."

I smiled. "They are. It was a great group tonight, including an 82nd birthday and a 50th wedding anniversary."

"I sure hope they don't go too far into the early morning hours with their partying," Bettina muttered. "I'd like to get some sleep."

Yeah, I thought. *You're staying here for free and you're complaining?* But I simply stated on my way to the kitchen, not even caring if it turned out to be wrong, "I'm sure they'll be quiet soon." I began to make myself a cup of tea, but the opened bottle of Merlot on the counter beckoned to me, so I poured a glass of that instead. I didn't want to, but I knew it was the polite thing to do, so I offered some to my guests.

"Anyone want a glass of wine?"

"No thank you," came the chorus from the other room. Wow, hell must have installed an ice rink that night. I shrugged and took my glass to the living room, happy that my favorite chair was available. I flopped into it, keeping my glass steady, and propped my feet up on the ottoman. Then I started to giggle quietly as my mind wandered. Ottoman. Archduke Otto. Princess Bettina. The Duchy of Harmonica. Memories of an old Monkees episode came to mind. My life had indeed become a sitcom. Or maybe a dramedy. Definitely not a romcom because that would require…well… romance. I had a vague memory of romance from the past. I sipped my wine. Fatigue was making me punchy.

"What are we watching?" I asked because I was unable to identify what was on the television screen.

"A movie." Taylor spoke without taking her eyes from the screen.

Yeah, I can see that, I thought to myself. I was going to ask for more information when the music built up and a vicious dog appeared to attack someone. I let out a tiny yelp and averted my eyes.

"Cujo." Bettina added the missing detail without looking away from the bloody scene. *Cujo,* eh? Yeah, not my thing. I stood, got my bottle of wine from the kitchen, and headed to bed.

"Goodnight all. I'll see you in the morning." No response. Wow. Yet another Monkee reference popped into my mind from the episode where everyone was hypnotized by their television.

I stifled a shiver and found solace in my bedroom, shutting the door firmly behind me and placing my wine bottle and glass on the bedside table. Movement caught my eye as I was turning on the lamp, and Chester poked his head out of my closet. I smiled and felt instantly better. "Hello my little furry friend. How are you?"

I'm okay, but I was afraid there was a snarly dog in the house.

"Just on the television screen." And then I saw Susie standing outside my private sliding glass door, his tongue lolling and his tail wagging hopefully. I unlatched it and let him in, in spite of the fact that he could have gotten inside on his own in his usual ghostly manner. He instantly nosed at my hand for pets, which I generously applied to his thick coat. "Hi Cujo," I teased him as we touched noses and his long tongue snaked out to lick my chin. "Were you scared too?" I patted the bed and he jumped up, made three tight turns, and plopped down in a rather large dog-ball, emitting a little moan of comfort as he settled. Chester hopped up beside him and nestled near the big dog's belly. Susie nosed him a bit and gave him a single lick before putting his head down and closing his eyes. Chester reached up with his paw and gave the dog's face a few gentle pats before he too settled down.

I could still hear the horror from the television in the other room, so I slid a new CD into my little portable. Raiatea Helm was a local singing sensation in the islands, and Davy shimmered in just as the first song began to play. He greeted Susie and then Chester first before even acknowledging that I was in the room.

"Hello." I grinned at him as I settled into my rocking chair.

"Hi." He seemed quite distracted as he picked up the CD case and looked at the front and back of it. "Rah-something Helm. I've never heard of her." He listened carefully again. "She has the voice of an angel," he exclaimed, his eyes wide. "And a face to match," he added as he looked at all the photos of her.

I chuckled because I could tell he was smitten, and I thought it was cute. "There's a song on that CD where she holds the longest note I've ever heard. It has to be more than 15 seconds. Someday I should time it."

Now it was his turn to chuckle. "Right."

"You don't believe me?" I leaned over and skipped to the song "Kalama'ula" so that he could hear for himself, and I pointed out the stanza I'd mentioned. Then I sat back as his eyes grew wider and wider.

"Wow."

"There's that witty repartee I love so much," I deadpanned. He glanced over at me and stuck his tongue out. "She's really got you tongue-tied, hasn't she?" I was giggling now, amused to see this side of him. "Maybe you should shimmer over to Oahu and look her up in Honolulu," I teased.

Those thick eyebrows of his arched up, disappearing beneath his long hair. "That's where she lives?"

Now I laughed. "Yeah. That's what I've seen whenever she's mentioned in the news. And she *is* mentioned... quite frequently."

"The local darling," he mused.

"The local darling with a Grammy nomination. She didn't win, but no one seems to care much. It was a big deal for Hawaiian music, until they eliminated the category."

"Wow." Davy's lack of one of his usual glib responses was entertaining, to say the least. "How do you pronounce her name?"

"Helm."

He poked my bare foot. "You know what I meant."

I grinned. "Near as I can tell it's ry-ah-tay-ah." I could see his lips move as he practiced.

But to further seal the deal, so to speak, although I think he was sold on her already, I skipped ahead to her version of the Etta James classic "At Last" and watched his face.

He let himself down onto my bed, his back propped up on my pillows, and his mouth open in awe. Yes, she was that good.

"And you should hear her sing it live," I added when the song was over and he stared at me. Actually, he stared right through me, seemingly lost in thought. "I've only heard her live performance on a YouTube video, but it was pretty phenomenal."

"Show me," he demanded, and then softened it. "Sorry. Could you please show me?"

"You're really stuck on her, aren't you? How cute."

"Shut up and just show me, please? She's got quite the voice."

I reached between my mattress and boxspring and pulled out my laptop that I'd stashed there. Hey, I was rooming with Satan's Sisters and I didn't trust them. At all. Would you? I booted up the lappie and set it on the bed in front of us. Susie raised his head briefly, slightly disturbing a sleeping Chester, who muttered in a nearly perfect imitation of Steve Martin... with a British accent... *Do you mind?* before settling again. Susie sniffed at the back of the laptop and, satisfied that it wasn't going to kill us all, went back to sleep with his head on his crossed paws. I heard Chester chuckle at Susie's worries about imagined enemies.

"Hey... You worry at ceiling monsters, so I don't think you'd better criticize Susie for being cautious."

Hmph. Chester yawned, already bored with the conversation.

Thank you, a male voice said in my head.

"You're welcome," I replied automatically. Wait. Who was I replying to? I studied Susie's face for a few seconds. *Nah, couldn't possibly be*, I thought to myself. And then Susie winked at me, but was it a conscious movement or just another one of those curious instances where dogs sometimes blink one eye at a time. "Susie?"

He raised his head and panted a few times, then swallowed, his giant tongue slurping his drool. Eww. *Hey, my drool is perfectly clean.*

Now the dog was talking to me? "No, no, no."

My full name is No Dammit. It's better than Susie, but both are a bit unconventional, don't ya think?

Holy crap! Susie just answered me back in my thoughts, exactly like Chester did!

Don't get yer panties in a bunch, he "said" in a distinctly southern accent. Southern? *I don't talk as much as Chester.*

It *was* him! "Why me?"

"Why you what?" Davy asked distractedly.

"Susie just talked to me. With a Southern accent. Although I didn't hear a *y'all* to verify that, but as far as I can tell, it was Southern."

"You're all annoying," Davy muttered and poked my earbuds into his ears in order to watch his YouTube video. When I saw that he was completely tuned out, I picked up my current library book, *Malice In Maggody*, by Joan Hess. It was a fun read, full of quirky characters and a touch of humor, all taking place in a land far away... well, far away for me: it was Arkansas. I wondered if people from Arkansas sounded like Susie. I peered at him over the top of my book, but he slept soundly.

I rocked and read and sipped my wine, then rocked some more, and still read and sipped. I loved my rocker. It reminded me of my mom, and I often flashed back to the hours she had rocked me in her own rocking chair. Every child should grow up with a parent or grandparent who rocked them... frequently.

I'd read several chapters before I realized Davy was still watching videos. I reached over and pulled out one of his earbuds.

"What happened to you?" I asked as he turned to see why he'd lost an earbud.

"The usual trap." He grinned sheepishly. "One video led to another, which led to more. I love this girl's voice though!"

I smiled as I put his earbud back in for him and returned to my book for a while. The Raiatea Helm CD had finished while he was busy watching videos, so I played something safer, *Sgt. Pepper's Lonely Hearts Club Band*. I already knew he liked The Beatles.

It was getting late and I began to yawn. I slipped out of my room to brush my teeth and change into Uncle Wally's big tee-shirt that I liked to sleep in sometimes. On the way back to my room, I heard the television still going, but it sounded like *Cujo* had ended and the news was on. Good. Less disruptive noise. I peeked into the living room and bid Bettina and Taylor a good night. They were still distracted, so I hustled back to my little sanctuary.

"I think we have grumpy house guests," I whispered to Chester, who also ignored me. If I hadn't been so sleepy I might have felt insulted. I patted Susie's head. "Goodnight, good pup." I made Davy move to my rocking chair before I climbed into bed, pulling Chester closer to snuggle. "Goodnight Davy," I called over my shoulder.

"Goodnight." He had stopped watching videos, but was playing around on the internet, so I just tucked in with the critters and fell into a luxuriously deep sleep that was interrupted only slightly and infrequently by the tapping of the keys on the laptop. As I drifted off I wondered idly if ghosts actually needed sleep, but strongly doubted that this particular specter was the one to test that theory on. He was an energizer bunny.

NINE

Dental Puns and Turkey Jerky

Early Sunday morning, Kalei, Lani, and I were loading our cars with food for the homeless encampment, Hale Maluhia, which loosely translated to *House of Peace*. In addition to the weekly meal, we had been instrumental in connecting various community leaders and service providers to the encampment. It could easily have been a full time job if I didn't already have one, yet I loved helping them. "I'll meet you there," I called to Kalei as he lugged a big pot of vegetable curry and brown rice to his car. Lani was behind him with an enormous box of cookies.

"Aloha, Macca-Roon," Makala called to me upon my arrival at the camp. She'd given me that nickname because I'd brought Lani's cookies on the first day, and everyone had fallen in love with the gooey delights. Even once they'd met Lani and were able to give proper credit to our expert baker, the nickname had stuck. Makala was one of the elders at the camp. Joe, a veteran Marine, and Kai, an Air Force veteran, were the equivalent of her second in command. All were highly respected by the camp residents because they only stepped in when there were issues that threatened to upset the balance they all sought to keep.

"Aloha, Makala," I answered while hugging her just as Joe and Kai approached to greet me as well. Together we were unloading my little Roomba when Kalei and Lani arrived with their own packed vehicle. Members of the camp assisted, and the buffet was set up quickly while I helped some of the kids dish out the dry kibble I had brought for their various dogs and cats. Extra bags were kept out of the pets' reach in one of the converted buses the government had decommissioned for use in camps such as this one.

Kalei and Lani had to head back to Hale Mele, but I stayed to dine with my friends. Kalei loaded up the cleaned pots, pans, and serving utensils from the previous week while Lani exchanged hugs with all those they'd become close friends with. Makala even rubbed her expanding belly and gave it a kiss.

"Hello little keiki," she spoke to the unborn baby, which caused me to grin.

We waved goodbye to Kalei and Lani and then got in line for food. I took a small helping of pasta salad and a heap of green salad too, then joined Makala, Joe, and Kai on a rough blanket they'd spread under the big monkeypod tree.

"How has your week been?" I asked the three of them.

"Week been good," Makala spoke between bites.

"That doctor who volunteers here fixed her up with some medicine for her arthritis." Joe nodded enthusiastically.

"Yes." She flexed her fingers for me. "Look! No pain!"

"That's wonderful! It must make your lei-making a little easier then?"

She nodded happily. "Very good stuff, that medicine."

"And we're happy when she's happy." Kai grinned, showing his missing tooth. "And the dentist is gonna fix my teeth!"

"Wow! What will he do?"

"A bridge, he said. We begin next week. I'm happy."

"Yeah." Joe teased. "Then he'll be able to eat those ribs and corn on the cob we have every day." Kai gave him a playful punch on his shoulder.

"Shaddup you. I will be happy to bite into a sandwich, that's all."

"I wonder if it will be a toll bridge." Joe was cracking himself up with his teasing. I admit, I was chuckling too. "Bridge over River Kai," he continued. Makala began to laugh too, and nearly spit out her pasta.

"Stop it. Both of you," she said. "Old woman tryin' t'eat."

But Joe winked at me before he answered "I think we should get Kai a little plaque for his tooth."

I groaned at the pun but it didn't stop him. "The dentist said he's going to get to the root of Kai's problems."

"Stop! Stop!" Makala was demanding as we all laughed.

"You are such a funny guy." Kai chuckled. "But one more tooth joke and I'll give you such a drilling!"

This caught Joe off guard, and he sat in stunned silence for about two beats until he began to laugh so hard that he flopped back on the blanket. Makala looked at me then, shaking her head.

"And they supposed to set examples for the keiki. Tsk, tsk, tsk." Her eyes gleamed in fun though.

As usual, spending time with my friends buoyed my mood, and I found myself singing with the radio on the way home. Davy and Mr. Pinckney shimmered and blipped in, Davy in the front seat, Mr. Pinckney hunched in the back compartment.

"Hello gentlemen." I smiled at Davy and sent a smile to Mr. Pinckney via the rear view mirror, but their faces were glum.

"You need to go directly home." Davy's voice was soft but serious.

"I had planned to," I began. "But why? What's going on?"

"They found Annie's body." He put his hand on my arm. I eased the car to the side of the road and shut off the motor. You've heard that term " the silence was deafening," right? Well, it can be. I felt like my ears were plugged, and then I realized I was holding my breath. I let it out with a whoosh.

"Were you there?" I asked.

"Yeah." Davy still had his hand on my arm, but he ran it down to my hand and held it on the console between us.

"Was it bad?"

"Yeah."

I gulped. "Do you think she suffered?"

He shook his head several times before responding. "I couldn't tell. Neither of us could."

"Any clues to the…" I couldn't finish the sentence.

"None that we could tell from the police. They're remaining very quiet. I get the feeling they have a suspect but aren't ready to show their hand just yet."

I nodded. "Do you think it's Bettina?"

"I don't know, Babe. Just be careful, okay?"

I nodded again. "You'll be around?"

"We want to poke around some more, but we're only a goldfish away."

"Okay. Thank you."

He leaned over and kissed my cheek just before they shimmered and blipped away. I spent precious time taking some calming breaths and rubbing my hands over my face. A sharp rap on my window caused me to jump; it was a local police officer. I rolled down my window.

"Just checking on you, ma'am. Is everything okay?" I glanced in my rear view mirror and saw his squad car.

"Yes, I…" What the hell should I say? "I had to make a call." I lifted my phone and wiggled it as emphasis.

"Oh, very well then." He patted the car door. "I'll let you be on your way."

"Thank you," I muttered as I started the car. The air conditioning needed a few minutes to cool, so I kept the window down. The wind on my skin felt refreshing though, so I turned off the artificial cool and enjoyed the island air. It was a cleansing sensation, and I breathed deeply a few times, even cracking a little smile of pleasure. But then I remembered Annie was gone, and from what I could tell by Davy's face, it had been brutal. The tears began to roll down my face, quickly followed by wracking sobs. I had to pull over again, but this time I chose a parking lot instead of the side of the road. I cried until I thought I had no tears left, and then I cried some more.

When I finally arrived home I sat in the parking lot for several minutes to regain my composure. The radio was playing oldies for the day and, of all things, "Act Naturally" came on. I'd never been a fan of the song, but the words went right to my heart. All I gotta do is "Act Naturally."

"You had a hand in this, didn't you Davy?" I even cracked a smile.

Anything I can do to help, you know. He was a sweetheart… most of the time. And a scamp for the remainder.

Trying to keep that smile on my face, I locked the car and walked slowly down the stairs to my bungalow, hesitating before opening my front door. I was relieved to see the place was empty so I deposited my bag and checked on Susie and Chester. Chester was asleep on my bed and I made certain that the sliding door was open for him as he awoke, stretched, and followed me around. Susie's absence was not alarming since I knew he could manage no matter what he was up against. I'd seen him jump right through a solid door just to protect Kalei, Lani, her mother Lehua, and me not that long ago. He was a true hero in my eyes. But seeing that Chester was fine was a relief. Frankly, I wasn't very trusting of Princess Bettina right now, and my critters' safety was top priority.

As I hurried to the front desk, Chester was right on my heels trotting one cat-length behind so that my flip flops wouldn't smack him on the chin. The little scamp stayed with me the whole way.

"C'mon little guy," I encouraged him to keep up just to see if he would continue his little dog act. When we reached the front desk I turned and picked him up, snuggling my face in his lush orange striped fur for comfort.

"Is everything okay?" I heard Bennie and looked to him behind the front desk.

"Yeah." I squeezed my eyes closed for an instant to fortify myself against the tears that were hiding right behind. "Chester is acting a little clingy." As I quickly thought *I'm only saying that as a smokescreen*, the big feline responded understandingly with a slow-blink. I slow-blinked right back at him. "I think he missed me."

I turned to look at my right-hand guy; he wasn't buying it. I sighed, set Chester on the floor, and crooked my finger at Bennie to lead him to our very private, extremely secure, and oh so official meeting area — the laundry room.

"Davy told me they've found Annie's body," I began as the door clicked firmly closed behind us. "I suspect the police will arrive within the next couple days." He looked aghast as he studied my face. I reached out and grasped his arm before continuing as it dawned on me. "Oh! But they won't be coming for me!" He was visibly relieved, expelling the breath he had apparently been holding.

"Your family then?" He still looked stricken.

I heaved a deep sigh. "I guess. I don't know for sure. And I just can't even recognize them as family anymore."

"Oh Macca." He gathered me in his arms and I let him, relishing the protection those arms afforded.

"My mind has already accepted that she's gone, but my stubborn heart isn't ready."

"Do you really think it's one of her family?" He was aghast at the idea.

"Yeah. I do. I sort of suspect Bettina. She's just so... angry at life."

His eyes widened. "Are you sure?"

"No. I'm not, but I'm definitely watching my back. If not Bettina, could it be a one-off madman who killed Annie? Or someone stalking her? I haven't heard of any such person, so I'm skeptical."

He sank onto the stool that we kept near the laundry folding counter and stared at the floor. "I don't know how you hold it together."

"I'm not sure I really am."

He moved to put his arm around me again and I leaned into him. I felt him kiss the top of my head, so shoot me, but I simply let him do it. I needed comforting. I needed every ounce of comfort I could find. Did that mean I was using him? I gulped. That was a discussion I would need to have with myself later, in private.

"You've really had a rough time these last years. I hope this is the end of it."

"I do too. It's coming time to plan for futures, to enjoy the present, and let the past be only memories that don't intrude, but instead awaken the soul." Where exactly did that come from? I froze for several beats and suspected my father. *Really Dad?* I heard a chuckle in my mind and wanted to throttle him, but I just went with it for the sake of appearances.

"Bettina and Taylor were here for lunch, and now I think they're down at the beach."

"Oh good, and thank you. I just need to have some time away from them."

"I understand."

I felt like he was on the verge of offering more than I could handle, so I sidestepped a bit. "I'm going to hide for a bit so I can get my head together."

"I suggest you go for a run then." He tilted his head and smiled sweetly.

"Good idea and thank you." I kissed his cheek and immediately berated myself for doing so, not wanting to lead him on. I made my escape and ran back to the bungalow to put on my running shoes then stopped near the imu oven. Chester sat on the grass and watched me as I stretched. "I'll be back. I promise." I gave him a loving pet and then hit the path. I ran and ran, and then I ran some more. I felt the endorphins kick in and ran even harder and faster. By the time I returned to my bungalow I was panting and pleasantly exhausted. I walked the perimeter a few times to cool down, then stretched again before I hit the shower. I scrubbed and rinsed all the stress away. Or so I hoped. I dressed in a yellow tank top and black shorts, with black flip flops to complete the ensemble. The result in the mirror was that I looked like a bumblebee. Good, I chuckled to myself. Bumblebees are important creatures; they pollinate crops and flowers, and basically provide that all living creatures be fed. I gave my reflection one last nod and headed back to work.

Chester caught up with me. *I'm going to nap in the laundry room. Don't lock me in, okay?*

"Okay," I whispered, stroking his cheek before heading to the kitchen to help Lani and Kalei prep for dinner. I stole a glance at the reservation list and saw Bettina and Taylor were on it, along with three other couples and cash guests from the neighborhood. I recognized the names since they had become semi-regulars. We referred to them as "The Kalei and Lani Fan Club." It warmed my heart that the two of them were developing a following; they had certainly earned it.

Having a nearly full house gave me the perfect excuse for not joining Bettina and Taylor; I was just going to be too busy. Aww shucks. Yeah, sarcasm button still engaged.

Just before the dinner hour, I went back to my place to change. I chose a turquoise print crinkle skirt that draped nicely down to mid-calf, with a lighter turquoise tank top. I rarely strayed from what I jokingly referred to as my uniform. I twisted my still-damp hair into a clip on top of my head and then added a bracelet and some chandelier earrings that sparkled next to my regular earrings. Black flip flops seemed fitting, and I noticed that my dark turquoise toe nail polish matched my ensemble. Imagine that. I'd often found myself wearing fire engine red polish against a fuchsia skirt, a combination that was not only blinding but cringe-worthy. When I emerged from my room, Bettina was just coming out of hers, all dressed for dinner in a light cotton pants outfit.

"You look very nice." I smiled, for she really did.

"Thank you." She seemed caught a little off guard by the compliment.

"Did you have a good day?"

And then she actually smiled. It was just a tiny smile, but it nearly lit her entire face. "I did. We went to Parker Ranch again and drove around. Then we came back and spent the afternoon at the beach. It's a lovely little spot, and so private!"

I nodded, pleased that she'd enjoyed her day. "It certainly feels private, even though it isn't."

Taylor emerged from the bedroom next, dressed in a short denim skirt and a peasant blouse. "Hi!"

"Hello! I was just hearing about your day. You enjoyed the beach then?"

"Yeah, except there was an old couple down there without clothes. I didn't think it was right, but we were clear on the other side so I just tried to ignore them."

I turned back to Bettina and grinned nervously. This was an interesting development. "Did either of you recognize them?"

"It was the couple celebrating their 50th wedding anniversary."

My hand flew to my mouth as I began to laugh. "Oh my. That's Jean and Bill Willton. I am just a little shocked, and a whole lot envious that they feel such freedom. I'd be mortified."

Bettina chuckled too, but Taylor wasn't impressed. "Who wants to see all those wrinkles in the sun though?"

"But at least they were very *tanned* wrinkles," Bettina mused. "Like turkey jerky left out to… jerky a little too long," she added and I continued to laugh.

"Well, there's a beach up the road a bit if you'd prefer," I managed to say once I found some sense of propriety again.

"You mean you're not going to do anything about them?" Taylor's irritation sounded in her tight voice.

"If they're not bothering anyone, no."

"They're bothering me." The petulant child in the 28-year-old body pouted, and I stared her down until she was the first to turn her head away. I was amazed at the quiet strength and calm of my voice as I responded. How I was able to pull it off, I'll never know, but later I would wish I could harness it for future situations.

"Well, you won't find a legal nude beach in the islands, but officials tend to look the other way. In fact, there's a very popular beach down near the Volcanoes National Park where nude bathers aren't harassed as long as they behave appropriately. I see no reason to deviate from that practice."

Bettina sighed wearily. "Stop behaving like the spoiled brat that you are, Taylor."

Her words surprised me, but I remained silent. The younger woman steamed and turned her fury on her mother. "Right, Mother, because you're so well behaved. Tell me, Mom, where were you when we were supposed to meet at the hotel during the time that Grandma went missing?" And although her angry words were directed at her mother, I saw her side-eye glances at me. She seemed to be saying the words and performing, so to speak, for my benefit.

Bettina blanched but quickly recovered. "I told you. I went to the lounge and had coffee." Her voice was icy, her face set in her usual mask that hid her true feelings. "Where were you?"

"I was waiting for you in the great room, like we'd arranged. You didn't show up for thirty minutes."

Whoa. Was I seeing an interrogation of sorts going on right in front of me? "Excuse me, but I need to get to work." And get the hell out of the company of these objectionable women. I stepped aside and hit the wooden path at a fast walk.

"Are you okay?" Lani asked me, a tiny frown on her lovely face as I skidded to a stop in the kitchen.

"Yeah." I gave a single laugh, completely devoid of mirth. "I just need to stay away from my mother's friends."

She smiled slyly. "I get it. They're no longer chosen family then."

"No way. We need to chlorinate that particular gene pool."

And then I had to smile when she laughed, a sound so musical that she brought the lightness back. I hugged her and she squeezed back so hard that I knew I was in the correctly chosen family this time.

I threw myself into the evening's work, stealing a bite now and then from my own small plate I'd set aside in the kitchen. I idly wondered where Davy was and hoped he was obtaining information.

We were serving a choice of shrimp bisque or garden salad to begin, followed by a choice of mahi-mahi crusted with macadamia nuts, grilled pineapple chicken, pasta primavera, or slow-cooked pot roast with root vegetables. For dessert, Kalei and Lani had made a few goat cheese cheesecakes with a bananas foster sauce, and a dark chocolate molten lava cake with coconut ice cream. I was hoping there'd be a lava cake or five or six leftover, but they were going fast.

I peeked at Bettina and Taylor a few times and couldn't believe they appeared to be chatting amiably. I just didn't get that duo. One minute they're insulting each other and the next they're casual friends again. No, that couldn't possibly be what I wanted in my life. I was pretty much done with them, especially if one of them had killed Annie. She had been prickly at times, but no one deserves to have their life ended so tragically. I studied Bettina's face when she was focused on her food.

Had she killed her own mother? The thought chilled me to the bone. I nearly jumped out of my skin when Lani came up behind me and put her hand on my shoulder.

"Oh! Sorry," she chuckled. "Just wanted to tell you I stashed a molten lava cake for each of us."

"Lani, you're a gem! Thank you." I began to dream of that gooey fudgy center, which nearly caused me to drool.

When the last dish was put away, the final leftover stashed, and the guests who lingered over drinks had moved over to the bar or out to the pool, we got our lava cakes out of the warming oven. I peeked out at Sam and Bennie at the bar and waited until guests were deep in conversation with each other or otherwise distracted, then took two of the cakes out to them, stashing them on the lower part of the bar's work area.

"Oh wow." Sam stared at it with a big grin on his face. "That is righteous!" His surfer lingo always made me smile, even though it sounded like it was left over from some 1980s sitcom.

"Thank you," was Bennie's simple reaction, but his childlike smile told me he was thrilled in his own quiet way.

"Compliments of Lani and Kalei, of course, but Lani is the one who set aside enough for all of us."

"I'll be sure to thank her," Sam mumbled around a giant hunk of the chocolate cake that had already made it to his mouth. Bennie laughed at him but then quieted as he stuffed some cake into his own mouth. They both had sighed happily when the fudgy center oozed out. I left them to their joy and went back to the kitchen to join Lani and Kalei who were just cutting into their own cakes.

"Oh my…" the melted fudge center nearly dribbled right out of my mouth as I ate. "It's heavenly. Thank you so much." And then we all ate in silence, the scraping of spoons against plates the only sound in the room. I about died laughing when Kalei picked up his plate and licked it.

"Kalei! What are you doing?" Lani asked the big man between giggles.

"Waste not, want not," he said slyly between licks. She and I exchanged glances. I shrugged. When in Rome… we followed his lead and did the same thing.

"No regrets," I murmured.

"Nope," Lani agreed. "Not a one." I giggled at the smear of chocolate on the tip of her pert nose. Kalei swooped in and licked it off which sent me into gales of laughter.

When I went out to get Sam and Bennie's dishes, I ran back to the kitchen and urged Lani and Kalei to come look. The three of us peeked through the door and saw first Bennie, pouring wine for a customer, then sweet Sam; he too happened to have a big smear of fudge on the tip of his nose.

Lani squealed and covered her mouth. "He licked the plate too!" We backed into the kitchen, letting the door swing shut before bursting into laughter.

"I'm not licking that off," Kalei spoke through his own chuckles.

This was my chosen family. This was where I belonged, and who I belonged with. Warmth spread through me and I sighed contentedly.

TEN

Arrest Warrant and a Royal Crown

I awoke the next morning to warm breath on my face and whiskers tickling my nose. Chester.

"Hungry, big guy?" I opened one eye at a time to peer at him.

Yeah. But I have a request.

Oh no. "And what might that be?"

I think I'd like to try seafood flavor again.

I chuckled and kissed his little wet nose. "I don't have any cans of seafood flavor, but I think I can give you some leftover mahi-mahi from last night." I had been the one to package the leftover fish from last night that Kalei intended to miraculously turn into appetizers and patties for today.

Whoa. Real fish? Get up. Get up now. And then he must have realized how desperate he sounded and added, *Please.* Very un-Chesterish.

I rolled out of bed, threw on a pair of flannel jammy pants and a hoodie, then slipped into last night's flip flops. "Be right back," I promised and trotted quietly out of the bungalow and to the back door of the main kitchen. My keys jangled in the still morning air as I fumbled at the lock. Once inside, I opted not to turn on the overhead light. Grabbing a small bowl, I quickly filled it with a piece of the mahi-mahi from last night's meal and made a note on the message board that I'd taken it, before hurrying back to my bungalow. I rinsed off all the macadamia nuts before chopping it up and scraping it into Chester's dish. The entire time he marched behind me, his tail twitching, his vocalizations becoming more and more urgent.

"Just a sec, Chet," I laughed quietly. "I want to be sure it's easy for you to eat."

Just gimme the damn food. I haven't eaten in twelve whole hours.

"Oh don't give me that. I saw you munching your crackers."

You weren't supposed to see that. Now you must die. But first... hand over the fish.

I giggle snorted as I placed his full dish on the floor and let him go for it. At first he sniffed it all over, then looked up at me.

"Go ahead," I tried to encourage him.

No, it's all good. I'm just so... overwhelmed. With pleasure.

His words could not have made me happier. I watched as he chowed down on the mahi-mahi. He ate and ate until it was all gone. Then he sat in a patch of early morning sun shining through the sliding glass door in the living room and groomed every part of himself.

"Happy?"

Very. He continued to lick.

"Well, it's a large body you've got there, so your 'bath' could take a while. I have to get ready to go to work."

No response. His eyes were closed and he was in that cat-zen zone as he groomed himself. I shrugged, still amused, and went off to shower and dress for the day.

A few minutes later I was entering the daily data for inventory and heard voices in the front of our reception area. My phone buzzed, indicating a text, just as I rose to my feet to investigate.

Cops are here.

The text from Bennie was short and to the point. Oh crap. It was beginning.

I snapped my laptop shut, tucked it behind the bar for safekeeping, and hurried to the front desk. Detective Green stood with the same detectives from the southern region, along with two uniformed officers and the crime scene techs.

"May I help you?"

"If I may?" Detective Green asked the other officers as he stepped forward, "Ms. Liberty, these officers have a warrant for the arrest of Mrs. Bettina Haas-Lundgren." I grasped the edge of the front desk to steady myself because, although I had suspected her all along, it was still a shock to hear the words.

"Okay." The roaring in my ears was distracting, but I got the feeling my voice was just barely above a whisper. I glanced at Bennie and then led the way to my bungalow. Opening the door, I expected the place to be quiet, but instead I found Bettina and Taylor fully dressed and engaged in yet another petty argument. They froze when they saw the platoon of police officers behind me. Okay, so it wasn't technically a platoon, but it was as near to one as I would ever see in my living room. Or so I hoped.

I watched in horror as Bettina was read her rights, handcuffed, and marched out to a waiting squad car, memories of my previous brush with the police causing me to freeze in my tracks. When I found my voice again I called out to her, "Don't worry. I'll call Rob Parker Kula. Everything will be okay." She only nodded, her fear palpable.

The detectives handed me yet another warrant and proceeded to bring in their techs once again to search Bettina's and Taylor's room. I couldn't fight it, of course, but I also couldn't stay quiet, "Please don't make as big a mess as you did the other day, okay?"

They didn't promise, but I did catch one tech shooting me a sympathetic smile.

I lifted my eyes to Taylor and was shocked to see an amused expression on her face. I only saw it for a fleeting moment before she noticed me looking her way. In slow motion, or so it seemed, she turned to face me directly. I found it curious and realized I'd tilted my head, as if to listen carefully, but no one was speaking. I experienced a brief shock though when I heard in my head a single word, *Good*. But where the hell did that come from? It had sounded like Taylor's voice, but her lips had not moved.

"What?" Her abrupt question, spoken in the petty manner of a sulking adolescent, brought me back to earth.

"Nothing," I stammered. "I just assumed you would be upset. Most daughters would be."

"Mind your own business!" She turned on her heel, fled to the bathroom, and slammed the door. Shocked, I shook my head and wondered if she'd regress all the way back to toddlerhood by dinner. Regardless, her behavior was puzzling. I pulled my phone out of my pocket and placed a call to Rob as I wandered back to the bar to retrieve my laptop.

"They've arrested Bettina," I told him when he answered. I heard him sigh on the other end.

"They really don't have much evidence against her, but they're desperate. I guess murder isn't good for the tourist industry."

"I guess not." I matched his sigh.

"I've got her covered," he promised. "I'll keep in touch."

"Thank you."

I disconnected the call just as I reached the front desk.

"I saw them take her away." Bennie's eyes were wide.

"Yeah. Rob is handling it."

"Is Taylor okay?"

I frowned. "Honestly? I don't know how Taylor is. Or even who she is. She's either hard to read or on an emotional roller coaster."

"Maybe both," he added.

"Maybe." But I wasn't convinced. Taylor was a puzzle with a bunch of pieces missing, and many of the other pieces were broken. I tried to throw myself into work to keep from thinking about it all, but the distraction of knowing the techs were making a mess in my bungalow was immense. Just as I was on my way to check on things at home, one of the techs stopped in.

"We're done."

"Thanks. Did you take anything?"

He held up a couple of plastic evidence bags containing papers and a book. "Just these."

I sighed and headed to my place to survey the damage, but I was pleasantly surprised to find that they had not left the same horrendous mess as before. Taylor was sitting on the sofa watching television.

"Could you help me clean up the mess? It's not as bad this time," I asked the back of her head.

"Nope. It's all yours," she spoke to the television. I guess she felt that an old episode of *Friends* was more important.

I shot a few evil thoughts her way, including the desire to yank out her hair and slap her silly but instead I headed to Davy's bedroom to clean up. She had given up any sort of license to that room by sitting on her bum and being an ass. I am easily amused I guess, because I chuckled at my bum and ass reference. Taylor was hereafter simply a very short-term guest. It only took about twenty minutes to clean the room this time, and for that I was thankful.

Late that evening I was sitting in my bedroom with Susie and Chester, having just returned my other companions, Winston and Marley, to their shared cage. They gave me the impression that they all felt the need to protect me. From what, I wasn't sure, nor was I too worried. Davy shimmered in, a solo trip again.

"They arrested Bettina," I spoke quietly enough that the television in the next room where Taylor was sitting would cover my voice.

"I know. I saw her. She seemed quite stoic."

"I don't envy her sitting all alone in a cell."

"Oh, she's not alone." There was a bit of an evil gleam in his eye. "I left Mr. Pinckney with her."

I laughed softly. "Aren't you just a dear. Poor Mr. Pinckney. He won't show himself though, will he?"

Davy laughed along with me. "No. Just observing. D'ya think he'll be safe with her? I mean… is invisibility enough?"

"Your guess is as good as mine."

I smiled at the vision of the elder ghost in my head before another thought came to me and wiped that smile from my face. "Have you heard any information about Annie?"

He sat beside me on the arm of my chair and took my hand in his. "She was… hit in the head several times. They aren't sure with what though."

Biting my lip, I was speechless but felt tears gathering in my eyes. "No one should die like that."

"No," he agreed. "They think she lived for several hours, and they seem to think that they'll know more soon."

I felt the blood drain from my face at the thought. "Where did they find her?"

"In some heavy brush near the crater. Her paints and canvas were not far from her body."

I leaned my face into the soft velvet of his eight-button shirt; this one happened to be black. I glanced and saw he was wearing tailored grey slacks and the standard white boots.

"You sure look nice tonight." I formed the words around a forced smile, still feeling the weight of Annie's death, but wanting to lighten my mood.

"Well thank you." He kissed the top of my head, his arm around my shoulder and one leg swinging from his perch on my chair.

"Heavy date then?" I loved teasing him, but he was the master at it, while I was only a novice.

"Yeah." He smiled down at me. "Right here." He pulled a small package out of his pocket again; it fit in the palm of his hand. This time there was no guessing game for he simply opened my hand and placed the parcel on my palm. "For you. My favorite innkeeper."

"Aww. Thank you." I beamed up at him before untying the slim strip of ribbon and opening the fragile paper. Inside was another tiny replica, but this one was a ceramic pillow upon a wooden base holding a very detailed enameled royal crown. "Oh Davy... It's beautiful!" I turned it around and around and held it up to the lamp on the table beside me. The tiny jewels shimmered in the glow. "I guess this means you've been to England recently?"

"Yeah. A quick trip."

Although I was curious about his trips all over the world, I respected his privacy, so I didn't ask for details. If he wanted to share his stories of travel with me, I knew he would.

"I love it! I will put this right next to my cherry tree on the window sill." I pulled on his arm to bring him down to my level and gave him a kiss on the cheek. "Thank you."

Frankly, I was quite touched that he thought of me when he was busy elsewhere; it warmed my heart. I put my fingers to my lips to indicate "quiet" and we tiptoed out to the kitchen. Well I tiptoed; he just sort of floated. She remained glued to the television as I scooted past. I placed the jeweled crown beside my cherry tree in the kitchen window and admired the effect of the moonlight upon the two. I turned and gave him another quiet kiss on his cheek, grabbed two glasses and a bottle of

Pinot Grigio from Uncle Wally's wine refrigerator, and then stole past Taylor once again. She was still watching old shows but had moved from *Friends* to *Seinfeld*. Safely back inside my room, I turned to open the bottle of wine and froze. I'd forgotten the corkscrew. "Damn," I muttered, causing Davy to chuckle.

"No sweat." He grinned, casually passed his hand a few times over the bottle, eased the cork out, and placed it on the table.

"Wow. Neat trick."

He winked then. "I'll teach you someday, but not for many, many years."

"I will hold you to that." I watched as he poured our two glasses.

He lifted his glass and I followed suit. "To Annie, and the truth, wherever it may be found," he whispered and we touched glasses.

We sat together in my room, sipping wine and whispering about life, death, rights, wrongs, and then, just for fun, the possible reasons there were interstate highways in Hawai'i. I mean, think about it for a minute: inter-state. The whole subject had us giggling like crazy as we came up with similar absurdities. Do you have any idea how hard it is to giggle in a whisper?

When I saw it was getting late, I cracked the sliding glass door and made sure Chester could get to his litter box before I headed to the bathroom to get ready for bed. I washed my face, brushed my teeth, and changed into a big sleep shirt. When I returned, Davy was petting Susie, and Chester had fallen back to sleep in the chair I'd been occupying.

"Thief," I muttered at the cat, but he didn't even crack an eyelid. Susie circled a few times on the big dog bed near the closet before settling as Davy and I enjoyed the last of the wine while sitting cross-legged on the floor. I had begun to get sleepy when he suddenly ramped our conversation up again.

"Ever wonder why a piece of freight that is transported by car or truck is called shipping, but if it's transported on a boat it's called cargo?"

I began to giggle again, burying my laughter behind my hand, and so it was that I found out that it is far better to end a day laughing rather than crying.

ELEVEN

A Bag of Booze and Miss NastyPants

When I awoke the next morning, Davy was gone, but the pillow he'd used was still warm. It was a bewildering concept indeed but there were many of those and I pondered them in the shower. I dressed in blue shorts and a blue striped tee-shirt, then slipped my feet into flip flops printed with pink and blue flowers. Really. If you saw my closet, you'd see that it's all shorts, tees, tank-tops, and a multitude of flip flops. I guess you could call me a collector because every time I see an interesting pair of the lightweight footwear for sale, I grab them. Some people collect stamps. I collect warm-weather wear.

I began to feed Chester his standard chicken flavored food and he seemed quite happy with it again. *I had a little tummy ache yesterday after eating fish, so I'll stick with what I know for now*, he told me quite simply.

"Okay then. Chicken it is." I dished up a quarter of a can and topped off his crackers before heading out to the front desk. Bennie was just arriving as well, uncovering Winston and Marley and setting up their perch with fresh food and water.

I'm a pretty bird. I'm a smart bird. Cheer up Sleepy Jean. We had tried to redirect Winston away from so many historical quotes to things that were more fun. Davy had been very handy teaching him the words to a few songs, and for Marley, the melodies. However, Marley still preferred reggae music and she whistled her favorite, "I Shot the Sheriff" as I walked by. I felt that was almost fitting for the week, except for the shooting part of course.

"Good morning," I said to Bennie as he shuffled paper into folders.

He turned his head briefly and gave me his thousand-watt smile. "Good morning, Macca."

I plopped my laptop on the bar in my usual spot where I could see the entrance to the reception area and also the door to the kitchen, with the pool area at my back. This was probably my favorite part of the common area when the folding storm shutters were fully opened. The designers had truly known what they were doing, and it was obvious that they'd had a deep understanding of island life.

Lani and Kalei arrived with a couple of mesh bags of fresh produce. "Good morning," they said in unison, but it came out as a beautiful harmony due to the island lilt of their voices.

"Good morning you two! How are you?"

"Ready to roll," Kalei said in his usual exuberance. The man loved to cook, and it showed in his food. Lani just smiled and shook her head, shooting knowing looks at her husband's retreating back.

"He's making fish balls today, thus the 'roll' pun." Lani rolled her eyes and smiled.

"Oh Kalei… You are too funny," I called to his retreating back. He looked over his shoulder and waggled his eyebrows.

"Get in that kitchen, Big Man." Lani cracked the imaginary whip in her usual loving way and he scooted along.

"And how are you and your little one?" I stage whispered to her just as he passed through the kitchen door.

"Life is good again. No morning sickness!"

"Yay!" I knew she had been having a difficult time, and this was fantastic news.

"I've been feeling well for a couple weeks but I was afraid to say anything and disturb the gods and make it all come back again," she chuckled as she spoke.

"I'm just glad you're feeling better."

"Mahalo, Macca. Hey, you want to beat up some dough again today?" She arched a brow.

"As a matter of fact, I do." We made a date of sorts that I would arrive to beat the crap out of a big mountain of dough in an hour. She then followed her husband into the kitchen, and I turned back to my purchase orders and other daily document management on my laptop.

I was interrupted by the sound of the FedEx truck arriving in the parking lot above so, being nosy, I twirled on my barstool, hopped off, and took a few steps to see what was up. Bennie was just signing for the package when I got there, so I peeked at the label while he finished up with the driver. I found it intriguing that she was peering around as if looking for something or someone, but she finally went on her way, trotting up the stairs back to the parking lot. The package was for the Morrison family and Bennie handed it to me to deliver. They'd been receiving little things for their new house, and each package was another step closer to them moving out of the inn and into their spectacular custom home.

With a bounce in my step, I carted the box to their bungalow and knocked.

"Good morning Macca," Jack greeted me, but his eyes lit up when he saw the box. "Oh! This is a gift for Rick," he whispered and then called over his shoulder that he'd be right back. "It's our anniversary next week," he explained as he walked with me back to the front desk.

"Aww, you sly devil, you!"

We used scissors from the front desk and opened the box. Inside was yet another box which he pulled out and opened. It was well packaged with bubble wrap and packing paper; inside was a very classy looking bronze sign that said *The Morrisons*, with their wedding date etched below their name.

"Jack, that's beautiful!"

"You think he'll like it mounted by the front door of our new house?"

"I think he'll love it!"

"Thanks! I need to hide this now."

"Do you have a place you can stash it?"

"Yeah. I do."

We stood together admiring the plaque before I realized something. "Jack, would you mind if I kept the FedEx box?"

He had a puzzled look on his face. "No, but why?"

"I have a certain little cat who hasn't had a proper box to love in many months."

He chuckled and handed the cardboard container over to me. "It's all yours, with our regards."

"Thank you so much! I'm sure he'll appreciate it."

Dramatically pressing the back of his hand to his forehead, he responded, "I just don't know how I'll live without that box though. It's quite the sacrifice, you know."

He winked before turning to leave, his laughter fading away on the breeze. I folded the flaps down on the FedEx box and took it to my own bungalow, quickly stashing it in my closet before rushing back to continue my work for the morning.

Later in the kitchen, I beat the daylights out of the mound of bread dough just as I'd promised. I pushed, rolled, punched, and repeated for a good ten minutes. Lani finally intervened, a sly smile on her face. "We don't want to kill it, just beat it into submission."

I chuckled and nodded, then gave custody of the giant blob back to her. "Anything else I can help with?"

"Yes. Could you please empty the last of the wine bag into the marinade?" Kalei pointed to the box of wine on the work table.

"Sure!" It was another therapeutic job I was more than happy to help with. I pried open the flap of the box and pulled the plastic pouch out, thinking about the bad reputation boxed wine often has. Some of it is fantastic and reasonably priced too. The fact that it was in a vacuum sealed pouch allowed it to stay fresh for far longer, which was especially helpful in commercial kitchen settings. In addition, the box itself was fully recyclable.

I grasped the plastic pouch with one hand, wrapped my fingers around it to force the wine into one end, and squeezed while opening the spigot, thus allowing the wine to be forced out and into the marinade container. I repeated this process until the pouch was empty. "There," I beamed. "All done. Just like milking a wine cow."

Lani and Kalei froze for just a beat before bursting into laughter. "I never thought of it that way, but you've got a good point there, Macca," he chortled. I felt myself blush but laughed with them.

"Leave it to our Macca to come up with something that sounds so absurd but true." Lani gave me a one-armed hug as she passed by me.

"Thanks folks. I'm here all week," I responded with a chuckle, borrowing a line Davy frequently used.

Out of the corner of my eye I saw Kalei open a drawer, pull out a large pair of scissors, and place them unceremoniously on the table. I looked into his eyes and could swear I saw them twinkle.

"I just usually cut the tip off and pour," he deadpanned.

I felt the blush seep up my neck and onto my face. "Oh." Then I laughed at myself and shook my head. "I trust we won't discuss this again, right?"

Kalei winked and gave me a casual hug. "Discuss what?"

"Exactly." With twitters of laughter we all went back to work.

About an hour later I saw Taylor leave the bungalow, her keys in hand. She'd been so closed down since Bettina's arrest, and I couldn't really tell what was going on beneath the surface. Was this how she showed that she missed her mom, or was it something else? I wondered if planning a casual dinner in the bungalow for just the two of us might help break the ice that had developed, melted, and developed again.

When I had finished with my paperwork, I stashed my laptop between my mattress and box spring again and told Bennie I was heading to a local market, one which had the best selection of organics and vegetarian products. I checked with Lani and Kalei to be sure they didn't need anything, even though I knew they'd just gone to the farmers' market earlier, and it turned out that the timing of my question was good because Kalei told me he needed more coconut milk. I put it on my list and headed out.

Grocery shopping was an enjoyable task for me, but that was most likely due to the fact that I usually only cooked for one or two people, and even then, only a few times a week. I wandered the produce section and saw that Japanese eggplant was on special. I grabbed several along with some fresh tomatoes, a couple of zucchinis, a garlic bulb, flat leaf parsley, a sweet onion, crimini mushrooms, and some baby greens. Then

I headed to the dairy section and found fresh mozzarella, a small wedge of Romano cheese, and a log of local goat cheese, all vegetarian friendly. In the canned goods section I snagged tomatoes and baby corn, then veered to the next aisle to get the coconut milk for Kalei. I hadn't planned on getting any bread since Lani's taro rolls were so good, but as I strolled past the bakery I saw that they had freshly baked baguettes, so I had to have one. Turning toward the checkout stand I found mini pies. I selected a fresh coconut cream pie for two and nearly squealed. I loved coconut cream pie.

I checked out and put a hefty ding in the debit card balance. Grocery prices were one of the most difficult things to get used to here on the island, but I usually worked with more local ingredients which were less expensive. Tonight though, I wanted to make a nice dinner with ingredients I knew from childhood. Hey, this was for my comfort too.

Back at the inn I delivered the coconut milk to Kalei and then headed back home to put my groceries away. As I was leaving to return to help Lani, Taylor arrived home with a large paper bag. As she moved, the bag's contents clanged together, and I detected the sound of bottles.

"Oh, let me get the door for you." I swung it open and she marched into the tiny kitchen. I had to follow her simply out of overwhelming curiosity. She pulled out bottles of Makers Mark, Stoli, Tanqueray, and, ugh, totally out of character, a bottle of Bailey's Irish Cream. "Wow. Having a party?"

"Yeah." She was sullen again. "Tonight. Wanna join me?" There was no mirth, no party attitude in her voice though.

"Sure. How about I make the two of us some dinner too?"

She shrugged her shoulders. "Whatever. I could eat a peanut butter sandwich even."

Oh dear. "No. I went to the market and I'd like to make dinner for us tonight, if that's okay."

She stopped loading her bottles into the cupboard and stared at me with a slight frown and a tilt of her head, as if she didn't "get" me any more than I "got" her.

"That would be…" she began, "well, that would be really nice, Macca. Thanks."

Wow. I actually got a polite response from her and didn't want to mess it up so I simply smiled and responded.

"You're welcome. I'll call you when dinner is ready."

She let out one single bark of a hollow laugh. "I might be blotto by then, but sure."

"Well, don't get 'blotto' right away. I'll bring you some snacks from the main kitchen." If I was going to the trouble of preparing this meal I wanted her sober enough to help eat it.

And then she flashed a smile. "Thank you." She reached out and put her hand on my arm. "I really mean it. I know we've been difficult, I know you hadn't planned on house guests… or police… or anything. So, thank you."

I just nodded and patted her hand. "I have to work for a bit, but I'll be back. I promise."

She watched me as I turned and I let out a long breath on my way back to the main kitchen. As I helped set things up for the evening, my mind was on the Taylor-Bettina dynamic. I realized I was exceedingly distracted as I couldn't even remember having finished some of my duties, but the proof was right in front of me. Before guests could begin to arrive, I headed back to my place and took a shower. It felt good to let my crazy hair loose and put a flowing sundress on before hitting my own little kitchen.

I pulled all my ingredients out and began slicing, dicing, and chopping. I sliced the Japanese eggplant and the zucchini into thin ribbons while the canned tomatoes simmered on the stove with mushrooms, onions, garlic, and spices. In a small casserole dish I layered the sauce, eggplant, and zucchini slices with mozzarella and goat cheese combined, and then repeated the process until the dish was filled like a lasagna without the noodles. Popping the casserole into the oven for a good long time, I then turned to the salad fixings and simply sliced a few leftover mushrooms, some of the baby corn from the can, and grabbed a couple of pepperoncinis from the refrigerator, which I sliced and added to the salad bowl of field greens. Turning to the dressing, I made a lemon rosemary vinaigrette and stored it in a small jar. I sprinkled the remaining goat cheese over the top of the salad and popped both the jar of dressing and the bowl into the fridge to hold until dinner. I chopped some tomatoes and left them in a pile on the cutting board, for they retained their flavor at room temperature. Then I mixed a little garlic, butter, and olive oil in a tiny saucepan and let it simmer for a few minutes. Slicing the baguette, I planned to quickly toast each slice and dip them in the bubbly garlic mixture just before dinner was served.

As I cleaned up all the utensils and dishes from the prep work, I idly wondered where Taylor was. I peeked out to the pool area and saw her sitting with a pitcher of some sort of mixture and a glass. She was sunning herself and drinking. I let out my breath and had a brief instance of wonder at just how drunk she'd be in an hour. I found Lani's leftover mini-pizza snacks from lunch that I'd promised and took a few out to her. Sitting in the lounge chair beside hers, I offered her some.

"Oh, thanks." She actually took two and ate heartily. When she reached for the remaining two mini pizzas I reached for her pitcher of alcohol.

"Why don't we go inside and we can have some dinner soon, okay?"

"Okay." She seemed to have lost her spirit and as she followed me I was reminded of a pound puppy. She was one mixed up cookie though.

I sat her at the little table in the dinette and gave her the last of the mini-pizzas. Lani always made these for the kids at lunch time, but we adults loved them as well.

"It smells good in here," she said, devouring the little appetizers.

"Thanks. Lasagna is in the oven, Willow-style."

"Cool." She peered at me then as she chewed. "Do you miss your mom?"

"Daily. And my dad too."

"Hmm…" And that was all she said. I didn't want to push, for there was plenty of time for her to open up once there was food. Right then I was more determined to keep her from getting so drunk that she couldn't eat. Hey, I worked hard on that dinner and I didn't want it to be ignored.

I stashed her pitcher in the refrigerator and served her a tall glass of Kalei's magic iced tea, a sure-fire way to keep her hands busy and the alcohol at bay.

"What did you do today?" I gently posed the question.

"I went to the liquor store and bought booze. You?"

"I worked, went to the grocery store, and then came home and worked some more before cooking dinner."

"Doesn't it drive you nuts to be working all the time?"

"Not at all. The inn has become my passion. And my livelihood. And one last link to my Uncle Wally."

She sipped her iced tea, her eyes never leaving my face. It was a little unnerving. I was relieved when the timer dinged, telling me the veggie lasagna was nearly done. I grated some Romano cheese generously over the top and returned it to the oven. When the cheese had melted sufficiently I sprinkled freshly chopped parsley over the top before placing it on a rack on the counter to let it "set" while I tossed the salad with the dressing. The baguette slices toasted in the oven and I reheated the garlic mixture to dip them in. At last it all came together, and I placed the dishes on the table before us.

"Dig in," I encouraged. While she dished some salad onto her plate, I cut into the lasagna and put one slice on her plate and one on my own. Then I added some salad for myself before picking up my fork to chow down. I was starved, and Taylor seemed quite eager to eat as well.

"Hey," she remarked, cutting a third bite from her square of lasagna. "This is really good!"

I guess she was shocked that I could cook, but I tried to brush it off by simply thanking her. The food had turned out to be quite good and I enjoyed every morsel before using a hunk of the garlic bread to mop up any remaining sauce. Yep, I could eat this every day... if I wanted to increase my body weight three times.

I sat back in my chair with my iced tea. "Rob Parker Kula is meeting with your mom tomorrow and he'll let us know what's going on."

"What's to know? She killed my grandmother and now she's incarcerated." She stood up and took her iced tea to the sink and returned with a glass of the mixture from her pitcher that I'd confiscated at the pool.

"Do you really think she did it though?" I felt Bettina was quite capable of murdering her mother, given the aura of anger she frequently gave off, but I wanted to get her talking.

"Yeah. She can be very mean, you know."

"Really?"

She took a big drink of her alcoholic concoction and leaned forward as if sharing a secret in the middle of a crowd of onlookers. "Once I stole a toy, and she marched me right back to the store and not only made me return it but also made me apologize too." She took another sip. "I was humiliated and she didn't care."

Whoa. This was like a *Twilight Zone* episode with an evil child who always got her way, or *else*. I frowned and gently waded in. "And?"

"And what?" She actually hiccuped then. I had always thought that was just a Hollywood reaction to alcohol.

"And is there more to that story?"

"No. Why should there be?"

I looked sideways, momentarily wondering if there was a hidden camera or something and I was getting punked. "Because that was a very typical parent-type thing to do."

Her face went from placid to angry. "Oh, you're one of *those* people. Always having to be right."

Wow. I sat back, landing hard against the back of my chair. "And what do you think she should have done?"

"Overlooked it, just like Gran and Dad did."

This was a big insight into this family's life. Overlook? With my lips clamped tightly I put my hands up to stop her, not wanting to wade any further into this mess without the chance to have a good long think on it. I was ready for Taylor to go home. Permanently.

I stood and began to clear the table. "So, you're on her side I take it?" Taylor asked between sips of her cocktail. I glanced down at her and frowned at the slight smirk on her face. This was one creepy person.

Giving myself time to think, I carried both plates and all the utensils to the sink and began to scrape and rinse before I replied. "I think her demand that you return a stolen object and apologize for your bad behavior was the right thing to do."

"Well aren't you just Miss Penny Perfect," she was slurring her words.

Shaking my head, I let loose with a long-suffering sigh. It wasn't worth arguing with an unstable person, and I was convinced she had issues. Then I stole a glance at my little gifts from Davy on the window sill and thought to myself, *Give me strength.*

"And," she continued, "can you wipe this table? It's got sticky stuff on it."

I glanced over and saw she was indicating her own mess she'd made, so I tossed the damp dishcloth to her. "Here."

She cringed and picked up the corner of the cloth as if it were covered in mud and dropped it on the floor. "I don't do domestic. That's your shtick."

Whoa. She picked up her pitcher and her glass and went out to the back deck. My little home was peaceful again, albeit temporarily. I idly wondered if I could serve Little Miss NastyPants an eviction notice. The toxic environment was getting to me.

After the dinner dishes were cleaned up and the kitchen back in order, I wandered over to the main dining room to see if they needed help. Sam and Bennie seemed to have things in order, so I checked in with Lani and Kalei in the kitchen.

"How's it going?"

"We're fine." Lani looked up from plating dessert and smiled. "I thought you were making dinner for you and Taylor?"

"Yeah. I did. But I had to get out of there."

"I was wondering if you can unchoose family?" Kalei chuckled.

"As a matter of fact I'm currently in the process of writing an eviction notice in my mind, along with a divorce decree of sorts to 'unchoose' her as family." I swear I moaned, but I suspect it sounded more like a whine.

"If you need me to, I'll gladly witness the documents for you," Lani teased as I assisted her with the fruit garnish on each plate. "Wanna help me serve these out?"

"Sure."

We began to carry the desserts, using our backs to open the swinging door while laden with five to six plates each. I was getting good at this waitressing scene under her tutelage, and it was far more pleasant than listening to the bratty toddler who was staying in my bungalow.

When I finally did return to my own kitchen, I cut myself a bit of pie and took it to my bedroom.

"There's a little coconut cream pie in the fridge if you want," I said as I passed Taylor sitting in front of the television, her drink still in her hand.

"Thanks," she responded, her eyes never leaving whatever show it was she was watching. I continued on to my little sanctuary and enjoyed my pie in peace, Chester and Susie joining me, watching every forkful from the plate to my mouth. I gave each a little piece of the crust and they seemed satisfied. It was nice to end the day in their company and not hers.

TWELVE

Freddie Krueger and Protective Beasties

Tuesday morning dawned bright and early, unlike me, who awoke in a cloud of confusion. I'd had a dream that was much like the Small World ride at Disneyland, on a never ending loop of annoyance. The discussion Bettina had been having with Taylor the other night regarding the fact that the two of them were separated for thirty minutes was the main theme. Bettina claimed to have been in the lounge, while Taylor said she was in the great room, but something didn't ring true, and I couldn't put my finger on it.

I showered, dressed, and headed to the reception area where I could find some privacy in order to call Rob. On the way I let Marley and Winston out and refreshed their food and water. Winston fluttered to the perch but Marley landed on my outstretched arm.

"Well hello you beautiful little thing," I murmured to her. She leaned toward me and I was amazed to see her cuddle under my chin and give me a sort of snuggle. "Aww. Aren't you sweet?" I stroked her beautiful feathers, a deep periwinkle color in the early hours. Whispering praise to her, I gave her head tiny kisses. "Gee Winston, how come you never give cuddles?"

I'm a pretty bird.

"Yeah, yeah, pretty bird." I reached over and stroked the feathers on his chest and he stretched his neck to allow me to reach below his beak. "And a ham too."

I do not like green eggs and ham. I do not like them Sam I am.

"Well that's new." I set Marley beside him on the perch and began opening the storm shutters before placing my call to Rob. Even though it wasn't yet office hours, I knew he would be at his desk already, and I was pleased when he answered on the second ring.

"Hey Macca." I could hear the smile in his voice.

"Hi Rob." I matched his tone. "I'm sorry to bother you, but did Bettina make a statement to the police about the thirty minutes when she and Taylor were separated?"

"Yeah. That was documented. Taylor claimed to have gotten a candy bar and then sat in the great room to wait for her mother and grandmother to show up. Her mother was thirty minutes late, and of course Annie never showed."

"And Bettina claimed to be in the lounge having coffee."

"Right. And no staff can verify either account."

"Damn," I swore under my breath.

"Exactly."

"When does she find out about bail?"

"Tomorrow morning. Are you attending?"

"Where is it?"

"Your old stomping grounds in Hilo."

"Ha ha," I deadpanned. "But I do know it all too well."

"Are you attending?"

"I'd like to try, yes."

"Good. It's important to show support, as you know."

Yeah, it was, and I remembered that my only support had been Rob, Alex, and Davy who was invisible to others, while Bettina would only have Rob and Mr. Pinckney. The difference was that the latter would remain invisible to her, offering no support at all, just acting as a spy and reporting to Sherlock Jones.

"Okay. Thanks Rob. I will try to get someone to cover for me so I can attend tomorrow."

"No problem. How is Taylor doing?"

"Better than I expected. And it's weird. Actually *she's* weird, and I'm not good with roommates."

He chuckled and I could hear someone calling his name in the background. "Gotta go, Macca. I'll call you when I have more information."

"Bye!" I ended the call and slipped my phone into my pocket just as Bennie was arriving for the day.

"Oh! Thanks for opening. Couldn't sleep?"

"No. I slept, but I had to make a call and needed privacy."

"That's in short supply these days, huh?"

"Very. Hey Bennie… Do you think you can cover for me tomorrow? I want to attend Bettina's bail hearing and give moral support."

"Consider it done!"

And it was then that I realized I'd have to carpool if Taylor was going, and even worse, I'd have to ask her if she was going, which meant she would most likely go, and… ohmygosh. Just shoot me now.

"What's wrong?" Bennie must have seen the stricken look I imagined was plastered on my face.

"I may have to spend nearly all that time in the car with…"

"No!"

I nodded. He froze for several seconds before crushing me into a hug, and I admit, I hugged him back. "I don't wanna. I don't," I kept repeating.

"I know. But you're you, and so you will do it, and you'll try to make the best of it." He held me at arms' length and looked me in the eye. I could only nod. I was engulfed in my own misery.

I trudged back to my bungalow and was relieved that there was no movement from Davy's room. It still *was* Davy's room, but it was temporarily contaminated… I mean… occupied... by Taylor. I checked on poor Chester who had become accustomed to living in my bedroom, and I found him staring at his empty food dish.

"Oh Chet!" I stooped to pet him, and he gave me a glare that could have singed hair. "I'm so sorry." I rattled the crackers in his dry food bowl to no end; there had been no canned food and he was going to make me pay.

You swine.

"You learned that from Davy, and I'm going to throttle him for that."

Doesn't matter. You're still a swine. You went to work and did not give me my chicken flavored stuffs.

"Stuffs?"

Hey, those are human words. You want to speak Cat? We can begin lessons immediately.

Whoa, he was incredibly grumpy this morning. I sort of felt his pain myself. "What's eating you today?"

I hate living in one room. I don't know how I did it in our old home and that was three rooms! I don't like this one bit.

"No one is forcing you to live in my bedroom."

He gave me a scathing look, if cats could actually do that, and... this one seemed to have that particular talent.

Am I'm supposed to live and be happy around the likes of her? She's so rude and mean.

"I know sweetie. I'm sorry. I'm pretty miserable too."

Good. I want you to suffer as much or more than I am.

Gee. What a nice guy. Not. "And where is Susie?"

Chester made a sound very similar to that noise he made when puking up a hairball. *Really?*

He got smart and headed out at first light. I'm not sure we'll see him again until she is gone.

"I owe you one, Chet. I really do."

Yep. And I take notes and keep records.

I giggled, imagining him scribbling on a piece of paper.

Not that way, you… human.

I still laughed, because not only did I have a cat who could communicate with me, but he had a wicked sense of humor. That's my boy.

Damn straight.

Man, I just couldn't get away with private thoughts anymore!

I took his little ceramic dish to the kitchen and filled it with his canned food. I always mashed it up because once he told me that dumping it out of the can was for the bourgeoisie crowd. Yes, he actually said that. Blew my mind too.

All I heard as I sat in my rocking chair was "nom, nom, nom." I gazed out the window, listening, while trying to find our little slice of peace again. It wasn't easy though. It seemed like every time that peace seemed imminent, something would intrude into my thoughts. Murder. Lies. Deception. Really? Life was far too short to dwell on such drivel. Drivel? It's not drivel at all! Yes, I was having an argument with myself. In my mind. Pathetic.

You are not pathetic. You're just… conflicted. Yep, Davy was in my head again too. It was getting to the point where I was considering charging rent, or a luxury tax. I sighed loudly, hoping it would chase Davy away, and went back to work.

Being Ming's day off, I grabbed the service cart and began at the first bungalow. By the time I got to Number 4, Bennie had joined me and we finished the last few bungalows together. Even Sam came to help at Number 6 and scrubbed the bathroom. What a team we were! By late morning we were done, and I began to launder the resulting mountain of sheets and towels. I know I should have been full of dread toward the massive chore, but instead I found a rather zen-like rhythm. Transfer wet laundry to dryer. Push button. Load washer. Add soap. Run washer. Transfer to dryer. Push button. Repeat. But when it came time to start folding the sheets I was usually swearing and grunting. Hey, swearing and grunting helped me focus and work faster. Ming had shown me her trick of using the door of the dryer and the clothesline stretched from wall to wall to fold and hold. I was rockin' it too! I had my earbuds firmly in place and was bouncing to Elton John's *Goodbye Yellow Brick Road* album.

"Now it's all over, Danny Bailey… And the harvest is in…" I was singing and dancing in place as I processed the laundry when I suddenly felt eyes on my back. I pulled one earbud out and whirled to see that it was Taylor. "Oh, sorry." But I really wasn't.

"There's not much to eat in your fridge."

And? But I kept silent.

"What should I do?" She sure was good at whining.

134

How about… grow the hell up? But instead, I smiled before responding. "The lunch buffet begins in…" I checked the time on my phone before slipping it back in my pocket. "…twenty-two minutes."

She made one of those childish smirky-faces that brought out a desire to smack it right off her face. "And what if I don't want to wait?"

"There's some leftover veggie lasagna in the fridge in the bungalow."

She made another face that caused me to think vile thoughts. Instead of voicing such thoughts, I just shrugged and turned back to my work. I was quite proud of myself for showing restraint. There was still a lot to do and I wouldn't have time myself to eat for at least two more hours, therefore I had little sympathy for her bitchiness. I smiled though when I heard her stomp off. Macca 1, Taylor 0.

Wash, dry, fold, repeat. I was back at it and when the laundry was all done, I grabbed a banana from the buffet and reluctantly returned to my bungalow. Susie and Chester were sunning themselves on the back deck, but the sliding door to my bedroom was cracked just enough for them to come inside if they needed. However, since there were several bowls of fresh water scattered about the property for them, I felt certain that they wouldn't have come inside without me there while Taylor was with us. Cowards.

Speaking of Taylor, she was cemented in front of the television again with a very old rerun of *Law & Order* blaring away. I liked that show, but not at the deafening volume that she had it set. I stood behind her, hands on hips, and glanced at the clock. Dinner set up needed to begin soon, giving me barely enough time to put my feet up, have a glass of iced tea, freshen up, and change my clothes, but I knew there was one unpleasant task that required my immediate attention, and I was dreading it. I dove in anyway just to get it over and done with.

"Taylor!" I had to speak up in order to be heard above the din of Detectives Lennie Briscoe and my personal favorite Ed Green running after a suspect while yelling "Stop! Police!"

She turned around and yawned, a look of extreme boredom on her face. "Oh hi."

"Yeah, hi." I couldn't believe this woman was my age. She acted like an angst-filled, unmotivated teenager. I remember, because I was one not that long ago. "Are you going to your mother's bail hearing tomorrow?"

She stretched, still seated with her back to me. "I hadn't thought much about it."

"Really? Okay. Let me know once you've *thought* about it."

I turned on my heel to go to my room, but she called after me. "Wait. Why are you asking?"

I ignored her, slammed my door, stripped out of my sweaty clothes, and threw on my little cotton robe to head to the bathroom. I hadn't intended to shower a second time, but I suspected it might make me feel better both emotionally and physically. Standing under the cool spray, scrubbing with citrus scented soap, and washing away all my troubles was the perfect foil to the funk of the day — or the week — and it had been a long one already.

Afterward, I dashed across the hall in my little robe and ducked into my room to dress properly. Well, properly for me. I don't believe I'd ever been accused of being "proper" per se. Per se? Have you ever really broken that term down? If you look it up in Websters you get that mumbo jumbo that causes your brain to want to implode: by, of, for, or in itself; intrinsically. Um. Yeah. Wait. What?

To continue, I don't believe I'd ever been accused of being "proper," OR cerebral... exactly. Yay! That word "yay" was way more "me." So... what was I saying again? I was finding myself more easily distracted these days. I blamed my mother's chosen family who had descended upon me, but in reality I'm sure the various unconnected murders in and around Hale Mele had been a horrible influence as well. Still, I'm an ex-L.A. girl, so I can handle anything. Right? Right? Crickets.

Babe, you're losin' it. Davy spoke in my head.

"Yeah, and I can blame you for part of that, buddy." And... more crickets.

Life on the island was supposed to be peaceful, slow, easy-going. It was promised in all the brochures. I was still waiting for the peaceful part.

I took Chester's dish into the kitchen, passing by more of Lennie and Ed yelling on the television and Taylor zoning out in front of it. I mashed up his chicken flavored food, peering at the tiny buffalo on the label and wondering just how many buffaloes little cats had ever taken down in a hunt. Life is full of mysteries.

I scooted back to my room and set the dish on my dresser where Chester could eat without fear of the giant Susie inhaling it in one gulp. I peeked out the open slider and caught Chester's eye. He slowly rose and walked toward me as if there were a million hours in the day. Once inside, he gracefully hopped up to the tall dresser and took two licks.

This is good. Thanks.

I chuckled. "You're welcome. See you after the dinner service."

Mmffmmbkk

What? When he finally swallowed, he repeated it in a more intelligible manner, albeit still only in my mind.

I'll be on the back deck.

That's what he'd said? Wow. I'd been way off. I thought he'd been swearing at me. "Okay then. See you later."

I ducked out the front door, ignoring Taylor watching Detective Briscoe rein in Ed yet again. It was my personal opinion that he had saved his partner's ass a number of times in that show. Maybe that's what I liked about Ed; he was a roller coaster ride.

As I entered the main kitchen I was struck by the sense that it was a sanctuary. If I was here, no one but employees could interact with me. I paced around, my eyes on the floor of the kitchen itself, the store room, and even the walk-in cooler, to determine if there was space for a cot and a sleeping bag. Not really. Oh well. It had been a nice thought. And then I flashed on the character Quasimodo, dragging along and calling, "Sanctuaaaaary." All of a sudden I identified with the guy. How's that for scary? A little giggle escaped my lips and I blushed, despite the fact that there was no one else in the room. But knowing how many people seemed to be in my head too often, it was probably not completely insane. Yeah... the men with the white coats were coming, of that I was certain.

You're coming unglued, Monkee Paw. This time I heard Dad in my head, and I waved him away with my hand. Yeah, like that works.

The back door opened, startling me out of my reverie.

"Oh, sorry." Kalei looked embarrassed for me. "Didn't mean to scare you."

"You're fine. I was just lost in thought." I looked around and observed two pots bubbling on the stove, several large bowls of fresh fruit salad, and the enormous urn of Kalei's finest, his specially made iced tea, the recipe for which had been carefully guarded for years. "Okay. What can I do?"

"Lani has a few trays of unbaked taro rolls rising on the back table, and the oven is hot. Want to get them going?"

"Of course!" Happy to be assigned a task, I got to work setting the beautiful purple dough balls to baking. Once they were in the oven, Lani had arrived with a small net bag nearly bursting at the seams with produce.

"Hi Macca!" She raised the bag to show me. "We needed additional ingredients for salads so I hopped over to the farm stand. I put the receipt in your inbox."

"Thank you. You're so efficient." And I really meant it. My true chosen family, working together like the parts of a well-oiled machine.

We worked as a team to get the food prepped, and the tables set. When the guests arrived we began to seat them and take orders. Sam was handling the bar on his own tonight, as Bennie had needed to take a little time off for personal family business, but once I'd taken order tickets back to the kitchen, I stepped in and helped deliver the drinks as he mixed them. I spent most of the evening dashing back and forth between kitchen and bar. Once the last guests had moved to the pool area with their cocktails and all the service had been cleared, I plopped into a chair to catch my breath. Sam dropped into one nearby, and tiny Lani perched on a barstool, her legs swinging like a little girl, a cute but incongruent image against her protruding belly. Kalei brought out a small plate of cookies and we noshed in silence. This was how we wound down after each dinner service.

"As always, thank you all." I looked around at each loving face and smiled.

"I love my job." Sam sat back, grinning. "But tomorrow is my day off so I'm goin' surfin' of course."

Kalei laughed and shook his head. "What a surprise. Sam is going surfing," he teased, slapping his friend on the back.

"Dude, it's a great reminder of how tiny we are when sitting on a board beyond the waves."

I nodded, understanding him completely, despite the fact that I had never surfed and never would. There were too many unknown things out there beneath the surface that bite or sting. The most you'd catch me doing was taking a swim in our little cove, staying closer to shore.

Kalei stood quickly and went to Lani who was resting her head on her arms. "You okay, ku'u aloha?" I recognized the term of endearment that he frequently used, meaning something like "my love."

"I'm fine, Big Man. Just tired."

He rubbed her expanding tummy so tenderly and I stood, ready to put an end to yet another day. "Time for you to take her home, Kalei." I went to her side and gave her a gentle hug and then cleaned up the cookie plate and napkins while the three of them called goodnight and headed out.

When I emerged from the kitchen, the big storm shutters around the dining room were closed and there was only a single safety light on by the reception desk beyond. All of a sudden the building was eerie. It never had been before. I shook my head and chalked it up to exhaustion along with creepy pseudo-relatives. I stopped and listened though. For a moment I thought I heard a heart pounding, but it was my own. I tilted my head to listen, and a chilling picture invaded my thoughts; Freddie

Krueger with those weird finger thingies standing with that other guy in the hockey mask. I shook it off, only to replace it with the imagined sound of a chainsaw being revved. "Stop it, Macca," I scolded myself just a little too loudly. I was walking toward the safety light and the main door when a shadow flitted past on the other side. I tried to picture the supplies at the desk that could act as a weapon and could only come up with the metal two-hole punch. I snatched it up, disappointed in how lightweight it was, but held it high anyway as I opened the front door a crack.

I peered left and right and saw Winston and Marley's empty cage with the cover on the ground. Damn! Stage whispering, I called their names. "Winston! Marley!" The air was silent around me until a startling noise caused me to turn just as a great fluttering of wings descended upon me. I think I jumped a couple of feet and even screeched as Winston landed on my head, clutching my hair with his claws.

Bad guy. Bad guy. Sleepy Jean. Cheer up. It stings.

"Shhh," I admonished him once my heart began to settle again. Marley fluttered in and landed on the cage, climbing down and around to enter through its open door. She whistled a few bars of "Don't Worry, Be Happy," and I grimaced. "That's not a Bob Marley song! It's Bobby McFerrin." She didn't seem to care. I put my arm up for Winston to jump on it and then settled him inside the cage where he belonged. The two birds huddled together. "Sorry, sweeties. Goodnight." I latched their door and shook the cover out before draping it across them. Then I returned my evil two-hole punch of doom to the desk and closed up for the night. Perhaps Sam had forgotten to put the birds to bed. I had to assume that was the reason for the scare-fest my fine feathered friends had brought down upon me. "I'll get you for that," I promised them under my breath and headed to my bungalow, chastising myself in my thoughts.

The television was still blaring but now it was *I Love Lucy*, the episode where they're dressed as Martians on top of the Empire State Building... one of my favorites. I stopped to watch for a minute, grinning at their made-up words. "It's a moo-moo..."

And then I realized Taylor wasn't in the room. I knocked on her bedroom door but got no response. A chill ran down my back. Had she seen the shadow? Or had she *been* the shadow? Had she let the birds out? I locked the front door and the sliding doors to the deck. Chester was in my room but Susie was nowhere to be seen. As Chet had indicated, our ghost dog wasn't having much of our houseguest. I wasn't too worried because of that key word: ghost. I pulled my phone out of my pocket and texted Sam.

Did you put the birds in their cage?

He replied quickly and in typical Sam-the-Surfer fashion reverted to shortcut texting.

Yeah. R they OK?

So, Sam's question proved that someone else had indeed let them out. I texted back.

Yes, they got out but they are back now. Thx.

His response was fast. I could sense the concern in his next text.

How they got out??????

I knew he was worried just by counting his question marks and not from his lack of grammar, which was a standard Sam-thing. I tapped a quick reply.

I don't know but I think someone was prowling around.

His next response was so Sam-like but not what I wanted. I didn't want to put anyone out because of my possible overreaction.

I be rt there.

Crap! I tapped as rapidly as I could, my thumbs growing tired.

No! We're fine now.

Just go home and enjoy your day off tomorrow.

Thanks again. We got this.

His response was fast, yet I still sensed tension.

OK but call me I be there. Bennie too.

Whew. I'd hoped I had convinced him that there was no danger.

I will. Thanks.

Simultaneously relieved and unnerved, I connected my phone to the charger in my room. I wandered back to the empty living room to turn off the television, my thoughts filled with our compassionate crew, always looking out for one another. I jumped, nearly out of my skin, when there was a loud rapping on the sliding glass door. There stood Taylor. I tossed the television remote on the sofa and opened the door for her, my senses on high alert. "Where'd you go?"

"I took a walk on the beach." She was all smiles. "Why did you lock me out?"

"I didn't know you were out," I lied. I don't lie well, so I turned my back to her and locked the slider once again.

"I couldn't stand to be trapped in this hovel a minute longer," she whined.

I fumed. "The Hilton is a brief drive away if you'd prefer," I said through clenched teeth.

She laughed, but it wasn't a happy sound. "Like I'd spend money when I have free digs here."

"Your free… digs… are available as long as you treat them with some respect and also an understanding that we all work hard to maintain this… hovel. You, on the other hand, haven't lifted a finger since you got here. If you want high class and room service, you'll need to find other arrangements." Whoa… I have no idea where that strength came from, but I was damn proud of myself and this inn. As I pondered my next move, Susie appeared on the other side of the slider I'd just locked. I turned and let him in before locking up again. I could feel his tense body as he took his place at my side and kept his attention on Taylor.

"Fine. Be a bitch. Everyone is a bitch to me." She was shaking with rage.

"Your grandmother is dead and your mother is in jail and all you can think about is yourself. You should be ashamed, but I don't think you know how to be even remotely human." I was on a roll. Susie leaned against my leg but stayed alert. He was "claiming" me against her.

I watched as Taylor worked up some crocodile tears. It took her a long time for any kind of moisture to appear in her eyes, and none of it ever hit her cheeks. Macca 2, Taylor 0.

"Everyone hates me. I'm going to bed." She flounced into her borrowed room and slammed the door.

I let out a huge breath and dropped to my knees to give Susie hugs and pets and to coo at him. "Good boy." His tail thwapped hard against the coffee table. "Sleep with Chester and me?" I walked toward my room and he followed, his huge tongue lolling out the side of his mouth. It was only then that I realized I hadn't checked to see if Chester was in my room. I dashed the last few feet and swung the door open so hard it banged against the wall.

What?! Can't a guy sleep without caterwauling — and don't even get me started on that word — going on in the next room and then the door slamming open?

He was curled up on my bed, his head on one paw. I didn't care how grumpy he was; I kissed him on top of his hot-headed little noggin.

My head is not hot.

"It is, in that you know how to be a grump. In fact, Grumpy Cat has nothing on you."

Hmph. Of course not. That cat is not grumpy, just looks like it and rakes in the bucks. Totally against feline policy. When he had finished his mini-rant he settled again and closed his eyes. Susie looked from him to me, then back to him. I just shook my head and the big dog sighed. He understood.

You're a sourpuss, cat. Susie chuckled — an odd sound, all things considered.

Susie settled on his bed near my closet, and I slipped into my tee-shirt. No Davy tonight, but I had Susie and Chester. And then I remembered the empty FedEx box. I retrieved it from my closet and put it on the bed next to Chester. He looked up briefly, eyeing the box with some interest that I was sure he would never admit to. I crawled into bed and turned the light off. As my eyes adjusted to the dark, I saw the big orange cat move stealthily over to the box and settle himself inside. I heard a low groan of pleasure, and soon he was purring again.

I fell asleep and dreamed of warrior women with their men and protective beasties, together fending off grumpy relatives. An easy win.

THIRTEEN

Power Banks and Thai Iced Coffees

I awoke the next morning to the blaring of the television in the next room. Again. Glancing at my phone and trying really hard to chase away the desire to throw it against the wall, I saw that it was time to begin the day. Susie and Chester barely moved when I tossed back my blanket and rolled out of bed. I stumbled to the living room and stood between Taylor and the television.

"Are you going to your mother's hearing this morning? Because I am, and I'm leaving at 7:00, so if you want to go together, I need to know, and you need to be ready by then."

She sighed then and tried to look around me at the television. This was ridiculous.

"Well, I hadn't decided, really."

"Taylor! You really need to get it together. You can't just sit in front of the television all the time."

And then it happened. She began to cry. Big and loud, tears and real sobs. I quickly moved to sit beside her, my arm around her as I let her cry it out. This woman and her family had my emotions on a yo-yo, set on a never-ending loop of "Around the World." Oh how I craved "Rock the Baby" instead.

"Yes. I'll go with you to Mom's hearing," she choked out between sobs.

"Okay." I patted her back as I spoke. "Then you'll be able to see her and you might feel better." I tried to soothe her, but she cried even harder. "Taylor, are you sure you want to go," I asked because now I was beginning to doubt her reasons.

"Yeah." She sat back, wiping her face with her hands. "I really need to. I don't want to very much though." I suspected that was the first truly honest thing she'd said in her nearly three decades of life.

"Just imagine how she's sitting alone in a tiny cell, wondering what will happen. Seeing your face will certainly cheer her, don't you think?"

She sniffed, an unattractive sound. I looked around, desperately seeking tissue but knowing full well that it was out of reach. "Can I come with you?" Her question was in the form of a whimper.

"Of course! You don't mind riding in my little Roomba though, do you?" Dial back the enthusiasm, Macca, I chided myself.

"No. I don't want to drive myself."

"Okay then... Can you be ready in time?"

She nodded and squeaked out one word. "Yeah."

I waited for her crying to stop before standing up. "We'll leave at 7:00," I reminded her.

"Okay." She got up and trudged to Davy's room. Yeah, there was no way I was ever going to call it anything else, and I silently yearned for the days when we could return to our normal lives.

Blowing out a huge but perhaps premature breath of victory, I went off to shower and dress.

On my way to the kitchen I hollered at her through Davy's door. "Remember, 7:00," and wondered if I was beginning to sound like a parent.

"Okay. I'll be ready."

I took care of Susie and Chester before making myself a cup of tea. I heard her fumbling around in her room and then saw her dash across the hall to the bathroom. Good. I sipped my tea and munched a rewarmed poi roll. I placed my tea mug in the nearly full dishwasher, turned it on, and wadded my little napkin into the bin before marching over to the bathroom where I pounded on the door a few times.

I checked the clock on my phone again. "It's now 6:55. I'll see you at the car. And I will leave at 7:00." I meant it. Yep, parenting skills. I shouldn't need them.

I grabbed my purse and headed for the stairs. I could see Bennie arriving and opening up Winston and Marley's cage. We exchanged waves and I took the stairs two at a time. I disconnected dear little Roomba's charging cord, stowed it, and climbed in. I looked at my phone for the time. My deadline came and went. I was just beginning to back out when Taylor's head appeared at the top of the stairs. She was winded but opened the door and plopped into the passenger seat.

"Geez. This thing is small."

"Yep. It is. It's one of the many efficient ways of the future. Taylor, meet Roomba."

"Whatever."

"Don't insult him. We're counting on him to get us there and back."

"Do we have to stop somewhere and rewind the rubber band or something?"

"We will plug him in when we get to the charging station near the government buildings."

"Near? You mean we'll have to walk?"

"Yeah… just a couple of blocks. It won't kill you."

She grumbled and put her seatbelt on.

I sighed and pulled onto the road. It was going to be a long trip, except that I noticed she fell asleep after only twenty minutes. Small mercies. I listened to the radio and was both amused and intrigued by some of the interviews on the public station. It sure helped pass the time. Of course the spectacular views at every turn in the road were always awe-inspiring to me as well and today was no different.

Taylor awoke and was sullen and silent, so I simply watched the road, with an occasional glance to the sea on the left, the lush vegetation on the right, or the volcanoes in the distance. The violet sky had slowly turned to cornflower blue, the oranges and pinks of dawn gone as the sun reached higher above us. When I lost interest in the interviews on the radio, I switched to a music station and hummed along. Glancing toward Taylor, I saw that her head was back against the headrest and she was asleep again. That buoyed my mood, and I tapped my fingers on the steering wheel as we zipped along.

Arriving at our destination, I drove around to find a spot with a charger and pulled into one that even had a tree that would throw a little shade for later. I turned off the engine just as Taylor awoke. "We're here already?" she asked.

"Yeah." I smiled. "You slept almost the whole way." Feeling thankful for that, I got out, stretched my legs, and connected Roomba to the charging unit. Taylor came up beside me and watched in boredom, which was quickly becoming her standard.

"Where's the courthouse?" She was peering in all directions.

I pointed ahead and we began to walk. The air was a comfortable temperature, not too hot yet. I'd been prepared though and wore a sleeveless cotton shift in a subtle print of tiny blue and green leaves. I carried a little sweater of white cotton knit in case the air conditioning inside the court was blowing an arctic gale as in most large government buildings. And out of respect for the hallowed halls of wherever we were going, I wore flat but strappy sandals; sadly, the flip flops had to stay home for today.

Taylor was dressed in a pink cotton blouse, white cotton pants, and matching slip-on Vans in pink and white. She looked great, but I wondered why one purchases a very limiting pink and white shoe. I chalked it up to large amounts of money and gave a shrug in my mind. At least they'd be able to pay my friend Rob Parker Kula's fees. We walked, we crossed streets, and we walked some more.

By the final approach to the courthouse, Taylor was complaining loudly.

"Suck it up, buttercup," I muttered, less than enamored once again with this family. I'd distanced myself from them in my head because I was beginning to understand that what they were today must have been far different than what my mother had seen in her youth.

We found our way to the correct courtroom according to the information that Rob had given me, and we took a seat near the wall as opposed to the aisle, in hopes that Bettina would see us as soon as she entered. Waiting for several more defendants to come and go was hard on the patience, and it was pretty discouraging to see that the judge barely lifted his head to look at anyone. Instead, he constantly referred to his laptop or his notes. Hell, he almost could have phoned in the job just as well.

Beside me, Taylor's head was bowed, her purse lying open on her lap with her hands inside. I peeked just a little bit and could see the glow of her phone. She was switching back and forth between texting with someone and playing a game. Good. It's always a smart move to keep a toddler occupied when the adults around them were busy.

I zoned out after the third DUI case was presented for bail or otherwise. Then came a couple of burglaries.

Taylor leaned toward me and whispered, "Do you have a power bank?"

"A what?"

"A power bank. You know… a portable charger?"

"Um… no." I really had no need for such luxuries. I plugged my phone into my charger at home each night and used it primarily for business purposes with the exception of a few games now and then. And texting? I only did that for work. Otherwise, I preferred to talk face to face with everyone most of the time.

Nah, you do just fine, Babe. I heard a sweet Mancunian voice in my head and I felt a smile grow from the inside out.

Where are you? I answered him back in my thoughts.

California, by the ocean.

I looked east and smiled. *Have fun. Hope to see you soon.*

You got it.

I almost chuckled then, realizing I just had a conversation with someone in my head, but quickly remembered we were in public, so I stifled the laughter by sucking my lips in. I kept looking at the clock as minutes ticked by. Finally, a mere twenty-five minutes late, Rob Parker Kula entered and took a seat at the table in front of us.

"Pssst." Yeah, not original or eloquent, but it still got his attention. He turned around and gave me a grin and winked. I returned his smile, but then a shackled Bettina was brought in. I elbowed Taylor to get her attention and loudly cleared my throat. Bettina glanced up and saw us, then tried to smile, but instead her lips quivered and tears made tracks down her cheeks. She looked like hell, dark circles under her eyes, no makeup, hair just hanging limp, and of course the requisite wrinkled clothing, the same outfit she'd been wearing when she was arrested. It was a blast from my own past.

Taylor finally looked up from her phone and waved to her mother, as if she were coming home from school for the day. Bettina hardly seemed to notice her daughter though; instead she was smiling widely at me through her tears. So, I blew her a kiss, and she did something my mother had often done: she mimicked catching it and holding it to her heart. I nearly lost my composure and had to swallow a few times to chase the tears away. Taylor looked back and forth between us and, not wanting to be outdone, pathetically blew her mother a kiss as well. Bettina, good sport, caught it too and held it to her heart.

Taylor squirmed happily in her seat, all grins and imagined fist bumps. Yeah, too little, too late, in my opinion, having just witnessed her previous lackluster performances. I wasn't fooled. There was something off-putting here and I was determined to figure it out.

Poor Bettina received what I felt was the harshest decision by this laptop-loving judge. Remand, no bail. Trial was set for thirty days. I was heartbroken for many reasons, the loss of Annie at the forefront being the most painful. Equally troubling were the collective thoughts of Bettina in that hellhole they call jail, the idea that Taylor could be my roommate for that amount of time, and the rising number of charges for which Rob could be billing their family were all nearly paralyzing. I'm sure a look of fear and horror was frozen on my face as she was led silently crying from the room.

Crime of passion? Or an innocent being charged with a crime she didn't commit? Both theories could be valid. So now what was I supposed to do? I had a long drive home ahead of me to think on it.

But for now, Rob turned to me. "I'm sorry, Macca." He held my hand, not in a handshake, but in the manner of a loving friend. "It's just that not many murders take place in the park."

"I know you did your best because that's who you are, and... I thank you."

He reached across that silly little thigh-high fence between the important people and just us supporters and gave me a really tight hug. "I'll see you soon, right?"

"Yes. Dinner in a couple weeks, and I'm really looking forward to it," I responded and he gave me his usual twinkly grin. "Give a hug to Momi for me in the meantime?"

"Will do." He packed his briefcase and exited the courtroom.

"Wow. Very chummy there," Taylor sneered.

I ignored her words and began to herd her out into the bright sunlight. "He and his wife are very dear friends," I responded at last, even though I should have just ignored her.

The walk back to the car was a lot more leisurely than earlier but little Roomba was right where I'd left him, still attached to the charger by his electrical umbilical cord. *Good boy*, I thought to myself with a little smile.

As I got onto the main road, our destination just seemed like an awfully long way. "Are you hungry?" I asked Taylor as she slumped in her seat.

"Yeah. Starving."

"Me too. I think it's time for lunch."

I pulled off the main road, headed a couple of blocks toward Hilo Bay, and found a parking spot. I pointed to Delilah's, a cafe down the block, and we began to walk.

"What kind of food do they serve here?" Taylor looked wary of my choice for lunch, but I'd eaten here before and liked the vegetarian options. There were plenty of non-vegetarian dishes too.

"Thai fusion, and there are a lot of great choices."

She shrugged. "Sounds good actually."

I chose the vegetarian wrap while Taylor decided on the Thai chicken pizza. At my suggestion, she and I each had a cup of the coconut soup, one of their specialties. We also sipped Thai iced coffee, one of my very favorite treats.

It was a relief when we dug into our food and Taylor ooohed and aaahed after each bite. I chuckled a few times, enjoying my own wrap and soup. The grilled tofu had been marinated in their special peanut sauce, and the brown rice with vegetables made it quite a substantial meal. Taylor's pizza looked great, with the exception of the chicken part, but the red curry, spinach, and dollops of cooling yogurt appealed to me.

"I was worried about the pineapple with the yogurt and the pumpkin," she said between bites, "but it's heavenly." She dunked a bite in some extra sauce. "The sweet, tart, salty, spicy notes just make you go back for more, even when you're full. Man, this could be dangerous for someone on a diet." She gave a relaxed and genuine laugh, and it was contagious.

"I'm really happy you like it!"

"Great choice, Macca. Really. People back home would never believe these combinations though." She mopped her forehead with her napkin before adding, "And just the right amount of heat. Who is the woman that owns this place? I think I want to marry her." The tension of the morning in court dissolved in that instant as we enjoyed fits of quiet laughter. People nearby turned and smiled, so we took the volume lower, not wanting to disrupt the lunch hour in one of my favorite little hole-in-the-wall cafes.

Both of us ended up taking nearly half our lunch home, which I stashed in the insulated bag I always kept in the back of Roomba, left over from R2, my previous Smart Car, and before that my rental car which had borne the ridiculous name of car-scooter-skateboard-skate. Ahh, good memories. I silently thanked my previous Smart Cars for giving their lives that I might live. Or something.

With the Thai iced coffee in our bellies, we had to make a couple of pit stops on the way back to Hale Mele, but the laughter continued. Every little thing we witnessed had us laughing. Frankly, it was extremely therapeutic.

"Did you know," I began, laughing as I pulled back into traffic after a pit stop, "I used to sneak Dad's coffee when he wasn't looking?" I chuckled at the memories of my reconnaissance missions of childhood, waiting silently until he was distracted or in another room, then… gulp. I got really good at it over the years too.

Taylor burst into laughter as well before telling me about her own spy-works. "I used to wait until my parents were distracted, then take sips of their cocktails. I'd fall into bed on Friday and Saturday nights completely blitzed, but wake up the next morning with no trace of a hangover. It wasn't until I was an adult that I realized how fortunate I was back then."

I joined in her laughter but secretly felt so sorry for her situation. What a crappy way to grow up… getting drop-dead drunk off her parents' vice. And before she could even drive a car. I sent a mental message up to my parents thanking them for their actual…. well… parenting.

You made parenting a joy, I heard Mom's voice in my head. I smiled and nodded that I heard her, and then she continued, taking a little wind out of my sails. *Yeah, but don't let your head get too big over that revelation, okay?*

I nodded very slightly, the smile almost comically wiped off my face. Tough love, ghost-style. It sucked.

Ignore them. I have bigger news. Davy was now in my head. I really needed to start charging rental fees.

And what is that, Davy?

Bettina didn't do it.

What? But he was gone again. What the hell? *How can you leave me hanging like that?* I shouted the words in my mind. Yeah, try to

149

figure that one out. I dare ya.

I glanced at Taylor from the corner of my eye. She had plugged her phone in to charge it and was busy texting again, so I just enjoyed the reverse angle of the scenery along the way home. My thoughts were crowded with Bettina's situation, and I visualized her sitting in a cell like I had not too long ago. It was chilling.

I was thankful when we were finally back at Hale Mele, my home sweet home. Taylor closed herself up in her borrowed room, and I headed to the reception area to catch up with Bennie and let him know the outcome of the hearing. Finding myself slipping into sadness again I decided I could use some of those old endorphins so I went for a run.

On the path I saw the rocking chairs again, this time all rocking in unison. *How did you manage that?* I asked Davy in my head.

Magic. The word floated away, accompanied by his trademark laugh. I couldn't help but smile and pushed on to clear my mind. Running was not only physically good for me but also mentally clarifying, and I began to feel my mood lift.

FOURTEEN

Steak Sauce and a Free Mai Tai

The very next day we had a new family checking in, and they were an interesting trio to say the least.

The Digby family hailed from Detroit, Michigan, and included husband and wife Dale and Nancy, and young adult son Connor. I estimated the younger Digby to be around nineteen, with long and floppy hair that mostly covered his eyes. He kept his nose stuck in his iPhone and stood several feet away from his parents as they checked in, transferring his weight back and forth between his right foot and left, rather like he was pacing impatiently in place. I watched from my spot at the bar, my overworked laptop whirring softly in front of me.

"Welcome to Hale Mele," Bennie greeted them. "You're the Digby family, right?"

Dale nodded and began the sign-in process by filling out the registration card and pulling out his credit card while Nancy seemed to be inspecting the premises. I'm sure my face registered shock as she drew a small napkin from the stack by the rarely-empty coffee urn and began to wipe the counter down. I tried valiantly to hide behind the laptop, but I soon realized she was only focused on the countertop. I'm sure it sparkled plenty, having just cleaned it myself not even an hour ago, yet the look of peace on her face seemed to indicate that she wasn't disapproving of the place but rather simply pacifying herself.

"We're still taking reservations for dinner." Bennie began his usual welcome points. "Will you be joining us this evening?"

"Yes." Dale spoke his first word since his arrival with a booming voice that startled me out of my fascination with his wife's obsession with dust mites and germs. The volume of Dale's voice caused Bennie to drop his pen, and he fumbled to retrieve it before adding them to the reservation list.

"What's for dinner?" Young Connor had the same booming voice, but his eyes never left his iPhone.

"Tonight will include a choice of fish, vegetarian fare, and I believe our chef has roast beef with pineapple in the imu oven outside," Bennie's voice was a whisper in comparison.

"Sounds good," Dale yelled. "Nancy, come." He turned to his wife who had dropped the pristine napkin into the small trash receptacle. I almost expected him to whistle to her, holler "Good girl," and pat her on the head. Bennie turned to me and covered up a grin before helping them

151

take their luggage to their bungalow, thus allowing me to finish my supply orders. I idly wondered if Nancy could speak. On the other hand, she might have been waiting for the order to do so, which would once again be followed by a pat on the head. Maybe she'd even get a treat.

"Connor!" Dale boomed at his son, shaking me out of my short reverie. "Put that blasted phone away or I'll toss it into the Pacific the first chance I get!"

But Connor ignored him and continued staring at his phone while following his parents slowly down the walkway. It was my guess though that Mr. Digby seemed to have made that threat before and never followed through on his promise. Empty threats by parents were something I saw frequently but had never experienced myself. Mom and Dad had excellent follow-through, much to my horror during childhood.

Oh yes… This was going to be an interesting group. When Bennie returned he was shaking his head and laughing. "We might have to issue ear plugs to the other guests."

I joined in his laughter. "Let's place them at one of the open air tables this evening so they don't shake the place down with their ear-splitting volume."

"I'm not sure that will help, but it's worth a try," he sighed. "I wonder if they're stage actors or something?"

"Hell, they could project to the nosebleed seats at Aloha stadium." I referenced the venue in our state capital on the neighboring island of Oahu.

He chuckled again. "Without even leaving the inn." He picked up the telephone and mimicked into it, "What? You'd like us to what? Tell our guests to keep it down? Sorry, I can't quite make out your words for all the noise over here." He slammed the phone down and I tried to muffle my raucous laughter.

Kalei and Lani came out from the kitchen, the latter wiping her hands on a dishcloth. "What was that all about?"

"Our newest guests. Got earplugs?" Bennie asked as we got our laughter under control. "You heard them in the kitchen?" he asked. "I'll bet you had the blender, the food processor, the radio, and the dishwasher all going at the same time and it didn't deafen the noise. Am I right?"

By now the laughter was tickling at Lani as well, and Kalei soon joined in.

"You'd better amplify your drumming this Saturday during the luau show," I teased.

"Maybe I should have a full percussion band accompany Lani's dancing," Kalei chuckled.

"How on earth are we going to keep the other guests happy?" Lani's eyes glowed with laughter.

"Free drinks," I stated the obvious and our laughter gained momentum again.

True to my promise, we began handing out free Mai Tais, Piña Coladas, and Sam's own version of Spicy Mangotinis for the first time that evening. The volume in the dining room and the open area adjacent was indeed thunderous during the dinner service. I saw Davy shimmer in, his expression a combination of horror and disgust.

"What the hell is going on here?" he hollered to me over the din. At that point Mr. Pinckney blipped in with a loud thud. Well, it was loud to Davy and me even though no one else could hear it.

"Oh dear," he murmured and blipped right out again. Davy sighed and shook his head.

"He'll never learn. I'm convinced." He slapped his hand over his face. I swear, the whole evening was a vaudeville show. I expected someone to march back and forth with a potted plant that grew bigger and bigger each time. "When does the trapeze act come on?" Davy added, and I snickered, shaking my head. On one shake I could see Bennie watching, clearly able to see Davy. I smiled at him warmly. These men just had to get along. Period. I tilted my head to the kitchen door and nodded, indicating we should move to the semi-privacy of the employees only area. Davy followed my lead and both Kalei and Lani turned around to greet him. It was surreal to me that Davy could now be seen by some others, but he seemed to embrace it.

"I've got a hot idea for a new television show called 'The Shouting Family,'" Davy began. "But you have to watch it with the sound muted. It doesn't matter, you'll hear them anyway."

"What's that? I can't hear you." Kalei's eyes sparkled with mischief.

"Ha ha ha." Davy winked. "The big guy is a comedian."

Kalei chuckled, shook his head, and went back to his task. It was then I noticed that Lani had earplugs in.

"Where did you find those?" I gave her a little squeeze about her shoulders.

"Big Man cut the cords off an extra pair of earbuds from his mp3 player."

"Aww, what a guy." I patted Kalei's back. "Got any more?"

"Sorry. Used the last pair for Mama here." He winked at his tiny wife as she moved about the kitchen, plating and arranging food, even humming to herself. "And I wish we could put soundproofing around her belly too." He gave Lani's expanding middle a loving caress as he moved to the walk-in cooler for supplies.

"Only six days left of their visit," I teased and slapped Davy's hand as he tried to steal a piece of pineapple from a plate.

Lani placed the last of the items on three plates and grinned wickedly at me. "For The Shouting Family, if you're brave enough."

"Oh, I'll get you, my pretty, and your little dog too," I cackled while loading two plates on my left hand and arm and taking the third in my right. I used my hip to bump the swinging door open and saw Davy trying to sneak the pineapple again. "Hey! Knock that off," I yelled, and he snatched his hand away, whistling oh so innocently at the ceiling.

Walking swiftly toward the farthest table, I saw Neatnick Nancy wiping the surface down. Again. Stifling a sigh, I put on my brightest smile. "Good evening Digby family!" I placed the plates in front of each individual as had been outlined on their ticket: fish for Nancy and roast beef for Dale and Connor. "Is there anything else I can get you?"

"Steak sauce," Connor yelled directly into his plate, his iPhone having been momentarily replaced by food.

"And another Mai Tai," Dale thundered. I nodded at each and turned to Nancy, but she was busy arranging her flatware and water glass.

I gave the drink order to Sam, then snaked my arm through the kitchen door and grabbed the steak sauce before Kalei could object. He, like many chefs, was often offended by the idea of people covering his food with condiments.

Returning to the bar, Sam handed me the Mai Tai and I placed it next to the steak sauce on a small tray and delivered both to The Shouting Family. Nancy was eating very methodically, one thing at a time, then turning her plate. I raised my eyebrows and turned back to the kitchen. I gave the Morrisons a passing greeting along the way and bumped the swinging door open again. Davy froze where he was standing, his right cheek ballooned out. I glanced down at the dinner plates on the workstation and saw one was missing pineapple. "You're incorrigible."

"I mnowm," he said around the slab of fruit in his craw.

I replaced the pineapple, checked the ticket, and grabbed all the plates for the next table. Lani helped me serve the Morrisons, our largest group at two adults, two children, and a baby, who, surprisingly, could sometimes eat more than the two children. Combined. I guess babies are like that. Lani always liked to linger a bit with them and chat with the kids. Mommy-in-training. I smiled and headed back for the last group of plates, catching Davy sneaking a French fry.

"Knock it off! Go to your room!"

"I can't. You gave it away."

"Oh yeah. Okay then, here," and I handed him his own small plate of fries, plucking two to replace the one he'd stolen, and then delivered the final meals.

Back in the kitchen, Lani had begun assembling dessert plates as Kalei tackled the usual mess created by mealtime prep. Davy was leaning over the workspace watching her expert placement of the food with an artist's touch.

"Stop drooling, Chef Davy," I teased. He stood up quickly with a "hand caught in the cookie jar" grin, shimmered out for only a second or two, then shimmered back in dressed in full chef attire, including a big floppy hat; I recognized it from one of the episodes of The Monkees. Lani glanced up at him and giggled bashfully, her cheeks reddening. She and her mother both became fangirls in Davy's presence, and he played it to the hilt. I simply shook my head and rolled my eyes.

"Those are gonna fall out yer head one of these days if you keep doin' that, y'know." He laid on the heavy accent whenever he had an audience.

I stuck my tongue out at him and Lani giggled again. I escaped to the dining area and scooped up plates as they were emptied, checking on our guests' desires for drinks, coffee, or anything else in the process, and then taking dessert orders. Back in the kitchen, I deposited the dirty dishes and gathered dessert plates instead. This went on for several minutes as I tried to keep up with Lani's plating. When at last all dishes had been collected and guests were taking coffee and drinks out to the benches and chairs around the pool, Lani and I began to clean tables and chairs with assistance from Bennie. Kalei cleaned the kitchen according to health department rules while Sam focused on the bar. Usually my mind was blank as we went about these frequent and familiar tasks, but on this night I happened to be reflecting on my life now compared to the boring existence I'd been living in Los Angeles. Yes, it was a lot of work to operate an inn, and meal service was quite intense at times, but the rewards were huge. I felt such satisfaction.

But then my mind drifted to Bettina in jail, and Davy's words, "She didn't do it," were ringing in my memory. Then who did? It was then that I decided that as soon as I had another day when I could beg off my chores I'd take a solo trip down to Volcanoes National Park and take a look around. Maybe I'd even ask a few questions. Right now though, the only question I could muster was what day in the busy week ahead might be available for this sleuthing.

FIFTEEN

A Cheshire Cat and the Disorient Express

Waking earlier than usual the next morning, I showered and sat on the deck. Before me was a bowl with chunks of melon floating on a cloud of lime yogurt, accompanied by my standard cup of tea. The mix of sweet and tart made my taste buds pucker happily. Taylor's door had remained closed, and I relished the solitary serenity as I watched the sky and the sea beyond; it was going to be another warm day with no threat of rain in the clouds. That usually meant people scattered to do their sightseeing, and I hoped this day was no different because it was Ming's day off and I needed to get the bungalows cleaned. Not my favorite part of innkeeping, but I still seemed to enjoy it more these days than in the past. I liked to think it was because I was pleased to make people comfortable, but instead I wondered if I was simply becoming the Domestic Goddess my mother had always tried so hard not to be. In fact, she had worked tirelessly to show the child-me that women could be whatever they wanted. I decided right then, spooning yogurt and melon into my mouth before a fantastic view, that anything other than running Uncle Wally's little slice of heaven wouldn't net me any more happiness than I already felt each day. But the real test was when I asked myself if I'd rather clean or be on the beach. My immediate reply always favored the beach. Ahh, I was my mother's daughter after all.

"Hey there!" Davy's imitation of The Shouting Family made me jump which knocked the spoon out of my now empty bowl, clattering to the deck.

"Dammit." I laughed. "You scared the hell out of me."

He chuckled as he drew the other chair close and sat with me, a cup of tea in his hand. "Sorry. Not sorry," he teased, having picked up yet another modern expression in a manner I found almost annoying. He picked up the dropped spoon, took my bowl from me, and placed both on the table, all in one smooth move. He really was just a nice guy with a big heart, but also a child who loved to pull pranks. I couldn't help but smile, feeling very Cheshire Cat-ish.

"What?" His smile reached from his mouth up to his big brown eyes, the lovely crinkle lines deepening along with the pronounced lines on either side of his mouth. He was just too cute for his own good sometimes.

"Just thinking," I felt a blush rise from my neck up to my forehead.

"Yeah, I heard. I'm a nice guy and a little brat. Oh, and I'm cute."

"I did not say any of that," I responded, but he had me chuckling too. "But your snoopy ways need a leash," I teased.

He chortled some more in that endearing raspy manner that made anyone and everyone want to laugh right along with him.

"What's up for today?" He crossed his sixties white booted ankles on the arm of my chair and leaned back.

"Ming's day off. Six bungalows. Must annihilate the dirt."

He threw his head back and laughed fully. "Sounds like a fantastic day. May I join you?"

I was surprised. "Yes! You can even help."

"Ha! Psych." Another irritating expression from what… the eighties? "I'm going to Pennsylvania. Got a date with a lovely old house."

"Really? Does the house dance? Cook? Clean?"

He stuck his tongue out at me. "No to all of that. I'm just checking in on it… and some people I care about."

My heart tugged my lips into a smile then. I found his compassion for his friends and loved ones incredibly endearing. And a whole lot of sexy. *Stop that, Macca*, I chided myself in my mind.

"Yeah." He peered at me from the corner of his eye with an impish smirk. "Stop that, Macca. You'll give an old man ideas," the words at odds with his youthful appearance. He waggled his eyebrows and I knocked his feet off my chair, causing his front chair legs to land hard on the deck with a loud thunk. "Hey!"

Now it was my turn to laugh as I stood and collected the dishes. "Give my regards to… Pennsylvania." I winked at him as I carried the dirty dishes into the kitchen with him on my heels. Once inside though, I whispered quietly, knowing that Taylor was close by in her room.

"By the way..." He leaned against the kitchen counter and held his closed fist out. I put my hand under his to catch the tiny package which he dropped into my palm. It was lovely blue paisley tissue wrapped around an artfully crafted little statue of four horses — one red, two brown, and the fourth gray — with their heads together affectionately.

"Oh Davy." I turned it around to see it from all angles, "It's beautiful. Thank you." I kissed him on the cheek, and he put his arms around me, hugging me tightly.

"I got to visit some of my horses. It made me think of you, and that looks like a few of them."

"You miss them."

He pulled away. "I do miss them, but I see them."

"But… I know it's different. It must be."

He nodded a little sadly but shrugged. "It is what it is, right?"

I kissed his cheek again and then placed the little horses next to my other gifts. They seemed to fit perfectly between the cherry blossom tree and the crown. The loving look on Davy's face told me this one was extra special, but as usual, I never pried into his personal life.

I glanced up at my mother's teapot clock on the wall and realized I was late. "Yikes," I squealed. "Gotta get to work."

"I've got to go too. I'll see you later." He kissed my forehead, and I gave his hand a brief squeeze before dashing out the door to begin cleaning the bungalows. A quick check told me that all guests except The Shouting Family had left the property, so I began to methodically clean, beginning with Number 6. As I trundled down the path with the service cart, I cursed under my breath; why did I always forget to ask Davy important questions like, "If Bettina didn't kill Annie, who did?" But then I saw The Shouting Family at the pool and all such thoughts flitted away. Dale was reading the paper at one of the tables that Neatnick Nancy was busy wiping down. Thank you Nancy Digby, for one less surface I needed to clean. Connor was floating on a raft in the pool with his eyes glued to the ever-present phone in his hand.

"Get that phone outta your face," Dale shouted again to Connor, his own eyes never leaving his newspaper. A brief thought flitted through my mind that Dale's use of his paper as a wall was just as bad as Connor's attention riveted to his phone. Lead by example, my family had always believed. As I turned the corner to head into their bungalow, Connor's response to his father was lost on the breezes. Small mercies and all that.

Just out of habit, I knocked on their door and called out, "Housekeeping," as I opened the door, knowing full well that there would be no response. I stood rooted to the spot just over the threshold and allowed my jaw to hang open as I gazed inside; the place was immaculate. Not even a magazine or book was out of place. I put my nose in the air and detected only freshness; a breeze kissed my face as it blew in from the kitchen. Rounding the corner, I could see an equally spotless dining area and the same in the kitchen itself. Not a dish out of place, or a crumb, or a piece of lint. I suspected all germs had fled in fear at the sight of Neatnick Nancy and her Hollering Boys. Wow. I checked the dishes in the cupboard to see if anything was needed, as sometimes things were broken, and our practice was to replace them without a word, but all was in its place and filled to capacity.

"Wow." This time I said it out loud. I checked the trash: empty. I did put fresh kitchen linens out and placed the old ones, only slightly used, into the laundry bag. Oh well. Sure made my job easy, but I also felt a little guilt gnawing at me.

Starting in the second bedroom, I noted the bed was neatly made, but I stripped it anyway and replaced the sheets. In the master, I repeated these tasks before heading to the single bathroom. Again, the towels were hung nicely, spotless. I briefly wondered if she'd washed them already early this morning, but instead I just tossed them in the laundry bag with their other not-soiled linens and hung a fresh set. The sink, counter, tub, and shower were sparkling. Oh, Ming was going to regret having this day off. I only hoped that whatever drove Nancy Digby's quest to obliterate all dirt would continue to do so for Ming's benefit every other day of their stay. The idea made me chuckle as I shut the bungalow door behind me and propelled the service cart to the next. The Morrisons, with their two kids and baby, were always tidy, but I welcomed the obviously used linens that needed replacement. After all, I needed a purpose to the day and this was it. The family had been staying with us for so long that they treated their bungalow with the same amount of love and care with which I knew they'd treat their new home once it was ready for them to move in.

It was nearly one in the afternoon before I was done with the cleaning and able to begin the third load of laundry. As I waited between shifts of linens from washer to dryer to folding table to shelf, I sat at the bar near the front desk and worked my inventory on the laptop. It was when I was making a note for Lani's request for produce that I realized I'd skipped lunch. This being the one day of the week that we didn't provide a noon-time buffet, I peeked inside the walk-in cooler and found enough leftovers to create an egg salad sandwich with a side of melon. Instead of going to a dining table, I perched at the center workstation to eat. It was better to stay out of hearing distance from The Shouting Digbys. I giggled at the absurdity of the name. They could be a double-bill with the Traveling Wilburys, but the former would have been far less entertaining than the latter. Completely satiated by my quick lunch, I fed the melon rind and eggshells into Kalei's compost bin, rinsed my plate, and deposited it into the commercial dishwasher. As I settled back in front of my laptop, Lani and Kalei arrived to begin dinner prep.

"Aloha, Macca." The big man grinned as he passed, and Lani briefly put her hand on my back as she followed.

"Aloha my friends. " I patted Lani's hand on my shoulder just as she let it slide off and they disappeared into the kitchen. I snapped my laptop shut, stowed it in my own bungalow, then returned to finish the last of the laundry and to restock the service cart. It had been a full day and it was only mid-afternoon.

I hadn't seen Taylor since starting my day, but I found her glued to the television set yet again. I mumbled a greeting, knowing I'd receive no response, and headed to my bedroom to change into a swimsuit. I was in need of a refreshing dip in the sea. I yanked my black tank suit out of the overstuffed bureau drawer and slipped into it. The vibrant orange and yellow hibiscus screenprint splashed on the front was a statement that was usually unlike me, but today it just felt right. I brushed my unruly hair out and quickly braided it before grabbing Uncle Wally's Bugs Bunny beach towel; I'd written my name on the hem, just to be sure it never ended up with the extra beach towels we kept on hand for guests. I headed down the path to the steps and from there, to the beach, stopping to hang my towel on a funky little dried frond of a palm tree that I'd long ago adopted as my own personal clothes hook. I knew I'd be sad once it finally crumbled and fell off, but for the time being it was perfectly placed at eye level near the bottom of the stairs. I pulled my sunglasses off, rested them on top of the palm "hook," and walked out of my flip flops, leaving them in the sand at the base of the tree.

I was never one to dive into the ocean because I felt a great respect for all those living within it and had once, as a little girl, jumped in and landed on a jellyfish. Not fun. It had stung me up and down both my legs and caused excruciating pain. Mom had hustled me to the lifeguard station, and the tall blond lifeguard had made my six-year-old heart go pitty pat as he rinsed my legs with lots of fresh water. And while the fresh water helped, the special attention and loving care of the tanned beach god had distracted me long enough to not feel the pain... for a few minutes at least. Jellyfish stings are not fun. And contrary to that old scene in the television show *Friends*, urine was deemed no more effective than fresh water, but registered high on the scale of yuck.

Since that fateful day, I had taken the more cautious method of entering the ocean, walking slowly and staying vigilant for critters of any sort. While they had every right to be there, I did not, so I was respectful of the inhabitants. For this, some people had called me ridiculous in the past, but those people no longer had a place in my life. If nothing else, Mom and Dad had taught me to stick to my convictions and all else would fall into place. They were pretty smart actually, and their influence had provided me with a core "mission statement" for myself, the one and only Macca... or so my parents assured me. I had frequently reminded them that there was indeed another Macca, very famous in his own right, but they always claimed that he had only been the inspiration, and that I was the artist with a blank canvas for my life from the minute I was born. Every day I had at least one thought, whether fleeting or more deeply, about how lucky I was, in spite of the occasional rough patches.

All these thoughts flitted through my mind as I walked into the gentle surf of the great Pacific Ocean before me. For me, swimming was another one of those Zen moments, a time for meditation, and I did just that as I eased out far enough beyond the break of the gentle waves. I turned south and, keeping my body parallel to the shore, I swam slowly at first, the salt of my sweat from the day mixing with the salt of the sea. Ashes to ashes, dust to dust, some may say, but also, salt to salt. This was more therapeutic than bathing, but a shower would follow. For now it was just me and the sea, a cleansing at the feet of the gods. Kalei and Lani's friendship had showed me enough of Hawaiian culture that I gave a brief thank you to the various gods and goddesses of the land and sea as I cleared my head.

As I turned around at the imaginary southern line of our little cove, I glanced up and saw movement at the top of the stairs. A slight figure stood there, as still as a statue. I hesitated briefly and tread water as I tried to identify the mysterious visitor, a tiny flutter of wariness preying on my mind. Giving up, I began to swim again, catching sight of the figure each time I turned my head to take a breath; the person was descending slowly like a claymation figure.

I took a few more strokes and opened one eye as I took a breath. The figure had descended a little again. I kept wondering who it might be. He or she didn't act like the average guest who just comes down for a dip in the sea, but I chalked it up to someone perhaps a little unsure about the vast sea before them. Continuing on, I tuned out the stranger because I was beginning to feel my muscles relaxing, my strokes getting longer the farther I swam.

Turning at the northern version of our imaginary line, I reached further and hit my perfect pace. My mind went blank and my years of meditation kicked in. I paid no attention to the possibility of jellyfish or other critters, no attention to the rise and fall of the swell that would become a small wave, no attention to the sand below my body, and definitely no attention to the stranger who had been descending the stairs.

I wrung my braid out as I waded through the low surf back to dry sand. My body was tired from the workout, but my mind was clear. Heading back to my palm tree "hook" I glanced around, happy to see I was alone again. The figure that had been on the stairs was nowhere to be seen. And neither was my towel. Or my sunglasses. And my flip flops were gone too! I slowly turned around, peering up and down the beach and into the thick foliage at the base of the cliffs. Muttering curses under my breath, I headed up the stairs in my bare feet, water dripping off my hair and my swimsuit. The scattered broken sea shells were like the Legos of nature, and my feet kept finding them. "Ouch. Ouch. Ouch," I chanted. What bugged me most though was the absence of Uncle Wally's Bugs Bunny beach towel. Every time I lost a memento like that it felt as though another little piece of my heart was taken. Sing it, Janis! But I was in no mood for music.

I stopped at the top of the stairs and briefly showered the sand and salt off before heading to my bungalow, dripping water along the way and still cursing under my breath. Taylor was gone and the television was mercifully dark. I knocked on her door but there was no answer. Good. She was on her own for the evening then. I grabbed clean clothes and hopped in the shower for a proper wash, then mopped up the puddles I'd made. I wanted my Bugs Bunny towel back, dammit. I put fresh food down for Chester and cracked the sliding glass door for him before heading over to the reception area.

The pool area was empty, as this was the time most people prepared for dinner or other evening excursions around the island. I'm not sure what drove me, but something seemed to be calling me to the pool. Silently, I lifted the lid to the towel bin and peeked in. There were several of our standard white towels so I dug below those and froze. There was my Bugs Bunny towel, my name printed boldly as proof of ownership. Maybe the person who had come down the stairs simply thought someone had left it behind on the beach, but where were my sunglasses and flip flops? Towel in hand, I slowly turned to view the area and wondered if I was being watched.

"Macca?" Kalei's voice made me jump. "Oh, sorry," he continued. "Didn't mean to startle you."

"It's okay." I then motioned him toward the kitchen where we could speak privately.

"What's going on?" he asked once the door swung shut, his brow wrinkled with concern.

I told him about the bird cage the other night and about what had happened today, showing him the towel I'd found in the pool bin. "Although the pranks, or whatever you want to call them, are nothing serious, it's really rather creepy."

Lani had joined us and rested her hand on my arm. "I think it's creepy too."

"I'll tell the rest of the team about it because we all need to be a bit more alert around here," Kalei added. I nodded, my mind wandering a bit.

"Could it be Taylor just being mean?" Lani asked.

"That's been in the back of my mind, yes," I confirmed and saw her shudder.

Kalei put his arm around his wife. "Lani said…" He looked at her and waited for her to nod encouragement. "…that there's something very dark about her."

"Dark?"

"Something isn't right in her head, I mean," Lani explained.

I chuckled, an unusual sound devoid of the usual mirth. "That I can agree with."

"Be careful, Macca," Kalei urged, looking troubled.

"I will." I turned to go back to my bungalow, but a sudden flash of a thought caused me to detour, so I jogged up the stairs to the parking lot and identified all the cars. My own Roomba, the Morrisons' Odyssey, and The Shouting Family's rental were nearby, with employee vehicles on the far side. Taylor's rental was nowhere to be seen. I wondered what time she had left the premises and where she had gone. Frustrated, I turned and trudged back down the stairs to my bungalow, wishing it was all mine again. I was quite done with having house guests, with the exception of the one ghostly guest. Unfortunately, his visits had been less frequent these days.

After showering and dressing to work the dinner service, I headed back to the main kitchen to help Kalei and Lani. I found Susie hanging around at the back door near the Imu oven when I stepped out to dump some scraps in Kalei's compost bin.

"Hey Susie." I stopped to pat his head and stroke his ears. "You waiting for scraps?"

No. Just standing guard, I heard him in my head. And while this information was encouraging, it was still odd to have added yet another voice to my growing cast of characters. This was giving new meaning to the term theater of the mind.

"Well…" I hesitated just a beat. "Thank you." I tossed him a hunk of carrot from the scrap bin before dumping the rest into the compost and returning to the kitchen.

As I set the tables in the dining area, I noticed Chester sprawled on the pavement near the pool, his tail repeatedly smacking angrily on the ground, his ears in constant motion. So he was on guard duty too, I supposed. I sighed and just hoped Glory wouldn't appear as well; there's no way to explain away the sudden appearance of a 1,200 pound horse. Wait. Does a ghost horse actually weigh 1,200 pounds? Pondering such a subject proved it was destined be a very long night.

When dinner service was over and the facilities were prepped for the next day, Kalei and Lani waited to walk me to my door. We put Winston and Marley to bed in their cage and locked up. I put a hand up to stop Kalei and Lani briefly though, and ran up the stairs to the parking lot. Taylor's car was still nowhere to be seen, and I breathed a heavy sigh of relief before returning to the waiting couple at my door.

"All clear." I wiped my forehead, still damp from the heat of the kitchen work.

"She's not here?"

"No, thankfully. I think I'll just turn in."

"Lock your bedroom door? Please?" Lani implored me, her soft hands on my arm, the weight of sheer comfort.

"I will. I promise." I nodded emphatically as I spoke. Susie and Chester strolled over, waiting to be let in.

"And keep your security detail with you." Kalei's grin shone in the moonlight as he leaned down to give each critter a pat. I nodded, opened the door, and let Susie go in first, knowing he would do a quick search of the premises. I waved to Kalei and Lani and closed my door, locking it against... whom? The one person I was beginning to suspect already had her own key. I shrugged. It just felt good to go through the motions.

In my room, I refreshed the food for Susie and Chester. They trotted behind me, close on my heels, as I went back and forth between the kitchen, the bedroom, the bathroom, and back to the kitchen, an ever-connected train. The Disorient Express. I giggle-snorted and poured myself a glass of white wine before we choo-choo'd back to my room where we locked ourselves in for the night. Chester climbed into his FedEx box and Susie curled up on his bed by my closet and the sliding glass door. I slipped into a comfortable sleep shirt and crawled between the sheets, turning out the bedside lamp and picking up my Kindle to read. I believe I managed two pages before I put the device down and allowed myself to fall asleep to the sound of quiet snores from Susie and the soft rumble of Chester's purrs.

SIXTEEN

Twirling Socks and a Floating Tea Mug

I was dreaming of soft clouds and blue skies when I felt someone shaking me, urgently calling my name. Forcing my eyelids open, I came nose to nose with Davy. Of course you wouldn't ever hear me complaining about that view, but I digress.

"Good morning," he said, sounding far too chipper for my liking. He kissed my forehead and flopped on the bed beside me, giving it a few extra childlike bounces.

"Stop that!" I rubbed my face. He gave the bed two more bounces, that impish grin of his firmly in place. "Oh my God. You're so incorrigible," I continued.

"Contrary to the exclamations of beautiful ladies in the past, I am not God. I am, however, incorrigible, or so I've been told many times."

He was relishing this. How can an insult end up being that enjoyable? I turned over and buried my head under my pillow. "Go away, and take that inflated ego with you."

He pulled the pillow away and tossed it on the rocking chair. "Nope. Not going away."

I groaned when I saw the time. "It's too early!"

"No it's not. It's time to watch the sun rise. Time to experience the birth of a new day. It's time…"

"Oh stop it. I'm up, I'm up." I rolled out of bed. Chester lifted his head from his FedEx box, grumbled something unintelligible, and went back to sleep. I stumbled about the room, pulling on my lightweight sweatpants and a hoodie over my sleep shirt. Davy was pawing through my underwear drawer. "What are you doing?" I asked, appalled at the invasion of privacy. But he answered by way of tossing me a pair of fuzzy socks, which bounced off my face and landed in my hands.

"Good catch. Sort of." He chuckled. "You'll need those. It's a bit breezy out there."

I hopped on one foot, trying to slip a sock on the other, then fell against the closet door. Oh good. Propped against it, I was then able to put both socks on. Hey, I wasn't totally awake yet.

Susie followed us out the sliding glass door and lay at our feet when we settled in the two comfy chairs. I tucked my stockinged feet up under me and pulled my hoodie closer. It was breezy and dark. I equate dark with cold. It's hard to unthink a lifetime of conditioning, but I was working on it. In reality, it was probably about 70F/21C. That last bit of information was thanks to Davy, who was always switching back and forth from Celsius to Fahrenheit in a grand attempt to thoroughly confuse me. I was especially convinced of this during times of interrupted sleep, such as this morning.

Davy poked my shoulder and pointed out to sea, then ran his hand down my arm to gently grasp my hand. A line of pink tinged light barely whispered on the horizon, turning the black night sea to a metallic gray. I held my breath as the colors slowly changed and spread. Pinks, corals, deep magenta, and fuchsia ebbed into the darkness, slowly brightening both the sea and the sky. I took a deep breath and let the tension leave my body.

"It's like a tie-dyed canvas," he whispered.

"On hand-painted silk," I added, and he squeezed my hand. When the sky reached a pale blue with pastels spreading abroad, I sighed deeply. "Thank you for waking me up to see this." I smiled and gave his hand a reciprocal squeeze.

He smiled broadly, the sweetness spreading to his eyes, and then he stretched his closed hand out to me. "I brought something for you."

I held my own hand out and he dropped another tiny gift from his fist. It was wrapped in what looked like sandwich paper, and I chuckled. "A miniature sandwich?"

He grinned and shrugged his shoulders. "It was the only wrapping I could get."

I opened the sandwich wrapper to find a lovely hand carved wooden Amish buggy and a white horse. "Oh Davy." I brought the wooden piece to my nose and took a deep breath. "I love the smell of carved wood." I turned my face to look at him, and my heart caught. He was staring at the carving, a sort of dreamy, hazy look on his face. "This is meaningful to you too, isn't it?"

He raised his eyebrows and they disappeared into his long hair. "I had a similar buggy."

"And horses," I whispered. "Thank you, Davy. Really. It's beautiful!" I leaned over and kissed his cheek. "And thank you for the sunrise. There's no one else I'd rather share it with."

"You're welcome." His voice was thick but he smiled through it, and then he sat up straight and cleared his throat. "Actually, I have news as well."

I sat up a little straighter in my seat too. "Is Bettina okay?"

He gave a quick grin then. "Mr. Pinckney said she's fine, and he's decided she's boring." He chuckled before continuing. "Pot and kettle there, frankly."

"Boring? How can one *not* be boring in a jail cell?" I chuckled.

"Good point." He grinned. "But my news is that the police found Bettina's camera. The problem is, the memory card wasn't inside."

I frowned. "Where did they find the camera?"

"In the laundry of the hotel where the ladies were staying. A worker reported it."

I stared out at the view, thinking nearly deep thoughts. Hey, it was still early. Suddenly I turned to stare at Davy. "It could be here somewhere in Taylor's belongings!"

"Why do you say that?" He had an almost make-believe suspicious look on his face, and I knew he was a better actor than that, so I had a feeling I was on the right track.

And then words came out of my mouth before I could even think. "Because I think Taylor killed Annie and framed her mother." My hand flew to my mouth. "Where did that come from?"

Davy was grinning at me, a look of supreme satisfaction on his face. "Look at you, going all prescient on me!"

"Wait a minute," I frowned. "Why did you tell me Bettina didn't do it?"

"To keep your thoughts open. You have the answers inside you, just let them speak to you."

"What?" I was thoroughly confused.

"You have a gift. You need to open up and let it free."

"But what if I don't want this gift?"

He grinned then and gently pointed at my chest. "Your heart won't let you turn your back on it if it means helping others. You know that."

I rubbed my face and ran a hand through my unruly hair, a simple, sometimes alluring move, right? Except that my fingers got caught and I spent the next seconds trying to free them, giving me time to process his words.

When I looked up, Davy was grinning and shaking his head. "Affectations and you? Oil and water, Babe. Oil and water. Just be you."

My cheeks burning, I stood abruptly, a thought invading my momentary embarrassment. "I need to find out if Taylor is here." I trotted down the deck stairs, passed the reception area which was still all buckled up, then up the other stairs to the parking lot. Quite pleased with myself at the realization that I wasn't even winded, I surveyed the lot. Her rental was parked at the end. Damn.

My return to the deck where Davy awaited was just a bit slower. "She's here," I whispered as I headed inside. The bathroom hadn't been touched and Taylor's door was closed. "Double damn," I whispered again. Back in my deck chair beside Davy I sighed loudly. "I'll watch for her to leave."

He patted my hand. "Whistle for me when she does."

"Whistle?"

"Yeah. You know... put your lips together and... blow."

"Har-de-har. But I don't know how to whistle. I never learned."

"What? How can that even be? I thought everyone knew how to whistle," he continued to tease.

I shook my head. He put his fingers between his lips and blew out the loudest, shrillest, most eardrum-shattering shriek of a whistle. "Holy crap." I clapped my hands over my ears as he laughed at my ineptitude, my weak reaction, or both. "You could summon an army with that sound!"

"Okay, never mind then. Just call out to me."

"That I can do."

"Right. Then I'm out of here. Got things to do. People to see. Bullies to spook and taunt. You know, the same old thing." His eyes twinkled and I chuckled quietly. "Love ya Babe." He whispered as he stood and kissed my forehead.

"Love ya right back," I spoke in a hush as he shimmered out, leaving me alone with Chester and Susie. "Hungry?"

Yes please, the well mannered dog replied.

Of course, the less well mannered cat snorted. *And breakfast is late. Again.*

Behave yourself, Susie grumbled, and Chester replied with a half-hearted hiss and a gentle swat on the big dog's nose. Susie then plopped his giant paw on the cat's head.

"I see nursery school is in full swing for the day," I muttered as I rose to prepare their meals.

After the kiddies were fed, I sliced a banana into a small bowl of Grape-Nuts and added some milk while water boiled for a cup of tea. Standing up, I munched and crunched my breakfast, using the extensive chewing time to make my tea. *Do you still suck the milk out of the cereal while you chew*? I heard the question in my head, the voice distinctly that of my mother. Chuckling, I nodded my answer, my mouth full of banana and cereal. I heard a responding titter in my head, a sound similar to the tinkling of glass wind chimes in a gentle breeze.

There was no sign of movement from Taylor as I finished my quick clean-up of breakfast dishes, then brushed my teeth. Once I was fully dressed I headed out to start the day. I released Winston and Marley from their cage and stowed the cover. They made a gentle ruckus as they flew and fluttered about, stretching both their wings and their vocal chords at the same time. I watched them for a good five minutes, feeling my mood lifting again after having it temporarily darkened by thoughts of Annie's murder.

Throwing open the doors and shuttered windows, I thought about Taylor, Bettina, and Annie. Where to search for that memory card was what was crowding my mind as I booted up the main computer before placing my own laptop on the bar adjacent to the reception area. I began to work on the inn's email and then the purchase orders for supplies.

Bennie was whistling as he sauntered through the door. Great, everyone could whistle except me. I licked my lips and puckered but only air came out.

"Morning." Bennie was smiling. "Whatcha doin'?"

"Trying to whistle."

He chuckled. "I thought everyone could whistle," he taunted as he lugged the large coffee urn to the kitchen in order to make his magic Kona elixir for staff and guests alike. He reappeared and set the urn on the counter in the reception area, plugging it in to allow it to perk. Soon the enticing smell of dark roasted fresh coffee filled the area. My mind wandered away from my tasks and all thoughts of memory cards until Bennie brought me a mug of the magical potion.

"That'll get your motor revving." He smiled and began to tap keys on the desktop computer, a rapid fire rata tat tat sound.

"Thank you. You are today's hero." I held the mug under my nose and breathed deeply before taking a tentative sip of the steaming brew to test the temperature, then I blew on it a few times more before proceeding. After a few swallows, I turned back to my work, and more than an hour later I caught movement out of the corner of my eye. Taylor approached and poured herself a cup of Kona.

"Morning," she addressed me, ignoring Bennie.

"Good morning." I noticed she had her purse with her. "Going somewhere?"

"Yeah. I bought a tourist package that includes a submarine tour in Kona followed by a *real* luau." I heard the sneer in her voice when she mentioned the luau and did my best to ignore it, which wasn't difficult when I remembered that such a package was extremely pricey.

"Wow. That's a pricey endeavor."

"I can afford it now."

"Oh really?"

"Yeah. With Mom going down for Grandma's murder, the estate goes to me."

The words she chose were interesting yet chilling. Not... *Since Mom killed Grandma... but... With Mom going down for Grandma's murder.* My eyes narrowed as I studied her. "Yeah. I can see you're really broken up about it," I deadpanned, staring her down and daring her to respond. Instead she turned on her heel.

"See you tonight."

"Yeah." I watched her go and then quickly finished up my tasks before closing the laptop and tucking it under my arm. "Bennie, I've got some stuff to do in my bungalow. Give me a call if you need me."

"Okay." He was engrossed in whatever was showing on his monitor, so I scooted home.

Davy! I yelled in my mind, and he shimmered in.

"She's gone?"

"For several hours, yes!"

"Brilliant!" We headed to her room. Our plan to methodically search every inch was pretty much destroyed when we saw the mess it was in. Clothing was strewn on the bed, the floor, the chair, and heaped in the closet. Dirty dishes were stacked on every other available surface. I groaned.

"So do I clean it up and let her know I was in here, or take a chance on her not noticing that things might be in different positions?"

We both stood with our hands on our hips as we surveyed the mess and then looked at each other.

"Clean it up," we spoke in unison, and I chuckled. After all, I could claim Ming cleaned the bungalow while on her rounds. Davy began with the dirty dishes, stacking them and carting them to my little kitchen. I could hear him singing as he rinsed the dishes and stacked them in the dishwasher. "It's a little bit me, and it's a little bit you... boom boom boom... too."

Giggling softly, I could even imagine him dramatically jabbing two fingers in the air. I picked up clothes and hung them on hangers or folded and stacked them in the dresser. The advantage I had was that I could also take the time to paw through anything in the closet and dresser. I checked every pocket and all the folds and hems of each piece of clothing.

Davy soon joined me and began to check under the mattress, tidying after ourselves as we went along. We checked the pillows, window coverings, paintings on the walls, the rugs, chair cushion, and the baseboards. We crawled on our hands and knees and checked under the furniture and inside the closet. We flipped through the pages of every magazine and book, felt under lamps and inside lampshades, and came up with zero. Sitting on the floor, we stared at each other.

"What have we missed?" Davy muttered. I flopped backward and lay on the floor, staring at the scene. Then I remembered the ceiling fan joke I'd played on Davy. Jumping to my feet, I dragged the chair next to the bed, climbed up, and stood on tiptoes. I felt the top side of each fan blade.

"Wow. If this ceiling fan is this dusty after only just a couple of weeks, I can't imagine how bad the fan in the living room is," I mumbled. Davy trotted out the door and returned with a dust cloth. "Thank you!" I began to run the cloth over the top of each blade, working blind. Suddenly I felt the cloth snag on something. "Ohmygosh," the words came out in a rush of breath. I stood higher on my toes, and Davy put his arms around my legs to support me. My fingers inched along the surface until I felt a piece of something curled up. It was just close enough to the edge that I was able to give it a tug. I stared at the piece of tape in my hand which was attached to a memory card. Speechless, I just held it out to Davy.

"Bravo!" He took it and carefully held just the tape between his fingers. I briefly pondered the existence of ghostly fingerprints when it suddenly became apparent that we both had a more urgent thought.

"Laptop!" We sang out in unison.

I quickly put the chair back where it belonged, snatched up the filthy dust cloth, and followed Davy to my room where we booted up the laptop. Carefully peeling the tape off, we used my tweezers to hold the card by the edges, feeding it into the SD card reader, then into the laptop's USB port. It took quite a while to copy hundreds of photos and videos onto my hard drive, and once the procedure was complete I gingerly replaced the memory card on the piece of tape, still making sure to keep my fingerprints off the card itself. I stuck the tape to a piece of paper, folded it, and put it inside an empty envelope.

"Do we look at the photos first or get this to the police?" I wondered aloud.

"It will take hours to study each photo. Call your boyfriend Detective Green."

Appalled, I shrank back from him. "He is not my boyfriend!"

Davy was chuckling and scrolling through photos. "Just call him."

"Okay, but he is not my boyfriend. He's not even my friend-friend."

"Fine. Call him anyway."

"But that was a rotten thing to say," I muttered as I scrolled through my contact list and placed the call. Davy's shoulders shook with laughter, and I gave him a solid punch on his arm.

"Ouch." He rubbed his bicep. "You have pointy fists."

Remarkably, I was able to get through to Detective Green on the first try. Even when I was accused of murder not too long ago he would never have answered my call so quickly, and within the hour I had a house full of police personnel. I showed them where I found the memory card taped to the top of the fan blade as Davy shimmered away.

"What made you look there?" Green asked me.

I put on my most confident face and kept my response short while silently apologizing to Ms. Karma and the universe. "I was cleaning." He gave me a sideways glance so I pulled the filthy dust cloth that had been hanging out of my now equally filthy back pocket. He raised his eyebrows briefly but turned back to the techs who were taking photos of the room yet again. Since this poorly chosen family of mine had come to visit there had been far too much police presence.

Detective Green followed me out to the living room and we stood there waiting for the techs to finish their job. His eyes followed the gently twirling socks on the fan hanging from the high ceiling in the living room.

"Do you also dust that one?" His skepticism was palpable, but I kept a brave face.

"That one only gets done once in a while since it requires such a tall ladder." I thought that sounded plausible enough and he seemed to accept it. Whew, a bullet dodged.

"Then how did the socks get there?"

"Um… practical joke. *Private* practical joke." I turned to the kitchen to make some tea and was relieved when he didn't follow. My hands were shaking as I put the kettle on and opened the lid of my tea canister. I studied the intricate and colorful design of the hinged tin container just to focus and settle my nerves. It had been my mother's since before I was born, and it never failed to bring a smile to my lips and warmth to my heart every time I viewed it, but today I was deeply missing my mom.

I'm here, Monkee Paw.

But not really, I lamented in my thoughts, and I felt her fade away. The whistling of the kettle brought me out of my reverie, and I emptied the hot tap water that I'd used to warm the Brown Betty teapot. I'd fallen in love with a similar teapot that Lani used in the main kitchen and had recently found one of my own in a second hand store. I tossed the tea bags in and poured the boiling water over them, then left it to steep under a quilted tea cozy while I gazed at the little collection of Davy's gifts on the sill. I couldn't help but smile away my melancholy feeling.

I felt him shimmer in beside me, his hand on my back. "You did the right thing, Babe."

"I know," I responded in hushed tones, "but it doesn't make me feel that much better."

He rubbed my back and I took deep breaths. My cell vibrated in my pocket and Davy took a few steps away from me to allow me to answer the call. It was Bennie asking why the police were here. As I explained, I watched absentmindedly while Davy prepared two mugs of tea, added milk, and handed one over to me while he dumped a couple pounds of sugar into his own. I inhaled the warm steam from my cup and felt myself relax. Satisfied that I was okay, Bennie promised to handle the front desk while I waited for the police to finish. It was going to be a long day since this was delaying not only my normal work but also the review of the hundreds of photos and videos now residing on my laptop. It was then I heard my name being called from the living room. I motioned to Davy to keep himself and his seemingly floating tea mug in the kitchen, set my own mug down, and rounded the corner to find Detective Green standing with a lab tech.

"Oh, there you are," he began, acting as if he didn't know I was in the kitchen. I considered this briefly; this man was a mystery I didn't care to solve. "Just wanted you to know that we've got everything. We'll be leaving now." He was all business again, which suited him better than his out of place friendliness.

"Thank you." I showed them out the door, latching it firmly behind them with a heavy sigh. Now there was work to do. I glanced at the time and my heart began to race. "Davy! We have housework to do!" He shimmered in beside me. "Good shortcut." I grinned. We quickly set Taylor's borrowed room to rights again, removing fingerprint dust and straightening all of her items that had been moved by the techs. It only took a few minutes with both of us working together, and it wasn't long before we were back in my bedroom with the laptop, pouring over the photos, leaving the videos for last.

I glanced at the clock, as my estimation of Taylor's return time was edging closer. The photos consisted mostly of landscape shots including panoramic views of lava trees and close-up images of tropical flowers. Nothing really jumped out at us, but I found the anomaly of heavy winter wear — parkas, jeans, hats — to be quite foreign to me in this tropical climate. Yet, viewing photos of Annie smiling for her daughter behind the camera tugged at my heart. Finding no clues in the photos, we switched our attention to the videos, which proved to be ever the more heart-wrenching. We could hear Bettina's voice behind the camera as she filmed Annie standing at her portable easel, paintbrush in hand. Annie dabbing at colors on a palette and then applying them to a small canvas.

Annie pointing to the steam vents and then toward the lava trees. Annie calling to Taylor as the younger family member surreptitiously slid something into her oversized coat pocket. Wait, what? We backed it up several times and watched again, unable to identify the fairly large item. The world slowed down as I heard the recording of Taylor's voice telling Bettina that she was returning to the hotel, and Bettina suggesting they meet in the lounge, but Taylor saying she'd call her cell instead. I turned and met Davy's eyes.

"Taylor has been lying all this time." He frowned.

"And Bettina let her; she didn't dispute the lie."

"Wow," we whispered in unison. This was chilling evidence.

"What on earth do you think she…" but before I could finish my question, Davy jumped up as if stung by a bee.

"Bloody hell!" Davy looked to me, fear and sadness in his eyes. "Gotta go." He shimmered out without any further explanation. I was left staring at the empty space he'd left behind. It was Chester jumping up onto my lap that brought me out of my stupor.

He did have to leave. It was unavoidable.

I only nodded, idly stroking his orange fur. He stayed on my lap, purring loudly as I finished watching the remaining footage. Although I found nothing more disturbing than the previous, I felt it was vital to view each file. When at last I was able to close the laptop, I felt stowing it between mattress and box spring, my usual habit, wouldn't be quite safe enough. I moved all the files to a single folder and set the permissions to private, password protected using an obscure code word, and then carried it with me to the reception area.

Bennie was staring intently at the monitor as I rounded the desk to peer over his shoulder at the list of vendors we used. "What's up?"

"Oh." He made a sound of irritation in the back of his throat. "The prep sink in the kitchen keeps backing up. Kalei and I tried to plunge it but…"

"Again?"

"Yeah. Time to call the plumber. Sorry."

I gave his shoulder a pat. "We knew it was coming. Better now than over the weekend."

"This is true." He picked up the desk phone and began to dial.

"I have to go down south tomorrow and will be gone all day." I watched as he nodded. I'd left my destination vague,

"I've got you covered," he whispered just before he greeted the person on the other end of the line. I stowed my laptop in the safe and proceeded to the kitchen to assist in meal prep for the evening ahead. My thoughts were whirling as I attended to the now familiar tasks. By the time the evening was over and the premises were cleaned and closed up for the night, it was quite late. I walked with Kalei, Lani, and Sam up to the parking lot, checked to see that Taylor's rental car was there, said goodbye to my friends, and then headed back to my bungalow.

Steeling myself for her presence, I was pleasantly surprised that the television was dark and the only lights on were the usual ones I left for myself. Taylor's door was closed and I could see light under it. I quickly fed Chester and Susie then reheated a cup of tea for myself before we retired to my bedroom.

The next morning, Roomba and I pulled out of the parking lot just a few seconds past way-too-early. As I had expected, Taylor's rental car remained in its spot at the very end of the parking lot.

The trip down to Volcanoes National Park was peaceful at that hour, and I drove at my own pace. I used the quiet time to think and create a plan of action for the day. Not too far into my journey, my phone buzzed in the drink holder. I pulled over to the side of the road where there was a safe turnout and set the brake before answering.

"What's up Bennie?"

"Detective Green is here. He asked for Taylor," Bennie continued, "but he gave me a message for you as well."

"Yeah? What's going on now?"

"Bettina tried to commit suicide yesterday. She's okay, but they've got her in the infirmary under watch."

I let out a long and heavy sigh. "Oh no." I rubbed my face as if I could erase this news. "Okay Bennie. Thank you for letting me know. Did Detective Green get the news to Taylor, too?"

"Yeah, and she split a couple of minutes ago. Had a beach bag slung over her arm but went toward the parking lot."

"Really broken up, I guess." I allowed the sarcasm to drip from my words.

"I'm sorry, Macca." Bennie's voice was like a balm to my troubled heart.

"Thanks. I'll see you later."

"Afternoon or evening?"

"Probably late afternoon."

We ended the call, and I called out to Davy in my mind. He shimmered in beside me and reached out to hold me; I felt comfort in his arms and hoped no one was watching.

"She's okay, Babe. She's awake and functioning."

"What did she do?"

"She tore her shirt and tried to hang herself."

I shuddered and he held me tighter. "Is that why you left so suddenly?"

"Yeah. Pinckney called out to me."

"Do you think I could see her?"

"No. No visitors. I'm sorry. I heard the instructions being dictated."

"Okay." I sighed heavily.

We sat together in the silence for what seemed like a long time. It was Davy who broke the spell. "Are you okay?"

I nodded and wiped my eyes with the sleeve of my tee-shirt. He tenderly kissed my cheek before shimmering out. I sat for a minute to compose myself before turning back onto the road. Veering off the main highway in Hilo, I stopped at a small natural grocery store that I'd visited in the past. Their freshly made food selection in the deli included vegetarian fare and I opted for a breakfast burrito and a cup of matcha tea. Sitting at a small table in the soft sunshine of morning, I sipped and ate. The eggs, spinach, tomatoes, and brown rice in the burrito were a tasty and filling meal. After I tossed my wrappings into the trash, I lingered in the sun a little longer while finishing my tea before climbing back into Roomba.

As I was waiting to pull into traffic, my attention was briefly caught by a vaguely familiar car that whipped by. Although out of sight in a second or two, I could have sworn it was Taylor barreling down the highway in her rental car. Traffic was picking up, and soon the vehicle in question was long gone, yet I still found myself watching for it as I made my way to the park.

I stopped at the visitor center, put on my seldom-used heavy coat, and picked up a map which I used to refresh my memory while leaning against little Roomba. I had a rough idea of where I wanted to go so I stowed the map in my pocket and climbed behind the wheel again. Starting at the hotel where Annie, Bettina, and Taylor had stayed, I walked around the grounds before heading inside. I visited the lounge where Bettina had claimed to have stopped for coffee. I didn't feel much of anything, so I poured a cup of coffee for myself and took it to the great room where Taylor said she'd been waiting for her mother. Sitting on one of the many comfortable wicker chairs, I sipped my coffee while enjoying the sweeping views of the steam vents spouting out of the crater.

As I cupped my hands around the warm mug of coffee, the scene before me began to shift, dissected by wavy lines and a sort of haze. I tried to blink, but some unknown but paralyzing force kept them wide open. The scene shifted again and I could see Bettina sitting in a chair in front of the large fireplace I'd noticed in the lounge. Another shift in the

176

view before me and Annie was sitting at her easel, dabbing first at her palette, then her small canvas. The scene took a dizzying turn and showed me that Taylor was creeping up behind her grandmother. Something large in her hands was slowly raised above her head and brought down forcibly. Again and again. I think I yelped and coffee sloshed onto my hands. What the hell had I just seen? Imagination? Or… something else. Was this the "gift" I was supposed to have? If so, I wanted nothing of it.

I stood up, wiped my hand on my pants, and set the mug down in the area designated for dishes to be bussed. Just a little shaken, to say the very least, I headed out of the hotel and back to my car. My hands were unsteady as I inserted the key in the ignition. Based on the vision, or whatever it was, I knew exactly where I needed to go, so I pointed Roomba that way and headed out.

Just a few minutes later I was walking along the path that would lead me past the steam vents. Something, some *force,* drew me there, the vision in the big window playing on a loop in my mind. It was quiet, with only the occasional tourist here and there. Turning slightly off the larger path, I came upon the area I'd seen in my shifting vision. Rooted to the spot where I stood, I took a few steadying breaths and closed my eyes.

Macca, I heard in my thoughts. *You shouldn't be here, sweetheart.* The voice was distinctly Annie's. I kept my eyes closed.

But I need answers, I responded in my mind.

It's not safe.

Why not? She was quiet for a long period, but I felt a patience beyond my usual character.

Because the truth is ugly. The truth is dangerous.

I think I know.

Then you mustn't let her know that you know.

I won't.

It's too late. The voice of her thoughts rose in panic. *She's here. You must go! Now!*

Hearing the crunch of gravel I turned around to see Taylor approaching. Her body language spoke of calmness, but her face was reminiscent of that scene in *The Shining* where Jack Nicholson uses an axe to break through the door. I found myself holding my breath before speaking, a fear rising from deep within. "Taylor." Even I heard the quaver in my voice. "What are you doing here?"

"Following you."

"But… why?" I tried to put forth my best innocent act.

"Because you have something of mine and you're going to give it to me." Her voice was chilling in its monotone, totally devoid of... humanity.

"I don't have anything of yours." I frowned. I was telling the truth actually, since the memory card was in the custody of the police. She stood still, her cold hard eyes filled with disbelief.

"The memory card. From Mom's camera. Where is it?"

Feeling my ears redden, I tried to gloss over it. "I have no idea. Where did you leave it last?" I thought if I made light of it she'd give up.

"You know damn well where I left it. It was taped to a blade of the ceiling fan."

I forced a chuckle then. "Why would you do that? And how did you even reach it?"

"I want it now." The chill in her words caused a shiver to run up my spine.

Standing tall, I took a deep breath. "I gave it to the cops already. You're too late."

"You're lying. I saw you blow past the station where I was waiting, so I followed you."

"When I found the memory card I called them and they picked it up and did another search of your room."

"Liar! I always knew you were stupid and this just proves it. You made me do this. Never forget that."

She covered the few feet between us so quickly that I only had time to take one step back just before she shoved me, hard. Having been unsteady on one foot, the force made me stumble. "Hey! Knock it off!" I pulled out the anger from our childhood, from those times when she would bully me. "Taylor, I have..." She cut off my words by grabbing a handful of my unruly hair and yanking me to my knees.

"You stupid bitch," She spoke so lowly, her face inches from mine, her teeth clenched. "I want that memory card now!"

"You're hurting me." I groaned and imagined hundreds of follicles giving up the fight to ease the pain on my scalp. If only. "I don't have it." Trying with all my might to stay calm, I grasped her hand that was wrapped around my hair, worrying that if I retaliated with the same anger she exhibited, the situation would escalate.

Childhood scenes, previously suppressed, now exploded in my mind. Taylor stealing my toys and then threatening me with bodily harm if I told the adults. Pushing me down the front steps and laughing when I cried over the resulting skinned knee. Holding my head under water in the public pool until the lifeguard saved me and ejected her from the facility. Blaming me for the lamp that she purposely broke. This flash flood of memories was so overwhelming that I stopped fighting against her brutal grip. *Goldfish*, I whispered in my thoughts, just as her other hand arced, bringing something hard down on my head and bashing me again and again until I could feel nothing. I had a vague sense of Davy's shimmer, but I feared it was too late. I never saw him appear.

SEVENTEEN

Killer Pillow and a Guardian Monkee

When I rose from the dead, for my first thought was that I had indeed died, I was enveloped in darkness. There wasn't even a glimmer of moonlight or human made light either. Unable to lift my arms, I couldn't even tell if I could see the hand in front of my face, as the old saying goes. I tried to speak, but there was something blocking my mouth. The searing pain that told me I was still alive, and perhaps wishing otherwise. It was then I realized that my eyes weren't even open, and in fact seemed to be glued shut. *Oh boy*, I thought. *What kind of a royal mess did you get yourself into this time, Macca?*

Panic began to rise inside, trying to bubble up through my blocked mouth. What *was* that in my mouth? Claustrophobia exploded in my mind like Saturday night fireworks against a black velvet sky. I couldn't see, couldn't speak, and was mostly unable to move. A rather manic mantra born of this realization ran through my head: *I'm going to die. I'm buried alive and I'm going to die.*

At last I felt a hand clasp mine as fingers stroked my arm. "Shh." It was Davy's voice. "It's okay, Babe." I felt his lips on my cheek. "You're in hospital," he stated in his oh-so British and comforting manner. "You're going to be fine, and I'm right here."

Why can't I open my eyes? I asked him in my thoughts. *What's this in my mouth? I can't swallow. I'm going to suffocate. What the hell happened?*

I heard him chuckle gently, a surprisingly soothing sound as he squeezed my hand. "You won't suffocate. Your eyes are swollen shut and there's a ventilator inserted down your throat to breathe for you." I felt his lips on my hand then.

I want it out.

"The doctor will remove it when it's safe to do so. When he's sure you can breathe on your own."

What happened?

"You don't remember?" He kept a gentle but firm pressure on my hand.

No. I… What the hell was the last thing I remembered? *I was feeding Chester and Susie.*

"That's the last thing you remember?"

Yes. I think so. I don't know!

He patted my hand and made soothing noises that were anything but. I felt tears squeeze out of my eyes, drip down my temples, and roll uncomfortably into my ears. Davy wiped them away.

"You had a… an accident and hit your head. But you'll be okay. You'll recover fully, I heard the doctor say it. Twice."

I sensed a tinge of worry in his voice which caused more tears to slip out. He was wiping them away when I heard the sound of a door opening. *I'll be over in the corner*, he whispered in my mind, which even in my current state I found mildly amusing. Nobody puts Davy in the corner. Yes, I was losing my mind.

The squeaky sound of multiple pairs of shoes on the floor told me several someones were standing beside me, one taking my hand.

"Are you awake, Miss Liberty?" Recognizing a voice from my past, I squeezed Dr. Lee's hand as hard as I could. Returning the squeeze, I could hear the smile in his voice. "Ahh, very good. I don't know why I keep having you here in our hospital, injured at the hands of evil, but I sure wish you'd knock that off."

I squeezed his hand again as he continued. "I'm going to examine you, and if I'm correct in my estimations, we'll remove the ventilation tube so you can talk. And drink. And eat too, when you're ready."

I squeezed his hand once more. It was unnerving to be examined while unable to see or talk, but of course I hadn't much choice and endured it as bravely as possible. Deep down though, I was terrified. I could hear the low murmurs of voices as the nurse or nurses responded to Dr. Lee's comments and questions.

You're doing well. Davy was in my mind again and I welcomed him there. Somehow he even managed to hold my hand and whisper to me as they removed the tube. It wasn't fun at all, but he made it easier with his support. When at last I was free of the great plastic snake, I tried several times in vain to swallow. The nurse spoke quietly and guided a straw to my lips. Still unable to open my eyes, I found my lips fumbling to sip the water, and it was bliss when I did finally get a couple of tiny swallows.

It was then that the pain I'd originally felt slowly grew in my head, searing my brain. I tried to speak but it only came off my dry lips as a puff sound.

"Are you feeling pain, dear?" The nurse was a smart cookie. She placed a cool pack across my face.

I made the puff sound again and heard the doctor order something. I sure hoped it was drugs. Within seconds I began to feel floaty and decided to sleep.

When I woke up again my sense of time was distorted, but I sensed movement beside me. I tried once more to open my eyes, to no avail. My lips were so dry and cracked, my mouth full of scorched earth at the end of the world. Overly dramatic? You bet. I learned from the best, and he was at that moment holding my hand.

Are you awake? Davy's thoughts came to me.

Yes. How long was I asleep?

I don't know exactly. Several hours maybe.

Letting that sink in for a few beats, I tried to lick my lips. *So thirsty.* Suddenly the straw was between my lips and I gulped hungrily.

"Not too much all at once," he whispered then and pulled the straw from my lips.

My head felt thick. And hot. *Why is my head so hot?* It was easier to communicate with thoughts.

You're heavily bandaged.

I am? Why?

You had an accident.

Where? He sighed heavily and I sensed he was unhappy. Was he upset with me? I asked him in my mind. *Are you mad at me?*

A little.

Why?

Because you went off by yourself like the impulsive twit that you are and got yourself in trouble. Again.

I did?

He growled. Or there was a bear in the room. Not being able to see, I decided to assume it was him. *I think you should sleep,* he growled some more.

Okay. But I felt tears creeping out of my eyes and he gently wiped them away.

It's okay, Babe. Don't cry. Please. I didn't mean to make you cry. You just scared me, that's all. But he held me while I wept anyway, until merciful sleep arrived.

Once again I awoke disoriented. The room was silent and obviously deserted. I attempted to open my eyes, but the swelling was still far too heavy. Unable to reach the remote-button-call-thingy, even if I could see it to find it, I just lay there in misery, calling out a few times with a mouth that was a sandbox. I gave my weak body a stern talking to before making the effort to lift my arm and feel around for the remote-button-call-thingy. What *do* they call those? I slowly patted the bed around me, making a grumbling sound deep in my throat the entire time, and came up empty. Add exhaustion to the pain and I was nearing a point of breakdown. I felt the shimmer beside me just as I was about to dissolve into tears of frustration.

"Why didn't you call me?" the familiar Mancunian accent implored. I lifted my hand and touched the comforting velvet of his sleeve. Holy cow, I loved that shirt. And him.

"I didn't want to pester you," I whispered through a rough throat.

"Pester me? You, who constantly called me *The Pest* for the longest time, didn't think that a simple calling out for help was acceptable?" He was chuckling in his endearingly raspy manner and I had to smile, even though it hurt my face.

"I was just looking for that thing that you push a button to call for a nurse."

"You mean... a *call button*?" I may have had a head injury, but his sarcasm wasn't lost on me.

"Smartass. Yeah. That thing."

He placed it in my hands and directed my finger to press on the button. "It's the top one." And he shimmered away, his laughter fading in the darkness.

"You just wait until I can open my eyes again," I mumbled just as the door whooshed open.

The nurse fussed around me and I found it comforting, almost parental. She set the call button right near my side and guided my hand to it so I could easily find it next time. A fresh cool pack was placed across my eyes before she fetched more medication to ease my pain and let me sleep. As I drifted off I realized that I had no sense of day or night and it was unnerving. It was then I had to face the truth: I was a control freak. Brief thoughts of a 12-step program for that affliction were chased away by dreamless sleep.

When next I awoke, I tried to remember the events leading up to my current situation. I even squished up my face, trying to force the memories, but all I got was a shimmer at my side and a laughing Davy kissing my cheek.

"Hey, you left here laughing at me. Don't come back doing the same thing, buster!" I was all whispering bark and no bite, of course.

"Want me to leave then?"

"No," I sulked.

I felt the bed shift a bit and reached out to find his velvet sleeve again and the leg of his pants as he perched on the edge. "How are you feeling?"

"Restless and tired and hurting and... blind."

"You're not blind. Your eyes are still swollen."

"Whatever."

I heard him chuckle again as he put his hand on my cheek. "Your inner teenager is showing."

"Shut up."

"I rest my case." He kissed my cheek. "Just checking on you. Now I gotta go."

"Again?" Even I heard the whine in my voice.

"I'll be back." And he shimmered away.

Left alone, the pain in my head became my main focus, so I pushed the call button for the magic meds.

I was in and out of sleep more times than I could count and was beginning to believe I'd been in this state for weeks on end. One of those times when I awoke from my drug induced vegetative state, I felt a certain shift of the energy in the room. "Hello?" I was calling out to anyone within earshot but was greeted with silence. Something told me that the silence was a lie; there was someone with me, and it wasn't a friendly force. I began to fumble for my lifeline, the call button, but it wasn't in its usual spot. "Who's there?"

"You look like shit." It was a woman with a hard voice.

"Who are you?"

"Can't see, huh? What a shame." But there was no compassion in her voice, only mockery. "The perfect Macca can't see." She clucked her tongue.

"I asked who you are." I put a lot more strength behind the question than I was feeling.

"Taylor."

"Taylor who?"

I could feel her leaning against the bed's safety rail and heard her derisive laugh. "Awww, did we lose our memory? How… fortunate. For me that is. How I enjoyed scaring you when you were swimming, stealing your stuff. Oh, and I love your sunglasses. They're mine now. The flip flops though? Too tacky for me. I chucked them in a dumpster. And too bad I ran out of time or I would have taken delight in the death of your dumb birds. Letting them out was as far as I got."

And then it dawned on me. Taylor. Bettina. Poor Annie. The memories came flooding back and the tears ran unchecked. "You're a monster." I spit out the words.

"Aha, memory coming back, hmm? Too bad for you." In a half beat my face was covered with something soft but dense, perhaps a pillow? She must have put her weight into it, and I began to thrash as my oxygen was cut off. Frantic, I grabbed at the bed, patting all over the area where I thought the call button should be. My hand beat a frenzied rhythm on the mattress until suddenly I found it. Holding the device firmly in my hand, I used every ounce of strength and leverage to arc it right into the area where I estimated her head was, and I felt a deep satisfaction when it connected with my target. Her weight on me fell away and I stabbed at the call button. I was reaching up to grab the killer pillow away from my face when the door whooshed open and I heard raised voices. Soon my room felt full of humanity as more people were called to help. The nurse pulled the pillow away from my face and checked my vitals, clucking away in a soothing and motherly manner. "You're safe now," she murmured.

It worked. "Will you be my mother?" I asked her, only half joking.

I felt her cool hand on my cheek. "I would be honored to be the mother of such a brave young woman."

I felt Davy's shimmer. *She's right*, he whispered in my thoughts. *I'm so proud of you.*

"Did they catch her?"

"Joe, an orderly who is our hero in the ward, has her tied up, dear," my new mother cooed. "You're safe now," she repeated that last part, and that's when I began to cry great wracking sobs. I cried for Annie, crushed under blows similar to my own, her life plucked away ruthlessly. I cried for Bettina, mistakenly incarcerated for a crime her daughter had committed. For Bettina, now motherless, and oh, how I knew of that pain. For Bettina again, wondering if she had suspected her daughter all along, and as a result had tried to kill herself. Bettina, all alone, like I had been before Davy rescued me so long ago.

I'm right here. I'm not leaving. He was in my thoughts again.

I answered back. *Promise?*

I promise.

I slept long and hard after my ordeal, but fortunately it was a dreamless sleep. When I awoke I was ravenous. Miraculously, I was able to open my eyes just enough to let some light in despite the stabbing pain after so much darkness.

You have company, Davy sent his thoughts to me.

"Hey," someone spoke quietly beside me. It hurt to turn my head so I attempted to peer out of the corner of my slits for eyes but could only make out vague human shapes, all with dark hair. I took a stab at it though.

"Is that who I think it is? Kalei, Lani, Bennie?" I felt a smile on my lips, spreading like warm butter on a fresh biscuit. A sense of hunger briefly flitted through my mind.

Hearing multiple breaths being let out, I relaxed, knowing I'd gotten it right even before they began clamoring to answer me all at once.

"You are in a mountain of trouble young lady," Lani teased before kissing my cheek.

"I'm so sorry."

"Yeah, well, you're grounded for two weeks," Kalei joined in, also following it with a kiss.

"Practicing that Daddy stuff, I see." I grinned.

"Macca..." Bennie held my hand. "Don't you ever do that again. You hear?"

"I promise. Never again. I'm no Nancy Drew. I get it now."

"Nancy who?" they asked in unison, then chuckled.

"Kalei, you aren't by chance packing an omelet in your pocket, are you?"

"Hungry? Let's get you some food." I could hear him talking to someone near the door before he returned to my side. Shortly after, a nurse arrived carrying a tray.

"Wow. That's some fine service." I laughed weakly.

"It's just broth and jello." The nurse seemed apologetic.

"She's vegetarian." Kalei ran interference.

"Oh! That's right. I'll return in a couple minutes." And off she went. True to her word, she returned quickly with a mug of vegetable broth and a glass of cranberry juice. She helped me adjust the bed so that I was in a nearly upright position, and then she moved the food closer to me.

I chose to drink the broth first, and had taken my first sip before she even got out the door. She chuckled as my delight over the food made me exclaim after the first sip. "Oh my," I kept saying with each subsequent sip. It was indeed heavenly. I drank it all, then sank back on the pillows and let out a contented sigh.

Lani moved the tray away from my bed and smoothed my blanket. I closed my swollen eyes and promptly fell asleep. When I awoke sometime later I was alone.

"Some hostess you are, Mac," I mused.

"You're a fine hostess." I heard his voice before the shimmer.

Davy took my hand and kissed my cheek before taking a seat beside my bed.

"Thank you. How are you?"

"How am I?" He made a snorting sound. "I'm fine. I'm not the one who was beaten and then smothered."

"I wasn't smothered. She only tried."

"She tried and you clocked her." He grinned. "Man, you swung that so fiercely you knocked her out! Remind me never to piss you off!"

He had me chuckling. "I have a certain Guardian Monkee who empowers me, I guess."

"Guardian Monkee? I kinda like that." He shimmered into his Monkeeman suit, complete with thick black eyeglass frames, and preened a bit. "Guardian Monkee!" He puffed out his chest. "Able to shimmer in at the drop of a goldfish!"

He adjusted the thick glasses and opened his mouth to continue, but I interrupted. "Are those *spook*tacles?"

He gave a dramatic sigh that spoke volumes to my lack of ghostly knowledge. "I'll have you know that these are my special x-ray vision glasses." He stared at my body until I laughed, pulling the blanket up to my chin. "Fine then." He averted his stare.

"I defeated Monkeeman, my Guardian Monkee, with… a *blanket*?" I began to giggle then.

"You've learned our secret, that blankets are our kryptonite, and now you must pay the price… with fifty kisses!" He swooped in and kissed my cheeks and nose and then licked my face from my chin to my eye. "That last one was from Susie. He sends his love."

His sense of fun was refreshing and uplifting at the same time. He had me laughing openly and sporting a vastly lighter mood as a result. "I see right through you, you ghostie!" He joined me in laughter. You know that old saying about it being the best medicine? It's true.

"Yeah, you weren't laughing so much in the am-boo-lance," he countered, and I let out a groan.

"Oh, you lift my spirits." And the punfest continued.

"You were in grave danger, you know."

"I knew you wouldn't let me make a *specter*cal of myself."

"I *demon*strated my devotion to you."

"You were e*thereal* thing."

Soon we were both groaning and laughing at the same time until I realized we were getting louder and louder. Not that it mattered if Davy was loud of course, but a nurse might find it strange that I was laughing so hard. Life with a ghostie was both glorious and complicated. I turned on the television and found an old rerun of *The Golden Girls* even though our laughter had settled down a bit.

"I'd *wraith*er watch *I Love Lucy*," Davy started up again, and the television was the perfect cover for our giggles.

The door suddenly whooshed open and the nurse came in, glancing up at the television as she approached my bed. "Nice to hear you laughing." She smiled in a way that oozed comfort. "I love *The Golden Girls* too. That Sophia is a crack-up!"

"I like her too."

Davy faded to the far corner while the nurse checked my vitals and fussed with the bandage around my head. "Dr. Lee and Dr. West will be in to see you soon."

"Who is Dr. West?"

"The neurosurgeon who performed your surgery."

"Oh. Thank you."

When she left, I gingerly turned my head toward Davy as he came back to perch beside me. "She rained on our parade," he exclaimed in a bit of a pouty voice, and I chuckled.

"We have had many parades, and will have many more. By the way, what day is it?"

"Tuesday."

His response left me puzzled though since I had no recollection of which day I went to Volcanoes National Park. I tried to frown but it hurt too much. "How long have I been in the hospital?" I figured a more direct question would be better.

"Nine days."

"Nine?" I yelled before lowering my voice. "Days?" He reached for my hand while nodding. I used my free hand to reach up to my head again, exploring the thick bandaging as best I could. "How...how bad is my injury?"

"She tried to kill you and she nearly succeeded... twice." He was interrupted by the appearance of Dr. Lee and another man whom I assumed to be Dr. West. Davy faded back to the corner again as I checked the new doctor out; I couldn't help myself. He was tall and nicely built, with hair the color of wheat, a strong jawline, and broad shoulders.

"Good afternoon." Dr. Lee squeezed my hand. "This is Dr. West."

"Hello," I croaked. Where had my voice gone? "I was just wondering how long I've been here?" I figured it didn't hurt to confirm what Davy had told me. "And how bad my injuries are?" That was the real puzzler for me.

Dr. Lee leaned against the foot of the bed reviewing my chart while Dr. West pulled up one of those stools on wheels and settled on it. "You've been here nine days, and you had surgery on the first day to repair the damage to your skull," Dr. Lee began before handing over the rest of the explanation to Dr. West.

I tried my hardest to follow the doctor's explanation but a fog seemed to have settled behind my eyes. All I heard were terrifying terms like depression fracture, some other kind of fracture I couldn't understand, and EEG. EEG I knew, so I tried to focus as he continued. "...showed no long term effects."

"The EEG?"

"Yes."

"So... I'll be okay?"

He smiled then for the first time. "You're young, in good general health, and apparently extremely lucky. So yes, you are expected to make a full recovery."

His smile was contagious, and I felt my face react in kind, followed by a heat that rose from my neck up to my cheeks. *Stop it, Macca*, I scolded myself.

Yeah, stop it, Macca, Davy injected into my thoughts.

Jealous.

Am not.

Are too.

"Any more questions?" Dr. West brought my attention back to the room.

I did have another question, but I felt a little silly asking. I swallowed my feelings though and plowed on. "When will the bandages come off?"

He smiled that thousand-watt smile again before responding. "Well, unless you really love the mummy look, we can remove them today if you'd like."

"I really would like that. It's... itchy. And hot."

He chuckled and pressed the call button for the nurse before he stood to attend to the bandage. It wasn't long before I felt the coolness of the air conditioning on my head. There appeared to be five million miles of bandage on the bed and the nurse magically appeared to dispose of it.

It wasn't easy, and it took all my restraint, but I refused to bring my hand up to my head until the doctors and the nurse were finished and left me on my own once again. The room was dim, the silence broken only by the occasional announcements on the PA system outside my door. I put the television back on and took a deep breath. Dorothy and Sophia were arguing about silliness when I slowly reached up to touch my now naked and partially hairless head. I patted my scalp tentatively a few times, biting my lower lip, then laid back on my pillow and closed my eyes. I was whole. Some might say I wasn't perfect, but perfect is a ridiculous notion. I fell asleep and dreamed of Wonder Woman teaming with Monkeeman.

When I awoke the room was darker than I'd remembered, like the earth had hiked up her skirts and fled from the sun, stopping in only the blackest part of the universe. My arms were weighed down by invisible forces, and it took all the energy and strength I could muster just to bring one hand to my head. With a drunken-like stagger, my fingers found my forehead and did a happy little tap dance for there was nothing amiss there. With tentative movements I pushed my fingers farther up toward my scalp, or I should say, where my scalp should have been. Instead, it was a gaping open wound and my fingers came away from the concave half of my head dripping with blood. I screamed. I kept screaming until my voice was raw and no further sound escaped.

"Miss Liberty." Someone was calling my name, a cool hand on my warm cheek. "Miss Liberty, Macca," she continued. I opened my eyes to a bright room, the nurse's concerned eyes boring into mine.

"Oh my God." I let out a breath. It must have been a terrible dream, and the relief was like the nurse's cool touch and flooded throughout my body.

"You were having a nightmare," the nurse stated the obvious.

"Yes. It was horrible." And then I remembered the concave skull, and my hand flew weightlessly up to my head. My very rounded head. Of course there was no hair on that side of my scalp, and the crusty bumps of stitches seemed to make a gruesome zig zag, but it was fully intact otherwise. A little laugh bubbled up, bursting out of my mouth with sheer hysterical relief, and growing in strength until my eyes watered. The nurse either understood or at least had the heart to pretend to, and she held my hand while she smoothed my blankets, never taking her eyes off of me. When my hysterics died down I was spent, and still the kindly nurse watched me, a warmth glowing from her gentle but wise eyes. I found myself mesmerized by the polished ivory of her face, for it seemed totally devoid of any makeup yet glowed of morning dew. I couldn't help but smile, and it was mirrored in her own.

"I could tell you were struggling." Her voice was smooth like her skin.

I nodded, swallowing hard as the memory of the dream returned. "My head was… part of it was missing."

Her smile never wavering, she glanced at the top of my head, then looked back into my eyes. "I can assure you, it's all there, and in fine working order." She spoke not with a condescending tone, nor a lie of appeasement, so I believed her implicitly and let out a relaxed sigh. "Now," she continued, tucking in the ends of the blanket, "perhaps you should rest?"

"I don't want to sleep though," I whispered with an edge of panic to my voice.

"Just rest." She dragged the call button/television remote closer to my hand. "Watch a little TV if you'd like, and call if you need anything."

I answered her with a smile and a nod, and she gave my hand a final squeeze before leaving me with my electronic friend, the sitcom. I flipped through the channels and settled on an old episode of *Cheers*, losing myself in the quiet hilarity of Norm, Sam, Carla, and Diane. Davy shimmered in and crawled onto the bed to watch with me.

"Where have you been?"

"Checking on Bettina and Taylor."

"Taylor can go to hell. How's Bettina?"

"Pretty upset but also relieved. She'll be released soon and Rob or Alex will pick her up."

"I guess they'll take her to my place…" My words trailed off.

"Most likely. It's up to her though."

"What do you mean?"

"She's feeling pretty awful about what Taylor has put you through."

"Well, it would be pretty cowardly of her to avoid me. I don't think that's the Bettina I know. Or… knew. I don't know any of those people now."

He kissed my cheek and held my hand as Sam and Diane had a slap fight on the small screen. The vast disparity between onscreen and reality was unsettling, and I squirmed a bit. "Are you okay?" He rubbed his thumb across my cheek.

"Yeah. Or I will be."

"Give it time. And I'm not going anywhere. Even when it looks like I'm not here? I am."

"I have a question though. How did the orderly know to come into my room when Taylor was trying… to smother me?"

He smiled, just a little shyly, and totally out of character. "I whispered in his ear. He was a little freaked out afterward, poor guy." He chuckled. "But he acted first, and saved your life."

I smiled then and kissed his cheek too. "You both did. Thank you." We turned back to the television and lost ourselves in *Cheers*. Or I lost myself. I suspect Davy was busy elsewhere even though he was lying next to me. How *did* he do that?

EIGHTEEN

A Walking Piña Colada and a Naked Noggin

The inn never looked so welcoming to me as it did the day I finally arrived home. The drive had been long and hard though, with Bennie driving Roomba while Kalei followed in his own car with me riding shotgun. The two men had taken it upon themselves to get Roomba out of car-jail and charge him up, but they insisted I ride with Kalei in his larger sedan to lessen the bumpity bump of the roads. I was still suffering from headaches and muscle pain, so I didn't put up any sort of fight. I dozed a few times as well. During my wakeful times I could sense Kalei watching me out of the corner of his eye. No matter how much I tried I was unable to assure him that I was fine.

"We're home," Kalei whispered as he gently touched my shoulder to wake me from one of my many naps. I sat up straighter and peered around at the full parking lot and saw Bennie parking Roomba at one of the charging docks. My face warmed and I felt a wide grin spreading.

"Home," I breathed. "That sounds so... comforting."

"Come on then." He helped me out of the car, and we met up with Bennie who was carrying a plastic bag of my few belongings from the hospital. Flanking me like large mother hens, they helped me down the stairs, and for this I was thankful because I was still in fact a bit unsteady on my feet. When they started telling me how many steps were left and warning me to walk gently though, I began to chafe a bit at their over protectiveness. When Kalei took to tiptoe-running ahead to open my front door, the absurdity hit me and I began to giggle. The big man reminded me of Big Bird on Sesame Street, but I would never let him know that.

"What?"

"It just tickled me to see you scamper ahead like that," I lied, sort of. I didn't want to insult the guy. His smile was my reward for the little white lie. Sometimes we must, right?

Behind Kalei, the warm light spilling from my open door caught my attention; my sanctuary awaited. As I crossed the threshold, I heard a strong "meow" coming from the sofa. Chester was perched on the back of the cushions with all his legs tucked beneath his body like a giant orange loaf of bread.

"There's my boy." I reached out to give his cheek a little scratch, and we met each other in a gentle head-butt.

I missed you, Mom, but I'll deny I ever admitted that. He sent his thoughts to me in his special manner.

"I missed you, big guy." I gave him a gentle kiss on his head and listened to his purrs for a bit before Lani came barreling in, her large tummy arriving a second before the rest of her. She squealed and wrapped her arms around me, squeezing tightly. I squeezed right back!

"Oh Macca. I have been so worried! But you look..." She held me at arm's length and blushed. "You look like you're on the mend."

"I am." I chuckled at her quick save. I had managed to tie my remaining hair into a sort of lopsided ponytail, and I had been told my face was still bruised and swollen. I hadn't bothered to hobble to a mirror to confirm the situation because honestly I didn't care. Hair grows back. Swelling goes down. Discoloration fades to normal. Eventually. All it would take was time, and I was alive so I had plenty of that.

"Now," Lani continued, "let's chase these men back to their work and get down to our own business."

"Excellent idea." We both turned and stared at Bennie and Kalei who reluctantly left us to our tasks. During one of the many lengthy conversations Lani and I had enjoyed while I was hospitalized, I had asked for her help. "Did you bring it?"

She pulled an electric clipper from her apron's oversized pocket and held it aloft. "Let's sit on the deck. I will do the clean-up afterward. Not you," she emphasized, and I didn't object.

Lani dragged a kitchen chair out to the deck and draped a small sheet around me. "It's a new crib sheet, not yet washed and prepared for the keiki, so I figured what better way to christen it, yes?"

"I will have so many connections to this keiki. I can hardly wait to hold her. Or him."

"But for now, we have work to do. Shall we begin then?"

"I'm ready." I was rather excited about it actually. It would be part of a new beginning. She turned the clippers on and slowly eased the remaining hairs from my scalp. The light brown and golden streaks fell onto the sheet and the deck around us. The day was lovely with very little breeze and the temperature was mild. I couldn't stop smiling and my heart felt light. I was so happy to be home.

"It's a little cooler," I remarked with a giggle when she was done.

"It's very... white." Lani returned my giggle.

"Never seen the sun."

"Make sure you use plenty of sunscreen!"

"I will. I always do... on the rest of me that is." We giggled as the clippers continued to buzz. When at last the buzzing stopped, Lani warmed some coconut oil in her hands and applied it to my cue ball head, avoiding the large area of zig zag stitches.

"That will help with any feelings of razor burn, if it occurs."

"Thank you. And it has no smell!"

"New brand of coconut oil we're trying. So far, I love it."

"So do I. I was beginning to feel like a walking Piña Colada."

She leaned down and kissed my cheek. "And you are just as beautiful as one."

I knew that was both a compliment to me as well as a nod to Sam's excellent alcoholic concoctions; he always used bright garnishes of fruit and edible flowers atop the frothy blends.

My dome thoroughly oiled, I relaxed while watching Lani clean up. She gathered her items and stood before me.

"Thank you, Lani, for everything." I was feeling weary and apparently it was obvious.

"I believe you should crawl into your own bed and take a rest. Ming changed your bedding and your bath towels, but remember to keep your stitches dry, okay?"

"A nap sounds good. A shower is for another day, but I see a bath in the near future."

"Perfect idea! And you know to tell us — any of us — if you need anything. And I do mean anything! Even if you want a cup of tea, we will be there in an instant to help. Promise?"

"I promise." I couldn't help but love my dear friend even more. Her baby didn't know it yet, but what a lucky child it would be.

I sat on the deck for a little longer, enjoying the breeze, the view, and life in general. Sometimes it takes a near tragedy to give you a greater appreciation of life, but I vowed not to put myself in danger ever again.

My eyelids began to feel heavy, for that's what the sea air does, so I crept to my bedroom and stretched out on the bed, pulling a light cotton throw over me. Chester hopped up and settled beside me with his head on my arm. His purrs soon lulled me to sleep.

When I peered at the clock later it told me I'd napped for more than two hours. I stretched for a while and felt my muscles loosen; the idea of a hot bath sounded like a day at the spa. In the bathroom I ran the hot water and encountered my first mirror since my injury. My face was bruised, swollen, and discolored, and my head naked except for the long, ragged line of stitches. I shrugged and climbed into the tub, easing my aching body into the hot water, willing the soreness away.

When I was dressed in my normal shorts and tee shirt, I felt almost like myself again. I pulled open the top drawer of my dresser and thumbed through the very small stack of scarves and bandanas I'd collected over the years. Choosing a large cotton scarf with white plumeria scattered on the pale blue background, I tied it around my head and knotted it in the back. Satisfied that it would keep our guests from freaking out, I added just a little bit of lip gloss before realizing how absurd it was against the multicolor bruises on my face. "Ah, you're beauty pageant material there, Mac," I teased myself.

Yes you are, I heard Davy in my head. He'd been suspiciously absent all day, but I was doing well and surrounded by people eager to help me. I knew I could reach him if I needed to with just a single thought sent his way.

I took a deep breath and slowly hobbled to the reception area. I could see that the dining area was already set up for the dinner service, and I glanced at the time on Bennie's computer to see that people would start arriving within the next hour.

And speaking of Bennie, he must have heard me bumbling about with the coffee urn and trying to pour myself a cup with shaky hands.

"What on earth are you doing?" he gently scolded while taking the cup from my hand, filling it, adding milk, and handing it back.

"Just trying to get back into the world of the living."

He gave me a sideways look as he stepped behind the counter to check his computer. "That would be funny if it didn't have so much truth to it."

"I'm sorry." I took a sip and made a small sound of delight. "Oh, I've missed this elixir. At least I think I missed it. I don't remember much."

"The mind works in mysterious ways to protect us from unpleasant memories."

"I guess I also missed the departure of Neatnick Nancy and the Hooligans?"

"Yeah." He chuckled, shaking his head. "We would have celebrated but we were a little busy… and a whole lot distracted."

I put my hand on top of his as it rested on his mouse. "I'm so sorry I worried everyone."

"We're just relieved that you're okay." His smile made his dark brown eyes twinkle, and in one fluid move he pulled me close and held me. I put my arms around him and rested my head on his shoulder. When we pulled away, he held me by the upper part of my arms and smiled again, gesturing to my scarf. "By the way, love the do-rag."

"It's covering up my naked noggin." I laughed.

"I heard about that. I'm sure you're beautiful bald, or with a Mohawk, or even green spiky hair."

I shrugged and felt my cheeks flush. "Thank you."

He briefly touched my chin before the phone rang and he returned to his duties. I took my coffee and wandered into the kitchen.

"Macca!" Kalei boomed as his cleaver came crashing down on a huge cabbage.

Lani came out of the cooler with a couple jugs of juice, and in one smooth motion Kalei swept them out of her hands and deposited them on the work table.

"Macca!" Lani's voice didn't boom, but was full of the same warmth. "Love the scarf! Very chic," she teased.

"It's a good thing I have several scarves, but I might want to head to town tomorrow and pick up a few more since I'll be wearing them daily. The only problem is that I don't feel up to driving yet. Want to come along?"

"Great idea! Girls' day out." She turned to her husband. "You can hold down the fort for a few hours, right Big Man?"

He swept her into his arms and laid it on thick "Yes my love, but I will miss you every second of your absence."

She snorted. "Right. Keep that in mind when you'll *really* miss me after the baby is born and you're listening to a squalling infant."

"It will be the sound of angels singing, I'm sure."

"Oh brother. He's laying it on thick." I giggled and she eyed him suspiciously.

"Yeah, he's up to something." She swatted his arms away, and he had the good sense to exaggerate his innocent look. I always loved watching them together, and I felt a warm glow of happiness at being home.

I spent the next couple of hours performing limited duties in addition to receiving hugs and greetings from employees, friends, and guests. Even Susie, Winston, and Marley welcomed me home in their own special ways, but by the time dinner was in full swing I was running on empty and let Bennie know.

"Then you should definitely go rest," he instructed. "We've got it all under control, and yes, we'll come to you if we have a problem, okay?" He was shooing me out the door.

"I hate that my phone is gone."

"It's not gone. The police have it. Rob has a copy of the inventory of evidence the police logged and he's working on getting at least some of it released."

I felt my eyebrows arch up almost to where my hairline should have been. "Wow, thank you! That's great news."

"You're welcome. Now go rest." He shooed me further out the door and guided me to my bungalow.

"Why do I feel like you're trying to get rid of me?" I was teasing but actually rather tickled at his insistence.

"Not at all, but I have learned how to deal with your stubbornness."

"Pure brute force? That works for you?" I was teasing him and hoped he knew it. His responding chuckle was reassuring.

"With you, any means will do." I saw that he was teasing right back. It warmed my heart, and I waved him away.

"I can go home by myself." I feigned indignation. "I'm a big girl."

"That you are," he whispered so softly I barely caught it.

"What did you say?" I only asked so I could hear it again.

"Never mind. Scoot." He turned on his heel to get back to work, leaving me with a smile on my face. *I think he likes me*, I thought, and giggled in my mind.

Oh my God, knock that off, Davy responded in kind, and I giggled outwardly, receiving a glance and a smile from Bennie as he disappeared into the reception area.

That's Goddess, I corrected Davy and went inside to find Susie and Chester waiting for me on the sofa. I joined them and we snuggled together to watch television. I figured that if I fell asleep it would be fine because I always loved a good nap before going to bed.

The next morning was dark and cloudy, and the weather channel forecast indicated a tropical squall on its way to dump its load on our part of the island, so Lani and I got an early start. I had opted for the paniolo look complete with a red bandana on my head instead of a cowboy hat, a red plaid short sleeved shirt, and faded denim shorts. Of course no outfit of mine was complete without the mandatory flip flops, and today's were red.

We chatted and giggled all the way to town. Lani chose a centrally located parking spot, and we slowly meandered in and out of a few shops. I collected several scarves and bandanas, including one with sock monkeys printed all over it. Lani's eagle eye spotted a scarf with paw prints around a border that surrounded a cluster of orange cats, and I squealed a little before tucking it over my arm with the others. After I'd paid for my scarves, our next stop was the general store where I purchased a cheap pay-as-you-go phone because I wasn't entirely sure I'd ever get my original phone back, although I remained hopeful.

We strolled down the street to a coffee shop for a sit and sip, and an ice cream snack. It was luscious and cooling, and I needed to rest. We stopped for fresh produce on the way to the car, then headed home.

"Tired?" Lani watched me as she started the car.

"Yeah. I'm thinking a nap is on the menu for the afternoon."

"Great idea. I'll put your new scarves in the laundry for you. And do you want me to give your new phone to Bennie to get it set up?"

"Yeah. Thanks. I'm ready to find my old energy again. This is starting to depress me."

"Give it time. You had quite a trauma."

I simply nodded and watched the scenery zip by. Before I knew it we were home. I took the stairs slowly, Lani mother-henning me along the way. I didn't mind it though, because I knew it was done out of love. And pregnancy hormones.

There was a note on my door from Bennie.

Macca -
Bettina called. Will be here
today at 4 to talk to you.
- Bennie
P.S. I hate this old-school
method of communication.
Get a phone!

I chuckled at his P.S. before considering Bettina's impending visit. Why did it give me a sick feeling? Perhaps the emotional wounds were deeper than my head wound.

I gave Chester a little pet as I passed by on the way to my bedroom, and he jumped from his perch on the back of the sofa to follow me in. On the other side of the bed I could see two large ears through the sliding glass door; Susie was on the deck peering in.

"Hey buddy." I opened the door and he trotted in, settling in his own large bed in the corner. As his big head came to rest on his equally big paws he let out a groan. "Rough day?" I gave his head a pat and stroked his fur.

It's exhausting worrying about you, he responded in my mind, the southern accent thick.

"I'm okay. Really."

But you weren't.

"But now I am."

He huffed, then groaned, and then flopped on his side with his tongue lolling out of his mouth and onto his bed. *Could you just stay home? Forever? Please?*

"I can't promise that, but I can assure you I'm done trying to solve mysteries. That's best left to the experts."

Well… Okay. Can I have a treat then?

"Yes. You both can."

HA! Thanks, man. Great job! Chester chimed in.

"Conspirators, the both of you. Playing on my sympathies!"

198

No, not playing. I really have been worried. The treats are just a bonus. Susie was apparently a con artist too.

I had to chuckle as I dug out a treat for each and handed them over. Susie's was gone in one gulp while Chester worried at his for several seconds before chomping into it.

I stretched out on the bed as Chester cleaned his face. It always amazed me how one little snack could cause an entire body to require a full cleaning. I drifted off to sleep and awoke to find myself on my side with Chester curled up against my stomach and Susie stretched behind me, his mammoth head resting on my neck. My bodyguards.

When at last I was able to extricate myself from the tangle of animals, I washed my face, brushed my teeth, then re-tied my bandana.

I left the critters snoozing on my bed and wandered over to the reception area. Winston and Marley welcomed me from their open perch just outside the main door.

Bluebird... homecoming queen, Winston sang a little, and with Marley's accompanying whistling it created an off-key harmony. I giggled and bobbed my head to their beat and they mimicked me.

"Hello my feathered buddies, how are you?"

I'm a pretty boy.

"Yes you are. And you're pretty too, Marley."

"Macca!" Bennie called to me from inside the reception area, then quickly stepped outside to find me.

"Yes?" My relaxed state was the opposite of his agitation.

"Sorry. I'm crazy busy and I know Bettina will be here soon. I just wanted you to have your new phone, all set up." He handed me the little device and I tucked it in my pocket.

"Thank you so much for doing that."

"You're welcome, but I admit it wasn't entirely selfless. It'll be much easier to contact you now. Writing notes is not my thing."

"Aw, didn't you ever pass notes in school?" I asked him, a tease in my voice.

"Yes, but the key words there are *in school*. As in long ago." He chuckled and whipped back inside to return to work. I followed him slowly and poured myself a cup of coffee. Briefly perusing the papers that had been stuffed into my inbox, I found requests for supplies, invoices for shipments received, etc. Same old incredibly welcome routine. I sipped my coffee a few times before deciding to plunge right back into work, but in the quiet of my own bungalow. Letting Bennie know he could reach me there, or on my new phone, I took my stack of papers and headed home to my laptop.

As I worked through each task my mind would occasionally wander. How awkward would it feel to be face to face with Bettina again? She'd seemed so hostile at times. Would she take any of her circumstances out on me? I felt I was pretty much the innocent here, but I know mothers can have very strong and sometimes blinded views of their kids. I chewed my bottom lip. A lot.

Later that afternoon I heard a knock at my door, causing my stomach to lurch as I rose to answer it. I greeted Bettina with a wide grin which slowly faded as I took in her appearance. She wore a fairly basic Hawaiian muumuu and flip flops, and her hair was limp and dull.

We stared at each other for what seemed like a long time. Her usual grumpiness was long gone and in its place she looked haggard, defeated, and seemed to have aged twenty years or so. I noticed her eyes flitted over my bandana-covered head. Where I had previously steeled myself to be strong and not let her steamroll me, I now felt all that planning melting away like a candle left too long on its own. I took two steps and wrapped my arms around her, which unleashed a sudden round of sobs from her, muffled against my shoulder.

I was overwhelmed with pangs of guilt, but why? I didn't cause any of this. Did she blame me? Did she think I blamed her? Did she just miss her mother?

Just hold her and don't think so much, Davy scolded.

I didn't respond, but I obeyed his command. We were going to have a long talk about this obeying crap though.

Some other time. And then I felt him leave my thoughts. Whew. But the vacancy was filled almost immediately.

Tell her you love her, my mother implored.

I shushed my mother's thoughts away. That's a tricky thing, you know, to shush someone in your mind.

Don't you shush me, young lady.

Mom. Let me handle this.

Okay, but I'll be here.

Great. I should charge rent in my head.

Chester popped in out of nowhere. *May I just add that I do not want that woman Taylor back here. Ever.*

Don't worry. I'm pretty sure she'll be in prison for a long time.

Just make sure she is.

Like I had control over this. Okay, I wondered... Who's next? But it was mercifully silent inside my head, giving new meaning to the term *empty thoughts.*

As Bettina's crying quieted little by little, I continued to hold her and just waited. I didn't let go of her until she made the first move. When she did, she lifted her head from my shoulder, still clinging tightly, and whispered, "You're so much like Willow."

"Thank you. What a lovely compliment."

She slowly pulled away, letting her hands trail from my back to my upper arms, holding me just slightly away from her body. "And I'm sorry..." She paused to gulp emotions back. "...for the pain my daughter caused you. And me. Us."

"It's okay."

"No, it's not, but thank you."

"Well, I accept your apology, although you're not the one who should be apologizing to me."

"I know." Taylor's name went unspoken for the time being, which was just as well under the circumstances.

"And I'm glad you weren't successful... in your cell... with your... um... shirt."

She sighed and shook her head. "I've had a lot of time to think about that; I was desperate and felt so hopeless, but now I have a court appointed therapist that I will see each week."

"Oh, I'm very happy to hear that, Bettina."

We stared at each other for a while before we both smiled. The idea that a new road lay ahead of us fit comfortably in my heart. "Would you like a glass of wine? Or I can find champagne, and we can talk?"

"I'd love to talk, and I'd give my left foot for a glass of wine."

We giggled and walked arm in arm to my small kitchen. I gathered wine glasses and a bottle of Sauvignon Blanc while she splashed cold water on her tear-stained face. I opened the wine and handed both the wine and the glasses to her after she had finished dabbing at her damp face with a paper towel. From the refrigerator I retrieved a little pu-pu platter that Lani had prepared, and we headed out to the deck.

"Oh, that looks lovely." Bettina smiled when she saw the platter of snacks. I'd now seen her smile more than the entire time they'd stayed here, and I was grateful for that refreshing change.

"Lani takes good care of us."

"She's a gem."

"That she is," I responded, although I was surprised by her statement. Her family had treated my friends almost like slaves while they were staying here. I took a seat and lifted my glass at the same time Bettina did, and we chuckled.

"To the truth," Bettina said.

"And new beginnings," I added. She nodded and we clinked glasses before sipping.

"Oh, that's delightful." She tasted the wine again. "Very light and refreshing in this tropical weather."

"It's a label my Uncle Wally had stocked up on. I like it too." From the platter I selected a slice of cucumber with a dollop of cream cheese and a roasted red pepper sliver on top and took a bite. "Also refreshing." I grinned as Bettina took one as well.

"Oh my God. After the meals in jail I will never take food for granted again. I just stopped eating."

"I noticed you lost a little weight. I did too, when I was… there."

She closed her eyes and let out a sigh, savoring the food before meeting my gaze. "Yes. I thought of you often in my cell. So many innocent people end up like that, but I knew Rob got you out, so I had faith. Sometimes it waned though, and that's when I thought of you. I figured you had to be strong, so I would be too. I guess that means you kept me sane." She said the last bit so softly that I barely heard her.

She swiped at her eyes before taking another sip of wine, but the weight of her words formed a knot of remembrance in my stomach. Those had not been pleasant days for me either. "How did you know about my situation? About me being in jail?"

"Mom heard about it and followed the news online. All of it. She searched your name and gathered all the information she could and shared it with us."

Wow. This was pretty eye-opening. I had gotten the idea that Annie hadn't paid my family any attention except on the occasions when we visited.

"I was jealous of your family for a long time, something I'm not proud of," she continued, her eyes cast downward.

"What changed?"

"My daughter came along, but then she turned out to be less of a source of pride and more a cause of stress. I was frequently getting her out of sticky situations. At one point I stopped saving her neck and tried to get Mom and my now ex-husband to stop too, but she had them both wrapped around her little finger."

"What did you do?"

"I sat back and let them. What could I do? I told them all of the devious and many times illegal things she was doing, but they either didn't believe it or didn't care. Mom said, 'Blood means everything and we protect our own.'"

She took another sip of wine before reaching for a mini macadamia nut cheese ball and popped it into her mouth. She chewed slowly, pleasure showing in her eyes. I took one too, and relished the contrast of the soft cheese with the crunchy macadamias.

"Oh Lani," I whispered nearly to myself, "you've done it again."

"She does have a magical touch, and so does Kalei." Bettina smiled as she popped another cheese ball into her mouth. "Your whole staff is remarkable, Macca. You've got a wonderful place here, people and all." Her face grew dark with emotion again. "And I'm sorry we made everything so difficult." She reached out and squeezed my hand, tears dampening her eyes again. "How can I ever make it up to you?"

"I think you just did." I squeezed her hand too.

There was a comfortable silence between us then as we sat sipping, noshing, and gazing at the lovely view. I, for one, never tired of that view.

"This is so… therapeutic." Bettina seemed to be making a similar observation.

"I regenerate right here on this deck nearly every day."

"You're very lucky."

"I know." I poured a little more wine into her glass. "Bettina, what will you do now?"

"I don't know yet. I mean, Mother is gone, Taylor is locked up, and my ex-husband thinks I'm to blame for all this."

I frowned. "What exactly do you mean?"

She sighed heavily. "He says a good mother would have stayed in jail to 'take the rap,' as he put it, for our daughter."

Sitting up straight, my tongue was tied for only a few seconds because... well… you know me. "He wasn't serious, was he?"

"Dead serious. He said it was better to waste my worthless life than Taylor's bright future."

"Wow." My word was more like an exhale than actual speech. I leaned back hard in my chair, for the enormity of the words from someone she once loved and trusted were unbelievable. Well, nearly. Knowing the family as I did, it was actually quite believable, but no less chilling.

"Yeah." She gave a little mirthless laugh. "Real stand-up guy that Stu is, right?"

"Oh Bettina." I reached over and grasped her hand again. "I'm so sorry."

"Thanks, but I've had a lot of time to think, and there's a new Bettina in town now. In fact, I'm going to make a fresh start, get a job, call myself Tina, cut my hair — a life makeover you could say."

"Good for you!" I was pleased to see her grin, and I jokingly pointed to my head then. "I got a new haircut too." And we laughed together comfortably until she suddenly became serious again.

"I'm so sorry she hurt you, and I'm sorry she killed my mother, but very grateful that you survived."

"I know, Bett… I mean, Tina. I know. And please don't blame yourself. Taylor herself told me a few stories about how your mother and your husband always tried to make excuses for her and that they didn't like you trying to discipline her. They made a mistake. Unfortunately, Annie paid the ultimate price for that behavior."

Tina-Bettina nodded. She'd always be Bettina to me, but I decided I would try to use her new name, for her sake.

"Taylor has always believed I'm the bad guy." She said it in such a casual manner, as if stating that butter is often spread on toast.

"But I think your mother and Stu did her a disservice. Really."

She peeked at me over her wine glass and nodded. "Taylor is damaged. I will take some of the blame for that. But it's also due to my mother and Stu's overly indulgent parenting with her."

I continued to give her the lead, and she took it.

"I mean, I was indulgent when she was little, but then I saw her doing things that weren't what I would consider normal for a preschool child."

"Like what?"

"I got to her preschool early one day to surprise her and watched her use her shoelaces to tie a little boy to the jungle gym. I was so shocked that I went immediately to the teacher in charge and demanded they call Taylor in to question her. It turned out that the teacher in charge was another of Stu's side-Barbies, and she refused to reprimand Taylor. Later she called him to report me for false accusations against my own daughter."

"Side-Barbie?" I giggle snorted into my wine glass and that got her giggling too.

"Yeah, I came to refer to all of them as SB's in my mind." And it was then that we both dissolved into fits of laughter. It was very cathartic. Although I'd only met him a few times as a child, I'd always found Stu disgusting, and Tina-Bettina's revelations proved it was even worse than I'd imagined.

"How long did he have… SB's… that you knew of?"

She picked up a cherry tomato stuffed with a green olive mousse, popped it in her mouth, and chewed before responding. "Let's just say that I caught him making a date while we waited for our flight home. On our honeymoon."

"Oh, wow! I'm so sorry!" I reached for her hand and grasped it.

"I was a fool," she spoke in a voice choked by emotion. "But Mom and Dad said the wedding had sealed the deal, and the gifts had been given by all the right families so, like a good and obedient and truly stupid daughter, I stayed with him."

"And then there was Taylor." It took me several seconds to realize that I'd said it out loud. "Oh! I'm so sorry!"

"No, don't be. That's what I… and Mom… always loved about you and your mom. You spoke the truth."

I chomped on my lower lip. "Still… I'm sorry." It came out as a whisper.

"I know. And thank you."

I emptied the last of the wine into both our glasses and then stilled, the empty bottle suspended over my own glass. "Tina? Please stay the night. I have your room still."

"Oh, thank you, but I've intruded far more than I should have and…"

"No! Really. Please stay? And… I mean…" I gulped. "Please stay until you have all your details arranged, or when you figure out what your next steps are. However long it takes. Please?"

When she covered her face with her hand, I wasn't sure what was happening until I saw her shoulders shake. I got up from the table, set the empty wine bottle down, and moved to her side to put my arms around her. I just allowed her the time to quietly let go.

It was several minutes later before she calmed and I took my seat again. I handed her napkins as needed and ran for more wine, which I believe was needed even more than the napkins. This woman had a lifetime of atrocities against her, built up and barricaded inside. But the tiny crack in the dam was widening.

"Macca, I would dearly love to stay for a few days, just until I can figure out what I need to do, and balance that with what I want to do."

"Then… welcome home, Bett… Tina."

NINETEEN

Spotted Flip Flops and a Tipsy Mohawk

The next morning I woke up very groggy, but I knew that I had to get up and begin my chores. My "time off," while not voluntary, had to come to an end. I couldn't keep relying on everyone to cover for me. I swung my legs over and sat up, facing toward the sliding glass door and marveling at yet another beautiful morning, despite the fact that the sky was painted with streaks of gray and navy. A storm was toying with us again, but I found the weather to be just another charm on the island's bracelet.

Rubbing my eyes, I stood on wobbly feet and surveyed the rumpled bedding for a bit before I rousted Chester in order to set it right again. He stretched and yawned, then hopped back up on the bed and tussled with the sheets as I tried to smooth them. If you've ever tried to make a bed with a cat in the room, you'll understand. I finally left him in the bed with the sheets, a thin blanket, and lightweight cotton coverlet smoothed over him, creating a hill. A cathill. I amused myself far too much.

"You still alive in there?"

I'm inspecting the linens.

"I see. I shall call you Inspector Number 8 then."

Why that number?

"I don't know. It's from an episode of *Monk* and it was the first thing that came to mind."

You really need a life.

"You are my life."

Right.

"You could live outside if you'd prefer."

Nothing to see here. Move along.

Trading quips with a cat. Unbelievable. I mean really. No one would ever believe it. I chuckled and aimed my sore and tired body for the shower. With my bald head covered by a shower cap to keep the stitches dry, I realized how much easier my daily grooming had become. When I was dressed in light blue denim shorts and a powder blue and white paisley sleeveless cotton camp shirt, I selected from my array of flip flops.

Try the blue and white spotted ones, I heard Susie's southern drawl in my head.

"Ya think? It won't clash with the paisley?" And then I changed course as I realized I was asking fashion advice from a dog, which caused me to giggle. "Okay. The polka dot flip flops it is."

Is that what they call it? Polka dots? You humans are a weird bunch.

His serious tone caused me to chuckle as I slid the sliding glass door open. The cool air of the morning wafted in as I turned and checked on the lump in the middle of the bed. Yep, Chester Hill was still there, and still breathing.

"Come on out when you get hungry."

The only response was a gentle snore, so I headed to the living room and opened that slider too. Stormy mornings were great for airing the place out. Hearing a noise in the kitchen, I peeked around the separating wall to see Tina-Bettina bent over the open oven door.

"Good morning." I tried to speak quietly so that I wouldn't startle her, but she seemed aware of my approach.

"Good mo..." she began as she turned, but stopped cold when she actually saw me. I was suddenly self conscious, realizing I hadn't put on a scarf. My hand drifted to my naked head.

"I'm sorry. I know it's not the prettiest thing."

"No, no, no." She came to stand with me, a tray of what looked like biscuits in her potholder covered hand. "I just... it's still so shocking what my daugh... what Taylor tried to do... what she did to you. I'm so, so sorry." She set the tray of biscuits down.

"It's okay." I tried to make light of it. "And the stitches come out tomorrow!" Actually, they had been scheduled to come out a few days before, but the tussle with Taylor and the pillow had damaged a few so they'd tidied them up and given me three more days on my sentence. I was more than ready for them to go though, since they itched like crazy.

Tina-Bettina put one hand to my naked scalp and, ever so gently, caressed the newly exposed skin. "I'm so sorry, sweetie," she murmured just before she kissed my forehead.

"I know." Because "It's okay" wasn't what she wanted to hear. previous conversation. "And I'll be fine now. I promise."

"I know you will. You're a strong, young, vibrant woman, with your whole life ahead of you."

We wrapped our arms around each other, and I felt the tension ease in both of us again.

Tell her I love her, I heard Mom in my head and tried to shoo her away. *Tell her*, she insisted. I sighed and pulled away from Tina-Bettina, but before I could get a word out, the older woman remembered the biscuits she'd set down.

"Oh! I made breakfast! Sit!" I took a seat and watched while she bustled about, setting plates, biscuits, and fruit on the table, along with Lani's homemade honey butter. "Lani slipped me the bit of butter. Isn't it grand?"

"This is wonderful, Tina," I exclaimed as I bit into a buttered hunk of biscuit. "These are perfect — crunchy on the outside and fluffy on the inside."

"My grandmother taught me, oh so long ago."

I'd never met her grandmother, but I wanted to send a message to the universe that she was A-OK with me. *Message sent*, Mom responded in thought. Tina-Bettina poured tea for the both of us and we had a proper breakfast together.

Now, mom nagged as we were sipping the last of our tea. I sighed and just sort of jumped in.

"B… Tina… I need to tell you something."

She stopped with her mug nearly to her lips and stared at me, a look of dread on her face. "Did I do something wrong?"

I was going to have to get used to tempering things with this pound puppy. "No, no, no! Everything is great, but there's something I need you to know." I took a sip of tea in a feeble attempt to draw energy. "I seem to have the ability to communicate in an… unusual manner."

Seeing her frown, I tried to plunge on, but she jumped in before me. "Can you read minds?"

"No," I began, but realized that wasn't the whole truth. "Although some animals 'talk' to me in thoughts."

"You can talk to Chester and Susie? And Winston and Marley?"

"No. Winston and Marley remain beyond my reach." I hesitated. "It's just Chester and Susie who tell me their thoughts, but you don't seem too surprised." I twisted the napkin in my lap and studied it, giving her time for this to sink in.

"Wow." She let her breath out. "That's pretty amazing. And frankly, there were times when I thought you were talking to yourself a lot."

Yikes. "Well, there's more." I watched as her eyes widened. "My mom has a message for you." Tina-Bettina swallow hard, but she remained silent. "She said to tell you that she loves you."

"What?" The word sounded flat.

It was then that I felt a mini heat wave in the kitchen, and the air rippled just like a hot day on asphalt, but without that nasty tar smell. It was more like warm banana bread. Go figure. And there beside us was my mom as her beautiful, youthful self. She wore a butter yellow gauzy top and skirt, and a crown of flowers in her long and silky hair. Why did

I get Dad's hair, I asked myself for at least the millionth time before remembering I currently had none.

"Bettina..." Her voice was like the warble of a songbird. "I know what happened and I want you to know that I love you. You've done all you could with Taylor."

Tina-Bettina sat in stunned silence, her eyes never leaving my mom's spectral image. "Oh my heavens." She finally let her breath out as Mom grasped her hand. Tina-Bettina looked down at the ghostly fingers wrapped around hers. "You're... warm. And you smell good. How is this possible?"

"I keep asking that myself," I muttered, largely ignored by both of them.

"It's just the magic of the universe," Mom told her, and I rolled my eyes.

"That's what they all say," I muttered some more. Honestly, it was as if I wasn't even in the room, and then I realized I wouldn't be missed. Therefore, I quietly slipped away, put some food in Chester's dish, and took it to him in my room. He was still being a lump under the blanket in the middle of the bed, so I simply his breakfast it down by his water bowl.

From my bureau drawer I selected a long rectangular head scarf of soft cotton with a dusty blue on blue subtle stripe and wrapped it around my head a few times. I ended with a small knot at the base of my skull, leaving the ends dangling down my back.

When I returned to the kitchen it was empty of people, both ghostly and non-ghostly, but movement on the deck caught my eye. Tina-Bettina and Mom sat in the chairs, talking animatedly. I had to smile then, despite the little stab in my heart. Tamping down the bit of jealousy that threatened to rise up, I turned to the dirty breakfast dishes and quickly rinsed them, then loaded the little dishwasher. Unable to delay the workday any longer, I quietly slipped out to the deck to say my goodbyes.

"Oh hi, honey," Mom said, as if I had just returned home from school and she were not a ghost whose attentions were normally unattainable to me. "That scarf looks wonderful on you. Far better than your naked noggin."

"Thanks. I just wanted to say I'm going to work now."

"Thank you, Macca." Tina-Bettina reached out and squeezed my hand.

"You're welcome." I smiled meekly, avoiding my mother's eyes. It was then that Mom chose to rise before me and hold her arms open. I stared at them and at her, not quite trusting that this was real. "I thought that was against the rules."

"Rules are often bent, broken, and sometimes smashed to smithereens. You're my daughter."

I let her hold me for what seemed like a very long time, an odd heat from my head to my toes, rather like warming yourself over a campfire. When at last we separated, I felt a brand new sense of peace and happiness, with a side of fresh baked bread smell. "How did you do that?"

"Magic," she gave the standard response.

"Magic. Well, could you teach Davy that?" I teased.

"He taught me." She gave a Cheshire Cat smile.

"Then why on earth… or universe… hasn't he done that for me?"

"I believe he's letting you learn to find your own peace and happiness."

Whoa. That was interesting. And kind of deep. I realized I was frowning, and she reached up like she used to do when I was small and rubbed the frown lines away with her soft touch. I kissed her cheek. "I love you Mom."

"I know. I love you too."

"Wait," Tina-Bettina interrupted. "Who is Davy? Not *the* Davy? The Davy that my mom and your mom both adored?"

I gave a small laugh. "None other."

"Wow." She sat back and stared out to the sea. It's amusing that she seemed to find that more interesting than the fact that she was talking to both a ghost and a human who could hear animal voices.

"I think we just blew her mind." I smirked at Mom, but I grew serious then and touched her one last time before bidding farewell, grabbing my laptop, and heading to work. I swiped an errant tear from my eye as I hurried into the reception area and careened into Bennie when he turned away from the large coffee urn.

"Oops! Sorry," I squeaked as we backed up a little from each other. I was relieved he didn't have a cup of coffee in his hands.

"I was just setting the pot to brew," he explained.

"I didn't think anyone else was here yet."

"I got an early start today. The coffee will be ready in a few minutes."

I thanked him, retrieved the papers from my little mail slot, and got to work on orders, supplies, and inventory while sitting at the empty bar — a nearly normal day at the office. I heard Lani and Kalei arriving and we bid each other a good morning. Lani deposited her belongings in the kitchen and then returned to fiddle with the ends of my scarf.

"There. All done," she pronounced after a few tugs before heading back toward the kitchen. I put my hand up to feel what she'd done and found a perfectly round knotted rosette. I grinned.

"Thank you," I called to her.

"You're welcome," she called back just before the swinging door shut between us. It was a good thing *someone* had a bit of fashion sense around here, besides a giant dog that is. I chuckled to myself as I recalled Susie's wardrobe advice, but he hadn't been wrong. I smiled at the thought.

When I'd finished my paperwork, I helped Lani prep some veggies for Kalei's imu oven, then caught Ming in the laundry area and helped her juggle loads between the washers and dryers. By the time I could sit down for a breather, I realized I needed to lie down for one instead. My energy level was still very low, so I let Bennie know and headed back to my bungalow to rest. When I opened the door I was assaulted by noise. Tina-Bettina, Mom, and Davy were sitting in the living room, all talking animatedly at once, or so it seemed. They all stopped and turned their heads to stare at me at once.

"And I wasn't invited?" I was teasing, but also a little miffed that Mom had brought Davy in as well.

"Sorry, Monkee Paw." Mom smiled and patted the sofa beside her, inviting me, albeit a little late, to join them.

"Thanks, but I need to take a little nap."

"Oh, poor dear," she continued. "Have a good rest." She waggled her fingers at me in some sort of coquettish wave. When did she pick up that annoying habit?

"Thanks." I turned away and headed to my bed, suddenly sensing that Davy was hot on my heels, even stepping on one of my flip flops in the process.

"Oops. Sorry." He flashed his grin and I turned to let him into my room before shutting the door. Not that doors keep him out really. I guess it was more ceremonial than anything else, and I was too weary to think very hard on it. *"Flip flop I was taking a walk."* He began to sing his own variation on Bobby Darin's "Splish Splash." *"Long about a Hawaiian night…"* He trailed off as I shot him a look of annoyance borne of fatigue.

I pulled off my head scarf, walked out of my flip flops, and crawled up to my pillow from the foot of the bed, carefully avoiding the lump in the middle. Lazy cat.

I heard that.

I ignored him.

"You shouldn't be working so hard until you're stronger," Davy gently chided me.

"I know, but there's stuff to do."

"And others to do it."

"No. They've done enough." I turned my head to face him as he stretched out beside me, forcing Chester to squirm out the end of the bedcovers and settle into his FedEx box on the floor. "You all looked chummy out there," I continued as I watched the sizable feline.

"We've been building Bettina up, getting her to laugh and tell stories. She has a rough road ahead of her."

"I know, and thank you for that."

He stroked my cheek with the back of his fingers. "You look awfully tired… and extremely naked from the neck up."

I giggled. "You like this look on me?"

"I like all looks on you, but…" He was searching for the right thing to say that wouldn't hurt my feelings, but I was too tired to wait for him to find it.

"Yes, I will let it grow back," I answered his unasked question. "But when I got home I looked like I had a tipsy Mohawk that had lost its balance, slid off the top of my head, and rested above one ear."

He chuckled with that same raspy and endearing little sound, and I couldn't help but smile. And that's all I remembered, for I must have fallen asleep. When I awoke later, Chester was snuggled against my chest and Susie was stretched out behind me once again. Warm and furry bodies were comforting when you weren't feeling up to speed.

I got up, washed my face, slipped my scarf back on, and walked into the flip flops I'd previously walked out of, all as if someone had hit my "rewind" button. If only.

Mercifully, my living room was quiet and empty, and I noticed Tina-Bettina's door was wide open and equally empty. Glancing out the sliders, I saw the deck chairs were put back in place, and there didn't seem to be any sign of Bettina and the Ghosts. I chuckled then, imagining "Bennie and the Jets" when I heard singing in my thoughts.

B-b-b-Bettina and the Ghostssssss, oh but they're weird and they're wonderful…

Davy never failed to make me smile, and this instance was no exception. "Get out of my head, you ghost," I teased.

You love it. Admit it.

I smirked. "I do."

That's better. And then he began to sing again, this time the real lyrics. *Oh but they're so spaced out, B-b-b-Bennie and the Jetssssssssss.*

TWENTY

Chick-Shtick and Peach Fuzz

The next morning Tina-Bettina drove me to the local clinic to have my stitches removed. Copies of my records had been forwarded from the hospital so that we didn't have to drive all the way to Hilo, and for that I was thankful. At the clinic they discussed options for future surgery to lessen the scars. I listened, but firmly declined. I wasn't that into appearances, and I knew my hair would grow back eventually to cover the zig zag reminder. I smiled and thanked them. They were only doing their job. I was just happy that the wound had healed enough that I could take a shower and wash from head to toe. Simple pleasures, right?

A quiet mood descended upon me so I let Tina-Bettina chatter away on her own in the car. She told me she'd gone to her motel and checked out, retrieving her few belongings. She also planned to do a little more clothes shopping since her property was still tied up with the police. More importantly, she seemed encouraged by the visit with my mother and Davy, and for that I was thankful.

My new little phone rang while she was chattering, and when I saw it was Rob I excused myself and took the call. He wanted to talk to both of us so we agreed to meet with him at my place later that afternoon.

She went shopping after she dropped me at the inn. Frankly, I was happy to put my energy into daily chores. The less I was reminded of my attack the more content I was, and the doctor's appointment had brought back memories I didn't wish to keep.

Tina-Bettina returned just a few minutes before Rob arrived. The three of us sat in my living room, and I let Chester snuggle beside me on the sofa, my hand stroking his soft orange fur.

Rob got right down to business. "Taylor notified me that I've been replaced by another attorney."

"Oh no!" Tina-Bettina's hand flew to her mouth.

"No, it's for the best. I was getting ready to withdraw from the case anyway and hand it over to a colleague because one of the victims is a good friend of mine," and he patted my hand.

I smiled and felt some sort of odd relief. He caught my eye and returned the smile.

"Did she go with a public defender?" Tina-Bettina wrung her hands.

"No. She hired an attorney who specializes in cases involving defendants with mental illness."

The room was so silent that I could hear Susie panting on the deck.

Moving quietly, like a cat stalking a taunting blue jay, I got up to let him in and returned stealthily to my seat. The faithful dog sat beside me, his large head on my lap. Chester barely registered that I'd briefly left his side. My protectors were in place. Even though I knew I was safe, it was comforting anyway. I suspected they had reacted to the tension in my thoughts.

"Mental illness? She thinks she's mentally ill?" Tina-Bettina's frown matched my feelings. It was all just further manipulation on Taylor's part. What worried me though was the thought of her being acquitted and free again. Stranger things have happened in today's world.

"Yes. She's claiming childhood abuses have caused her undue stress and that she can't be responsible for her actions."

I couldn't help it. I burst out laughing in disgust but quickly reined it in and clamped my hand over my mouth.

"The only acts of abuse in her childhood were those that she carried out on her family with her manipulation and lies." Tina-Bettina was struggling to keep her own emotions in check.

Rob was unperturbed, a beacon of sensibility and strength. "Her new attorney had her examined by a doctor that he always uses for these cases, but a court appointed doctor will need to examine her as well."

"Wow. Please tell me that she won't get away with murdering my mother and nearly murdering Macca. Please?" Tina-Bettina's eyes filled with tears and I heard the words stick in her throat.

"I can't promise anything. We'll have to wait and see. But I just heard that the case was assigned to Judge Higashi who doesn't put up with nonsense like this. Let's hope she sees through it."

They discussed the trial date that had been set and made arrangements to attend the hearings. Me? I just sat there in stunned silence, and for some reason my head began to ache. As our meeting wound down and Rob was going out the door, I took to my bed for another little rest. Davy shimmered in and had to struggle to find enough room between the animals, who had loyally taken up their place on the bed with me. I might have found it humorous to watch him wiggle in between them if I hadn't felt so awful. Thankfully I was soon asleep with my three bodyguards surrounding me.

When I awoke, I snatched up my phone, saw that it was late, and knew that the dinner service must be in full swing. I jumped up, dog and cat scattering to give me room, and quickly changed my clothes, splashed water on my face, and put on a simple pink head scarf to go with my pink and yellow sun dress. I kept tripping as I tried to slide into my flip flops while on the run. Out of breath, I careened around corners and ran through the back door of the main kitchen. Lani and Bennie were bent over plates, arranging food.

"I am so sorry," I panted. They looked up casually.

"Hi Macca." Lani smiled. "We've got it under control. Did you have a good rest?"

"How did you know?"

Bennie chuckled. "There's a pillow crease on your cheek."

I grinned and rubbed my cheeks to get more blood flowing. "Yeah. I slept long."

"As you should," Kalei joined in. "You're not ready for active duty yet." He winked.

"But…" I struggled to get my brain in gear. "I want to be."

"Bored already?"

"No. I just want to keep my mind busy."

"Are you okay?" Lani stopped her work and peered expectantly at me, so I quickly filled them in on the latest news from Rob. Bennie reached for my hand and nearly crushed it, his eyes filled with worry. Lani used her birthing training to breathe through her anger, but it was the big man Kalei that made me jump as he pounded his powerful fist on the counter.

"Sorry." He hung his head. "I have little patience for someone who tries to kill one of my loved ones." He straightened his shoulders and turned back to his work at the stove. Lani wrapped me in a warm hug.

"It will all be okay," she said. I tried to believe her.

I held onto Lani's words as the days and weeks wore on, and I was beginning to think that this… injury had affected my mental well-being. I felt emotionally numb at times and wickedly terrified at others. I began to close all the window coverings in my bungalow each night in order to stop feeling like I was being watched. My heart would race whenever I was alone for too long. And the nightmares? Oh, where do I even begin with that?

Rob had connected me to a Victim's Assistance Representative and we met periodically. She'd given me a number I could call whenever I needed to confirm that Taylor was still incarcerated. The VAR also referred me to a therapist who specialized in situations like mine, but I nervously delayed calling for an appointment. It was Davy who stepped in.

"Babe, you can't live like this. This isn't living. This is simply existing. You deserve better. Please call the therapist."

"Do you have any idea how diagnosed mental issues follow you around for the rest of your life? Do you not understand that people are labeled forever?"

"Do you not remember the homeless people at Hale Maluhia? The ones you helped? The ones you got referrals for? Why is that okay for them but not for you?"

That stung. And it was a really good question. He left me alone for a few minutes, and I wrangled with the realization of my hypocrisy, a trait I'd always loathed. What was good for my friends at Maluhia should be good for me as well. I tapped the business card against my lips as my mind worked. Watching the socks go round and round on the ceiling fan brought a tiny bit of happiness back into my heart. It was these little things and also the people around me who made me smile, and that caused me to act. I placed the call and nervously made an appointment.

There was a kiss on top of my head and warm hands on my shoulders as Davy had returned and was standing behind me. "Well done, Babe. Well done," he murmured into my scarf and kissed my head again. But the appointment was just one more item of dread to add to the cloud hanging over me these days.

Davy accompanied me to the therapist's office several days later and silently held my hand in the waiting room, but he had the good sense to stay behind when I went in for my first session. I was grateful though when I found him waiting for me as I emerged into another room via the privacy door. I tried to duck my head so he wouldn't see my swollen eyes, but he knew me too well. I leaned against the wall and he held me until I was able to take a deep breath.

"Next week then?" he asked me about my next appointment while we drove back to the inn in Roomba.

"Yeah. And the week after. And the week after that." My words felt thick in my throat.

"I'll go with you as long as you'll have me."

While at a traffic light I turned to look at him and felt my eyes well again. "Always."

He chuckled. "You say that now, but I'll keep asking. There will come a day when you feel stronger."

"Maybe for the appointments, but I hope you'll always be in my life."

"I will."

Those two little words held so much promise that I felt some of the load lifting from my shoulders. When you start to feel down, you tend to create more worries than are real, and I'd been afraid he'd get tired of dealing with a basket case. Shame on me for ever thinking such a thing about him. "Thank you."

"You're welcome. So stop acting like a cotton-headed ninny muggins."

It was my turn to laugh. "You stole that line!"

"I did, and it's an excellent line to steal, and I'm very grateful that it was out there in the universe just waiting for me to take it." He squeezed my hand. "You know what else is out there in the universe?"

"What?"

"Mars. Mars bars, I mean. I'm starving."

He kept me chuckling all the way home, where we had some of the luncheon leftovers before I had to get back to work.

After several more weeks of therapist appointments, I was beginning to learn how to deal with some of my issues, and my hair was growing back too. One morning as I looked in the mirror, I realized that my mood seemed a little lighter, and perhaps I was ready to abandon the head scarf. My hair was less than an inch long and the zig zag scar was still easily visible, but I felt good. I put on my regular earrings but included some larger hoops that were threaded with a bunch of my silver charms I'd collected over the years. I shook my head a little and was delighted that they still jingled. Taking one last look in the mirror, I realized that I was pleased with the new me.

I fed Chester and Susie before heading to the reception area to begin the day's work. Bennie was just feeding Winston and Marley as I strolled in, my flips flops slapping a lively beat against the wooden floor.

"Good morning! My, you have a lively bounce to your flip flops today," Bennie called, and I saw him do a double take as he turned to look at me, a big grin spreading across his handsome face. "Wow. You look great too!"

I matched his grin and did an exaggerated little twirl without slowing my pace. "Why thank you, kind sir." I vamped a little and then giggled at the absurdity. I was not a vamper. Nor a flirter. I was just me, with the occasional foray into chick-shtick, and Bennie knew it, for he egged me on with a playful wolf whistle. Not to be outdone, Marley matched his whistle. Over and over again. And again. Winston joined in with his rendition of "Daydream Believer." Bennie brought me coffee, trying not to slosh the hot liquid as he laughed at the impromptu concert, and he gave me a little hug before he turned to his own duties at the computer. I went to work on the daily recording of inventory and orders.

Our FedEx delivery woman showed up with a fairly large stack of packages, but Sam trotted over before Bennie even had the chance to sign for the delivery.

"Aloha Macca." He shot the shaka sign. "Bennie." He nodded to

217

each person in turn. "Laura." He kissed the FedEx delivery woman's cheek and then blushed when he realized we were watching.

I saw Bennie chuckling and his thumbs flying on his phone, followed by the buzz on my own phone for an incoming text.

Laura is Sam's new gf.

I couldn't hold back my gasp of surprised pleasure at the news.

"What?" Sam glanced at me, suppressing a shy smile before turning back to Laura to say goodbye. His eyes followed her until she was out of sight.

"Nothing." I bit my lower lip to keep from giggling. As far as I knew, this was Sam's first love interest, but he was usually a very private person so I couldn't be sure. When I heard Laura's FedEx truck start up, I chuckled. "Aww, Bennie. Our little boy is growing up," I teased.

"Next he'll be wanting to borrow the car," Bennie added with a mischievous twinkle to his eye.

"Shuddup." Sam blushed and laughed, focusing far too intently on opening packages and stacking the packing slips for me. I saw a sly grin peeking out from his long hair as he was bent over his task. "By the way, you look great, Macca. Love the new 'do."

"Thank you, Sam," I beamed, which caused his blush to deepen.

I had a light lunch in my bedroom with Susie and Chester, and the late arrival, Davy. He picked at my fruit salad, popping a grape into his mouth now and then.

He reached over and gave one of my earrings a gentle flick with his finger. "You should wear these more often. They look great."

"They would just get in the way when I'm working, but I figured they'd draw attention away from my bald head or something."

He shook his head. "No, they just look great on you. You're still very obviously bald, except for some peach fuzz," he grinned and patted my head. "Soft."

I grinned back and playfully swatted his hand away, but he reached for my earrings and held the charms between his fingers. "These are cool," he continued. "Where did you get them?"

"Most are from my parents from my childhood. The Snoopy and the Woodstock charms were from Uncle Wally and Aunt Fran. My room at their house was filled with Snoopy and Woodstock stuff." Smiling at the memories, I let a happy sigh escape.

"You should definitely wear these more often. They give you sparkle." He reached over then and hugged me.

"These are happy memories too," I murmured into his velvet-clothed shoulder.

"We just make 'em up as we go along." He kissed my temple and squeezed me tighter. It was very comforting, until I caught him sneaking more of my fruit. I pulled away and smacked his hand. The moment had passed and we shared a laugh.

There was a knock at my bedroom door and I knew it must be Tina-Bettina. "Come in, Tina."

"I can't get used to the name change yet," Davy whispered just as the door opened and I shushed him.

Tina-Bettina popped her head in. "What time do you think we should leave tomorrow?" She had seemed increasingly nervous as the next day's trial loomed closer, while I had been trying hard to forget it. "Oh, and hello." She blushed. "Sorry to interrupt."

"You're not interrupting anything but Davy trying to steal my lunch" I deadpanned, flashing him a look that I was sure parents everywhere often utilized.

Tina and I then agreed on a very early departure time. "I'll drive," I insisted. "There's a charging station near the courthouse." Deja vu. Didn't I just do this with Taylor?

"Thanks. I'm not very comfortable driving here yet."

"No problem." I tried to give her a big reassuring smile, but I'm sure it fell flat because an actress I was not, and I was dreading the trial too.

She waved and left us alone again. I turned back to Davy "So much for that sparkle, yeah?"

"We'll just have to do something about that," he teased as he began to tickle me, making me squeal so hard I thought I would pee my pants. The thought of that was not attractive. He certainly had the gift of a magical touch. Yeah, I'm here all day, folks.

TWENTY-ONE

Aquarium Court and a Restraining Order

In a thick fog borne of dread, distraction, fear, and anxiety, I took my seat beside Tina-Bettina in the courtroom the next day. Davy shimmered in and sat beside me, cautiously peering around to be sure he wasn't noticed by any "sensitives" in the room. His resulting smile told me he was indeed undetected. He reached over and held my hand as it lay on my lap, his loving touch a constant reminder that I was safe. I found myself studying his hand at times until I could picture the details when I closed my eyes. It was a coping mechanism I'd learned from my therapist: find a tiny something that gives you a smile and study it as if your life depended on it. In this case, I feared it truly did.

After a few minutes I was ready to glance at my surroundings. There were only a few others sitting in the spectator area of the small courtroom. Thankfully it wasn't the same courtroom that I had been in, but close enough in appearance to cause me a few involuntary shudders, each being met with a squeeze of my hand from Davy.

Tina-Bettina and I both jumped a little in our seats when a door slammed somewhere beyond the courtroom. Still clutching Davy's hand, I used my other to reach out to Tina-Bettina and we held tightly to each other. The bailiff called the standard "all rise" and our little trio did just that, still physically connected by our hands. The large door opened and a tiny woman emerged dressed in a black robe. Her legs were bare and I noticed she was wearing black pumps with a medium heel. Her inky black hair was piled on top of her head with a wisp of fringe across her forehead. She had an air of all business about her, and I felt an inexplicable surge of comfort.

As she took her seat on the "bench" and banged her gavel, we all resumed our own seats while her dark eyes roamed the courtroom. Her vision bounced from the prosecutors and she frowned slightly when she saw the infamous defense attorney. I could only assume he was the one that Rob had told us about. The judge seemed less than impressed. As she tamped down her papers, her eyes scanned the rest of the room's inhabitants. When she turned her head my way there was eye contact between us and a slight smile on her face. She softly blinked her eyes, much like Chester did when he was trying to tell me his feelings. I squirmed a little, but smiled back, wondering what the hell that was all about, but I kept my smile in place until her eyes wandered to the rest of the courtroom.

At last the business of the day began. Taylor's case number was called, and I tuned out the details. When a door opened on the side of the room and Taylor was escorted in, her eyes narrowed when she spotted her mom and me. My own eyes glazed over right then and the surrounding sounds roared in my ears as if we were under water. Aquarium court. I felt Tina-Bettina squeeze my hand a few times and watched Davy rub his thumb over my fingers while the rest of the world fell away. At one point I heard muffled shouting, but I was paralyzed, stuck in some other dimension. Before I even knew it, Tina-Bettina and Davy were rising to their feet and pulling me up between them.

"What?" But my voice sounded far, far away.

"It's over for now," Davy whispered. Why was he whispering?

"Why isn't the judge on the bench?" I asked when I noticed she was gone. "And why do they call it a bench?"

"Shh," Davy whispered again, and the two of them hustled me out of the courtroom. I turned back to look one last time, but Taylor was gone, and only a handful of people remained. It was then that I locked eyes with a man; he was staring at me with such obvious disgust, bordering on hatred, and there was something vaguely familiar in his face.

"Come Macca," Tina-Bettina spoke sternly, pulling on my hand.

"But who... wait... is that...?" But she yanked me hard and I stumbled, struggling to stay upright, grabbing onto both Davy and Tina-Bettina to right myself. The man caught up with us easily though. Tina-Bettina swore quietly under her breath, and the hazy feeling began to fade away.

"Bettina." The man's tone was terse and sent a chill down my back when I recognized him.

"Stu," she responded in kind to her ex-husband. "You remember Macca," she added.

"Hi Stu," I muttered, my head still a little muddled.

"Macca." His stare was unsettling and I squirmed as his cold eyes bore straight into mine.

"Well, we have to go," Tina-Bettina said, trying to move me along while Davy made sure to keep me upright.

"I'll see you next week," Stu snapped at Tina-Bettina, his eyes still on me. Wait, next week?

"Yes," she answered, pulling on my arm, but I felt rooted.

"You shouldn't be here," Stu directed his words at me in a very low and menacing tone.

"She has every right to be here," Tina-Bettina stopped pulling and faced her ex like a mama bear.

"No, she shouldn't be here. If she had died, Taylor would be free."

Tina-Bettina went nose-to-nose with Stu. "You had better watch what you say. I want you to leave us alone. I have nothing to discuss with you. I don't want to see you, hear from you, or even think of you ever again."

"Fine. Don't show up next week. You don't care about Taylor anyway."

"You just worry about you, and stay away from us." She whirled around and yanked me toward the parking lot again, Davy supporting me.

"Are you okay, Macca?" I heard worry in his voice.

I nodded.

"Good. I'll see you back at the inn." And he shimmered away before I could respond. Tina-Bettina held my hand and draped her other arm around me, supporting me to the car where we disconnected the charger and then sat inside in silence for several minutes.

"I'm sorry I was so rough on you, but something happened to you in the courtroom," she finally spoke.

I slowly turned to look at her. "I have no idea what. I... I seemed to have spaced out or something."

"For two hours!" She looked so worried.

"Two hours?" I looked at the clock on the dash, but it was blank because I'd yet to turn the key.

"I'm worried about you. Let me drive us home."

"You said you don't feel comfortable driving here yet." But I really didn't feel up to driving either, so I'd already given in by the time she spoke again.

"I have to find a comfort level some time, and that time is now." She took my keys out of my hand and we got out to switch seats.

"What did Stu mean about seeing you next week?" I asked once we were on the road.

"The trial will continue next Wednesday. It looks like they may throw out Taylor's mental illness defense. Apparently two court appointed doctors' findings were enough to debunk the defense attorney's doctor."

"Wow." I felt relief wash over me like rain over a cool waterfall. Halfway home, I fell asleep. When I finally awoke, the view out the car window showed me we were just minutes from home. "Whoa." I rubbed my eyes. "I'm sorry I slept so much."

"It's okay." She smiled, eyes set on the road. "I haven't felt much like talking."

"What happened in court?"

"Court? I'm not sure what happened with you, but it was disturbing." She chewed her lip. "You completely tuned out."

"I did?"

She nodded before continuing. "Do you remember the confrontation with Stu outside the courthouse?"

"Yeah, that I remember. He hates me."

"He hates the world. You just happened to be standing in front of him at a time when he decided to spew, and I'm sorry for that. He has been full of hate for a very long time." She reached out and held my hand. "But you scared me today. Where did you go? I mean, where did your mind go?"

"I don't know. It was like time zoomed forward and before I knew it we were leaving the courthouse."

As we pulled into Roomba's parking space at home, I could feel Tina-Bettina's eyes on me. She hesitated a moment, chewing on her bottom lip. "If I may be so bold, you should call your therapist."

I stared ahead and let that sink in, and as I repeated her words in my head, I began to worry too. "I will," I whispered. She squeezed my hand and got out of the car. In a daze I followed her, and once in the bungalow I went to my room and sat for a while in the rocking chair. Finally I called the therapist and left a message.

The following day I was in her office, as she'd suspected I'd had some sort of dissociative reaction. Simply put, I'd shut down, which was my mind's defense against the stress of the situation. She and I discussed my feelings and fears, confronted them, beat the hell out of them in fact, and set a plan for future sessions as well. She gave me a few exercises to use when it was time to be in court again, and she even offered to accompany me. I decided then and there to get down on one knee and ask for her hand in marriage. Not really. But I did decide to bring her some baked goods next session.

Davy was waiting for me when I arrived home after that first "new" session.

"I'm okay." I tried to brush it off, but he scooped me in his arms and held me tight.

"It *will* be okay," he murmured into the side of my head, "but it's not okay yet. However, *I'm* here to stay."

"I know. Thank you," I whispered as a little of my bravado slipped. He simply squeezed me tighter and I relaxed into his arms and let him be my Guardian Monkee. After all, he did it so well.

When the next court date arrived, Tina-Bettina and I headed south again, accompanied by Davy. My therapist had made the decision on her own to attend, but she sat in the back of the courtroom. The comfort I felt by having them all with me was quite empowering, and I felt far more equipped to face the proceedings this time.

Stu arrived and sat behind his daughter, sending us nasty glances every few minutes. Rob and Alex slipped in as well just before the judge entered. My two loyal and loving attorney friends sat in the back with my therapist. It was as if I had brought my own cheering section, complete with invisible banners and balloons.

Opening statements were painful to listen to but I tried to keep up. Fortunately, both attorneys kept it brief.

The prosecutor had been informed of my issues, and so he had arranged to call me as the first witness. I took the stand with Davy close beside me, my very own Guardian Monkee sticking by me to ward off evil. I avoided Taylor's glare the entire time I was questioned and simply responded to the inquiries as best I could. I blocked out the sight of the jury as well, but I heard their gasps a few times and squeezed Davy's hand. When they passed the photos of my injuries around, I steadfastly averted my eyes. My therapist would nod and smile whenever I glanced her way. I even caught Alex slipping me a wink now and then. I was surrounded by strength and support. Poor Tina-Bettina was mopping her eyes every few minutes though, and my heart squeezed, wishing I could make her pain go away.

When it was time to answer the defense attorney's questions, I was a little less confident. Each time he tried to attack my memory of the incident, the prosecutor would object, and Judge Higashi would call "sustained." At one point the defense attorney became so belligerent, apparently trying to shake me to my core, that the prosecutor objected again and exclaimed, "Your honor, badgering the witness!" The defense attorney was admonished again and again. The sound of the gavel crashing against the judge's wooden desk began to grate on my nerves after a while. I felt a headache pounding behind my eyes but I worked hard to keep my focus on the job at hand. When I was finally able to return to my seat, Davy met me there and kissed my cheek while Tina-Bettina gave me a squeeze and whispered, "I'm so proud of you."

After a break for lunch, where I only munched a banana and one of Lani's mango macadamia nut muffins I'd brought from home, my therapist spent a few minutes congratulating me and giving me further encouragement. It was doubtful I'd be called back to testify more, so she said she'd see me at our next session and said goodbye. Alex and Rob checked on me just as she was leaving before they too headed out. After my banana and muffin, Davy shimmered in and walked with me back to the courtroom.

Tina-Bettina testified in the afternoon, and it was an ugly scene. I was shocked when the prosecuting attorney showed a plastic evidence bag to her, asking if she recognized the item of clothing encased. Tina-Bettina responded that it was her daughter's shirt she'd been wearing the day of Annie's disappearance. As it was taken over to the jury I had a chance to see it, and the sight of a horrendous amount of dried blood all over the front of it caused me to gasp. My hand flew to my mouth and I looked over at Tina-Bettina; her eyes glistened with tears and mine began to do the same. Sympathy tears. I had not known of the damning evidence, but it gave me further hope.

The prosecutor then asked if Tina-Bettina had been aware of Annie's decision to cut off Taylor's allowance once they'd all returned home. I was shocked when Tina-Bettina answered yes. I had not known any of these details before then. She gave me a look that was brimming with apologies. I gently shook my head and tried to smile, but the tears splashed down my cheeks. Davy squeezed my hand again, and courage flowed through me. I turned to stare at Taylor, seeing her for the evil little monster she really was.

When the prosecutor wrapped up his questions, the defense attorney took over. He had the nerve to criticize her parenting, and the prosecutor again had to raise objections for badgering. Judge Higashi finally fined the nasty little toad for contempt of court due to his constant harassment and total disregard for her warnings.

Tina-Bettina exuded confidence during the entire session and when she returned to sit with us I gave her a tight but warm hug.

"I didn't know," I whispered.

"I know. I'm sorry. I didn't want to give you gruesome details; you were struggling enough without knowing more about the monstrous behavior of my daughter."

"Thank you," I kissed her cheek and she smiled sadly.

When at last the day was done, Tina-Bettina and I headed home, with Davy promising to see us there.

"He's a good man...erm... ghost," she said in the car.

"Exceptional," I agreed, but said no more. And although I had not suffered any dissociative episodes, I was well beyond exhaustion and napped the entire way home.

Tina-Bettina returned to court each of the following days to watch the rest of the proceedings, including the introduction of the damning photo files we'd found hidden on top of the ceiling fan, but I opted to stay home and try to get back to some sort of normal life. She updated me each evening, and on the afternoon when testimony was completed and the jury given instructions for deliberation, she opted to stay in a motel room in Hilo. Her voice told me she was both weary and worried. I imagined it couldn't be easy to watch your child go through such a horrendous procedure, but I knew she realized that Taylor had brought it on herself.

The next day, late in the afternoon, I was helping Bennie and Lani set up for the dinner service when my phone buzzed; the jury was back, and Tina-Bettina's voice was unusually sharp, like that twang a guitar string makes when it has been over-tightened.

"Guilty," she uttered just that one word and seemed to work at catching her breath before continuing. "Second degree murder and attempted murder in the second degree, two counts. They're counting both attempts on your life separately. I'm so relieved it's over."

My legs turned to noodles, causing me to sink onto the nearest dining chair. "Oh my gosh," I whispered. "Really?"

"Really," she gulped. "Sentencing is tomorrow. I'm going to stay down here again. I'm too tired to drive home."

When she said "home" my heart instantly warmed. She'd been so supportive despite her own conflicted motherly feelings toward her daughter, and I loved her all the more for it.

"Okay. Call me when it's over."

"I will. And Macca?"

"Yeah?"

"I love you," and she began to cry. "And I'm so sorry she did this to you and to my mom."

"I love you too, and I know. It's not your fault." Yes, it was a little white lie because there was no way I was going to play the blame game about her parenting methods. It just wasn't my place to do so, nor would it accomplish anything but cause more misery.

"Stu is livid. I had to stay with the prosecutor until they could find a guard to escort me to my car. They even warned him that if he didn't check his temper he'd be put in a cell for the night. What a mess. I'm staying at the same motel as he is, just down the road. A police officer spoke with management and they assured my safety and moved me to another room on the other side from him."

"Okay, that's good, but call me tomorrow? Or call me tonight if you need. And don't even hesitate in calling the police if you feel threatened. Just stay safe."

"I will, on all counts."

Desperate for this entire ordeal to be over, I threw myself into my work around the inn. I tried not to think of Annie, who had died alone and cold. I tried not to think of Tina-Bettina, who had lost both her mother and her daughter, one to death and one to prison. I tried not to think of Stu, so angry and full of hatred. And most of all, I tried not to think of Taylor, so damaged by sheer overindulgence and privilege. Instead, I thought of Davy, who was my rock. Of Bennie, who was such a kind and loving man. Of Lani and Kalei, embarking on a new phase of their family. Of Alex and Rob and their lovely wives, whose professionalism had turned into friendship and love. Of Ming and Sam and Albert, who were the quiet members of my family. I made a mental note to give them a little more attention, for I'd noticed that it was the quiet ones who often got overlooked, that old squeaky wheel thing and all. And lastly, I thought again of Tina-Bettina, or I should say *Tina*, on the verge of her new life that I hoped would include me.

As all these things crowded my brain, I heard Dad's soft voice in my head. *Imagine all the people living life in peace. You may say I'm a dreamer but I'm not the only one. I hope someday you'll join us and the world will be as one.* Dad often resorted to quoting John Lennon. Those lyrics applied quite frequently, and this was one of those times. We had so much ahead, so much life to live and love to give, and I felt ready to embrace it. Dad began to sing, his familiar voice so gentle and comforting. *All you need is love. Love is all you need.*

Tina called the next day, her voice fraught with emotion. "The judge sentenced Taylor to life imprisonment for the combined offenses. There will be a hearing to determine what the minimum time will be before she can petition for parole, but Rob indicated he was fairly certain it could be as long as 20 to 30 years because of the three counts."

I sat in stunned silence. I was going to be safe from Taylor for a very long time.

"Are you there?" I heard Tina anxiously ask.

"Yes, just… shocked."

"Me too. But as much as I hate to say it, they've done the right thing. My mom is gone, your life has forever changed, and justice was necessary." And then she began to cry.

"Oh Bett… Tina, I'm so sorry."

"You have nothing to be sorry for," she choked and sniffled. "It's me who is sorry to have brought her here."

"You had no way of knowing how bad it would end up. It's not your fault."

"Perhaps, but I will accept partial blame for the person she has turned out to be, and she will need to change her ways if she ever wants to be released."

We were silent for a moment before she continued. "And Rob filed for a restraining order against Stu for me. Both Rob and Alex are such good guys. You're very lucky to have such supportive friends."

"That they are. I am rich with good friends." I found myself smiling as I thought of all of them, and it was like being bundled in a soft and warm blanket. "And I'm glad you took the steps for protection. It will let you breathe a little easier."

"Yes, and I barely slept last night. I was listening for any little noise."

"Well, come home tomorrow and I will make sure you have time for some uninterrupted rest."

"Thank you. And now, I'm going back to the motel to rest. I'll be home tomorrow afternoon but I may stop and do some thinking along the way."

"Stay safe, Tina. I'll see you soon."

Overwhelmed, I headed for my bungalow where I knew Chester and Susie would be waiting for me. Instead though, when I opened the door, it was Davy who was standing before me, his arms spread wide; I fell into his hug and let his magic wash over me. And as the year was winding down, I realized that all would be right in my world again.

That evening I dug through my closet and found the little cross stitch kit that Annie had bought for me that day in Kona. I turned on some soothing music and opened the package. The instructions were clear and simple, and I followed along. As the colors began to appear on the blank cloth, I felt a smile reaching from my heart to my face. I worked on the piece over the course of a few weeks, and when at last it was complete, I was filled with a sense of pride and accomplishment. I found myself gazing happily at the island scene, with the man and woman walking along the sand. Red trunks and a blue bikini. Of course, the subject on the canvas had hair while I was still very… bare.

When I had a few hours to myself one day, I took my finished project with me to an arts and crafts store in the village and found the perfect little frame for it. And while the shop offered to frame it for me, for a price of course, I decided that it was important to finish the piece myself. With my amateur hands I'd created the cross stitch, errors and all, and now I would frame it as well.

"It doesn't look half bad," I told Chester and Susie as I hung the framed cross stitch piece on the wall just below Annie's larger painting. "And now, this is Annie's Wall." I stood back and smiled, feeling warm and loved. Davy shimmered in behind me and wrapped his arms around my waist.

"It's very pretty." He smiled, his chin resting on my shoulder as we gazed at the wall together.

"Thank you. I think so too, if I may be so bold."

"It looks like us, doesn't it?"

"It does. That's why I chose it." I turned in his arms and gave him the biggest bear hug I could muster. "Thank you for being my friend."

He squeezed me tight. "You have no idea how easy it is to be your friend, do you?" He chuckled. "I think I love that about you."

And before we got too mushy, I pulled away and showed him my next cross stitch project that I'd picked up along with the frame. This one wasn't a "kit" like the other one, but from a chart that I'd purchased, along with the individual skeins of floss to use.

He laughed when he saw the chart, a man on a horse. "I changed the colors out a bit so that it would look like you and Glory."

"It will be brilliant, Babe. I know it will!" He slipped his hand into his pocket and withdrew another little wrapped gift. Taking my hand, he placed it on my palm and closed my fingers on it. "For you," he stated the obvious, but with a smile just for me. I matched that smile and unwrapped the gift. It was a small ceramic statue of a snow-capped mountain, a large evergreen tree, and a little girl about to splash in a puddle. She was wearing pink rain boots, a yellow slicker, and was carrying an open umbrella in a lovely shade of blue. I held it up to the light and turned it around and around to study the many details. It was quite intricate, especially for its small size.

"This is… this is beautiful." I shook my head and raised my eyes to meet his.

He grinned then and tapped my nose with his finger. "It reminded me of you. Even the unruly hair and the mismatched clothes." His eyes twinkled.

"Thank you, Davy! I think I will cherish this one the most." I was struck by a thought though. "Hey! Are you saying I wear mismatched clothes?"

"No, but I suspect you did as a child."

I blushed and ducked my head. "I did." I giggled and looked up shyly through my lashes. We stared at each other for a moment, and in his beautiful brown eyes I saw a lifelong friend. I hoped he saw the same in mine. I knew he'd keep his promise to be there forever. Right then I was even more convinced that I was the richest person in the entire world.

TWENTY-TWO

Aloha

A funny thing happened in those last few weeks of the year. Everything went well! Imagine that! The inn's business was booming, and I felt safe once again with Taylor behind bars. I continued to see my therapist each week, finally admitting to myself that it could be years before I might no longer need her.

Tina had headed back to the home she'd once shared with her mother and daughter, deciding to sell most everything and move back here to Hawai'i. She'd excitedly told me that she had already been promised first choice in a seaside townhouse complex that our long-term architect guest Rick Morrison had designed and was overseeing.

The Morrison family had finally been able to move into their dream home just a couple of miles from Hale Mele, where I visited them frequently. They had become part of my family as well.

A few wintry storms blew in over the volcanoes and deposited a lot of snow on both Mauna Kea and Mauna Loa. Rob and Alex called and had gathered some sleds, inviting me along with them and their wives. We bundled up and spent the day flying through the white stuff on Mauna Kea, then stopping for hot cocoa before sledding some more. It was a day made for children, both young and old, and I had a blast. At one point I was sledding a bit behind the others and guess who joined me then? Yep, that little Mancunian daredevil himself. We rode and floated over little moguls, laughing our fool heads off. It was a snowy rebirth for me, and I shed a lot of the emotional weight of the past year in just those few hours.

The mismatched socks, one polka-dot, one argyle, still spun lazily around on the ceiling fan in my bungalow. While I could have had Albert get the big ladder and take them down, I had little to no desire to do so. They offered both a happy memory and a nice little conversation piece on the occasion that I had guests in.

"I hope you keep them there forever," Davy had said one evening as we were eating at the little dinette table below the fan. "They remind me of an old friend of mine."

I didn't prod him for more information because I saw in his eyes that he was far away. It did appear that the memory was a happy one and I reached out to give his hand a squeeze. He turned his head, smiled at me and finished his meal. No further words were necessary.

One Saturday, Lani, Bennie, and I stole away from the inn for a few hours to enjoy Dr. Josh's wedding, leaving Kalei, Sam, Ming, and Albert to prep the evening dinner. The veterinarian's nuptials had been postponed once due to the busyness of his business, so to speak, and we were fortunate enough to be able to witness the exchanging of vows on a cool and crisp day. But as we walked from the church to the small hall for the reception, Lani gasped, stopped in her tracks, and stared at a small but growing puddle on the pavement.

"My water just broke!"

"No worries." I whisked her away, Bennie on our heels, "We'll get you to the hospital in no time!" Bennie kept pace behind us, his phone pressed to his ear as he told Kalei to meet us in the birthing center at the hospital.

Later that evening we all welcomed little Miss Alana into the world. Big man Kalei was overcome with tears of joy as he brought us into the room to meet her. When he picked her up he looked like a giant palm tree holding a tiny coconut. I stifled a chuckle because that tiny coconut he held was the most beautiful little creature I'd ever laid eyes on. Even Davy shimmered in behind me, cooing to the little one.

"She's gorgeous," he whispered, and I nodded.

Later, when we were all gathered around the hospital bed where Lani held Alana in her arms, I could almost see a halo of golden light surrounding them. Kalei took Alana from his wife and handed her into my arms. I felt the warm current from Kalei, Lani, and Alana spread to me, creating a bond that I swore would never be severed. As Alana settled in my arms, her snuffles and fussing diminished and she tried to look up at me.

"Hello my little Hawaiian warrior princess. I promise you that you'll always be safe with Auntie Macca. 'Anake will never let anything happen to you." She stared at me with her coffee bean eyes and I fell in love. "And Uncle Davy, Chester, and Susie will watch over you too," I whispered.

As the weeks passed, we were thrilled to be a part of little Alana's growth, and the village that was Hale Mele Inn helped raise her whenever necessary. Between all of us, and Lani's mom too, Alana received all the attention she needed, and then some. Even the mostly aloof Chester warmed to her, lying close beside the child whenever possible. And when Alana was in her little play seat, Susie would stand guard, even sometimes resting his massive head gently on the baby. Bennie taught Winston to say her name, and Marley whistled happy tunes to amuse her, delighting in her squeals of pleasure.

My head had finally healed and my hair was growing back faster than I expected, but the surprise of all surprises was that it was growing in smooth and silky. I no longer had to give myself a coconut oil treatment as frequently as before. I'd finally gotten my mother's hair, I mused to myself, and then wondered if she had somehow caused it. *No, I can't perform miracles*, she teased me in thought. Well, if I'd known this would happen I might have shaved my head years ago. Or maybe not.

I heard from Tina-Bettina now and then and was pleased that she was finding her way. She promised she still wanted to move to the islands but was quite busy selling her home and the majority of her belongings. Frankly, I was looking forward to having her nearby. The new Tina was definitely someone I treasured as a friend, and I understood her strong desire to return to the islands. After all, I'd grown up in Los Angeles where palm trees often swayed just to create their own breeze, which only served to relocate that big city stench that results from too many people crammed into 500 or so square miles of concrete and asphalt. In contrast, these island breezes were cleansing and intoxicating, and we were able to find peace and solitude when we so desired.

Davy, my very best friend, continued to keep me smiling, laughing, loving, and most importantly, grounded. His advice and support were something I'd come to rely on, especially since those were often dished out with a large portion of song, dance, theatrics, comedy, and just plain fun.

One afternoon when all the chores of the inn had been completed, Davy shimmered in dressed in his iconic red swim trunks and I donned my favorite blue bikini. We checked to be sure there weren't any guests hanging around, and seeing the pool deserted, we'd taken a quick dip to cool down.

Afterward we sat on my private deck sipping Kalei's phenomenal iced tea, still a hit with our guests and family alike. Chester and Susie were lazing nearby. A fly was cruising above their heads and Susie lifted his head to snap at it a few times. Chester soon joined in the lazy chase. The sound of two sets of snapping jaws struck us as extremely cheap entertainment and we found ourselves laughing at their antics.

One last snap of the big dog's mouth was successful though, and the fly ceased to exist. When our laughter died down, Davy swiftly got to his feet and gave both animals a loving pet before turning to me.

"Let's take a walk on the beach." He held out his hand for me to grasp as I uncurled my legs and let him pull me up beside him. He held tight to my hand as we slowly navigated the stairs behind my deck, down the main steps to the beach, stopping to enjoy the comforting breeze and spectacular view now and then. When our bare feet hit the sand, he pulled me a little closer, and we walked hand in hand with our feet slapping the edge of the surf. There wasn't a single person from the southern end to the northern end of "our" beach.

"This is forever, isn't it?" I beamed, finally feeling the security he'd brought me when I had been so alone.

"I keep saying so. Do you finally believe me?"

I grinned and nodded. "I'm sorry I took so long to believe you."

"Well, you wouldn't be you if you hadn't been so skeptical."

Chuckling, I bumped his shoulder with mine. "Are you saying I'm stubborn?"

"No, I wouldn't dare do that." He laughed and winked at me playfully. I found myself reflecting on this man beside me. First there was the man I'd come to know as his public persona, Davy, the charming entertainer. Then, as our friendship grew over the years, I had been allowed to see the private man behind the curtain, my dear friend David, with a heart as big as the vast Pacific whose endless waves currently lapped at our feet.

We walked a little farther before he spoke suddenly, in a very thick Mancunian accent. "Now then, shall we skip? Or walk sensibly?"

I felt as if a beam of light shone down upon us at that exact point in time, and my grin spread widely across my face. I tried to put on my best imitation of a British accent as I replied, "Why, I think we should skip, don't you?"

And skip we did, giggling and splashing each other in the surf, my Guardian Monkee and me.

Glossary of Hawaiian Words

Word	Pronunciation	Meaning
'anake	ah-nah-keh	Aunt
'ohana	oh-hah-nah	Family
'ono	oh-noh	Delicious
'aina awakea	eye-nah ah-vah-keh-ah	Lunch
akamai	ah-kah-mah-ee	Smart, intelligent, wise
aloha	ah-loh-hah	Hello, goodbye, love, affection, goodwill
'anakala	ah-nah-kah-lah	Uncle
auna (hula)	ow-nah	Native dance accompanied by chanting
hale	ha-leh	House
haole	hau-leh	Foreigner, Caucasian
heaiu	hay-yow	Ancient Hawaiian religious temple or area
ho'omaika'i-'ana	ho-oh-ma-ee-kah-ee-ah-na	Congratulations
hula	hu-lah	The dance of Hawaii that tells a story
imu	ee-moo	Underground oven
kahiko (hula)	kah-hee-koh	Native dance tells a story with music and movement
kalo	kah-loh	Taro plant
kane	kah-neh	Man, boy
kapu	kah-poo	Taboo, forbidden
keiki	keh-ee-kee	Child, children
kekui	keh-koo-ee	State tree of Hawaii, the nuts are often used for leis
koa	koh-ah	Native tree, often used for building and crafts
lei	lay	A garland of flowers, leaves, nuts, or shells
lomi-lomi	loh-mee-loh-mee	Raw salmon massaged and cured, with tomatoes, onions, peppers.
lua	loo-ah	Toilet, hole, cave
mahalo	mah-hah-low	Thank you

maile	mye-leh	Plant whose leaves are used for special leis
makai	mah-kah-ee	Toward the ocean (directional)
makuahine	mah-koo-ah-hee-neh	Mother
maluhia	mah-loo-hee-ah	Peace, safety (Hale Maluhia)
mauka	mau-kah	Inland, or toward the mountain (directional)
mele	meh-leh	Song
paniolo	pah-nee-oh-loh	Hawaiian cowboy
pikake	pee-kah-keh	Small, white, very fragrant flowers used for leis
poi	poy	A paste made of taro root
poke	poh-keh	A dish of diced raw fish with spices
pono	poh-noh	Righteousness
puakenikeni	poo-ah-keh-nee-keh-nee	Yellow to orange fragrant flowers used for leis. Name means "10 cent flower" because the leis used to be sold for 10 cents.
shaka	shah-kah	Pinky and thumb salute for hang loose or right on
wahine	wah-hee-neh	Woman, girl
wikiwiki	wee-kee-wee-kee	Fast, speedy

Place Names

Place Names	Pronunciation
Hi'ilawe (falls)	hee-ee-lah-veh
Hilo	hee-loh
Honoka'a	hoh-noh-kah-ah
Kahua	kah-hoo-ah
Kaluahine (falls)	kah-loo-ah-hee-neh
Kapa'ua	kah-pah-oo-ah
Kilauea	kee-lah-weh-ah
Kohala	koh-hah-lah
Kona	koh-nah
Oahu	oh-ah-hoo
Papakôlea	pah-pah-koh-leh-ah
Waimea	wye-meh-ah
Waipi'o	wye-pee-oh

Given Names

Hawaiian Name	Pronunciation
Kai	kye
Kalakaua	kah-lah-kah-oo-ah
Kalei	kah-lay
Kamehameha (King)	kah-meh-ha-meh-ha
Kimo	kee-moh
Lani	lah-nee
Lehua	leh-hoo-ah
Makala	mah-kah-la
Momi	moh-mee
Pele	peh-leh

Other	Pronunciation
Macca	MACK-kah (not Hawaiian, obviously, but I use John Lennon's pronunciation as my own personal guide)

ABOUT THE AUTHOR

Jerri Keele resides with her husband, a dog and a cat in Salem, Oregon. She has been a fan of Davy Jones since the age of nine, in 1966, when he first hit the scene as a Monkee. Since his sudden passing in 2012, she has worked tirelessly toward fundraising to help care for the herd of retired racehorses he left behind. The horses are under the watchful eye of his four daughters – Talia, Sarah, Jessica, and Annabel – who created the charity The Davy Jones Equine Memorial Foundation (DJEMF).